RENDELL IS AWFULLY GOOD . . . IN ANY RENDELL BOOK YOU KNOW THAT SOMETHING UNUSUAL IS GOING TO HAPPEN."

*The New York Times Book Review*

"When Rendell writes crime-from-the-criminal-point-of-view, she is gripping and creepy. When she writes straightforward detection starring homely, countryish Inspector Wexford, she is even better. Only P. D. James can rival Rendell for total, no-seams-showing command of the classic genre, and true mystery fans, unlike literary critics, would probably give Rendell extra points for unliterary economy and ease of her irresistible non-stop prose."

*The Kirkus Reviews*

By Ruth Rendell
*Published by Ballantine Books:*

TO FEAR A PAINTED DEVIL

VANITY DIES HARD

THE SECRET HOUSE OF DEATH

FROM DOON WITH DEATH

SINS OF THE FATHERS

WOLF TO THE SLAUGHTER

THE BEST MAN TO DIE

A GUILTY THING SURPRISED

DEATH NOTES

MASTER OF THE MOOR

# Wolf to the Slaughter

Ruth Rendell

BALLANTINE BOOKS • NEW YORK

ISBN 0-345-31744-0

This edition published by arrangement with Doubleday & Company, Inc.

Printed in Canada

First Ballantine Books Edition: October 1970
Fifth Printing: December 1983

'Tis all a chequer-board of Nights and Days
Where Destiny with Men for pieces plays:
Hither and thither moves, and mates, and slays,
And one by one back in the Closet lays.
*The Rubaiyát of Omar Khayyám*

I think the Vessel, that with fugitive
Articulation answer'd, once did live,
And merry-make; and the cold Lip I kiss'd
How many kisses might it take—and give!

*The Rubaiyat of Omar Khayyám*

# 1

They might have been going to kill someone.

The police would possibly have thought so if they had stopped the car that was going too fast along the darkening road. The man and the girl would have had to get out and explain why they were carrying an offensive weapon. Explanation would have had to come from the man, for the girl could not have answered them. In the gathering dusk, watching the thin rain trickle down the glass, she thought that the raincoats they wore looked like a disguise, gangster garments, and the knife unsheathed for use.

'Why do you carry it?' she asked, speaking for the first time since they had left Kingsmarkham and its street lamps drowned in drizzle. 'You could get into trouble having a knife like that.' Her voice was nervous, although the nerves were not for the knife.

He pressed the switch that worked the windscreen wipers. 'Suppose the old girl turned funny?' he said. 'Suppose she changed her mind? I might have to put the fear of God into her.' And he drew his fingernail along the flat of the blade.

'I don't like it much,' the girl said, and again she did not only mean the knife.

'Maybe you'd rather have stayed at home with him

1

liable to come in at any minute? It's a miracle to me you ever got around to using his car.'

Instead of answering him, she said carefully, 'I mustn't see this woman, this Ruby. I'll sit in the car out of the way while you go to the door.'

'That's right, and she'll nip out the back. I got the whole thing arranged on Saturday.'

Stowerton was seen first as an orange blur, a cluster of lights swimming through mist. They came into the town centre where the shops were closed but the launderette still open. Wives who worked by day sat in front of the machines, watching their washing spin round inside the portholes, their faces greenish, tired in the harsh white light. On the corner at the crossroads, Cawthorne's garage was in darkness, but the Victorian house behind it brightly illuminated and from its open front door came the sound of dance music. Listening to this music, the girl gave a soft giggle. She whispered to her companion, but because she had only said something about the Cawthornes having a party, nothing about their own destination and their purpose, he merely nodded indifferently and said:

'How's the time?'

'She caught sight of the church clock as they turned into a side street. 'Nearly eight.'

'Perfect,' he said. He made a face in the direction of the lights and the music and raised two fingers in a derisive gesture. 'That to old Cawthorne,' he said. 'I reckon he'd like to be in my shoes now.'

The streets were grey and rain-washed and they all looked the same. Stunted trees grew from the pavements at four-yard intervals and their struggling roots had made cracks in the tarmac. The squat houses, unbroken rows and rows of them, were all garageless and there was a car stuck half-way on the pavement outside nearly every one.

'Here we are, Charteris Road. It's number eighty-two, the one on the corner. Good, there's a light in the front room. I thought she might have done the dirty on us, got cold feet or something and gone out.' He put the knife into his pocket and the girl watched the blade flick back to bury itself in the shaft. 'I shouldn't have liked that,' he said.

The girl said quietly, but with an undercurrent of excitement in her voice, 'Nor should I now.'

The rain had brought night early and it was dark in the car, too dark to see faces. Their hands met as together they fumbled to make the little gold cigarette lighter work. In its flame she saw his dark features glow and she caught her breath.

'You're lovely,' he said. 'God, you're beautiful.' He touched her throat, moving his fingers into the hollow between the horizontal bones. They sat for a moment looking at each other, the flame making soft candlelight shadows on their faces. Then he snapped the lighter closed and pushed open the car door. She twisted the gold cube in her hands, straining her eyes to read its inscription: For Ann who lights my life.

A street lamp on the corner made a bright pool from the kerb to the gate. He crossed it and it threw his shadow black and sharp on this evening of blurred outlines. The house he had come to was poor and mean, its front garden too small to have a lawn. There was just an earth plot, an area ringed with stones, like a grave.

On the step he stood a little to the left of the front door so that the woman who would come to answer his knock should not see more than she need, should not, for instance, see the tail of the green car, wet and glistening in the lamplight. He waited impatiently, tapping his feet. Raindrops hung from the window sills like chains of glass beads.

When he heard sounds of movement from within, he stood stiffly and cleared his throat. The footsteps were followed by sudden illumination of the single diamond pane in the door. Then, as the latch clicked, that pane became a frame for a wrinkled painted face, businesslike but apprehensive, crowned with ginger hair. He thrust his hands into his pockets, feeling a smooth polished hilt in the right-hand one, and willing things to go right for him.

When things went wrong, hideously wrong, he had a terrible sense of fate, of inevitability. It would have happened sometime, sooner or later, this way or the other. They got into their coats somehow and he tried to staunch the blood with his scarf.

'A doctor,' she kept moaning, 'a doctor or the hospital.' He didn't want that, not if it could be avoided. The knife was back in his pocket and all he wanted was air and to feel the rain on his face and to get to the car.

The terror of death was on both their faces and he could not bear to meet her eyes, staring and red as if the blood were reflected in the pupils. Down the path, they held on to each other, staggering past the little bit of earth like a grave, drunk with panic. He got the car door open and she fell across the seat.

'Get up,' he said. 'Get a grip on yourself. We've got to get out of here,' but his voice sounded as far off as death had once seemed. The car jerked and shuddered up the road. Her hands were shaking and her breath rattled.

'You'll be all right. It was nothing—that tiny blade!'

'Why did you do it? Why? Why?'

'That old girl, that Ruby . . . Too late now.'

Too late. A blueprint for last words. Music came out from Cawthorne's house as the car went past the garage, not a dirge but music for dancing. The front door stood open and a great band of yellow light fell across the puddles. The car went on past the shops. Beyond the cottages the street lamps came to an end. It had stopped raining but the countryside was shrouded in vapour. The road was a tunnel between trees from which the water dripped silently, a huge wet mouth that sucked the car along its slippery tongue.

Across the band of light and skirting the puddles, party guests came and went. Music met them, hot dry music in sharp contrast to the night. Presently a young man came out with a glass in his hand. He was gay and full of *joie de vivre* but he had already exhausted the possibilities of this party. The drunk he spoke to in a parked car ignored him. He finished his drink and put the glass down on top of a diesel pump. There was no one to talk to except a sharp-faced old girl, going home, he guessed, because the pubs were shutting. He hailed her, declaiming loudly:

> 'Ah, make the most of what we yet may spend,
> Before we too into the dust descend!'

She grinned at him. 'That's right, dear,' she said. 'You enjoy yourself.'

He was hardly in a fit state to drive. Not at the moment. Besides, to remove his own car would necessitate the removal of six others whose owners were all inside enjoying themselves. So he began to walk, buoyantly and in the faint hope of meeting someone rather special.

It had come on to rain again. He liked the cool feeling of the drops on his hot face. The road to Kingsmarkham yawned at him. He walked along it happily, not at all tired. Far away in the distance, in the throat as it were of this deep wet mouth, he could see the lights of a stationary car.

> 'What lamp,' he said aloud, 'had destiny to guide
> Her little children stumbling in the dark?'

# 2

A high east wind blowing for a day and a night had dried the streets. The rain would come again soon but now the sky was a hard bitter blue. Through the centre of the town the Kingsbrook rattled over round stones, its water whipped into little pointed waves.

The wind was high enough to be heard as well as felt. It swept between the alleys that divided ancient shops from new blocks and with a sound like an owl's cry made leafless branches crack against slate and brick. People waiting for the Stowerton bus going north and the Pomfret bus going south turned up coat collars to shelter their faces. Every passing car had its windows closed and when cyclists reached the summit of the bridge over that rushing stream, the wind caught them and stopped them for a moment before they battled against it and wobbled down past Olive and Dove.

Only the daffodils in the florist's window showed that it was April and not December. They looked as sleek and smug behind their protective glass as did the shopkeepers and office workers who were lucky enough to be indoors on this inclement morning. Such a one, at least for the moment, was Inspector Michael Burden, watching the High Street from his well-insulated observatory.

Kingsmarkham police station, a building of startling modernity, commands a view of the town although it is separated from its nearest neighbour by a strip of green meadow. A horse was tethered there this morning and it looked as cold and miserable as Burden had felt on his arrival ten minutes before. He was still thawing out by one of the central heating vents which blew a stream of warm air against his legs. Unlike his superior, Chief Inspector Wexford, he was not given to quotation, but he would have agreed on this bitter Thursday morning, that April is the cruelest month, breeding, if not lilacs, grape hyacinths out of the dead land. They clustered beneath him in stone urns on the station forecourt, their flowers smothered by a tangle of battered foliage. Whoever had planted them had intended them to blossom as blue as the lamp over the canopy, but the long winter had defeated them. Burden felt that he might have been looking upon tundra rather than the fruits of an English spring.

He swallowed the last of the hot sugarless tea Sergeant Camb had brought him. The tea was sugarless because Burden preferred it that way, not from motives of self-denial. His figure remained lean naturally, no matter what he ate, and his greyhound's face thin and ascetic. Conservative in dress, he was wearing a new suit this morning, and he flattered himself that he looked like a broker on holiday. Certainly no one seeing him in this office with its wall-to-wall carpet, its geometrically patterned curtains and its single piece of glass sculpture would have taken him for a detective in his natural habitat.

He restored the tea cup to its saucer of black Prinknash pottery and his gaze to a figure on the opposite pavement. His own sartorial correctness was uppermost in his mind today and he shook his head distastefully at the loiterer with his long hair and his unconventional clothes. The window was beginning to mist up with condensation. Burden cleared a small patch fastidiously and brought his eyes closer to the glass. He sometimes wondered what men's clothes were coming to these days—Detective Constable Drayton was just one example of contemporary sloppiness—but this! An outlandish jacket of spiky fur more suited to an Eskimo, a long purple and yellow scarf that Burden could not excuse by connecting it with any university, pale blue jeans and suede boots. Now he was crossing the road—

a typical jay walker—and entering the station forecourt. When he bent down and snapped off a grape hyacinth head to put in his buttonhole, Burden almost opened the window to shout at him, but remembered about letting warm air out and stopped in time. The scarf was the last he saw of him, its purple fringe flying out as its wearer disappeared under the canopy.

Might as well be in Carnaby Street, Burden thought, recalling a recent shopping trip to London with his wife. She had been more interested in the cranky-looking people than the shops. When he got home he would tell her there was no need to go fifty miles in a stuffy train when there were funnier sights on her own doorstep. Even this little corner of Sussex would soon be infested with them, he supposed as he settled down at his desk to read Drayton's report on the theft of some Waterford glass.

Not bad, not bad at all. Considering his youth and his inexperience, Drayton was shaping up well. But there were gaps, vital facts omitted. If you wanted anything done in this world, he thought aggrievedly, you mostly had to do it yourself. He took his raincoat from the hook—his overcoat was at the cleaner's. Why not, in April?—and went downstairs.

After days of being almost obscured by muddy footmarks, the foyer's black and white checkerboard floor was highly polished this morning. Burden could see his own well-brushed shoes reflected in its surface. The long ellipse of the counter and the uncomfortable red plastic chairs had that chill clear-cut look wind and dry air give even to an interior.

Also contemplating his reflection in the mirror-like tiles, his bony hands hanging by his sides, sat the man Burden had seen in the street. At the sound of footsteps crossing the floor, he glanced up vaguely to where Sergeant Camb was on the phone. Apparently he needed attention. He had not come, as Burden had formerly supposed, to collect garbage or mend fuses or even sell shady information to Detective Sergeant Martin. It seemed that he was an authentic innocent member of

the public in some sort of minor trouble. Burden wondered if he had lost a dog or found a wallet. His face
was pale and thin, the forehead bumpy, the eyes far
from tranquil. When Camb put the receiver down, he
approached the counter with a curious sluggish irritabil-
ity.

'Yes, sir?' said the sergeant, 'what can I do for you?'

'My name is Margolis, Rupert Margolis.' It was a
surprising voice. Burden had expected the local brand
of country cockney, something to go with the clothes,
anything but this cultured effeteness. Margolis paused
after giving his name, as if anticipating some startling
effect. He held his head on one side, waiting perhaps for
delighted gasps or extended hands. Camb merely gave a
ponderous nod. The visitor coughed slightly and passed
his tongue over dry lips.

'I wondered,' he said, 'if you could tell me how one
goes about finding a charwoman.'

Neither dogs nor wallets, fuses nor undercover information. The man simply wanted his house cleaned.
An anti-climax or a salutary lesson in not jumping to
obvious conclusions. Burden smiled to himself. What
did he think this was? The Labour Exchange? A Cit-
izen's Advice Bureau?

Seldom disconcerted, Camb gave Margolis a genial
smile. The inquirer might have found it encouraging,
but Burden knew the smile covered a philosophical
resignation to the maxim that it takes all sorts to make a
world.

'Well, sir, the offices of the Ministry of Labour are
only five minutes from here. Go down York Street, past
Joy Jewels and you'll find it next to the Red Star garage.
You could try there. What about advertising in the local
rag or a card in Grover's window?'

Margolis frowned. His eyes were a very light green-
ish-blue, the colour of a bird's egg and like a bird's egg,
speckled with brown dots. 'I'm very bad at these practical things,' he said vaguely, and the eyes wandered over
the foyer's gaudy decor. 'You see, normally my sister
would see to it, but she went away on Tuesday, or I

suppose she did.' He sighed, leaning his whole weight against the counter. 'And that's another worry. I seem to be quite bogged down with care at the moment.'

'The Ministry of Labour, sir,' Camb said firmly. He recoiled, grabbing at fluttering papers, as Detective Constable Drayton came in. 'I'll have to see to those doors. Sheer waste running the heating.' Margolis made no move to go. He watched the sergeant twist the chrome handles, crouch down to examine the ball catch.

'I wonder what Ann would do,' he said helplessly. 'It's so unlike her to go off like this and leave me in a mess.'

His patience rapidly going, Burden said, 'If there aren't any messages for me, Sergeant, I'm off to Sewingbury. You can come with me, Drayton.'

'No messages,' said Camb, 'but I did hear Monkey Matthews was out.'

'I thought he must be,' said Burden.

The car heater was a powerful one and Burden found himself weakly wishing Sewingbury was fifty miles away instead of five. Their breath was already beginning to mist the windows when Drayton turned up the Kingsbrook Road.

'Who's Monkey Matthews, sir?' he asked, accelerating as they passed the derestriction sign.

'You haven't been with us all that long, have you? Monkey's a villain, thief, small-time con man. He went inside last year for trying to blow someone up. In a very small way, mind, and with a home-made bomb. He's fifty-odd, ugly, and he has various human weaknesses, including womanizing.'

Unsmiling, Drayton said, 'He doesn't sound very human.'

'He looks like a monkey,' Burden said shortly, 'if that's what you mean.' There was no reason to allow a simple request for official information to grow into a conversation. It was Wexford's fault, he though, for taking a liking to Drayton and showing it. Once you started cracking jokes with subordinates and being matey, they took advantage. He turned his back on Drayton to stare at the landscape of chilly fields, saying coldly, 'He smoked like a chimney and he's got a churchyard cough. Hangs around the Piebald Pony in Stowerton. Keep on the look-out for him and don't think you won't encounter him because you're bound to.' Better let him hear it and hear it without sentimentality from him than Wexford's highly coloured version. The Chief Inspector enjoyed the peculiar *camaraderie* he had with characters like Monkey and it was all right for him in his position. Let Drayton see the funny side and goodness knew where he would end up. He stole a glance at the young man's dark hard profile. Those cagey contained ones were all the same, he thought, a mass of nerves and complexes underneath.

'First stop Knobby Clark's, sir?'

Burden nodded. How much longer was Drayton going to let his hair grow? For weeks and weeks until he looked like a drummer in one of those pop groups? Of course Wexford was right when he said they didn't want all and sundry picking out an obvious cop from his raincoat and his shoes, but the duffel coat was the end. Line Drayton up with a bunch of villains and you wouldn't be able to tell the sheep from the goats.

The car drew up outside a small shabby jeweller's shop. 'Not on the yellow band, Drayton,' Burden said sharply before the hand brake was on. They went inside. A stout man, very short of stature, with a purple naevus blotching his forehead and the greater part of his bald pate, stood behind a glass-topped table fingering a bracelet and a ring.

'Nasty cold morning,' Burden said.

'Bitter, Mr. Burden.' Knobby Clark, jeweller and occasional receiver of stolen goods, shifted a step or two. He was too short to see over the shoulder of the woman whose trinkets he was pricing. His whole massive head came into view and it resembled some huge root vegetable, a swede perhaps or a kohl rabi, this impression being enhanced by the uneven stain of the birthmark.

'Don't hurry yourself,' Burden said. 'I've got all day.'

He transferred his attention to a display of carriage

clocks. The woman Knobby was haggling with was, he could have sworn, utterly respectable. She wore a thick tweed coat that reached below her knees although she was a youngish woman, and the handbag from which she had produced the jewellery, wrapped in a thin plain handkerchief, looked as if it had once been expensive. Her hands shook a little and Burden saw that she wore a wedding ring on each. The shaking might have been due to the intense cold of Knobby's unheated shop, but only nerves could have been responsible for the tremor in her voice, nerves and the natural reluctance of such a woman to be there at all.

For the second time that day he was surprised by a tone and an accent. 'I was always given to understand the bracelet was valuable,' she said and she sounded ashamed. 'All my husband's gifts to me were very good.'

'Depends what you mean by valuable,' Knobby said, and Burden knew that the ingratiating note, the servility that covered granite imperviousness to pleading, was for his benefit. 'I'll tell you what I'll do, I'll give you ten for the lot.'

In the icy atmosphere her quickly exhaled breath hung like smoke. 'Oh, no, I couldn't possibly.' She flexed her hands, giving them firmness, but still they fumbled with the handkerchief and the bracelet made a small clink against the glass.

'Suit yourself,' said Knobby Clark. He watched indifferently as the handbag closed. 'Now, then, Mr. Burden, what can I do for you?'

For a moment Burden said nothing. He felt the woman's humiliation, the disappointment that looked more like hurt love than wounded pride. She edged past him with a gentle, 'Excuse me', easing on her gloves and keeping that curious custody of the eyes that is said to be a nun's discipline. Going on for forty, he thought, not pretty any more, fallen on evil days. He held the door open for her.

'Thank you so much,' she said, not effusively but with a faint surprise as if once, long ago, she had been

accustomed to such attentions and thought them lost for
ever.

'So you haven't seen any of this stuff?' Burden said
gruffly, thrusting the list of stolen glass under Knobby's
bulbous nose.

'I already told you, young lad, Mr. Burden.'

Drayton stiffened a little, his mouth muscles hard.

'I think I'll take a look.' Knobby opened his mouth to
complain, showing tooth fillings as richly gold as the
metal of the clocks. 'Don't start screaming for a war-
rant. It's too cold.'

The search yielded nothing. Burden's hands were red
and stiff when they came out of the inner room. 'Talk
about Aladdin's cave in the Arctic,' he grumbled. 'O.K.,
that'll do for the time being.' Knobby was an occasional
informer as well as a fence. Burden put his hand to his
breast pocket where his wallet slightly disturbed the out-
line of the new suit. 'Got anything to tell us?'

Knobby put his vegetable-like head on one side.
'Monkey Matthews is out,' he said hopefully.

'Tell me something I don't know,' Burden snapped.

The swing doors had been fixed when they got back.
Now it was difficult to open them at all. Sergeant Camb
sat at his typewriter with his back to the counter,
one finger poised in the warm air, his expression be-
mused. When he saw Burden he said as wrathfully as
his bovine nature permitted:

'I've only just this minute got shot of him.'

'Shot of who?'

'That comedian who came in when you went out.'

Burden laughed. 'You shouldn't be so sympathetic.'

'I reckon he thought I'd send Constable Peach down
to his cottage to clean up for him if he went on long
enough. He lives in Quince Cottage down in Pump
Lane, lives there with his sister only she's upped and
left him to his own devices. Went to a party on Tuesday
night and never came back.'

'And he came in here because he wanted a *charwoman?*' Burden was faintly intrigued, but still they

didn't want to add to their Missing Persons list if they could avoid it.

'I don't know what to do, he says. Ann's never gone off before without leaving me a note. Ann this and Ann that. Talk about Am I my brother's keeper?'

The sergeant was a loquacious man. Burden could hardly help wondering how much Camb's own garrulity had contributed to Rupert Margolis's long diatribe. 'Chief Inspector in?' he asked.

'Just coming now, sir.'

Wexford had his overcoat on, that hideous grey overcoat which would never be at the cleaner's during cold spells because it was never cleaned. Its colour and its ridged, hide-like texture added to the elephantine impression the Chief Inspector made as he strode heavily down the stairs, his hands thrust into pockets which held the shape of those fists even when empty.

'Carousel for a spot of lunch, sir?' said Burden.

'May as well.' Wexford shoved the swing door and shoved again when it stuck. With a half-grin, Camb returned smugly to his typewriter.

'Anything come up?' Burden asked as the wind hit them among the potted hyacinths.

'Nothing special,' Wexford said, ramming his hat more firmly on his head. 'Monkey Matthews is out.'

'Really?' said Burden and he put out his hand to feel the first spots of icy rain.

# 3

That Chief Inspector Wexford should be sitting at his rosewood desk reading the *Daily Telegraph* week-end supplement on a Friday morning was an indication that things in Kingsmarkham were more than usually slack. A cup of tea was before him, the central heating breathed deliciously and the new blue and grey folkweave curtains were half-drawn to hide the lashing rain. Wexford glanced through a feature on the beaches of Antigua, pulling down an angle lamp to shed light on the page. His little eyes, the colour of cut flints, held a mocking gleam when they lighted on a more than usually lush advertisement for clothes or personal furnishings. His own suit was grey, double-breasted, sagging under the arms and distorted at the pockets. He turned the pages, slightly bored. He was uninterested in aftershave, hair-cream, diets. Corpulent and heavy, he had always been stout and always would be. His was an ugly face, the face of a Silenus with a snub nose and wide mouth. The classics have it that Silenus was the constant companion of Bacchus, but the nearest Wexford ever got to Bacchus was an occasional pint with Inspector Burden at the Olive and Dove.

Two pages from the end he came upon an article which caught his eye. He was not an uncultured man and the contemporary fashion of investment by buying pictures had begun to interest him. He was looking at coloured photographs, two of paintings and one of a painter, when Burden came in.

'Things must be quiet,' Burden said, eyeing the *Week-end Telegraph* and Wexford's pile of scattered

15

correspondence. He came up behind the Chief Inspector and glanced over his shoulder. 'Small world,' he said. Something in his tone made Wexford look up and raise one eyebrow. 'That bloke was in here yesterday.' And Burden stabbed his finger at the photographed face.

'Who? Rupert Margolis?'

'Painter, is he? I thought he was a Mod.'

Wexford grinned. 'It says here that he's a twenty-nine-year-old genius whose picture, "The Dawn of Nothing", has just been bought by the Tate Gallery.' He ran his eye down the page. ' "Margolis, whose 'Painting of Dirt' is contemporaneous with the Theatre of Cruelty, uses coal dust and tea leaves in his work as well as paint. He is fascinated by the marvellous multifarious textures of matter in the wrong place, et cetera, et cetera." Come, come, Mike, don't look like that. Let us keep an open mind. What was he doing in here?'

'Looking for a home help.'

'Oh, we're a domestic service agency now, are we? Burden's Buttling Bureau.'

Laughing, Burden read aloud the paragraph beneath the Chief Inspector's thick forefinger. ' "Some of Margolis's most brilliant work is the fruit of two-year sojourn in Ibiza, but for the past year he and his sister Anita have made their home in Sussex. Margolis works in a sixteenth-century studio, the converted living-room of Quince Cottage, Kingsmarkham, and it is here under the blood-red quince tree that he has given birth after six months' painful gestation to his masterpiece, or 'Nothing' as he whimsically calls it." '

'Very obstetric,' said Wexford. 'Well, this won't do, Mike. We can't afford to give birth to nothing.'

But Burden had settled down with the magazine on his knees. 'Interesting stuff, this,' he said. ' "Anita, a former model and Chelsea playgirl, is often to be seen in Kingsmarkham High Street, shopping from her white Alpine sports car. . . . " I've never seen her and once seen never forgotten, I should think. Listen. "Twenty-three years old, dark and exquisite with arresting green eyes, she is the Ann of Margolis's portrait for which he was offered two thousand pounds by a South American collector. Her devotion to Margolis's interests is the inspiration of some of his best work and it is this which, some say, led to the breaking off six months ago of her engagement to writer and poet Richard Fairfax." '

Wexford fingered his own sample of the glass sculpture which with the desk and the curtains had just been allocated to the station. 'Why don't you buy the *Telegraph* yourself if you're so keen,' he grumbled.

'I'm only reading it because it's local,' Burden said. 'Funny what goes on around you and you don't know it.'

Wexford quoted sententiously, 'Full many a gem of purest ray serene the dark unfathomed caves of ocean bear.'

'I don't know about dark unfathomed caves.' Burden was sensitive to criticism of his hometown. He closed the magazine. 'She's a gem all right. Dark and exquisite, arresting green eyes. She goes to parties and doesn't come home. . . . '

The glance Wexford gave him was sharp and hard and the query cracked out like a shot. 'What?'

Surprised, Burden looked up. 'I said she goes to parties and doesn't come home.'

'I know you did.' There was a hard anxious edge to Wexford's impatience. The teasing quality present in his voice while they had been reading was quite gone and from facetious mockery he had become suddenly alert. 'I know what you said. I want to know what made you say it. How d'you know?'

'As I said, genius came hunting for a charwoman. Later he got talking to Camb and said his sister had been to a party on Tuesday night and he hadn't seen her since.'

Wexford got up slowly. The heavy lined face was puzzled and there was something else there as well. Doubt? Fear? 'Tuesday night?' he said, frowning. 'Sure it was Tuesday night?'

Burden did not care for mysteries between colleagues.

'Look, sir, he didn't even report her missing. Why the panic?'

'Panic be damned!' It was almost a shout. 'Mike, if her name is Ann and she went missing Tuesday night, this is serious. No picture of *her,* is there?' Wexford flicked expertly through the magazine, having snatched it roughly from Burden. 'No picture,' he said disgustedly. 'What's the betting the brother hasn't got one either?'

Burden said patiently, 'Since when have we got all steamed up because a single girl, a good-looking, probably rich girl, takes it into her head to run off with a boy-friend?'

'Since now,' Wexford snapped. 'Since this morning, since this.' The correspondence, Wexford's morning post, looked like a pile of litter, but he found the envelope unerringly and held it out to Burden. 'I don't like this at all, Mike.' He shook out a sheet of thick folded paper. The glass sculpture, indigo blue and translucent, shed upon it a gleaming amorphous reflection like a bubble of ink. 'Things are slack no longer,' he said.

It was an anonymous letter that lay where the magazine had been and the words on it were handwritten in red ballpoint.

'You know what a hell of a lot of these we get.' Wexford said. 'I was going to chuck it in the basket.'

A back-sloping hand, large writing, obviously disguised. The paper was not dirty nor the words obscene. The distate Burden felt was solely on account of its author's cowardice and his desire to titillate without committing himself.

He read it to himself.

> *A girl called Ann was killed in this area between eight and eleven Tuesday night. The man who done it is small and dark and young and he has a black car. Name of Geoff Smith.*

Discarding it with a grimace, he turned to the envelope. 'Posted in Stowerton,' he said. 'Twelve-fifty yesterday. Not very discreet of him, writing it. In our experience, the usual line is to cut words out of newspapers.'

'Assuming the infallibility of handwriting experts?' Wexford scoffed. 'Have you ever heard one of those johnnies give a firm opinion one way or the other, Mike? I haven't. If your recipient hasn't got a sample of your normal handwriting you might just as well save your newspaper and your scissors. Slope backwards if you normally slope forwards, write large if you usually write small, and you're perfectly incognito, safe as houses. No, I'll send this down to the lab but I'll be very much surprised if they can tell me anything I haven't deduced for myself. There's only one thing here that'll lead me to my correspondent.'

'The paper,' Burden said thoughtfully. He fingered its thick creamy surface and its silky watermark.

'Exactly. It's handmade, unless I'm much mistaken, but the writer isn't the kind of man to order handmade paper. He's an uneducated chap; look at that "done it".'

'He could work in a stationers,' Burden said slowly.

'More likely work for someone who ordered this paper specially from a stationers.'

'A servant, d'you mean? That narrows the field a lot. How many people around here employ menservants?'

'Plenty employ gardeners, Mike. The stationers should be our starting point and we'll only need to tackle the high-class ones. That leaves out Kingsmarkham. I can't see Braddon's supplying handmade paper and certainly not Grover's.'

'You're taking this whole thing very seriously, sir.'

'I am. I want Martin, Drayton, Bryant and Gates up here because this is one anonymous letter I can't afford to treat as a practical joke. You, Mike, had better see what you can get out of the twenty-nine-year-old genius.'

He sat beside Burden behind the desk when they were all assembled. 'Now, I'm not taking you off your regular work,' he began. 'Not yet. Get hold of the electoral register and make a list of all the Geoffrey Smiths in the district. Particularly in Stowerton. I want them

all looked up during the course of the day and I want to
know if any of them are small and dark and if any of
them has a black car. That's all. No frightening of
wives, please, and no insisting on looking into garages.
Just a casual survey. Keep your eyes open. Take a look
at this paper, Sergeant Martin, and if you find any like
it in a stationers I want it brought back here for comparison . . .'

After they had gone, Burden said bitterly, 'Smith! I
ask you, Smith!'

'Some people really are called Smith, Mike,' Wexford
said. He folded up the colour supplement with Margolis's photograph uppermost and tucked it carefully in a
drawer of the rosewood desk.

'If I could only find the matches,' Rupert Margolis
said, 'I'd make you a cup of coffee.' He fumbled helplessly among dirty crockery, topless bottles of milk,
crumpled frozen food cartons on the kitchen table.
'There were some here on Tuesday night. I came in
about eleven and all the lights had fused. That's not unusual. There was an enormous pile of newspapers on
here and I picked them up and chucked them outside
the back door. Our dustbins are always full. However, I
did find the matches then, about fifteen boxes where the
papers had been.' He sighed heavily. 'God knows where
they are now. I haven't been cooking much.'

'Here,' said Burden and handed him one of the
match books the Olive and Dove gave away with drinks.
Margolis poured a percolator full of black liquid
sprouting mould down the sink. Grounds clung to the
sink side and to an aubergine floating in dirty dishwater.
'Now, let me get this straight.' It had taken him half an
hour to get the salient facts out of Margolis and even
now he was not sure if he had them sorted out. 'Your
sister, whose name is Anita or Ann, was going to a
party given by Mr. and Mrs. Cawthorne of Cawthorne's
service station in Stowerton on Tuesday night. When
you got home at eleven, having been out since three,
she was gone and her car also, her white Alpine sports

car which is usually parked outside in the lane. Right?'

'Right,' said Margolis worriedly. The kitchen had no ceiling, only a roof of corrugated metal supported by ancient beams. He sat on the edge of the table staring at the cobwebs which hung from them and moving his head gently in time to the movement of those swinging grey ropes, agitated by the rising steam from the coffee pot.

Burden went on firmly. 'You left the back door unlocked for her and went to bed but you were awakened soon afterwards by Mr. Cawthorne telephoning to ask where you sister was.'

'Yes. I was very annoyed. Cawthorne's a terrible old bore and I never talk to him unless I have to.'

'Weren't you at all concerned?'

'No. Why should I be? I thought she'd changed her mind and gone off somewhere else.' The painter got down from his perch and ran the cold tap over two filthy tea cups.

'At about one o'clock,' Burden said, 'you were awakened again by lights passing across your bedroom ceiling. These you assumed to be the lights of your sister's car, since no one else lives in Pump Lane, but you did not get up . . .'

'I went straight off to sleep again. I was tired, you see.'

'Yes, I think you said you'd been in London.'

The coffee was surprisingly good. Burden tried to ignore the incrustations on the cup rim and enjoy it. Someone had been dipping wet spoons in the sugar and at times it had apparently been in contact with a marmalade-covered knife.

'I went out at three,' Margolis said, his face vague and dreamy. 'Ann was there then. She told me she'd be out when I got back and not to forget my key.'

'And had you forgotten it, Mr. Margolis?'

'Of course I hadn't,' the painter said, suddenly sharp. 'I'm not crazy.' He drank his coffee at a gulp and a little colour came into his pale face. 'I left my car at

Kingsmarkham station and went to see this man about a
show I'm having.'

'A show?' Burden said, bewildered. The word con-
jured up in his mind visions of dancing girls and din-
ner-jacketed comedians.

'An exhibition, then,' Margolis said impatiently. 'Of
my work. Really, you are a bunch of philistines. I
thought so yesterday when nobody seemed to know who
I was.' He favoured Burden with a look of dark suspicion as if he doubted his efficiency. 'As I was saying, I
went to see this man. He's the manager of the Morissot
Gallery in Knightsbridge and when we'd had our talk he
rather unexpectedly gave me dinner. But I was absolutely exhausted with all this travelling about. This gallery man's a fearful bore and it got very tedious just sitting there listening to him talking. That's why, when I
saw Ann's car lights, I didn't bother to get up.'

'But yesterday morning,' Burden said, 'you found her
car in the lane.'

'All wet and revolting with the *New Statesman* plastered across its windscreen.' Margolis sighed. 'There
were papers all over the garden. I don't suppose you
could send someone to clear them up, could you? Or get
the council to?'

'No,' said Burden firmly. 'Didn't you go out at all on
Wednesday?'

'I was working,' said Margolis. 'And I sleep a lot.' He
added vaguely, 'At odd times, you know. I thought Ann
had come and gone. We go our own ways.' His voice
rose suddenly to a shrill pitch. Burden began to wonder
if he might be slightly mad. 'But I'm lost without her.
She never leaves me like this without a word!' He got
up abruptly, knocking a milk bottle on to the floor. The
neck broke off and a stream of sour whey flowed across
coconut matting. 'O God, let's go into the studio if you
don't want any more coffee. I don't have a photograph
of her, but I could show you my portrait if you think it
would help.'

There were probably twenty pictures in the studio,
one of them so large that it filled an entire wall. Burden

had only once in his life seen a larger and that was Rembrandt's Night Watch viewed reluctantly on a day trip to Amsterdam. To its surface, giving a three-dimensional look to the wild cavorting figures, other substances apart from paint adhered; cotton wool, slivers of metal and strips of tortured newspaper. Burden decided that he preferred the Night Watch. If the portrait was in the same style as this picture it would not be helpful for the purposes of identification. The girl would have one eye, a green mouth and a saucepan scourer sticking out of her ear.

He sat down in a rocking chair, having first removed from its seat a tarnished silver toast rack, a squashed tube of paint and a wooden wind instruments of vaguely Mediterranean origin. Newspapers, clothes, dirty cups and saucers, beer bottles, covered every surface and in places were massed on the floor. By the telephone dead narcissi stood in a glass vase half-full of green water, and one of them, its stem broken, had laid its wrinkled cup and bell against a large wedge of cheese.

Presently Margolis came back with the portrait. Burden was agreeably surprised. It was conventionally painted rather in the style of John, although he did not know this, and it showed the head and shoulders of a girl. Her eyes were like her brother's, blue with a hint of jade, and her hair, as black as his, swept across her cheeks in two heavy crescents. The face was hawk-like, if a hawk's face can also be soft and beautiful, the mouth fine yet full and the nose just verging on the aquiline. Margolis had caught or had given her, a fierce intelligence. If she were not already dead in her youth, Burden thought, she would one day be a formidable old woman.

He had an uneasy feeling that one ought always to praise a work when shown it by its creator, and he said awkwardly:

'Very nice. Jolly good.'

Instead of showing gratitude or gratification, Margolis said simply, 'Yes, it's marvellous. One of the best things

I've ever done.' He put the painting on an empty easel and regarded it happily, his good humour restored.

'Now, Mr. Margolis,' Burden said severely, 'in a case like this it's normal practice for us to ask the relatives just where they think the missing person might be.' The painter nodded without turning round. 'Please concentrate, sir. Where do you personally think your sister is?'

He realized that his tone had become more and more stern, more schoolmasterish, as the interview progressed, and suddenly he wondered if he was being presumptuous. Since his arrival at Quince Cottage he had kept the newspaper feature in mind, but only as a guide, as information on the brother and sister that could only have been elicited from Margolis after hours of probing. Now he remembered why that feature had been written and what Margolis was. He was in the presence of genius, or if that was journalist's extravagance, of great talent. Margolis was not like other men. In his fingers and his brain was something that set him apart, something that might not be fully recognized and appreciated until long after the painter was dead. Burden experienced a sense of awe, a strange reverence he could not reconcile with the seamy disorder that surrounded him or with the palefaced creature that looked like a beatnik and might be a latterday Rembrandt. Who was he, a country policeman, to judge, to mock and put himself among the philistines? His voice softened as he repeated his question.

'Where do you think she is, Mr. Margolis?'

'With one of her men friends. She's got dozens.' He turned round and his opalescent eyes seemed to go out of focus and into some dreamy distance. Did Rembrandt ever come into contact with whatever police they had in those days? Genius was more common then, Burden thought. There was more of it about and people knew how to deal with it. 'Or I *would* think so,' Margolis said, 'but for the note.'

Burden started. Had he also received an anonymous letter? 'What note? A note about your sister?'

'That's the point, there isn't one, and there should be.

You see, she's often popped off like this before and she wouldn't distrub me if I was working or sleeping.' Margolis passed his fingers through the long spiky hair. 'And I don't seem to do much apart from working and sleeping,' he said. 'She always leaves a note in a very prominent position, by my bed or propped up somewhere.' Memories seemed to come to him of such former examples of his sister's solicitude. 'Quite a long detailed note usually, where she'd gone and who with, and what to do about cleaning the place and—and, well, little things for me to do, you know.' He gave a small doubtful smile which clouded into sourness as the telephone rang. 'That'll be dreary old Russell Cawthorne,' he said. 'He keeps bothering me, wanting to know where she is.'

He reached for the receiver and rested his elbow against the chunk of mouldering cheese.

'No, she isn't here. I don't know where she is.' Watching him, Burden wondered exactly what were the 'little things' his sister would recommend him to do. Even so small a thing as answering the telephone seemed to throw him into a state of surly misanthropy. 'I've got the police here, if you must know. Of course I'll tell you if she turns up. Yes, yes, yes. What d'you mean, you'll be seeing me? I shouldn't think you will for a moment. We never do see each other.'

'Oh, yes, you will, Mr. Margolis,' Burden said quietly. 'You and I are going to see Mr. Cawthorne now.'

# 4

Thoughtfully Wexford compared the two sheets of paper, one piece with red ballpoint writing on it, the other new and clean. The texture, colour and watermark were identical.

'It was from Braddon's, after all, sir,' said Sergeant Martin. He was a painstaking officer whose features were permanently set in an earnest frown. 'Grover's only sell pads and what they call drawing blocks. Braddon's get this paper specially from a place in London.'

'D'you mean it's ordered?'

'Yes, sir. Fortunately they only supply it to one customer, a Mrs. Adeline Harper who lives in Waterford Avenue, Stowerton.'

Wexford nodded. 'Good class residential,' he said. 'Big old-fashioned houses.'

'Mrs. Harper's away, sir. Taking a long Easter holiday, according to the neighbour. She doesn't keep a manservant. In fact the only servant she does have is a char who goes in Mondays, Wednesdays and Fridays.'

'Could she be my correspondent?'

'They're big houses, sir, and a long way apart. Waterford Avenue's not like a council estate or a block of flats where everyone knows everyone else. They keep themselves to themselves. This char's been seen to go in and out, but no on knows her name.'

'And if she has a way of snapping up unconsidered trifles like expensive writing paper, her employer and the neighbours don't know about it?'

'All the neighbours know,' said Martin, a little discomfited by the paucity of his information, 'is that she's middle-aged, showily dressed and got ginger hair.'

'Mondays, Wednesdays and Fridays ... I take it she goes in while her employer's away?'

'And today's Friday, sir. But, you see, she only goes in mornings and she was gone before I got there. "I've just seen her go by", the neighbour said. I nipped up the road smartish but she was out of sight.'

Wexford turned his attention once more to the sheets of paper and to the lab report on that paper. No fingerprints had been found on the anonymous letter, no perfume clung to it; the pen with which it had been written was a cheap ballpoint such as could be bought in every stationers in the country. He had an inventive imagination but he could not visualize the concatenation of happenings that must have been the prerequisite to this letter. A ginger-haired charwoman, whose own conduct was apparently not above reproach, had seen something or heard something that had led her to write to the police. Such communication would necessarily be alien to a woman of her type, a woman found to be an occasional thief. And yet she, or someone closely associated with her, had written it. Fear or spite might have prompted her action.

'I wonder if it could be blackmail,' Wexford said.

'I don't quite follow you, sir.'

'Because we always think of blackmail being successful, or, at any rate, successful for a time. Suppose it isn't successful at all. Suppose our ginger-haired woman tried to put the squeeze on Geoff Smith, but he won't play. Then, if she's vindictive, she carries out her threat.'

'Blackmailers always are vindictive, sir,' Martin said sagely unctuous. 'A nasty spiteful thing, if ever there was one. Worse than murder, sir.'

An excessive show of respect always grated on Wexford, especially as in this case when it was associated with the imparting of platitudes he had heard a thousand times before. 'Here endeth the first lesson,' he said sharply. 'Answer that, will you?'

Martin leapt to the phone before the end of the second double peal. 'Inspector Burden for you, sir.'

Wexford took the receiver without getting up. The stretched coil lead passed dangerously near his glass sculpture. 'Move that thing,' he said. The sergeant lifted it and stuck it on the narrow window sill. 'Well?' Wexford said into the mouthpiece.

Burden's voice sounded dazed. 'I'm off to have a word with Cawthorne. Can we spare someone to come down here and fetch Miss Margolis's car? Drayton, if he's not tied up. Oh, and the cottage'll have to be gone over.' Wexford heard his tone drop to a whisper. 'It's a proper shambles, sir. No wonder he wanted a char.'

'We want one, too.' Wexford said crisply, 'a snappy dresser with ginger hair.' He explained. The phone made crackling sounds. 'What's going on?'

'The cheese has fallen into a flower pot.'

'My God,' said Wexford. 'I see what you mean.'

Mark Drayton came down the police station steps and crossed the road. To reach Pump Lane he had to walk the whole length of the High Street and when he came to Grover's the newsagent he stopped for a moment to glance at its window. It seemed incredible to him that Martin had for a moment considered this place as the possible purveyor of hand-made paper. It had the shady, almost sordid, aspect of a shop in the slum streets of some great city. A high brick wall towered above it and between it and the florist's next door a brown cobbled alley plunged deep into a dubious hinterland of dustbins and sheds and a pair of garages.

In the shop window the displayed wares looked as if they had been arranged there some years before and since left utterly untended. Easter was not long past and the Easter cards were topical. But it seemed to him that their topicality must be an accident in the same way as a stopped clock must be correct twice a day, for there were Christmas cards there as well, some fallen on their sides and filmed with dust.

Dying houseplants stood among the cards. Perhaps

they were for sale or perhaps misguidedly intended for decoration. The earth around their roots had shrunk through dehydration, leaving an empty space between soil and pot. A box containing a game of snakes and ladders had come open, so that the coloured board hung from a shelf. The counters lay on the floor among rusty nails, spilt confetti and shed leaves. Drayton thought he had seldom seen anything which could be regarded as an advertisement so repellent and so discouraging to those shoppers who passed this way.

He was going to walk on with a shrug of disgust when, through the dirty glass panel that separated this window from the interior of the shop, he caught sight of a girl behind the counter. He could only see her dimly, the shape of her, and her pale bright hair. But, as he hesitated, his interest faintly aroused, she approached the panel and opening it, reached for a pack of cards which lay to the left of the snakes and ladders box. That she made no attempt to retrieve the counters or blow the dust from the box lid annoyed him. He was meticulous in his own work, tidy, attentive to the tools of his life and his trade.

Because he felt distaste and a desire to make plain the disapproval of at least one potential customer, he raised his eyes coldly and met hers. At once he knew who she was. A face which had haunted him for four days and which was faintly familiar but not specifically identifiable was confronting him. He stared at her and felt the hot blood rush into his cheeks. She could not know that he had seen her before, or if she did know it, could not be aware of the thoughts, many of them dreamlike, searching, sensuous, which had accompanied his constant evoking of her image on to his mind's eye. She could not know it, but he felt that she must do so, that such vivid violent imaginings could not be contained within the brain that conceived them and must by some telepathic process be communicated to their object.

She gave no sign. Her grey eyes, large and listless, met his only for a moment. Then she took the pack of

playing cards, kneeling among the dust and the confetti
to reach them, and retreated to serve a waiting customer. Her legs were long and rather too thin. The dust
had left circular grey patches on her knees. He watched
the panel swing slowly shut behind her, its finger-
marked, bluish translucency obscuring all but the blur
of her silver-gold hair.

Drayton crossed the alley, avoiding puddles on whose
scummy surface spilt oil made a rainbow iridescence.
He glanced at the garage doors, wondering why no one
painted them when paint was cheap and the making of
things clean and fresh so satisfying. From the stall outside the florist's he could smell daffodils. They and the
girl he had just seen shared the same quality of untouched exquisite freshness and like the girl they flowered in squalor. The roughly made dirty wooden box
was to them what the sordid newsagents was to her, an
ugly unfitting background for breathless beauty.

Was everything he saw going to remind him of her?
Had he felt like this about her before Monday night? As
he came to the parapet of the bridge and looked down
the river path he asked himself the question again. Certainly he had noticed her shopping in the town. She was
the sort of girl any man would notice. For months now
she had held for him a vague attraction. Then, on
Monday night, he had passed this spot and seen her on
that path kissing another man. It had given him a
strange feeling to watch her, disarmed, vulnerable,
abandoned to a passion anyone walking by in the dusk
might witness. It showed that she was flesh and blood,
subject to sensuality and therefore attainable, accessible
to him.

Their figures had been reflected in the dark water, the
man's which he had disregarded, and hers, slim, long,
quivering. From that moment her image had haunted
him, lying just above the surface of his conscious mind
to trouble him when he was alone.

His own reflection, sharper and more real in the afternoon light than theirs had been at twilight, stared
back at him coldly from the stream. The dark Italianate

face with its guarded eyes and its curved mouth showed nothing of his thoughts. His hair was rather long, much too long for a policeman, and he wore a dark grey duffel coat over slacks and sweater. Burden objected to the coat and the hair, but he could find no fault with Drayton's economy of speech, nor with his reserve, although it was a different brand from his own.

The mirrored head and shoulders crumpled and retreated into the parapet of the bridge. Drayton felt in his pockets to make sure he had remembered his gloves. It was a formality only; he seldom forgot anything. He looked back once, but he could only see shoppers, prams, bicycles, a tall brick wall and an alley with wet litter on its cobbles. Then he made his way to the outskirts of the town and Pump Lane.

This by-way into Kingsmarkham's countryside was new to him, but like the other lanes it was just a tunnel between green banks topped with high trees, a roadway scarcely wide enough for two cars to pass. A cow peered at him over the hedge, its feet in primroses. Drayton was not interested in natural history nor given to pastoral reflection. His eye was drawn to the white sports car parked half on the verge, half on the road, the only man-made thing in sight. The cottage itself was not immediately visible. Then he discerned, among tangled greening hawthorn and white sloe blossom, a small rickety gate. The branches were spiny and wet. He lifted them, drenching his shoulders. Apple trees, their trunks lichened to a sour pulpy green, clustered in front of the house whose shabby whiteness was relieved by the flame-coloured flowers of a tall shrub growing against it, the quince—though Drayton did not know it—from which the cottage took its name.

He slipped on his gloves and got into the Alpine. Possessing little of his own, he nevertheless had a respect for material things. This car would be a delight to own, a pleasure to drive. It irked him that its owner appeared to have used it as a kind of travelling dustbin, throwing cigarette packs and match ends on to the floor. Drayton knew better than to touch more than was needful, but he had to remove the torn newspaper from the windscreen before he could see to drive. Hawthorn boughs scraping the roof hurt him almost as much as if they had scoured his own skin.

The temptation to take the longer way round by Forby had to be resisted. Traffic was not heavy at this time of day and his only excuse would be that he wanted to enjoy himself. Drayton had trained himself stoically to resist temptation. One, he knew, he would soon succumb to, but not such triviality as this.

There was a yellow and brown spotted fur coat slung across the passenger seat. It had a strong heady scent, the smell of a beautiful woman, evoking in Drayton's mind past and future love. The car moved smoothly forward. He had reached the centre of the High Street before he noticed the needle on the gauge climbing swiftly and alarmingly. It was almost at danger level. There were no service stations in this part of the main road, but he remembered seeing a garage in York Street, just past Joy Jewels and the labour exchange.

When he reached it he got out and lifted the hood. Steam billowed at him and he stepped back.

'Radiator's leaking,' he said to the pump attendant.

'I'll get you some water. She'll be all right if you take her slow. Far to go?'

'Not far,' said Drayton.

The water began to leak out as soon as they poured it in. Drayton was almost within sight of the police station. He passed Joy Jewels with its windows full of rhinestones on crimson velvet and he passed Grover's, but he did not look. Poetry was not among his considerable and heterogeneous reading matter, but he would have agreed that man's love is of man's life a thing apart. He would go there later when his work was done.

Cawthorne's garage was an altogether grander affair than the modest place to which Drayton had taken Anita Margolis's car. It commanded Stowerton crossroads. From the roof of the showroom to the pinnacle of the little glass cubicle where Cawthorne sat at the receipt of custom, hung a yellow and scarlet banner: *Treble stamps with four gallons*. These colours matched the paint on the eight pumps and the neon tubing on the arch to the service entrance. Burden could remember when, not so long ago, a copse of silver birches had stood here and he remembered the efforts of the rural preservation society to prevent Cawthorne's coming. The last of the birches huddled by the showroom wall like bewildered aborigines crowded out by a conqueror from the new world.

By contrast the house behind was old. A triumph of the gothic revival, it sported pinnacles, turrets, gables and aggressive drainpipes. Formerly known as Birch House, the home of two spinster sisters, it had been furnished by Cawthorne and his wife with every conceivable Victorian monstrosity. The mantelpieces were fringed and set about with green glass fluted vases, stuffed birds and wax fruit under domes. Cawthorne, after a dubious look at Rupert Margolis, took them into a sitting-room and went away to fetch his wife.

'It's the lastest fad,' Margolis said morosely. 'All this Victorian junk.' Above the fireplace hung an oleograph of a woman in grecian dress holding a lily. He gave it an angry glance. 'Cawthorne must be sixty and his wife's a hag. They're mad about young people. I expect the young people think they had this stuff for wedding presents.' And he laughed vindictively.

Burden thought he had seldom met anyone so uncharitable, but when Mrs. Cawthorne came in he began to see what Margolis meant. She was extravagantly thin and her dress had a very short skirt and very short sleeves. Her hair was tinted primrose and styled like the head of a feather duster.

'Why, hallo, Roo. You are a stranger.' Burden was suddenly sure that she had met Margolis perhaps only once before, and here she was giving him pet names like a character out of *Winnie the Pooh*. A lion hunter. She bounced into a quilted and buttoned armchair, showing a lot of scrawny leg. Margolis took absolutely no notice of her. "What's all this about Ann, then?'

'We hope you'll be able to help us, Mrs. Cawthorne,' Burden said heavily, but it was to her husband that he turned his eyes. He was an elderly, white-moustached man, with a decided military bearing. If the growing fashion among the young of wearing soldier's uniforms spread to older generations, Cawthorne ought to catch on. He would look fine in a hussar's tunic. 'You had a party on Tuesday evening, Mr. Cawthorne. Miss Margolis was invited. I understand she didn't turn up.'

'Right,' Cawthorne said briskly. 'She dropped in in the afternoon, said she'd be sure to be here. Never turned up. I've been damned worried, I can tell you. Glad to see you folk have been called in.'

'Yes, and Dickie Fairfax came all the way down from London just to see her.' Mrs. Cawthorne moved closer to Margolis's side. 'They used to be friends. Very close friends, I may add.' She fluttered beaded eyelashes.

'Fairfax, the writer?' Burden had never heard of him until that morning, but he did not wish to be branded a philistine for the second time that day.

Mrs. Cawthorne nodded. 'Poor Dickie was rather peeved when she didn't turn up and drifted away around eleven.'

'Left one of my best brandy glasses on a diesel pump,' said Cawthorne gruffly. 'Damned inconsiderate blighter.'

'But he was here all the evening?' Between eight and eleven, Burden thought. That was the crucial time if the anonymous letter was to be trusted.

'He was here all right. Came on the dot of eight and got started in on the hard stuff right away.'

'You are so mean,' Mrs. Cawthorne said unpleasantly. 'Mean and jealous. Just because Ann preferred him.' She gave a tinny laugh. 'She and Russell have a sort of thing.' Burden glanced at Margolis but the painter had gone off into a brooding abstraction. Mrs. Cawthorne thrust a bony finger into her husband's ribs. 'Or that's what he kids himself.' The blood rushed into Cawthorne's already pink face. His hair was like white wool or the coat of a West Highland terrier.

Suddenly Margolis roused himself. He addressed Burden, rather as if there was no one else in the room.

'Ann gave Dickie the out months ago. There's someone else now. I'm trying to remember his name.'

'Not Geoff Smith, by any chance.' Burden watched the three faces, saw nothing but blankness. He had memorized the message in that letter. *He is small and young and dark and he has a black car. Name of Geoff Smith.* Of course, it wouldn't be his real name. Smith never was.

'All right. That's all for now. Thanks for your help.'

'I don't call that help.' Mrs. Cawthorne giggled. She tried to take Margolis's hand but failed. 'You'll be lost without her, Roo,' she said. 'Now, if there's anything Russell and I can do. . . .'

Burden expected Margolis to maintain his silence, or possibly say something rude. He gave Mrs. Cawthorne a blind hopeless stare. 'Nobody else has ever been able to do anything,' he said. Then he walked out of the room, his shoulders straight. For a brief moment he had attained Burden's notion of the heights of genius. He followed, Cawthorne behind him. The garage owner's breath smelt of whisky. His was a soldier's face, brave, hearty, a little stupid. The military air about him extended, Bruden thought, even to his name. All those years ago his mother had called him Russell because it sounded so well with Cawthorne, auguring great things. General Sir Russell Cawthorne, K.C.B., D.S.O. . . . Burden knew something of his history. The man had never won a battle or even led a troop. He kept a garage.

'I'm looking for a Geoff Smith who might be a friend of Miss Margolis's.'

Cawthorne gave a braying laugh. 'I daresay he might, only I've never heard of him. She's got a lot of boy friends. Lovely girl, lovely little driver and a good head for business. I sold her that car of hers. That's how we met. Haggled, you know, drove a hard bargain. I admire that. Only natural she'd have a lot of boy friends.'

'Would you include yourself among them?'

It was grotesque. The man was all of sixty. And yet

boy friend could be applied these days to a lover of any age. It was in two senses a euphemism.

For a moment it seemed that Cawthorne was not going to reply and when he did it was not to answer the question.

'Are you married?'

'Yes. I am.'

'Horrible business, isn't it?' He paused and gazed lugubriously at a pump attendant giving green stamps with change. 'Growing old together. . . .Horrible!' He braced his shoulders as if standing to attention. 'Mind you, it's your duty to stay young as long as you can. Live it up, keep going, go around with young people. That's half the battle.' The only one he was ever likely to fight.

'Did you "go around" with Miss Margolis, Mr. Cawthorne?'

The garage proprietor brought his face and his whisky breath closer to Burden. 'Once,' he said. 'Just the once. I took her out to dinner in Pomfret, to the Cheriton Forest Hotel. Stupid, really. The waiter knew me. He'd seen me there with my wife, you see, and he said, "Will your daughter have the smoked salmon too, sir?" '

Why do it, then? Why make such a crass fool of yourself? Burden had no temptations, few dreams. He got into the car beside Margolis, wondering why the defenceless put themselves into the firing line.

There were pictures on the stairs and pictures on the landing. The light was fading and Sergeant Martin stumbled over a pile of washing on the floor outside Anita Margolis's bedroom door.

'No letters and no diaries, sir,' he said to Burden. 'I never saw so many clothes in all my life. It's like a—a draper's shop in there.'

'A boutique, you mean,' said Drayton.

'Been in many, have you?' Burden snapped. Drayton looked the type who would buy black nylon underwear for his women and not turn a hair. Through the half-open door, propped ajar with a gilt sandal, he caught sight of garments spread on the bed and hung, crammed closely, in two wardrobes. 'If your sister went away of her own accord,' he said to Margolis, 'she'd have taken clothes with her. Is anything missing?'

'I really wouldn't know. It's absolutely useless asking me things like that. Ann's always buying clothes. She's got masses of them.'

'There's just one thing,' Drayton said. 'We can't find a raincoat.'

Martin nodded agreement. 'That's right. Furs and suede things and all sorts, but no woman's raincoat. It was raining cats and dogs on Tuesday night.'

'Sometimes she takes clothes,' said Margolis, 'and sometimes she doesn't. She's quite likely to have gone just as she was and buy anything she needed.'

Leaving them to finish their search, Burden followed the painter downstairs. 'She had money, then?' The woman in the portrait, the woman who possessed this vast and apparently expensive wardrobe, would hardly be content with something off the peg from Marks and Spencers. Or was the lover expected to cough up? In this set-up anything was possible. 'How much money did she have on her?'

'One of her cheques came on Monday. She has this money of her own, you see. My father left all his money to her. He didn't like me and I couldn't stand him, so he left it all to Ann. They pay it out every three months.'

Burden sighed. Anyone else would have spoken of a private income, of payments made quarterly.

'Do you know how much this cheque was for?'

'Of course I do,' Margolis said crossly. 'I'm not a half-wit. It's always the same, five hundred pounds.'

'And she had this cheque with her?' Here, at last, was something for him to get his teeth into. The beginning of a motive loomed.

'She cashed it as soon as it came,' Margolis said, 'and she put the money in her handbag.'

'All five hundred!' Burden gasped. 'You mean she set

off for a party with five hundred pounds in her handbag?'

'Bound to have done. She always carried it about
with her,' Margolis said casually, as if it were the most
natural thing in the world. 'You see, she might be out
and see something she wanted to buy and then she'd
have the money on her, wouldn't she? She doesn't like
paying for things with cheques because then she gets
overdrawn, and Ann's rather middle-class in some
ways. She gets worried if she's overdrawn.'

Five hundred pounds, even if it was in fivers, would
make a big wad in a woman's handbag. Would she be
careless about where she opened the handbag and to
whom she revealed the contents? The woman was
thoroughly immoral too. Decent women had clean tidy
homes. They were either married or had jobs or both.
They kept their money in the bank. Burden thought he
could see just what had happened to Anita Margolis.
She had gone into a shop or a garage on her way to the
party, opened her bag and its contents had been seen by
that villain Smith. A good-looking plausible villain,
probably. Young, dark and with a black car. They had
gone off together and he had killed her for the money.
The letter writer had got wind of it, maybe tried blackmail, blackmail which hadn't worked?

But a casual pick-up would be next to impossible to
find. A regular boy friend, especially if he was down on
his luck, might fill the bill.

'Have you remembered the name of Fairfax's suc-
cessor?' he asked.

'Alan Something. He's got no money and he's very
provincial. I don't know what she sees in him, but
Ann's rather inclined to go slumming, if you know what
I mean. Fitz something Fitzwilliam? It isn't exactly
Fitzwilliam but it's something like that. I've only spoken
to him once and that was enough.'

Burden said tartly. 'You don't seem to like anyone
very much, sir.'

'I like Ann,' Margolis said sadly. 'I tell you who
might know. Mrs. Penistan, our late char. I should go

and ask her, and if she's just pining to come back and clean this place, don't discourage her, will you?

A chill grey drizzle was falling as they emerged from the cottage door. Margolis accompanied Burden to the garden gate. 'You haven't found a charwoman, then?'

From behind him the painter's voice held a note of childlike pride. 'I put an advertisement in Grover's window,' he said. 'I wrote it on a little card. Only half-a-crown a week. I really can't imagine why people spend all that money on the agony column of *The Times* when this way is so cheap and easy.'

'Quite,' said Burden, stifling an incipient desire to roar and stamp. 'This Mrs. Penistan, she hasn't got ginger hair, has she?'

Margolis stood against the hedge, picking the new shoots off a hawthorn bush. These he put into his mouth and began to chew them with evident relish. 'She always wore a hat,' he said. 'I don't know what colour her hair is, but I can tell you where she lives.' He paused for congratulation perhaps on this unlooked-for feat of memory. Burden's expression seemed to gratify him, for he went on, 'I know that because I drove her home once when it was raining. It's in Glebe Road, on the left, past the fifth tree and just before you get to the pillar box. Red curtains downstairs and . . .'

Burden cut him short with a snort of exasperation. If this was genius he had had enough of it. 'I'll find it.' He could have recourse to the electoral register himself. Penistan was surely as rare a name as Smith was common.

# 5

Mark Drayton rented a room down by Kingsmarkham station. His landlady was a motherly woman who liked to make her lodgers feel at home. She hung pictures on the walls, provided flowered counterpanes and scattered little ornaments about like seeds. As soon as he moved in Drayton put all the vases and ashtrays into the bottom of the cupboard. There was nothing to be done about the counterpane. He wanted the room to look like a cell. Someone—it was a girl—had told him he had a cold nature and he had since cultivated his personality in this direction. He liked to think he was austere and without emotion.

He was very ambitious. When he had first come to Kingsmarkham he had set out to make Wexford like him and he had succeeded. He carried out all Wexford's instructions meticulously, absorbing the Chief Inspector's homilies, lectures, digressions and pleasantries with courteously inclined head. The district was now as familiar to him as his own hometown and he used his library tickets for works on psychology and forensic medicine. Sometimes he read a novel, but nothing lighter than Mann or Durrell. One day he hoped to be a commissioner. He would marry the right wife, someone like Mrs. Wexford, good-looking, quiet and gracious. Wexford had a daughter, a pretty girl and clever, they said. But that was a long way off. He had no intention of marrying until he had attained distinguished rank.

His attitude to women was a source of pride to him. Being intensely narcissistic, he had little admiration left over, and his idealism was reserved for his own career.

His affairs had been practical and chilly. In his vocabulary love was a banned verb, the most obscene of the four letter words. He had never used it between 'I' and 'you'. If he ever felt anything stronger than a physical need he called it desire with complications.

That, he thought, was what he felt for the Grover girl. That was why he was going into the shop now to buy his evening paper. Maybe she would not be there. Or maybe when he saw her close-to, not through glass or in someone's else's arms, it would all fade away. On the whole, he hoped that would happen.

The shop squatted under a towering wall of brown brick. It seemed to lurk there as if it had something to hide. A street lamp in a black iron cage stuck out beside its door but the lamp was still unlit. As Drayton opened this door a little bell made a cold tinkle. The interior was dim and it smelt unpleasant. Behind the paperback stand and a rusty refrigerator hung with lop-sided ice-cream posters, he could see the shelves of a lending library. The books were the kind you buy at jumble sales, nineteenth century three-volume novels, explorer's reminiscences, school stories.

A thin dried-up woman was behind the counter, standing under a naked light bulb. Presumably this was her mother. She was serving a customer with tobacco.

'How's the governor?' said the customer.

'Ever so bad with his back,' said Mrs. Grover cheerfully. 'Hasn't left his bed since Friday. Did you say Vestas?' Drayton noted with distaste the girlie magazines, the stand of paper patterns (two swinging mini-skirts to cut out and sew in an evening), the ninepenny thrillers, Ghosty Worlds, Cosmic Creatures. On a shelf among mock-Wedgwood ashtrays stood a pottery spaniel with artificial flowers growing from a basket on its back. The flowers were furred with dust like a grey fungoid growth. 'That's five and three, then. Thanks very much. It's what they call a slipped disc. He just bent over fiddling with the car and—crack!'

'Nasty,' said the customer. 'You thinking of letting your room again? I heard your young man had gone.'

'And good riddance. I couldn't take another one on, dear, not with Mr. Grover laid up. Linda and me have got enough on our hands as it is.' So that was her name, Linda. Drayton turned away from Ghosty Worlds. Mrs. Grover looked at him indifferently. 'Yes?'

'*Standard*, please.'

There was only one left and that in the rack outside the shop by the advertisement case. Drayton followed her out and paid for his newspaper on the doorstep. He would never go back in there, inefficient, ill-mannered lot! Perhaps he never would have done and his life would have pursued its ordered, uninterrupted course towards its goal. He lingered only for a moment. The lamp had come on and his eye was caught by a familiar name on one of the cards. Margolis, Quince Cottage, and beneath a plea for a charwoman. The door opened and Linda Grover came out. Even so quickly can one catch the plague. . . .

She was as tall as he and her short grey dress made her look taller. The damp wind blew the stuff against her body, showing the shape of her little breasts and the long slender thighs. She had a small head set on a thin neck and her pale hair was drawn back so tightly that it pulled the skin and stretched wide the smooth dove-coloured eyebrows. He had never seen a girl so completely clothed look so naked.

She opened the card case, removed one and replaced it with another. 'Raining again,' she said. 'I don't know where it all comes from.' An ugly voice, half-Sussex, half-Cockney.

'The sky,' said Drayton. That was the only answer to such a stupid remark. He could not imagine why she had bothered to speak to him at all, unless she had seen him that night and was covering embarrassment.

'Very funny.' Her fingers were long and the hand had a wide octave span. He observed the bitten nails. 'You'll get soaked standing there,' she said.

Drayton put up his hood. 'How's the boy friend?' he asked conversationally. Her reaction pleased him. He had flicked her on the raw.

'Is there one?' Her ugly accent grated on him and he told himself it was this and not her proximity which made him clench his hands as he stood looking at the cards offering prams for sale and council flats to be exchanged.

'A good-looking girl like you?' he said, turning sharply to face her. It was not Mann or Durrell, just standard verbal practice, the first preliminary love play.

'Get away.'

Her smile began very slowly and developed with a kind of secrecy. He noticed that she smiled without showing her teeth, without parting her lips, and it devastated him. They stood looking at each other in the rainy dusk. Drizzle spattered the tiers of newspapers. Drayton shifted his gaze rudely and deliberately back to the glass case.

'You're very interested in those cards, I must say,' she said sharply. 'What's so fascinating about a load of second-hand stuff?'

'I shouldn't mind it being second-hand,' he said, and when she blushed he knew she had seen him witness that kiss.

A charwoman with ginger hair. It might be. Everything pointed that way. Mrs. Penistan seemed to fill the requirements. She had cleaned for Anita Margolis, why should she not also clean for Mrs. Harper of Waterford Avenue? A woman who lived in unsalubrious Glebe Road might steal paper from one employer to write anonymous letters about another. In Glebe Road they were no strangers to crime, even to murder. A woman had been killed down there only last year. Monkey Matthews had once lived there and it was behind one of these squat stuccoed façades that he had mixed up sugar and sodium chlorate to make his bomb.

Burden tapped smartly on the door of the small terraced house. A light came on, a chain was slipped, and before the door opened he saw a little sharp face peering at him through the glass panel.

'Mrs. Penistan?'

Her mouth snapped open like a spring tap and there came forth a voluble stream of words. 'Oh, here you are at last, dear. I'd nearly given you up. The Hoover's all ready for you.' She produced it, an enormous, old-fashioned vacuum cleaner. 'I reckon it's a bit of grit caught up in the motor. My boys don't care what muck they bring in on their shoes. Won't be a long job, will it?'

'Mrs. Penistan, I haven't come to service your cleaner. I'm not a . . .'

She peered at him. 'Not a Jehovah Witness, I hope?'

'A police officer.' They sorted it out, Mrs. Penistan laughing shrilly. Even in her own home, she still wore her hat. The hair which showed under its brim was not ginger but grey. You could neither describe her as middle-aged, nor showily dressed. In addition to the pudding basin hat, she wore a cross-over sleeveless overall, patterned in mauve and black, over a green cardigan. Burden thought she was approaching seventy.

'You won't mind coming in the kitchenette, will you, dear? I'm getting me boys' tea.' On the cooker chips were frying. She lifted out the wire basket, replenished it with a fresh mound of cut wet potatoes. 'How about a nice cuppa?'

Burden accepted the offer and when the tea came it was hot and strong. He sat down on a grubby chair at the grubby table. The frowsty appearance of the place surprised him. Somehow he expected a charwoman's house to be clean, just as a bank manager's account should always be in the black.

'Smith?' she said. 'No, it doesn't ring a bell.'

'Fitzwilliam?'

'No, dear. There was a Mr. Kirkpatrick. Would it be him?'

'It might be.' Knowing Margolis, it very well might be.

'Lives in Pomfret somewhere. Funny you should ask about him because it was on account of him I left.'

'How was that, Mrs. Penistan?'

'I don't know why I shouldn't tell you. Missing, you

said? Well, it don't surprise me if he'd done her in like he said he would.'

'He did, did he?'

'Threatened her in my hearing. D'you want to hear about it?'

'I do indeed, but first I'd like to hear about her, what you thought of her, that kind of thing.'

'She was a nice enough girl, mind, no side to her. First day I came I called her Miss and she just screamed out laughing. "Oh, Mrs. P., darling," she says, "you call me Ann. Everyone calls me Ann." One of the free and easy ones she is, takes things as they come. Mind you, they've got money, got wads of it, but they're not always free with it, that kind. The clothes she give me, you wouldn't believe. I had to let most of them go to my granddaughter, being a bit past wearing them trouser suits and skirts up to me navel.

'She'd got her head screwed on the right way, mind. Very sharp way she'd got with the tradesmen. She always bought the best and she liked to know what she was getting for her money. You'd have to get up early in the morning to put anything over on her. Different to him.'

'Mr. Margolis?'

'I know it's easy to say, but I reckon he's mental. All of a year I was there and he never had a soul come to see him. Paint, paint, paint, all the blessed day long, but when he'd done you couldn't see what it was meant to be. "I wonder you don't get fed up with it," I says to him once. "Oh, I'm very fecund, Mrs. Penistan," he says, whatever that may mean. Sounded dirty to me. No, his mind's affected all right.' She piled the chips on to two plates and began cracking eggs which she sniffed suspiciously before dropping them into the pan.

Burden had just begun to ask her about Kirkpatrick's threats when the back door opened and two large bull-necked men in working clothes came in. Were these the boys who didn't care what they brought in on their feet? Both looked years older than Burden himself. With a nod to their mother, they tramped across the kitchen, taking no notice at all of her visitor. Perhaps they also concluded that he had come to service the vacuum cleaner.

'Hang on a minute, dear,' said Mrs. Penistan. A plate in each hand, she disappeared into the living-room. Burden finished the last of his tea. Presently one of the boys came back for the tea pot, followed by his mother, now all smiles.

'You can't get a word out of them till they've got a meal inside them,' she said proudly. Her son ignored her, marched off, banging doors behind him. 'Now, dear, you wanted to know about Mr. Kirkpatrick. Let's see, where are we now? Friday. It would have been last Wednesday week. Mr. Margolis had gone down to Devon for a painting holiday. I come in a couple of days before and I says to her, "Where's your brother, then?" "Dartmoor," she says, and *that* I could believe, though Broadmoor was more his mark.' She let out a shrill laugh and sat down opposite Burden, her elbows on the table. 'Well, two days later on the Wednesday there comes a knock at the door in the afternoon. "I'll go," she says and when she opens the door there's this Kirkpatrick. "Good afternoon," she says, sort of cool but in ever such a funny way I can't describe. "Good afternoon," he says and they just stand there looking at each other. Anyway, as I say, there's no side to her and she introduces me very nice. "Penistan?" he says. "That's a real local name. We've got some Penistans living opposite us in Pomfret," and that's how I know where he come from. Well, I was getting on with cleaning the silver so I went back into the kitchenette.

'No more than five minutes later I hear them go upstairs. Must be going to look at his paintings, I thought in my ignorance. There was paintings all over the place, dear, even in the bathroom. About half an hour after that they come down again and I'm beginning to wonder what's in the air. Then I heard them start this arguing.

' "For God's sake don't drool all over me, Alan," she says sharpish. "Love," she says, raising her voice. "I

don't know what that is. If I love anyone it's Rupert."
Rupert being her mental brother. Well, this Alan, he
flies right off the handle and he starts shouting. All sorts
of horrible expressions he used as I couldn't repeat. But
she didn't turn a hair. "I'm not ending anything, darling," she says, "You can go on having what you've just
had upstairs." I can tell you, dear, all the blood rushed
to my head. This is the last time you set foot in here,
Rose Penistan, I says to myself. My boys are very particular. They wouldn't want me going where there was
immorality. I was going to march right in on her and
that Kirkpatrick and tell her there and then when I
heard him say, "You're asking to get yourself killed,
Ann. I might do it myself one of these fine days."

'Anyway, the upshot was that he just went off in a
huff. I could hear her calling out after him, "Don't be so
silly, Alan, and don't forget we've got a date Tuesday
night." '

'Tuesday?' Burden interjected sharply. 'Would that
have been last Tuesday?'

'Must have been. People are funny, aren't they, dear?
As business-like as they come, she is, and good too in a
sort of way. Collected for Oxfam and the sick animals,
read the newspaper from cover to cover and very hot
about what she called injustice. Just the same, she was
carrying on proper with this Kirkpatrick. It's a funny
old world.'

'So you left?'

'That very day. After he'd gone she come out into the
kitchenette just as if nothing had happened. All cool
and serene she was, smiling and talking about the horrible weather her poor Rupert was having down on the
Moor. I don't know what it is, dear, but I reckon that's
what they mean when they talk about charm. I couldn't
have it out with her. "I'll finish out the week," was all I
said, "and then I'll have to give up. This place is getting
too much for me." And I never spoke a truer word.'

'Do you work anywhere else, Mrs. Penistan? Stowerton, for instance?'

'Oh, no, dear. It wouldn't be worth my while going

all that way. Not that my boys wouldn't fetch me in the van. Always thinking of their Mum, they are.' She accompanied him into the hall where they encountered one of her sons, returning to the kitchen with his empty plate. This he deposited silently on the table. Although he still took no notice at all of his mother, beyond pushing her aside as he passed through the doorway, the meal he had 'got inside him' had effected a slight improvement in his temper, for he remarked gloomily to Burden:

'Nasty night.'

Mrs. Penistan smiled at him fondly. She lugged the vacuum cleaner out of the way and opened the front door on to squally rain. Strange how it always came on to pour in the evenings, Burden thought. As he walked along Glebe Road with his head lowered and his collar turned up, he reflected on the awkwardness of questioning Kirkpatrick when they had no body and no more proof of death than an anonymous letter.

# 6

Two men called Geoffrey Smith lived in Kingsmarkham, one in Stowerton and two more in Sewingbury.
The only dark-haired one was six feet two; the only one
under thirty-five had a blonde beard; none possessed a
black car. The inquiry had been fruitless, as unsatisfac-
tory as the search of Margolis's house. His sister's note
had not come to light, but then neither had anything
else which might suggest foul play.

'Except the five hundred quid,' said Burden.

'A very nice sum to go on holiday with,' Wexford
said firmly. And then, with less certitude, 'Have we
worried Margolis in vain, Mike?'

'Hard to say whether he's worried or not. I don't understand the fellow, sir. One minute I think he's pulling
my leg and the next—well, he's just like a child. I daresay that's what they mean by genius.'

'Some say there's a knife edge between it and
madness, others that it's an infinite capacity for taking
pains.'

If there was anything Burden did understand it was
taking pains. 'It looks as if he pours that paint and
muck on like you or I might slop sauce on fish and
chips,' he said. 'All those paintings are beyond me. I'd
say they were just another way of conning the public.
How much do they charge to go into the Tate Gallery?'

Wexford roared with laughter. 'Nothing, as far as I
know. It's free.' He tightened the thin shiny rag he
called a tie. 'You remind me of that remark of
Goering's,' he said. 'Whenever I hear the word culture I
reach for my gun.'

Burden was offended. He went out into the corridor, looking for someone on whom to vent his temper. Bryant and Gates, who had been chatting up the sergeant, tried to look busy as soon as they saw him. Not so Mark Drayton. He was standing a little apart from the others, staring down at his feet and apparently deep in thought, his hands in the pockets of his duffel coat. The sight of his black hair sticking out over his hood lining inflamed Burden still further. He marched up to Drayton, but before he could speak, the young man said casually:

'Can I have a word with you, sir?'

'The only person you need a word with is a barber,' Burden snapped. 'Four words to be precise. Short back and sides.' Drayton's face was impassive, secretive, intelligent. 'Oh, very well, what is it?'

'An advert in Grover's window. I thought we might be interested.' From his pocket he took a neat flat notebook and opening it, read aloud: 'Quiet secluded room to let for evenings. Suit student or anyone wanting to get away from it all. Privacy guaranteed. Apply, 82, Charteris Road, Stowerton.'

Burden's nostrils contracted in distaste. Drayton was not responsible for the advertisement, he told himself, he had only found it. Indeed it was to his credit that he *had* found it. Why then feel that this kind of thing, so squalid, so redolent of nasty things done in nasty corners, was right up his street?

'Grover's again, eh?' said Wexford when they told him. 'So this is their latest racket, is it? Last year it was—er, curious books. This place gets more like the Charing Cross Road every day.' He gave a low chuckle which Burden would not have been surprised to hear Drayton echo. The fellow was a sycophant if ever there was one. But Drayton's olive-skinned face was wary. Burden would have said he looked ashamed except that he could not think of any reason why he should be.

'Remember the time when all the school kids were getting hold of flick knives and we knew for sure it was Grover but we couldn't pin it on him? And those magazines he sells. How would you like your daughter to read them?'

Wexford shrugged. 'They're not for daughters, Mike, they're for sons, and you don't *read* them. Before we get around to convening the purity committee, we'd better do something about this ad.' He fixed his eyes speculatively on Drayton. 'You're a likely lad, Mark.' It irked Burden to hear the Chief Inspector address Drayton, as he very occasionally did, by his christian name. 'You look the part.'

'The part, sir?'

'We'll cast you as a student wanting to get away from it all, shall we, Inspector Burden?' Still viewing Drayton, he added, 'I can't see any of the rest of us creeping nimbly in a lady's chamber.'

The first time they went to the door there was no answer. It was a corner house, its front on Charteris Road, its side with a short dilapidated fence, bordering Sparta Grove. While Burden waited in the car, Drayton followed this fence to its termination in a lane that ran between the backs of gardens. Here the stone wall was too high to see over, but Drayton found a gate in it, locked but affording through its cracks a view of the garden of number eighty-two. On a clothes line, attached at one end to the wall and at the other to a hook above a rear window of the house, hung a wet carpet from which water dripped on to a brick path.

The house was seventy or eighty years old but redeemed from the slumminess of its neighbours by a certain shipshape neatness. The yard was swept—a clean broom stood with its head against the house wall—and the back step had been whitened. All the windows were closed and hung with crisp net curtains. As Drayton contemplated windows, a curtain in one, probably the back bedroom, was slightly raised and a small wizened face looked out. Drayton put his foot on a projecting hunk of stone and hoisted himself up until his head and shoulders were above the grass-grown top of the wall. The brown simian face was still there. Its eyes met his and there appeared in them a look of terror, surely out of proportion to the offence or to the retribution for that offence that occupants of the house might be supposed to have committed. The face disappeared quickly and Drayton returned to the car.

'There's someone in,' he said to Burden.

'I daresay there is. Apart from the fact that we can't force an entry over a thing like this, making a rumpus would rather defeat the object of the exercise, wouldn't it?'

Theirs was just one of twenty or thirty cars lining Sparta Grove. At this end of the street there were neither garages nor space for them.

'Someone's coming now,' Drayton said suddenly.

Burden looked up. A woman pushing a shopping basket on wheels was opening the gate of the corner house. Her head was tied up in a coloured scarf and she wore a coat with a huge showy fur collar. As the door closed behind her, he said:

'I know her. Her name's Branch, Mrs. Ruby Branch. She used to live in Sewingbury.'

'Is she one of our customers?'

This use, on Drayton's lips, of one of Wexford's favourite terms, displeased Burden. It seemed not so much an accidental echo as a calculated and ingratiating mimicry of the Chief Inspector's racy style. 'We've had her for shoplifting,' he said stiffly, 'larceny as a servant and various other things. This is a new departure. You'd better go in and do your stuff.'

She subjected him to a careful and at first alarmed scrutiny through the glass panel of the door before opening it. The alarm faded and the door gave a few inches. Drayton put his foot on the mat.

'I understand you have a room to let.' He spoke pleasantly and she was disarmed. She smiled, showing excellent false teeth with lipstick on them. The scarf and the coat had not yet been removed and between the feather boa-like sides of her collar he could see a frilly blouse covering a fine bosom. The face was middle-aged—early fifties, Drayton thought—and bravely painted particularly about the eyelids. 'I happened to see your advert in Grover's window, Mrs. Er. . .?'

'No names, no pack drill, dear,' she said. 'Just call me Ruby.'

'O.K., Ruby.'

The door was closed behind him and he found himself in a tiny narrow hall, its floor covered in cheap bright red nylon carpet. On the threshold of the front room he stopped, staring, and his face must have shown his astonishment, for she said quickly:

'Don't take any notice of the bare boards, duckie. I like everything to be spick and span, you see, and I'm just giving the carpet a bit of an airing.'

'Spring-cleaning, eh?' Drayton said. All the furniture had been moved back against the walls. There was a three-piece suite, covered in moquette, whose pattern showed what seemed like, but surely could not be, blue fishes swimming through a tangle of red and pink climbing roses. On a huge television set stood a naked lady in pink porcelain whose eternally raised right arm held aloft a lamp in a plastic shade. The wallpaper was embossed in gilt and the single picture was of the late King George the Fifth and Queen Mary in full court regalia. 'I can see you keep it nice,' he said heartily.

'You wouldn't get things nicer in any of your hotels. When did you think of coming? Any night would be convenient to me.' She gave him a long look, partly coy, partly assessing. 'You'll be bringing a young lady with you?'

'If you haven't any objection. I thought perhaps this evening. Say eight till eleven. Would you. . .?'

'I'll get my things on by eight sharp,' she said. 'If you'll just tap on the door you needn't bring the young lady in till after I've gone. Some do feel a bit shy-like. Say a fiver?'

Burden had agreed to give him ten minutes. Things could hardly have gone more smoothly. He glanced up at the window and saw the inspector approaching the front door. That she had seen him too and knew who he was he guessed from the little gasp of fear that came from her.

'What's going on, then?' she said, her voice dying to a whimper.

Drayton turned and addressed her severely. 'I am a police officer and I have reason to believe you are engaged in keeping a disorderly house. . . .'

Ruby Branch sat down on the red and blue sofa, put her head in her hands and began to cry.

Drayton had expected they would simply take her down to Kingsmarkham and charge her. It was all cut and dried and there had been neither denial nor defiance. She had put the advertisement in Grover's window to m⌐ke a little extra money. What with freezes and squ⌐ ⌐es, it was a job to make ends meet. . . . Burden listened to it all. His eyes were on the scarf Ruby Branch had unwound from her head and was using to wipe her eyes, or perhaps on the ginger curls the removal of that scarf had revealed.

'You were a blonde last time I saw you, Ruby,' he said.

'Since when do I have to ask your permission when I want to have my hair tinted?'

'Still working for Mrs. Harper in Waterford Avenue, are you?'

She nodded tearfully, then glared at him. 'What business is it of yours who I work for? If it wasn't for you I'd still have my job at the supermarket.'

'You should have thought of that,' Burden said, 'before your little *contretemps* with six dozen packets of soap powder. You always were houseproud and it's been your undoing. Quite a vice with you, isn't it? I see you've been at it again.'

He stared at the bare boards and thence from Ruby's varicose veined legs in their thin black nylons to her suddenly terrified face. To Drayton he said conversationally:

'There's not many working women would find the time to wash a big carpet. Go over it with a damp cloth, maybe. That's what my wife does. Let's go outside and see what sort of a job she's made of it, shall we? It's not a bad morning and I could do with a spot of fresh air.'

Ruby Branch came with them. She tottered in her high-heeled shoes and it seemed to Drayton that she was dumb with terror. The kitchen was neat and fresh and the step so clean that Burden's not very dirty shoe made a black print on it. Of the man seen at the window— husband? lodger?—there was no sign.

Drayton wondered that the clothes line was strong enough to bear the weight of the carpet, for it was soaking wet and looked as if it had been totally immersed in a bath. The high wind hardly caused it to sway. Burden advanced on it curiously.

'Don't you touch it,' Ruby said shrilly. 'You'll have the lot down.'

Burden took no notice of her. He gave the carpet a twitch and suddenly, as she had predicted, the line snapped. Its load subsided with a squelch, half on to the path and half on to the lawn, giving off from its heavy soaking folds a strong animal smell of sodden wool.

'Look what you've done! What d'you want to come out here poking about for? Now I'll have to do it all again.'

'No, you won't;' Burden said grimly. 'The only people who are going to touch that are scientific experts.'

'Just giving it an airing?' Drayton exclaimed.

'Oh, my God!' Ruby's face had become a yellowish white against which the quivering red lips stood out like a double gash. 'I never meant any harm, I was scared. I thought maybe you'd pin it on me, maybe you'd get me for a—a. . . .'

'An accessory? That's a good idea. Maybe we shall.'

'Oh, my God!'

Back in the disarranged sitting-room she sat for a moment in petrified silence, twisting her hands and biting what remained of the lipstick from her mouth. Then she said wildly:

'It's not what you're thinking. It wasn't blood. I was bottling raspberries and I. . . .'

'In April? Do me a favour,' said Burden. 'You can take your time.' He looked at his watch. 'We've got a very slack morning, haven't we, Drayton? We can sit here till lunchtime for all I care. We can sit here till to-morrow.'

Again she said nothing and in the renewal of silence shuffling footsteps were heard outside in the passage. The door opened cautiously and Drayton saw a little man with thin grey hair. The face was the face he had seen at the window. With its prognathous jaw, its many furrows in dark brown skin, and its bulbous nose and mouth, it was not prepossessing. The terrified expression had undergone a change. The eyes were fixed on Drayton just as they had been previously, but the agony of fear had been replaced by a kind of gloating horror comparable to that of a man shown a five-legged sheep or a bearded lady.

Burden got up and, because the newcomer seemed inclined to make a bolt for it, closed his hand over the door knob.

'Well, if it isn't Mr. Matthews,' he said. 'Can't say I think much of your coming-out togs. I thought they made them to measure these days.'

The man called Matthews said in a feeble grating voice, 'Hallo, Mr. Burden,' and then automatically, as if he always did say it, just as other men say, 'How are things?' or 'Nice day', 'I haven't done nothing.'

'When I was at school,' said Burden, 'they taught me that a double negative makes an affirmative. So we know where we are, don't we? Sit down, join the gathering. There aren't any more of you, are there?'

Monkey Matthews skirted the room carefully, finally sitting down as far as possible from Drayton. For a moment nobody said anything. Matthews looked from Burden to Ruby and then, as if unwillingly compelled, back again at Drayton.

'Is that Geoff Smith?' he asked at last.

'You see,' said Ruby Branch, 'he never saw them. Well, come to that, *I* never saw the girl.'

Wexford shook his head in exasperation. His whole body had shaken with fury when Burden first told him, but now his anger had begun to abate, leaving a sour disgust. Four days had passed since Tuesday, four days of doubt and disbelief. Half a dozen men had been wasting their time, working in the dark and perhaps asking the wrong questions of the wrong people. And all because a silly woman had been afraid to go to the police lest the police stop a racket that promised to be lucrative. Now she sat in his office snivelling into a handkerchief, a scrap of cotton and lace streaked with make-up that the tears had washed away.

'This Geoff Smith,' Wexford said, 'when was the first time you saw him?'

Ruby rolled the handkerchief into a ball and gave a deep choking sigh. 'Last Saturday, Saturday the 3rd. The day after I put the advert in. It was in the morning, about twelve. There was a knock at the door and there was this young chap wanting the room for Tuesday night. He was dark and ever so nice-looking and he spoke nice. How was I to know he was a killer?' She shifted in Wexford's yellow chair and crossed her legs. ' "My name's Geoff Smith," he said. Proud of it, he was. I didn't ask him for his name. Well, he said eight till eleven and I said that'd cost him five pounds. He didn't argue so I saw him off the premises and he got into his black car.

'On Tuesday he came back like he said, at eight sharp. But I never saw any car this time and I never saw his girl. He give me five pounds and said he'd be gone by eleven and when I came back he *had* gone. Now, I'd left the room like a new pin, as good as a hotel it was. . . .'

'I doubt if the court will look on that as a mitigating circumstance,' Wexford put in coldly.

At this hint of the revenge society intended to take on her, Ruby gave another loud sniff. 'Well,' she gulped: 'they'd messed it up a bit, moved the furniture, and of course I started putting the room to rights. . . .'

'D'you mind sparing me all these asides? I'm a detective, not a domestic science examiner.'

'I have to tell you, don't I? I have to tell you what I did.'

'Tell me what you found.'

'Blood', Ruby said. 'I moved back the sofa, and there it was, a great big stain. I know I ought to have come to you, Mr. Wexford but I panicked, I was scared. All those convictions you've pinned on me. They'll get me for an accomplice or whatever it is, I thought. Then, there was him, Geoff Smith. It's all very well you saying you'd have looked after me. You and me, we know what that amounts to. You wouldn't have put a bodyguard on my place night and day. I was scared stiff.' She added in a querulous whimper, 'Still am, come to that.'

'Where does Matthews come into all this?'

'I was all on my own. I kept going to the window to see if I could see a little dark fellow watching the house. He's killed one girl, I thought. The odds are he won't think twice about finishing me off. George and me, we'd always been good friends.' For a moment Wexford wondered who she meant. Then he recalled Monkey's long disused christian name. 'I'd heard he'd come out and I found him in the Piebald Pony.' She put her elbows on Wexford's desk and fixed him with a long supplicating stare. 'A woman needs a man about at a time like that. I reckon I thought he'd protect me.'

'She wanted someone to protect her,' said Monkey Matthews. 'Can I have another fag? I hadn't got nowhere to go, being as my wife won't have me in the house. Mind you, Mr. Burden, I don't know as I'd have gone back with Rube if I'd known what was waiting for me.' He banged his thin concave chest. 'I'm no bodyguard. Got a light?' Unashamed, no longer afraid since he had been assured that any possible resemblance between Drayton and Geoff Smith was coincidental, he sat jauntily in his chair, talking with animation.

Burden struck a match to light the fourth cigarette he

had had since his arrival and pushed an ashtray pointedly towards him.

'It was blood on the carpet all right,' Monkey said. The cigarette adhered to his lower lip and the smoke made him screw up his eyes. 'I didn't believe her at first. You know what women are.'

'How much blood?' Burden asked tightly as if the very effort of questioning this man hurt him.

'Good deal. Nasty it was. Like as if someone had been playing silly beggars with a knife.' He shuddered, but he cackled at the same time. The cigarette fell. When he had retrieved it, but not before it had marked the carpet, he said, 'Rube was scared stiff of this Smith coming back, wanted to come to you. "That's no bloody good," I said, "not after all this time," but not being one to flout the law when it's a matter of real down-right crime I thought I'd better give you a hint there was a body knocking about. So I wrote to you. Rube had got some paper about. She always has things nice.'

He gave Burden an ingratiating smile, hideously distorting his face. 'I knew you'd only need a hint to get your hands on him. Anyone who finds fault with our local police, I always say, Mr. Wexford and Mr. Burden, they're real educated tip-top men. They'd be up in London at the Yard if there was any justice in this world.'

'If there's any justice in this world,' Burden said furiously, 'it'll put you away for the biggest stretch you've ever done for this.'

Monkey contemplated Burden's green glass statuette as if he hoped to identify it with some known form of human or animal life. 'Now don't be like that,' he said. 'I haven't done nothing. You could say I'd put myself out to help you. I never even set eyes on this Geoff Smith, but if he'd come back snooping around, I'd have been up the creek just the same as Rube.' He gave a deep theatrical sigh. 'It was a real sacrifice I made, helping you with your inquiries, and where's it got me?'

The question was rhetorical but Burden answered it sharply. 'A nice comfortable house to kip down in, for one thing. Maybe you're putting the squeeze on this

Smith and you only made your "real sacrifice" when he wouldn't play.'

'It's a dirty lie,' said Monkey passionately. 'I tell you I never saw him. I thought that young bloke of yours was him. God knows, I reckoned I could spot a copper a mile off, but then they tog themselves up so funny these days. Rube and me we'd been scared stiff and then there he was, poking his long nose over the wall. I tell you, I thought my number was up. Put the squeeze on him! That's a proper laugh. How could I put the squeeze on him when I never set foot in Rube's place before Wednesday?' More ape-like than ever, he scowled at Burden, his eyes growing bulbous. 'I'll have another fag,' he said in an injured tone.

'When did you write the letter?'

'Thursday morning while Rube was out working.'

'So you were all by yourself?'

'Yes, on my tod. I wasn't putting Mr. Geoff Smith through the third degree if that's what you're getting at. I leave that kind of thing to you.' Indignation brought on a coughing fit and he covered his mouth with deeply stained yellowish-brown fingers.

'I reckon you must have D.T.'s of the lungs,' Burden said disgustedly. 'What d'you do when you're—er, behind bars? Start screaming like an addict in a rehabilitation centre?'

'It's my nerves,' Monkey said. 'I've been a mass of nerves ever since I saw that blood.'

'How did you know what to put in the letter?'

'If you're going to trap me,' Monkey said with distant scorn, 'you'll have to be more bloody subtle than that. Rube told me, of course. Be your age. Young, dark and got a black car, she says. Name of Geoff Smith. Come in at eight and was due out at eleven.'

His dog-end was stubbed out on the base of the glass sculpture. Lacking for a brief moment its customary cigarette, Monkey's face reminded the inspector of a short-sighted man without his glasses. There was about it something naked yet unnatural.

'O.K.,' he said. 'You know all this about him, because Ruby told you, but you never saw him and you never saw the girl.' At the last word Monkey's indignant eyes wavered. Burden was not sure whether this was from apprehension or because he was in need of further stimulation. He snatched the cigarette box and put it in a drawer. 'How did you know her name was Ann?' he said.

# 7

'How did you know her name was Ann?' Wexford asked.

The look Ruby Branch gave him was one of simple incomprehension. She appeared not merely unwilling to answer his question; she was utterly at sea. With Geoff Smith and his description she had been on firm ground. Now he had plunged her into uncharted and, for some reason possibly known to her, dangerous waters. She turned away her eyes and contemplated one of her veined legs as if she expected to see a ladder running up the stocking.

'You never even saw that letter, did you, Ruby?' He waited. Silence was the worst thing, the thing all policemen fear. Speech, no matter how clever and how subtly phrased, is necessarily a betrayal. 'Geoff Smith never told you that girl's name. How did you know? How does Matthews know?'

'I don't know what you're getting at,' Ruby cried. She clutched her handbag and shrank away from him, her mouth trembling. 'All those sarcastic things you say, they go in one ear and out the other. I've told you all I know and I've got a splitting headache.'

Wexford left her and went to find Burden. 'I don't even begin to understand this,' he said. 'Why does Geoff Smith tell her his name? She didn't want to know. "No names, no pack drill" is what she said to Drayton.'

'Of course it's an assumed name.'

'Yes, I expect it is. He's an exhibitionist who uses an alias for fun, even when no one's interested.'

'Not only does he give his name unasked, he gives his girl friend's too.'

'No, Mike,' Wexford said crossly, 'my credulity won't stretch that far. "My name's Geoff Smith and I'll be bringing Ann with me." Can you visualize it? I can't. Besides, I've been over and over it with Ruby. I'd stake a year's salary on it. He never told her the girl's name and the first time she heard it was from me in there just now.'

'But Monkey knew it,' said Burden.

'And Monkey wasn't even there. I don't think Ruby's lying. She's scared to death and late in the day though it is, she's throwing herself on our mercy. Mike, would Ann Margolis go to a place like that? You know what the paper said. "Ex-model and Chelsea playgirl!" Why wouldn't she just take her boy-friend home with her?'

'She likes slumming,' said Burden. 'Margolis told me that. Smith, so-called, booked the room on Saturday. Anita knew Margolis would be out on Tuesday evening but she probably thought he'd come home fairly early. He didn't know and she didn't know the gallery manager would ask him out to dinner.'

'Yes, it ties up. Have they started going over Ruby's place?'

'Taking it apart now, sir. The carpet's gone down to the lab. Martin's found a neighbour who saw something. Old girl called Collins. She's waiting for us now.'

She was nearly as large as Wexford himself, a stout old woman with a square jaw. Before he began to question her, she launched forth on a long account of her suffering consequent on being Ruby Branch's next-door neighbour. Hardly an evening passed without her having to bang on the common wall between the houses. Ruby worked all day and did her cleaning after six. The television was always full on and often the vacuum cleaner at the same time. Monkey she knew. He had lived there from Ruby's arrival two years before until six months before he went to prison. It was disgusting, a crying scandal. As soon as she saw him come home

with Ruby on Wednesday morning she knew trouble
would start. Then there was a married niece and her
husband from Pomfret way—if they *were* married—
who came a couple of times a week, and who got
drinking and laughing until the small hours.

'That's who I thought it was I saw leaving on Tuesday,' she said. 'Staggering down the path and holding on
to each other. As much as they could do to walk it
was.'

'Two of them?' Wexford said, his voice rising. 'You
saw two of them?'

Mrs. Collins nodded emphatically. 'Yes, there was
two. I didn't look long, I can tell you. I was too disgusted.'

'Did you see them come?'

'I was in my kitchen till gone nine. I come into the
front and I thought, thank the Lord she's gone out.
There was dead silence until half past. I know I'm right
about the time on account of looking at the clock. There
was something on telly I wanted at twenty-five to. I'd
just got up to switch it on when there comes this great
mighty crash from next-door. Here we go, I thought,
more hi-jinks, and I banged on the wall.'

'Go on,' Wexford said.

'For two pins, I said to myself, I'll go in and have it
out with her. But you know how it is, you don't like to
make trouble with the neighbours. Besides, there was
three of them and I'm not so young as I used to be.
Anyway, I got so far as putting my coat on and I was
standing just inside the front door, sort of hesitating,
when I saw these two come down the path.'

'How well did you see them?'

'Not that well,' Mrs. Collins admitted. 'It was
through the little glass bit in the door, you see. They
was both in macs and the girl had a scarf on her head.
His hair was dark, that I do know. I never saw their
faces, but they were drunk as lords. I thought the girl
was going to fall flat on her face. And she did fall when
he got the car door open, fell right across the front seat.'
She nodded indignantly, her expression smug and self-

righteous. 'I gave them five minutes to get out of the way and then I went next-door, but there was no answer and I saw her come in myself at eleven. What's been going on? I thought. It wasn't the married niece from Pomfret. She never had no car. Couldn't keep money in her pocket long enough to get one.'

'This was a black car you saw them get into, Mrs. Collins?'

'Black? Well, it was under one of them street lamps, and you know what they are, make you go all colours.' She paused, searching in her mind. 'I'd have said it was green,' she said.

Linda Grover flushed when Drayton told her to take the advertisement out of the window. The blood poured into her madonna's face and he knew it was because his explanation had been too crude.

'Didn't you realize what it meant?' he said harshly. 'I should have thought one look at that old tart would have told you she wasn't a legitimate landlady.'

They were alone in the shop. She stood behind the counter, her eyes on his face and her fingers picking at the dog-eared corner of a magazine. 'I didn't know you were a policeman,' she said in a voice which had grown throaty.

'You know now.'

On his way here from Ruby Branch's house he had stopped at the library, not for the sake of the crime section this time, but to look at the big coloured books of paintings by old masters. There, amid the Mantegnas, the Botticellis and the Fra Angelicos, he had found her face under cracked haloes and he had stared at it in a kind of wonder before rage had taken over and he had slammed the book shut so that the librarian looked up with a frown.

'Is that all you came for?' Her first fright was gone and her voice took on an aggressiveness as he nodded. 'All that song and dance about an old advert card?' With a shrug, she walked past him and out of the shop, her body held straight as if she had an invisible weight on her head. He watched her come back, fascinated by the clean, pure curves of jaw and arm and thigh and by the small graceful movements her hands made as she tore Ruby's card into shreds.

'Be more careful next time,' he said. 'We'll be keeping an eye on you.' He saw that he had made her angry, for the colour faded utterly from her face. It was as if she had blushed white. There was a thin silver chain round her neck. As a schoolboy, Drayton had read the Song of Songs, hoping for something salacious. A line came back to him. He had not known what it meant, but now he knew what it meant for him. Thou has ravished my heart with the chain of thy neck. . . .

'An eye on us?'

'This shop's got a bad enough reputation as it is.' He didn't give a damn about the shop's reputation, but he wanted to stay there, hang it out as long as he could. 'If I were your father with a nice little business like this I wouldn't touch that filth.'

She followed his glance at the magazines. 'Some like them,' she said. Her eyes had returned to his face. He had the notion that she was digesting the fact that he was a policeman and searching for some brand mark he ought to carry about on him. 'If you've finished with the sermon, I've got Dad's tea to get and I'm going to the pictures straight after. Last house is seven-thirty.'

'Mustn't keep what's-his-name waiting,' Drayton sneered.

He could see he had nettled her. 'His name's Ray if you must know and he lodged with us,' she said. 'He's gone, left. Oh, come off it. You needn't look like that. I know you saw me with him. So what? It's not a crime, is it? Don't you ever stop being a cop?'

'Who said anything about a crime? I get enough crime in the daytime without the evenings.' He went to the door and looked back at her. The grey eyes were large and luminous and they had a trick of appearing always full of unshed tears. 'Maybe I wished I'd been in his shoes,' he said.

She took a step towards him. 'You're kidding.'

'Men usually kid you about that, do they?'

Her fingers went up to the little insincere smile that was just beginning and she tucked one of the bitten nails between her lips.

'What exactly are you trying to say?'

Now she looked frightened. He wondered if he had been wrong about her and if she were really as inexperienced and innocent as a tempera madonna. There was no gentleness in him and he did not know how to be soft and kind.

'If I'm kidding,' he said, 'I won't be outside the cinema at seven-thirty.' Then he slammed the door and the bell tinkled through the old sagging house.

'Believe it or not,' Wexford said, 'Monkey doesn't want to go home. He's had a nice comfortable bed at Ruby's and God knows how many free meals, but he'd rather spend his weekend in what he calls "this contemporary-type nick." He's scared stiff of coming face to face with Ruby. Just as well, since I haven't the faintest idea what to charge him with.'

'Makes a change,' Burden grinned. 'Our customers appreciating the amenities. Maybe we could get ourselves in the A.A. Guide, three-star hotel, specially adapted for those with previous convictions. Anything from the lab yet?'

'No, and I'll take my oath there won't be. We've only got Ruby's and Monkey's word that it was blood at all. You saw it, you saw what she'd done to that carpet. Char-ing may be a lowly trade, but Ruby's at the top of it. If I were Mrs. Harper I wouldn't grudge a few sheets of handmade paper to get my house cleaned like that. She must have nearly killed herself washing that carpet. The lab says she used every cleanser in the book short of caustic soda. Oh, sure, they can sort out the Chemiglo from the Spotaway. The trouble is they can't sort out the blood, can't even say what group it is.'

'But they're still working on it?'

'Be working on it for days. They've got buckets full of muck from the pipes and drains. I'll be very surprised if they find anything. It's my bet our couple never went anywhere but that room in which they doubtless left a couple of hundred fingerprints. . . .'

'All carefully removed by the Queen of Chars,' Burden finished for him. 'The girl may be still alive, sir.'

'Because they left together and because the man's getting her out of there at all seems to show regret at what he'd done? I've had all the hospitals and all the G.P.'s checked, Mike. They haven't had sight nor sound of anyone with stab wounds. And it must have been stabbing, a blow on the head and that much loss of blood and the victim would never have been able to stand up, let alone stagger to a car. Moreover, if she's alive, where is she? It may only be assault we're up against or unlawful wounding, but whatever it is, we have to clear it up.'

Monkey Matthews gave them a crafty look when they returned to him.

'I've run out of fags.'

'I daresay Detective Constable Bryant will get you some if you ask him nicely. What d'you want, Weights?'

'You're joking,' said Monkey, stuffing a grubby paw into his jacket pocket. 'Forty Benson and Hedges Special Filter,' he said importantly and he brought out a pound note from a rustling mass that might indicate the presence of others like it. 'Better make it sixty.'

'Should last you till breakfast,' said Wexford. 'Rolling in it, aren't you? I can't help wondering if that's Geoff Smith's fee for silence you're sending up in smoke.' Stroking his chin, his head on one side, he looked speculatively into the other's simian face. 'How did you know her name was Ann?' he asked almost lightly and with a deceptive smoothness.

'Oh, you're round the twist,' Monkey said crossly. 'You don't never listen to what you're told.'

When they came out of the cinema a light rain was falling, very little more than a clammy mist. Lamps glowed through the translucence, orange, gold and pearl-coloured. The cinema traffic coming from the car park swam out of the mist like subaqueous creatures surfacing with a gurgle and a splash. Drayton took the girl's arm to shepherd her across the road and left it there when they reached the pavement. This, the first contact he had ever had with her body, sent a tremor through him and made his mouth dry. He could feel the warmth from her skin just beneath the armpit.

'Enjoy the picture?' he asked her.

'It was all right. I don't like sub-titles much, I couldn't understand half of it. All that stuff about the woman letting the policeman be her lover if he wouldn't tell about her stealing the watch.'

'I daresay it happens. You don't know what goes on in these foreign places.' He was not displeased that the film had been sexy and that she wanted to talk about the sexiest part of the plot. With girls, that kind of talk was often an indication of intent, a way of getting on the subject. Thank God, it wasn't the beginning of the week when they'd been showing that thing about a Russian battleship. 'You thinking of nicking any watches?' he said. She blushed vividly in the lamplight. 'Remember what the character in the film said, or what the sub-title said he said. "You know my price, Dolores."'

She smiled her close-lips smile, then said 'You are awful.'

'Not me, I didn't write the script.'

She was wearing high heels and she was almost as tall as he. The perfume she had put on was much too old for her and it had nothing to do with the scent of flowers. Drayton wondered if her words had meant anything and if the perfume had been specially put on for his benefit. It was hard to tell how calculating girls were. Was she giving him an invitation or was the scent and the pale silvery stuff on her eyelids worn as a uniform might be, the battledress of the great female regiment who read the magazines she sold?

'It's early,' he said, 'only a quarter to eleven. Want to go for a walk down by the river?' It was under the trees there that he had seen her on Monday. Those trees arched dripping into the brown water, but under them the gravel path was well-drained and here and there was a wooden seat sheltered by branches.

'I can't. I mustn't be late home.'

'Some other night, then.'

'It's cold,' she said. 'It's always raining. You can't go to the pictures every night.'

'Where did you go with him?'

She bent down to straighten her stocking. The puddles she had stepped in had made dark grey splashes on the backs of her legs. The way she stretched her fingers and drew them up the calves was more provocative than all the perfume in the world.

'He hired a car.'

'I'll hire one,' Drayton said. They had come to the shop door. The alley between Grover's and the florist's next door was a walled lane that ended in a couple of garages. Its cobbles were brown and wet like stones on a cave floor that the tide has washed. She looked up at the high wall of her own home and at the blank unlit windows.

'You don't have to go in for a bit,' he said. 'Come under here, out of the rain.' There was no more shelter there than in the open street but it was darker. At their feet a little gutter stream flowed. He took her hand. 'I'll hire a car tomorrow.'

'All right.'

'What's the matter?' He spoke harshly, irritably, for he wanted to contemplate her face in repose, not working with anxiety, her eyes darting from one end of the alley to the other and up at the rain-washed wall. He would have liked eagerness, at least complaisance. She seemed afraid that they were watched and he thought of the thin beady-eyed mother and the mysterious father lying sick behind that brick bastion. 'Not scared of your parents, are you?'

'No, it's you. The way you look at me.'

He was nearly offended. The way he looked at her was something calculated and studied, a long, cold and intense stare that a good many girls had found exciting. A stronger desire than he had ever felt was increasing that intensity and making a contrived mannerism real. The poverty of her response almost killed it and he would have turned away from her to walk off alone into the wet night but for the two little hands which touched his coat and then crept up to his shoulders.

'It's you that frightens me,' she said. 'But that's what you want, isn't it?'

'You know what I want,' he said and he brought his mouth down on hers, holding her body away from the cold, clammy wall. At first she was limp and unresisting. Then her arms went round him with fierce abandon and as her lips parted under his, he felt a great thrill of triumph.

Above them a light appeared as a bright orange rectangle on the dark bricks. Before he opened his eyes Drayton felt it like pain on his eyelids.

She pulled away from him slowly with a long 'Aah!' of pleasure, a sigh of pleasure only begun to be cut short. 'They're waiting up for me.' Her breath was light and fast. 'I must go in.'

'Tomorrow,' he said, 'tomorrow.'

She could not find her key at first and it excited him to see her fumbling and hear her swearing softly under her breath. He had caused this sudden gaucheness, this disorientation, and it filled his masculine ego with the joy of conquest.

'Tomorrow, then.' The smile came, shy and tantalizing. Then the door closed on her and the bell made its cold harsh music.

When he was alone in the alley and the light from above had gone out, he stood where they had kissed and passed his forefinger across his lips. The rain was still falling and the street lamp glowed with a greenish sulphurous light. He came out into this light and looked at his finger with the long smear of pale lipstick. It was not pink but the colour of suntanned flesh and he fancied that with it she had left on his mouth something of herself, a grain of skin or a trace of sweat. On the front of his coat was a long fair hair. To have these vestiges of her was in itself a kind of possession. Alone in the wet street, he passed his tongue lightly across his finger and he shivered.

A cat came out of the alley and slunk into a doorway, its fur dewed with fine drops. There was no visible sky, just vapour, and beyond the vapour blackness. Drayton put up his hood and walked home to his lodgings.

# 8

To the south of Kingsmarkham and overshadowing the eastern and southern sides of Pomfret lie twenty or thirty square miles of pine woods. This is Cheriton Forest. It is a man-made plantation, consisting mostly of firs and larches and it has a stark un-English beauty, giving to the green plains beneath it the appearance of an Alpine meadow.

A new estate of small white houses has sprung up on the Pomfret side of the forest. With their coloured front doors and their decorations of cedar board they are not unlike chalets. To one of these, a yellow-painted house with a new car port, Detective Sergeant Martin took himself on Sunday morning, looking for a man called Kirkpatrick.

The door was opened promptly by a girl of about seven, a child with large eyes and a cowed look. Martin waited on the doorstep while she went to find her mother. The house was built on an open plan and he could see a little boy, as pale and wary as his sister, playing apathetically on the floor with alphabet bricks. The woman who came at last had a pugnacious face. She had the roseate breathless look of those who suffer from high blood pressure. Her blonde hair was dressed in tight shiny curls and she wore red-rimmed glasses. Martin introduced himself and asked for her husband.

'Is it about the car?' Mrs. Kirkpatrick said savagely.

'In a way.'

The children crept up to their mother and stood staring.

'Well, you can see he isn't here, can't you? If he's crashed the car I can't say I'm sorry. I'd say good riddance. I hope it's a total write-off. When he brought it home here last Monday, I said, "Don't think you'll get me to go joy-riding in that thing. I'd rather walk. If I wanted to make an exhibition of myself in a pink and white car with purple stripes I'd go on the dodgems at Brighton," I said.'

Martin blinked at her. He had no idea what she meant.

'The other thing he had,' she said, 'that was bad enough. Great old-fashioned black Morris like a hearse. God knows, we must be the laughing stock of all the neighbours.' She suddenly became aware of the staring listening children. 'How many times have I told you not to come poking your noses into my private business?' she said viciously. The boy wandered back to his bricks, but it took a savage push to move the little girl. 'Now, then,' she said to Martin. 'What's he done? What d'you want him for?'

'Just to talk to him.'

Mrs. Kirkpatrick seemed more interested in listening to the sound of her own voice and airing grievances than eliciting reasons from Martin. 'If he's been speeding again,' she said, 'he'll lose his licence. Then he'll lose his job.' Far from being concerned, her voice held a note of triumph. 'A firm like *Lipdew* aren't going to keep on a salesman who can't drive a car, are they? Any more than they're going to give their people great showy cars for them to smash to smithereens just when it takes their fancy. I told him so before he went to Scotland. I told him on Tuesday morning. That's why he never came in for his dinner Tuesday night. But he can't be told. Pig-headed and stubborn he is and now it's got him into trouble.'

Martin backed away from her. A barrage of gunfire would be preferable to this. As he went down the path he heard one of the children crying in the house behind him.

Monkey Matthews was lying on his bed, smoking, when Wexford went into the cell. He raised himself on one elbow and said, 'They told me it was your day off.'

'So it is, but I thought you might be lonely.' Wexford shook his head reprovingly and looked round the small room, sniffing the air. 'How the rich live!' he said. 'Want me to send out for more of your dope? You can afford it, Monkey.'

'I don't want nothing,' Monkey said, turning his face to the wall, 'except to be left alone. This place is more like a goods yard than a nick. I never got a wink of sleep last night.'

'That's your conscience, Monkey, the still, small voice that keeps urging you to tell me something, like, for instance, how you knew the girl's name was Ann.'

Monkey groaned. 'Can't you give it a rest? My nerves are in a shocking state.'

'I'm delighted to hear it,' Wexford said unkindly. 'Must be the result of my psychological warfare.' He went out into the corridor and upstairs to Burden's office. The inspector had just come in and was taking off his raincoat.

'It's your day off.'

'My wife was threatening to cart me off to church. This seemed the lesser evil. How are we doing?'

'Martin's been talking to Mrs. Kirkpatrick.'

'Ah, the wife of Anita Margolis's current boy-friend.'

Burden sat down by the window. This morning the sun was shining, not after the fashion of fitful April sunshine but with the strength and warmth of early summer. He raised the blind and opened the window, letting in with the soft light the clear crescendo of bells from Kingsmarkham church steeple.

'I think we may be on to something there, sir,' he said. 'Kirkpatrick's away, travelling for his firm in Scotland. He went off on Tuesday and the wife hasn't seen him since. Moreover, he used to have a black car, had it up until last Monday, when his firm gave him a new one, white thing apparently, plastered all over with advertising gimmicks,' he chuckled. 'The wife's a harridan.

Thought he'd smashed the car when she saw Martin, but she didn't turn a hair.' His face hardening slightly, he went on, 'I'm not one to condone adultery, as you know, but it looks as if there may have been some justi-fication for it here.'

'Is he small and dark?' Wexford asked with a pained look at the open window. He moved closer to the cen-tral heating vent.

'Don't know. Martin didn't care to go into too many details with the wife. It's not as if we've much to go on.' Wexford nodded a grudging approval. 'Ah, well,' Bur-den said, getting up. 'Margolis may be able to help us there. For an artist he's a rotten observer, but he has *seen* the man.' He reached for his coat. 'Lovely sound those bells.'

'Eh?'

'I said the bells were lovely.'

'What?' said Wexford. 'Can't hear a word you say for the sound of those bloody bells.' He grinned hugely at the ancient joke. 'You might have a look-in on Monkey on your way out. Just in case he's getting tired of hold-ing out on us.'

After careful examination by the police and a session at a garage to have its radiator repaired, Anita Margo-lis's Alpine had been restored to its parking place on the grass verge outside Quince Cottage. Burden was not surprised to find it there, but his eyebrows went up as he saw ahead of him the rears of not one white car but two. He parked his own behind them and came out into the sunshine. As he walked up to it he saw that the new arrival was white only in that this was its background colour. Along its sides a band perhaps a foot wide had been painted in bright pink, adorned with sprays of purple flowers. This particular shade of purple had been used for the lettering above it: *Lipdew, Paintbox for a Prettier You.*

Burden grinned to himself. Only a brazen extrovert would enjoy being seen about in this car. He glanced through a side window at the pink seats. They were lit-tered with leaflets and on the dashboard shelf were samples of the stuff the driver peddled, bottles and jars presumably, done up in mauve packages and tied with gold cord.

There could hardly be two cars in Sussex like this. Kirkpatrick must be somewhere about. Burden unlatched the gate and entered the cottage garden. The wind had scattered the petals of the quince blossom and underfoot the ground was slippery scarlet. When nobody answered the knock, he went round the side of the house and saw that the doors of the garage where Margolis kept his own car were open and the car gone.

Fat buds on the apple branches brushed his face and all around him he could hear the soft twittering of birds. The atmosphere and appearance of rustic peace was somewhat marred by the ragged sheets of paper, vestiges of Margolis's inexpert tidying up, which still clung to bushes and in places fluttered in the treetops. Burden stopped by the back door. A man in a stone-coloured belted raincoat was standing on a wooden box and peering in at the kitchen window.

Unseen, Burden watched him in silence for a moment. Then he coughed. The man jumped, turned to face him, and came slowly down from his perch.

'There's nobody in,' he said diffidently, and then, 'I was just checking.' The man was undeniably good-looking, pale, dapper and with curling dark brown hair. The chin was small, the nose straight and the eyes liquid and lashed like a girl's.

'I'd like a word with you, Mr. Kirkpatrick.'

'How d'you know my name? I don't know you.' Now that they were standing level with each other, Burden noted that he was perhaps five feet eight inches tall.

'I recognized your car,' he said. The effect of this was electric. Two dark red spots appeared on Kirkpatrick's sallow cheekbones.

"What the hell does that mean?" he said angrily.

Burden looked at him mildly. 'You said no one was in. Who were you looking for?'

'That's it, is it?' Kirkpatrick took a deep breath,

clenching his fists. 'I know who you are.' He nodded
absurdly and with grim satisfaction. 'You're a snooper,
what they call an inquiry agent. I suppose my wife put
you on to me."

'I've never seen your wife,' said Burden, 'but I'm certainly an inquiry agent. More commonly called a police
officer.'

'I overheard you asking the sergeant where you could
hire a car,' Wexford said.

'In my lunch hour, sir,' Drayton replied quickly.

Wexford shook his head impatiently. 'All right, man,
all right. Don't make me out an ogre. You can hire an
articulated lorry for all I care and you won't do it in
your lunch hour, you'll do it now. There are only three
firms in the district doing car hire, Missal's and Cawthorne's in Stowerton and the Red Star where you took
Miss Margolis's in York Street here. What we want to
know is if anyone hired a green car from them last
Tuesday.'

After Drayton had gone, he sat down to think it all
out and to try to solve the enigma of the cars. The man
called Geoff Smith had used a black car on Saturday, a
green one on Tuesday, if Mrs. Collins could be believed. He thought she could. Last night he and Bryant
had tested a black car under the pearly lamplight in
Sparta Grove and it had remained black. He had looked
at it through clear glass and through stained glass. No
amount of contriving or exercise of the imagination
could make it green. Did that mean the Geoff Smith
possessed two cars, or that on Sunday or Monday he
had sold the black one and bought a green? Or could it
be that because his new car was conspicuous, he had
hired the green one for his dubious and clandestine ad-
venture?

Drayton, too, asked himself these questions as the
tumultuous ringing of the church bells ceased and he
turned the corner into York Street. In the strengthening
sunshine the rhinestone ropes glittered at him from the
window of Joy Jewels. He thought of the silver chain

Linda wore around her neck and simultaneously of that smooth warm skin, silky to his touch.

He had to shake himself and tighten his mouth before going into the Red Star Garage. They showed him two ageing red Hillmans and he turned away to catch the bus for Stowerton. There he found Russell Cawthorne in his office. On the one bit of solid wall behind his head was a calendar of a girl wearing three powder puffs and a pair of high-heeled shoes. Drayton looked at it with contempt and a certain unease. It reminded him of the magazines in Grover's shop. Cawthorne sat up stiffly when Drayton told him who he was and gave a brisk nod, the C in C receiving a promising subaltern.

'Morning. Sit down. More trouble brewing?'

Affected old bore, Drayton thought. 'I want to ask you about hiring cars. You do hire cars, don't you?'

'My dear boy, I thought you were here in your official capacity, but if you just . . .'

'I am. This is an official question. What colour are they, these hire cars of yours?'

Cawthorne opened a fanlight. The fresh air made him cough. 'What colour are they? They're all the same. Three black Morris Minors.'

'Were any of them hired on Saturday, the 3rd?'

'Now when would that have been, laddie?'

'Last week. There's a calendar behind you.' Cawthorne's face darkened to an even maroon. 'It'll be in the book,' he muttered.

The book looked well-kept. Cawthorne opened it and turned back a few pages, frowning slightly. 'I remember that morning,' he said. 'I lost my best mechanic. Impertinent young devil, treating the place like he owned it. I gave him the push, lost my temper. . . .' Drayton fidgeted impatiently. 'About the cars,' Cawthorne said moodily. 'No, they were all in.'

'What about sales? You wouldn't have sold anyone a green car about that time?'

One of the veined, not very steady hands, went up to twitch at his moustache. 'My business hasn't been exactly booming.' He hesitated, eyeing Drayton warily.

'I'll tell you frankly,' he said, 'I haven't made a sale since Mr. Grover took delivery of his Mini in February.'

Drayton felt his face grow hot. The name was enough to do it. 'I want to hire a car myself,' he said. 'For tonight.'

Blustering, confident as only the weak can be, Alan Kirkpatrick stood defiantly in Wexford's office. He had refused to sit down and a constantly reiterated, 'Rubbish' and 'I don't believe it' had greeted Wexford's hints as to Anita Margolis's probable death.

'In that case,' Wexford said, 'You won't mind telling us about your movements last Tuesday, the night you had a date with her.'

'A date?' Kirkpatrick gave a short sneering laugh. 'I like the way you put it. I got to know that woman solely because I'm keen on art. The only way to get into that place and look at Margolis's pictures was through her.'

Burden got up from his corner where he had been sitting quietly and said, 'Interested in his work, are you? So am I. I've been trying to remember that name of that thing he's got in the Tate. Perhaps you can refresh my memory.'

That it was so obviously a trap did not derogate from its significance as a question and a question which, if Kirkpatrick were to sustain his role as a seeker after artistic enlightenment, must be answered. His soft mobile mouth twitched.

'I don't know what he calls them,' he muttered.

'Funny,' said Burden. 'Any admirer of Margolis would surely know "Nothing".' For a moment Wexford himself stared. Then he recalled the *Weekend Telegraph* lying close to his hand in the desk drawer. As he listened to the inspector who had suddenly launched into an esoteric review of modern art, he was lost in admiration. Instead of reaching for his gun, Burden had evidently reached for a work reference. Kirkpatrick, also perhaps overcome, sat down abruptly, his face puzzled and aggressive.

'I don't have to answer your questions,' he said.

'Quite right,' Wexford said kindly. 'As you rightly say, we can't even prove Miss Margolis is dead.' And he nodded sagely as if Kirkpatrick's wisdom had recalled him from sensational dreams to reality. 'No, we'll just make a note that you were probably the last person to see her alive.'

'Look,' said Kirkpatrick, on the edge of his chair but making no move to get up, 'my wife's a very jealous woman. . . .'

'Seems to be infectious in your family. I'd have said it was jealousy made you threaten Miss Margolis a couple of weeks ago.' Wexford quoted Mrs. Penistan. ' "I might kill you myself one of these fine days." Was last Tuesday one of those fine days? Funny way to talk to a woman you were only interested in because of her brother's painting, wasn't it?'

'That date, as you call it, she never kept it. I didn't go out with her.'

Ruby would know him again. Wexford cursed the paucity of their evidence. He did not think it would be an easy matter to persuade this man to take part in an identification parade. Kirkpatrick's confidence had been slightly shaken by Burden's questions, but as he sat down again some of his bravado seemed to return. With a look that was part impatience, part resignation, he took out a pocket-comb and began to arrange his curly hair.

'We're not interested in your wife's possible divorce proceedings,' Wexford said. 'If you're frank with us there's no reason why it should go further, certainly not to your wife's ears.'

'There's nothing to be frank about.' Kirkpatrick said in a less belligerent tone. 'I was going up North on Tuesday for my firm. It's true I'd arranged to meet Miss Margolis before I went. She was going to show me some of Margolis's—er, early work. He wouldn't have had it if he'd been there but he was going out.' Wexford raised his eyes and met Burden's calm, polite gaze. How green and gullible did this cosmetic salesman think they were?

This story which seemed to fill its teller with pride was so near what Wexford called the 'old etching gag' that he could hardly suppress a chuckle of derision. Early work, indeed! 'I was going home first for a meal but I was late and it was seven when I got to Kingsmarkham. Grover's were closing and I remember that girl made a bit of a scene because I wanted my evening paper. There wasn't time to go home then, so I went straight round to Pump Lane. Ann—Miss Margolis, that is— had forgotten all about me coming. She said she was going to a party. And that's all.'

During the latter part of this explanation Kirkpatrick's face had grown red and he fidgeted uneasily.

'It can't have been more than half past seven, if that,' Wexford said. He was wondering why Burden had gone to the window and was staring down, his expression amused. 'Surely there was time for your artistic researches, especially as you'd missed your evening meal?'

The flush deepened. 'I asked her if I could come in for a bit and then I said I'd take her out for a meal before the party. She had her ocelot coat on ready to go out, but she wouldn't let me in. I suppose she'd just changed her mind.'

Burden turned from the window and when he spoke Wexford knew what he had been scrutinizing. 'How long have you had this car?'

'Since last Monday. I sold my own and got this one from my firm.'

'So Miss Margolis had never seen it before?'

'I don't know what you're getting at.'

'I think you do, Mr. Kirkpatrick. I think Miss Margolis wouldn't go out with you because she didn't care to be seen about in such a conspicuous car.' The shot had gone home. Again Wexford marvelled at Burden's perspicacity. Kirkpatrick, who blushed easily at mild slights, had now grown white with anger and perhaps with mortification.

'She was a woman of taste,' Burden said, 'I shouldn't

be surprised to hear she burst out laughing when she saw all your pink and mauve decorations.'

Apparently this was the salesman's soft spot. Whether he was a connoisseur of modern painting or just a phi-landerer, there was no room in either image for this ridiculous vehicle. It was the scar of the branding iron, the yellow armband, the shameful card of identity.

'What's so funny about it?' he said aggressively. 'Who the hell did she think she was laughing at me?' Indigna-tion began to rob him of caution. 'It doesn't alter my personality, make me into a different man, just because I have to have a car with a slogan on it. I was good enough for her before, my money was good enough to spend on her . . . ' He had said too much, and his rage gave place to a sudden recollection of where he was and to whom he was speaking. 'I mean, I'd given her a few samples in the past, I . . .'

'For services rendered, no doubt?'

'What the hell does that mean?'

'You said she showed you her brother's paintings without his knowledge. A kindly act, Mr. Kirkpatrick. Worth a pot of nail varnish or some soap, I should have thought.' Wexford smiled at him. 'What did you do, borrow a more innocuous car?'

'I tell you, we didn't go anywhere. If we had, we could have gone in hers.'

'Oh, no,' Wexford said softly. 'You couldn't have used hers. The radiator was leaking. I suggest you got hold of a green car and used this to drive Miss Margolis into Stowerton.'

Still smarting from the derision his car had aroused, Kirkpatrick muttered, 'I suppose someone saw me in Stowerton, did they? Cawthorne, was it? Come on, you may as well tell me who it was.'

'Why Cawthorne?'

Kirkpatrick flushed patchily. 'He lives in Stowerton,' he said, stammering a little over the dentals and the sib-ilant. 'He was giving that party.'

'You were on your way to Scotland,' Wexford said thoughtfully. 'You must have made a detour to go through Stowerton.' He got up ponderously and went over to the wall map. 'Look, here's the London Road and you'd have to go that way, or East into Kent, if you wanted to by-pass London. Either way, Stowerton was miles off your route.'

'What the hell does it matter?' Kirkpatrick burst out. 'I had the whole evening to kill. There was nothing else to do. I didn't want to land up in Scotland in the small hours. I should have thought the main thing was Ann wasn't with me. My God, she wasn't even in Stowerton, she didn't go to that party!'

'I know,' Wexford said, returning to his chair. 'Her brother knows and Mr. Cawthorne knows, but how do you know? You never got back into Sussex till this morning. Now listen, an identification parade would clear the whole thing up. Do you object?'

Suddenly Kirkpatrick looked tired. It could have been mere physical exhaustion or that the strain of lying—and lying ineffectually—was telling badly on him. His good looks were particularly vulnerable to anxiety. They depended on a swagger in the tilt of his head, a laugh on his full mouth. Now there was sweat on his upper lip and the brown eyes, which were his most compelling feature, looked like those of a dog when someone has trodden on its tail.

'I'd like to know what it's in aid of,' he said sullenly. 'I'd like to know who saw me where and what I'm supposed to have been doing.'

'I'll tell you, Mr. Kirkpatrick,' said Wexford, drawing up chair.

'When am I going to get my carpet back?' said Ruby Branch.

'We're not cleaners, you know. We don't do an express service.'

She must be lamenting the days, Burden thought, when women wore veils as a matter of course, as often as not just to go out in the public street. He could remember one his grandmother had had on a toque, a thick, seemingly opaque curtain which when lowered was a perfect disguise for its wearer.

'Pity we're not in Morocco,' he said, 'you could put on your yashmak.'

Ruby gave him a sulky glance. She pulled down the brim of her hat until it almost covered her eyes and muffled her chin with a chiffon scarf.

'I shall be a marked woman,' she said. 'I hope you lot realize that. Suppose I pick him out and he escapes? The jails can't hold them these days. You've only got to look at the papers.'

'You'll have to take your chance on that,' said Burden.

When they were in the car she said diffidently, 'Mr. Burden? You never told me whether you're going to do anything about that other thing, that keeping a what-d'you-call-it house?'

'That depends. We shall have to see.'

'I'm putting myself out to help you.'

They drove in silence until they reached the outskirts of Kingsmarkham. Then Burden said, 'Be honest with me, Ruby. What's Matthews ever done for you except take your money and pretty well break up your marriage?'

The painted mouth trembled. There were calluses and the long grey indentations housework makes on the fingers that held the scarf to her lips. 'We've been so much to each other, Mr. Burden.'

'That was a long time ago,' he said gently. 'You've got yourself to think of now.' It was cruel what he had to say. Perhaps justice always is and he was used, if not to administering it, at least to leading people to its seat. Now, to find out what he wanted, he would lead Ruby away from it and cruelty would have to be his means. 'You're nearly ten years off your pension. How many of these women you work for would employ you if they knew what you'd been up to? They will know, Ruby. They read the papers.'

'I don't want to get George into trouble.' It took him, as it had Wexford, a moment's reflection before he remembered that George was Monkey's christian name. 'I was crazy about him once. You see, I never had kids, never had what you'd call a real husband. Mr. Branch was old enough to be my father.' She paused and with a tiny lace handkerchief dabbed at the tearstained space between scarf and hat brim. 'George had been in prison. When I found him he seemed—well, so kind of happy to be with me.' In spite of himself, Burden was moved. He could just recall old Branch, doddery and crotchety in advance of his years. 'Four quid George had off me,' she said unevenly, 'and all the drink I'd got in the place and God knows how many good dinners, but he wouldn't lie down beside me. It's not nice, Mr. Burden, when you've got memories and you can't help. . .'

'He's not worth your loyalty. Come on now. Cheer up. Mr. Wexford'll think I've been giving you the third degree. You never heard that Geoff Smith call the girl Ann, did you? It was made up to save Monkey.'

'I reckon it was.'

'That's a good girl. Now then, did you search the room at all when you'd found the stain?'

'I was too scared for that. Look, Mr. Burden, I've been thinking and thinking about it. George was alone in there for hours and hours on the Thursday doing that letter while I was out at work. I think he must have found something they'd left behind them.'

'I've been thinking, too, Ruby, and I think great minds think alike.'

When they got to the police station a dozen men were lined up in the yard. None was more than five feet nine and all had hair of shades between mid-brown and coal-black. Kirkpatrick stood fourth from the end on the left. Ruby came hesitantly across the concrete, cautious, absurd in her high heels and with her swathed face. Wexford, who had not heard her story, could hardly keep himself from smiling, but Burden watched her rather sadly. Her eyes flickered across the first three men on the left and came to rest for a brief moment on Kirkpatrick. She came closer and walked slowly down the line, occasionally turning to look over her shoulder.

Then she turned back. Kirkpatrick looked afraid, his expression bewildered. Ruby stopped in front of him. A spark of recognition seemed to pass between them and it was marked on his part as on hers. She moved on, lingering longest of all in front of the last man on the right.

'Well?' said Wexford just inside the door.

'For a minute I thought it was the one on the end.' Wexford sighed softly. 'The one on the end, was police Constable Peach. 'But then I knew I'd got it wrong. It must be the one with the red tie.'

Kirkpatrick.

'Must be? Why must it be?'

Ruby said simply, 'I know his face. I don't know none of the others. His face is kind of familiar.'

'Yes, yes, I daresay. My face ought to be familiar to you by this time, but I didn't hire your knocking shop last Tuesday.' Under the veil Ruby looked resentful. 'What I want to know is, is he Geoff Smith?'

'I don't know. I wouldn't know him if I saw him now. Ever since then I've been dead scared every time I've seen a dark man in the street. All I know is I saw that fellow with the red tie somewhere last week. Maybe it was Tuesday. I don't know. He knew me too. You saw that?' She made a little whimpering, snivelling sound. Suddenly she was a little girl with an old face. 'I want to go home,' she said, darting a vicious glance at Burden. He smiled back at her philosophically. She was not the first person to make a confession to him and then regret it.

Kirkpatrick came back into Wexford's office, but he did not sit down. Ruby's failure to identify him had restored his confidence and for a moment Wexford thought that he was going to add further touches to the image he had tried to create of himself as a patron or connoisseur of the arts. He picked up the blue glass sculpture and fingered it knowingly while giving Wexford a sullen glance.

'I hope you're satisfied,' he said. 'I think I've been very patient. You could see that woman didn't know me.'

You knew *her,* Wexford thought. You were in Stowerton and although you were not at the party nor in her brother's confidence, you knew Anita Margolis never went there.

Kirkpatrick was relaxed now, breathing easily. 'I'm very tired and, as I say, I've been particularly patient and forthcoming. Not many men who'd just driven four hundred miles would be as accommodating as I've been.' The foot-high chunk of glass was carefully replaced on the desk and he nodded as if he had just subjected it to expert evaluation. You poseur, thought Wexford. 'What I want now is a good sleep and to be left in peace. So if there's any more you want you'd better speak now.'

'Or else hereafter for ever hold your peace? We don't work that way, Mr. Kirkpatrick.'

But Kirkpatrick hardly seemed to have heard. 'In peace, as I say. I don't want my family bothered or frightened. That woman not identifying me should settle the matter for good and all. I . . .'

You talk too much, Wexford thought.

'The Vine had struck a Fibre; which about
If clings my being—let the Sufi flout;
Of my base metal may be filed a Key,
That shall unlock the Door he howls without.'

# 9

After the rain the town looked cleansed. The evening
sun made the pavements gleam like sheet gold and a
thin vapour rose from them. It was mild, warm even,
and the air heavy with damp. Excitement made a hard
knot in Drayton's chest as he drove up the High Street
in Cawthorne's hire car and parked it in the alley. He
wanted to fill his lungs with fresh air, not this cloying
stuff that made him breathless.

Seeing her was a shock. He had had fantasies about
her in the intervening time and he had expected reality
to disappoint. She was just a girl he fancied and would
possess if he could. It had happened to him a dozen
times before. Why then, although the shop was full of
customers and pretty girls among them, were they all
faceless, all so many zombies? The sensuality which had
flooded into him last night outside the shop and had
since been transmuted into a clinical tickling calculation
came back like a blow and held him, staring at her,
while the doorbell rang in his ears.

Her eyes met his and she gave him the faint secret
smile that was just a lifting of the corners of her mouth.
He turned away and killed time playing with the paperback stand. The shop had an unpleasant smell, food
stench that came perhaps from whatever they ate in
those back regions, the sickliness of unwrapped sweets,
dirt that filled up the corners where no one tried to
reach. On the shelf above his head the china spaniel still
carried his pot of dusty flowers. Nobody would ever buy
him just as nobody would buy the ashtray and the jug
which flanked him. What connoisseur of Wedgwood—

what connoisseur of anything, come to that—would even enter this shop?

More and more customers kept coming in. The constant tinkling of the bell set Drayton's nerves on edge. He spun the stand and the coloured covers flickered in a bright senseless kaleidoscope, a gun, a skull under a stetson, a girl who lay in blood and roses. His watch told him that he had been in the shop only two minutes.

Only one customer left now. Then a woman came in to buy a dress pattern. He heard Linda say softly, even scornfully, 'Sorry, we're closed.' The woman began to argue. She had to have it that night, a matter of urgency. Drayton felt Linda's shrug, caught a firm phrase of denial. Was it thus, with this cool dogged patience, that she habitually refused demands? The woman went out, muttering. The blind rattled down the window and he watched her turn the sign.

She came away from the door and walked towards him quite slowly. Because her face had lost its smile and her arms hung stiffly at her sides, he thought that she was about to speak to him, perhaps apologize or state conditions. Instead, without a word or a movement of her hands, she lifted her mouth to his, opening her lips with a kind of sensuous gasp. He matched his mood to hers and for a moment they were joined only by the kiss. Then he took her in his arms and closed his eyes against the parody that mocked him from the book jackets, the orgy of writhing lovers, coupling above, below, beside each other, a massed fertility rite in modern undress.

He released her and murmured, 'Let's go.' She gave a soft giggle which drew from him a low, reluctant laugh. They were laughing, he knew, at their own weakness, their defencelessness under the grip of emotion.

'Yes, let's go.' She was breathing hard. The short staccato giggle she had given had nothing to do with amusement. 'Mark,' she said, faintly interrogative, and then, 'Mark' again, as if the repetition of his name settled something for her. To him it seemed like a promise.

'We'll go to Pomfret,' he said. 'I've got the car.'

'To Cheriton Forest?'

He nodded, feeling a stab of disappointment. 'You've been there before?'

The implication in the question was not lost on her. 'With Mum and Dad on picnics.' She looked at him gravely. 'Not like this,' she said. It might mean so much or so little. It might mean she had never been there with a boy friend, with any man, to make love or just to walk hand in hand. Words were a disguise for thought and for intention.

She got into the car beside him and went through a small ritual of arranging her skirt, removing her gloves, placing her handbag under the dashboard. What strange compulsion women had with their genteelisms, their attention to their personal furnishings! And how seldom they abandoned themselves. The face which she had put on was not the one he had seen as they came out from their embrace, but a prideful smug mask arranged, as it were, in the framing of the car window so that the world might observe her serenity out in a car with a man.

'Where would you like to eat?' he asked. 'I thought of the Cheriton Hotel, just where the Forest begins?'

She shook her head. 'I'm not hungry. We could have a drink.'

A girl like this, had she ever been in such a place before? Could she resist being seen there? With all his heart he despised her for her origins, her poverty of conversation, the pitiful smallness of her world. And yet her physical presence excited him almost beyond bearing. How was he to endure an hour with her in an hotel lounge, what would they talk about, how could he keep from touching her? He had nothing to say to her. There were rules in this game, prescribed amorous badinage, corresponding to courtship in the ornithological world, a kind of dancing and fluffing out of feathers. Earlier in the evening, before he had come into the shop, Drayton had to some extent rehearsed these preambles, but now it seemed to him that they had passed beyond them. The kiss had brought them to the threshold. He longed for a little gaiety from her, a spark of joy that might change his excitement from lust into something more civilized.

'I don't know,' he said dully. 'The evening I get the car is the first one it hasn't rained for weeks.'

'We couldn't have come here without it.' Ahead of them the lights of Pomfret glimmered in the dusk through the greening trees. 'It's getting dark,' she said.

Driven to despair for something to talk about, he broke a rule. 'We've been questioning a fellow called Kirkpatrick today,' he said. It was unorthodox, perhaps even wrong, to talk police business. 'He's a customer of yours. D'you know him?'

'They don't give their names,' she said.

'He lives around here.' Exactly here, he thought. This must be it. The black escarpment of the forest rose before them and in front of it, lying like boxes dropped in a green meadow, were a dozen white and blue dwellings, styled 'village houses.'

'Oh, look!' she said. 'That car.' There it was on one of the drives, its pink and lilac turned sickly in the light of a porch carriage lamp. 'That's the man you mean, isn't it? Fancy driving around in a thing like that. I nearly killed myself laughing.' Her animation over something so puerile chilled him. He felt his mouth go stiff. 'What's he done?' she asked.

'You mustn't ask me that.'

'You're very careful,' she said and he sensed that her eyes were on him. 'Your bosses, they must think a lot of you.'

'I hope so.' He thought she was smiling at him, but he dared not turn. It came to him suddenly that her silence and her dullness perhaps sprang from the same source as his own and the thought rocked him. The road was dark here where the pinewoods began, too dark for him to take his eyes from it for an instant. In the distance, between black billows of conifers, he could see the lights of the hotel. She put her hand on his knee.

'Mark,' she said, 'Mark, I don't want that drink.'

It was nearly nine when the call from the station came through to Burden's house.

'Ruby Branch is back again, sir.' The voice was Martin's. 'She's got Knobby Clark with her and she wants to see you. I can't get a word out of them.'

He sounded apologetic and as if he expected a reprimand. But all Burden said was, 'I'll be straight down.'

At his throat, he could feel that odd little stricture, that nervous pull, which meant something was going to happen at last. His tiredness went.

Ruby was in the police station foyer, her attitude abject, almost martyred, and on her face an expression of stoicism. Beside her, on a spoon-shaped red chair inadequate to contain his bulky rotund body, sat the fence from Sewingbury. Looking at him, Burden recalled their last encounter. Knobby looked nervous now and he had the air of a suppliant, but on that previous occasion it was he who had been in a position to exercise scornful contempt, to bargain and reject. In his mind's eye, Burden saw again the shy ladylike woman who had come to sell the jewels that were her husband's gifts. His heart hardened and he was seized with a sudden anger.

'Well?' he said. 'What do you want?'

With a heavy mournful sigh, Ruby surveyed the colourful appointments of the hall where they sat and it was these she seemed to address. 'A nice way to talk when I've taken the trouble to come all this way. It's a real sacrifice I've made.'

Knobby Clark said nothing. His hands were in his pockets and he appeared to be concentrating on retaining his balance on a seat constructed for narrower buttocks than his own. The little eyes in cushions of fat were still and wary.

'What's he doing here? Burden asked.

An apparently self-appointed spokeswoman for both

of them, Ruby said, 'I guessed George'd go to him,
them being old buddies. I had a bus ride to Sewingbury after I'd been here.' She paused. 'After I'd been
helping you,' she said with heavy meaning. 'But if you
don't want to know, that's O.K. by me.' Clutching her
handbag, she got up. Her fur collar undulated at the
quivering of the big bosom beneath it.

'You'd better come into my office.'

Still silent, Knobby Clark hoisted himself carefully
from his chair. Burden could look down easily on to the
top of his head. All that remained of his hair was a
feathery tuft, again evocative of the stubbly crown on a
great misshapen swede.

Intent on wasting no more time, he said, 'Well, let's
see it, then. What is it?' He was rewarded by nothing
more than a slight tremor in Knobby's mountainous
shoulders.

'D'you mind shutting the door?' said Ruby. Here the
lights were brighter and her face looked ravaged. 'Show
it to him, Mr. Clark.'

The little jeweller hesitated. 'Now, look, Mr. Burden,'
he said, speaking for the first time. 'You and me, we've
had no trouble for a long time, have we? Must be seven
or eight years.'

'Six,' said Burden crisply. 'Just six next month since
you had your little spot of bother over receiving those
watches.'

Knobby said resentfully, 'That was when I come out.'

'I don't see the point of it, anyway.' Ruby sat down,
gathering confidence. 'I don't see the point of trying to
make him look small. I come here of my own free
will . . .'

'Shut up,' Burden snapped at her. 'D'you think I
don't know what's been going on? You're narked with
your boy friend, you want to do him down. So you took
yourself over to this little rat's shop in Sewingbury and
asked him just what Monkey Matthews flogged to him
last Thursday. Make him look small! That's a laugh. If
he was much smaller we'd trip over him.' He swallowed
hard. 'It wasn't public spirit, it was spite. Naturally

Clark came with you when you told him we'd got Monkey here. Now you can fill in the rest but spare me the sob stuff.'

'Knobby wants to make sure there won't be no trouble for him,' Ruby said, now reduced to a tearful whimpering. 'He wasn't to know. How was I to know? I left George alone for a couple of hours on Thursday while I was working, making money to keep him in luxury . . .' Perhaps she recalled Burden's caution as to sentimentality, for she went on more calmly, 'He must have found it down the side of one of my chairs.'

'Found what?'

A fat hand returned to a shapeless pocket, emerged and dropped something hard and shiny on to Burden's desk. 'There's a lovely piece of workmanship for you, Mr. Burden. Eighteen carat gold and the hand of a master.'

It was a cigarette lighter of gleaming red-gold, the length and breadth of a matchbox but thinner, its sides delicately chased with a design of grapes and vine-leaves. Burden turned it over and pursed his lips. On its base was an inscription: "For Ann who lights my life.'

A big split opened in Knobby's face, the rift in the mango that has grown too pulpy for its skin. He was smiling. 'Thursday morning it was, Mr. Burden.' The bloated hands spread and quivered. ' "Take a butcher's at this," Monkey says to me. "Where d'you get it?" I says, knowing his reputation. "All that glisters is not gold," I said . . .'

'But if it wasn't gold,' said Burden nastily, 'it could glister on till kingdom come for all you cared.'

Knobby looked at him narrowly. ' "My old auntie left it me," he says, "my auntie Ann." "Lively old geezer she must have been," I said. "She leave you her cigar case and her hip flask as well?" But that was only my fun, Mr. Burden. I never thought it was hot. It wasn't on the list.' His face split again, virtuously this time. 'I gave him twenty for it.'

'Don't be childish. I'm not senile and you're no philanthropist.' Again Burden remembered the woman with the jewels. 'You gave him ten,' he said contemptuously.

Knobby Clark did not deny it. 'It's my loss, Mr. Burden. Ten or twenty, it doesn't grow on trees. You won't make anything of it? No trouble, eh?'

'Oh, get out,' Burden said tiredly. Knobby went. He looked smaller than ever, yet he seemed to be walking on his toes. When he had gone Ruby put her ginger head in her hands.

'It's done then,' she said. 'My God, I never thought I'd shop George.'

'Hear the cock crowing in the distance, can you?'

'You're a hard man. You get more like your boss every day.'

Burden was not displeased at this. 'You can go, too,' he said. 'We won't say any more about the other thing. You've wasted enough public time and public money as it is. I should stick to char-ing in future.' He grinned, his good temper almost restored. 'You've got a genius for cleaning up other people's mess.'

'Would you let me see George?'

'No, I wouldn't. Don't push your luck.'

'I didn't think you would.' She sighed. 'I wanted to say I was sorry.' Her face was ugly and painted and old. 'I love him,' she said and her voice sounded very tired. 'I've loved him for twenty years. I don't reckon you can understand that. You and the others, it's a dirty joke to you, isn't it?'

'Good night, Ruby,' he said. 'I've got things to do.' Wexford would have managed things better. He would have said something ironic and tough—and tender. It was as she had said. He, Burden, could not understand, never would, did not want to. To him that kind of love was a closed book, pornography for Grover's library. Presently he went down to see Monkey Matthews.

'You ought to get yourself a lighter, Monkey,' he said through the smoke, viewing the litter of match ends.

'Can't seem to get on with them, Mr. Burden.'

'Not even a nice gold one? Or would you rather have the lolly?' He let it lie in the palm of his hand, then raised it to catch the light from the bare bulb. 'Stealing by finding,' he said. 'What a come-down!'

'I don't suppose it's any use asking you how you found out?'

'Not a bit.'

'Ruby wouldn't do that to me.'

Burden hesitated for a second. She had said he was getting like Wexford and he had taken it as a compliment. Perhaps it was not only the Chief Inspector's toughness he could emulate. He opened his eyes wide in wrathful indignation. 'Ruby? I'm surprised at you.'

'No, I don't reckon she would. Forget I said it. Different to that lousy old git, Knobby Clark. He'd sell his own grandmother for cats' meat.' With slow resignation, Monkey lit another cigarette. 'How long'll I get?' he asked.

The car lights were off. He had parked it in a clearing surrounded by dense trees, tall black firs and pines, grown for ship's masts and flagpoles. Their trunks looked grey but even these straight shapes were indiscernible a few yards in from the edge of the wood. Beyond them there was neither night nor day, only a dark labyrinth.

He held her in his arms and he could feel her heart beating. It was the only sound. He thought it would be dark when he opened his eyes—their kiss had been long and blind—and the pallid dusk was a shock.

'Let's walk,' he said, taking her hands. They were all right now. It had come right. He did not know why, but instead of triumph there descended upon him a subtle and hitherto unexperienced fear. It was not in any sense a fear of physical inadequacy, nor of psychological failure, but an apprehension rather of some terrible involvement. Until now his sexual adventures had been transient, sometimes gay, never the spur to introspection. But he felt that they had not in any way been a practice or a rehearsal. Indeed the feelings they had evoked and those by which they had been promoted were quite unlike the sensations he now had both in kind and in degree. He was totally engulfed by something new and terrifying. It might almost have been the first time for him.

'It's like a foreign country,' she said.

It was. An uncharted place, alien, with an untranslatable language. That she should feel what he felt, identically, telepathically, made him gasp. Then he looked at her and, following her gaze upwards to the crowns of the trees, knew with a sudden sense of letdown that she meant the forest itself, and not a state of mind.

'Have you ever been in one?'

'No,' she said, 'but it's like that. And it's like last night. Alone with you between high walls. Did you think of that when you brought me here?' They had begun to climb an avenue which, cutting into the hillside so evenly and precisely, resembled an incision in thick black flesh or a sewn wound. 'Did you think of that?'

'Perhaps.'

'That was clever of you.' She was breathing shallowly, although the ascent was steep. To the left of them and a little way ahead, a tiny footpath threaded between the trees.

'But there aren't any windows here, are there?' More than anything in the world, more at that moment even than absolute possession of her, he wanted to see that covert smile, that uplifting of the lips without parting them. She had not smiled at all since they had entered the forest and that look of hers was the essence, the very nucleus of her appeal to him. Without it he could kiss her, even achieve that culmination for which this visit had been contrived, but he would lose the savour and the scent and half his pleasure—or perhaps be saved. Already he was the slave of a fetish.

Echoing him, she said softly, 'No windows ... No

one to watch you or stop you.' She added breathlessly, turning to face him so that their bodies and their eyes were close, 'I'm tired of being watched, Mark.'

A little orange square in a wall, a bell that always jangled, a querulous voice calling.

'You're with me,' he said, 'and nobody watches me.' Usually he was subtle, but her nearness deprived him of restraint and brought out the swagger of the male animal. Before he could stop himself the appeal came out. 'Smile for me,' he said in a hard whisper. Her fingers closed on his shoulders, not firmly or passionately but with a light, almost calculatingly seductive pressure. The look in her eyes was quite blank and the invitation in them came entirely from the tremor of half-closed heavy lids. 'Oh, smile . . .'

Then suddenly he was rewarded. A terrible urgency possessed him, but for all that he took her slowly in his arms, watching the smile that was the focal point of all his desire, and then bringing his own mouth down to meet it.

'Not here,' she whispered. 'In the dark. Take me into the dark.' Her response was strong yet fluidic. The words, spoken against his lips, seemed to flow into his body like wine and fill him with heat.

The thread of a path beckoned him and he held her against himself, half carrying her into the deep shadows of the forest edge. Above them the pine needles whispered and the sound was like the distant voices of doves. He took off his coat and spread it on the sandy floor. Then he heard her whispering to him words he could not catch but which he knew were no longer hesitant or passive. Her hands reached for him to pull him down beside her.

The darkness was almost absolute and it was this anonymous secret blackness which she seemed to have needed just as he had needed her smile. Her coquetry, her shy silence, had given place to a feverish hunger. That it was neither false nor simulated he knew when she took his face in the long hands that had become strong and fierce. He kissed her throat and her breasts and she gave a long sigh of pleasure. The darkness was a warm river to drown in. They call it the little death, he thought, and then the power to think at all melted away.

# 10

There was scarcely any delay between his knocking and the opening of the cottage door. A bright shaft of sunshine fell upon a black and mauve spotted overall and a sharp red face.

'Turned up again like a bad penny,' said Mrs. Penistan. Burden blinked. He hardly knew whether her remark referred to his arrival or her own unexpected appearance. She clarified with one of her shrill laughs. 'I saw Mr. M's advert and I took pity on him, said I'd come back till *she* turns up.' Leaning towards him, her broom held aloft like a spear, she whispered confidingly, 'If she turns up.' She stood aside for him to enter. 'Mind the bucket,' she said. 'We're all at sixes and sevens in here. Good thing my boys can't see what I have to contend with. If they set eyes on this place they'd have their mum out of it before you could say knife.' Remembering the ox-like Penistan men, not surely conspicuous for filial piety, Burden could only give a neutral smile. Their mother thrust her face into his and with a laugh, this time so cheerful as to amount to glee, said, 'Wouldn't surprise me if there was bugs in them walls.' A shrill peal of giggles pursued him into the studio.

Her efforts seemed to have made as yet small improvement in the general dirty disarray. Perhaps she had only just arrived. Nothing had been tidied or dusted and to the normal unpleasant smell had been added a sour stench, possibly coming from the dregs which still remained in the dozen or so empty cups on the tables

101

and the floor. Here, as nowhere else, Ruby's vigour and acumen were needed.

Margolis was painting. In addition to the tubes of oil colour arranged about him were various small pots of unidentifiable matter. One seemed to contain sand, another iron filings. He looked up when Burden entered.

'I've decided not to think about it,' he said with as near an approach to firmness as could be imagined. 'I'm simply getting on with my work. Ann'll be back.' He added as if this clinched the matter, 'Mrs. Penistan agrees with me.'

It was hardly the impression Burden had received on the doorstep. Without comment—let the man be cheerful while he could—he held out the lighter. 'Ever seen it before?'

'It's a cigarette lighter,' Margolis said sagely. So might some authoritative archaeologist identify an obscure find in an ancient barrow.

'The point is, is it your sister's?'

'I don't know. I've never seen it before. People are always giving her things.' He turned it over. 'Look, it's got her name on it.'

'It's got Ann on it,' Burden corrected him.

A poised broom preceded Mrs. Penistan's entry into the studio. She seemed to find amusement not so much in her employer's remarks as in his very existence, for, standing behind him as he contemplated the lighter, she favoured Burden with a slow deliberate wink.

'Here, let's have a look,' she said. One glance satisfied her. 'No,' she said, 'no.' This time her laughter seemed aimed at his own gullibility, or possibly at his supposing Margolis to be capable of identifying anything. Burden envied her her ignorance. Not for her dilemma of wondering how to contend with genius.. Here was a man, inept in practical matters, vague in his speech; therefore he was a lunatic, affording mirth and a kind of rough pity. 'She never had nothing like that,' she said firmly. 'Her and me, we used to have our coffee break midmorning. Always had a cigarette with it, she did. You need one of them lighters, I said, seeing the way she got through umpteen boxes of matches. Get some young fellow to give you one. It was way back around Christmas, you see, and her birthday was in January.'

'So she may have had it for her birthday?'

'If she did, she never showed it to me. Never had a gas lighter, neither. My boy could get you one cost price, him being in the trade, I said, but she. . .'

Burden cut her short, his ears painfully anticipating the strident laugh the end of this story, however humourless, would certainly provoke. 'I'll see myself out,' he said.

'Mind the bucket!' Mrs. Penistan called after him cheerfully. He went out among the daffodils. Everything was gold this morning, the sunshine, the pale bright flowers of spring and the little object in his pocket.

Kirkpatrick's car was on his driveway. Burden edged past it, his coat brushing the lettering and the mauve flowers.

'He says he's ill,' Mrs. Kirkpatrick said in a loud harsh voice.

Burden showed her his card. It might have been an advertising brochure for all the notice she took of it.

'He says he's got a cold.' Into this last word she put an infinite scorn as if a cold were of all afflictions the least credible and the most bizarre. She let Burden in and, leaving him alone with the two wide-eyed silent children, said, 'You might as well sit down. I'll tell him you're here.'

Two or three minutes later Kirkpatrick came down. He was wearing a silk dressing gown under which he appeared to be fully clothed. Burden recalled similarly attired figures, but gayer and more debonair, who featured in those bedroom comedies of the thirties, still ruthlessly acted by local dramatic societies, to whose performances he was sometimes dragged by his wife. The setting of chintz-covered chairs and mock wood panelling enhanced this impression, but Kirkpatrick had a hangdog look. Had this been a real stage, the audience would have supposed him to have forgotten his opening lines. His face was unshaven. He managed a smile for his children and just touched the little girl's long fair hair.

'I'm going to make the beds,' said Mrs. Kirkpatrick. It was not, Burden thought, a statement normally capable of being interpreted as a threat, but she succeeded in putting into it an almost sinister menace. Her husband gave her an encouraging nod, smiling as might one who wishes to foster his wife's interests in some unusual intellectual pursuit.

'I'm sorry to hear you're feeling unwell.'

'I expect it's psychological,' Kirkpatrick said. 'Yesterday afternoon upset me a good deal.'

A psychological cold, Burden thought. That's a new one. 'Pity,' he said aloud, 'because I'm afraid you may have to go through the mill again. Don't you think it would be better if we were to stop this farce about your being interested in Miss Margolis for the sake of her brother's paintings?' Kirkpatrick's gaze travelled to the ceiling. From above violent noises could be heard as if his wife were not so much making the beds as breaking the furniture. 'We know very well you were her lover,' he said roughly. 'You threatened to kill her. On your own admission you were in Stowerton on Tuesday night.'

'Not so loud,' Kirkpatrick said, an agonized note in his voice. 'All right. It's all true. I've been thinking—that's why I feel so bloody—I've been thinking I'll have to tell you. It's not her,' he said, and he looked at the boy and girl. 'It's my kiddies. I don't want to lose my kiddies.' In a low voice he added, "They always give custody to the mother, never mind what sort of mother she is.'

Burden gave an impatient shrug. 'Ever seen this before?'

The colour which flooded Kirkpatrick's face was the outward sign of an emotion Burden could not define. Guilt? Horror? He waited.

'It's Ann's.'

'Sure of that?'

'I saw her with it.' Dropping pretence, he said, 'She flaunted it in my face.'

Although it was warm in the office, Kirkpatrick kept his raincoat on. He had come of his own free will, Burden told Wexford, to talk in comparative comfort away from his wife.

'Did you give this lighter to Miss Margolis?' Wexford asked.

'Me? How could I afford a thing like that?'

'Tell me how you know it's hers.'

Kirkpatrick folded his hands and bowed his head.

'It was about a month ago,' he said, his voice scarcely above a whisper. 'I called for her but she was out. Margolis didn't seem to want to know me and I sat out in the car waiting for her to come back. Not this car,' he said with a small painful frown, 'the other one I had, the black one.'

He sighed and went on, his voice still low, 'She came back in hers about half an hour later—she'd been getting it serviced. I got out and went up to her. That lighter you've got there, it was on the shelf in her Alpine and I picked it up. I knew she hadn't had it before and when I saw the inscription, 'For Ann who lights my life", well, I knew her and I knew what sort of terms she'd be on with the giver.' A tiny thread of hysteria crept into his tone. 'I saw red. I could have killed her then. Christ, I didn't mean that!' He passed his hand across his mouth as if by this action he could wipe away the injudicious words. 'I didn't mean that. You know I didn't, don't you?'

Wexford said very smoothly, 'I know very little about you, Mr. Kirkpatrick. You seem to have a split personality. One day you tell me Miss Margolis was merely the key into her brother's art gallery, the next that you were passionately jealous of her. Which personality is—er, the dominant one?'

'I loved her,' he said stonily. 'I was jealous.'

'Of course you were,' Wexford said scornfully, 'and you don't know a Bonnard from a bull's foot.'

'Go on about the lighter,' said Burden.

Instead of continuing, the man said wretchedly, 'My wife mustn't know. God, I was mad, crazy, ever to go near that girl.' Perhaps he noticed that Wexford made him no promises of discretion, noticed and understood the implication, for he said wildly, 'I didn't kill her, I don't know anything about it.'

'For a man in love you're not showing much grief, Mr. Kirkpatrick. Let's get back to the lighter, shall we?'

Kirkpatrick shivered in the warm room. 'I was jealous as hell,' he said. 'She took the lighter from me and looked at it in a peculiar way.'

'What d'you mean, a peculiar way?'

'As if there was something to laugh at,' he said savagely, 'as if it was all one hell of a big joke.' He passed his hand across his forehead. 'I can see her now in that spotted fur coat, beautiful, free . . . I've never been free like that. She was holding that little bit of gold in her hand. She read out those words on the bottom, read them aloud, and went on laughing. "Who gave it to you?" I said. "He's got a pretty turn of phrase, my generous friend, hasn't he?" she said. "You'd never think of anything like that, Alan. All you ever do is add two and two and make it come to about sixteen." I don't know what she meant.' His fingers had left white marks where they had pressed the skin. 'You talk about showing grief,' he said. 'I loved her all right, or I thought I did. If you love someone you ought to be sorry when they're dead, oughtn't you? But, my God, if I couldn't have her, just me all to myself, I'd rather she was dead!'

'What were you doing in Stowerton on Tuesday night?' Wexford snapped.

'I don't have to tell you that.' He said it limply, not defiantly. Then he unbuttoned his coat as if he had suddenly grown hot.

'I wouldn't do that,' said Burden, 'not if you're going. As you said yesterday we can't keep you here.'

Kirkpatrick stood up. He looked weary to the point of distress. 'I can go?' He fumbled with his coat belt, his fingers jerking. 'There's nothing more I can tell you, anyway.'

'Perhaps it'll come to you,' Wexford said. 'I'll tell you what, we'll drop by later in the day.'

'When the children are in bed,' Burden added. 'Maybe your wife knows what you were doing in Stowerton.'

'If you do that,' Kirkpatrick said fiercely, 'you'll lose me my children.' Breathing heavily, he turned his face to the wall.

'He can cool off in there with Drayton for company,' Wexford said over a cup of coffee in the Carousel Café. It was opposite the police station and he preferred it to their canteen. His entry always had the effect of clearing the place of less desirable elements and now they were alone with the espresso machine, the rubber plants and the juke box playing Mantovani.

'Funny Ruby recognizing him like that,' said Burden, 'yet not being sure she recognized him as Geoff Smith.'

'I don't know, Mike. According to your moral code and maybe mine too, his behaviour wasn't exactly ethical, but it wasn't suspicious. She wouldn't have taken much notice of him.'

'Enough to know he was short, young and dark. Kirkpatrick's not that short, must be five feet eight or nine. It's the alias that puzzles me. Smith's obvious, but why Geoff? Why not John, for heaven's sake, or William?'

'Maybe Geoffrey is Kirkpatrick's middle name. We'll have to ask him.' Wexford drew his chair in from the gangway. A slim fair girl in skirt and sweater had come into the café and was making for a table beyond the room divider. 'Little Miss Grover,' he whispered. 'Let off the lead for once. If her father was up and about she wouldn't have the chance to pop out even for five minutes.'

'I've heard he's a bit of a tyrant,' Burden said, watching the girl. Her expression was dreamy, far away.

'Wonder what he was up to, slipping a disc? It's not as if he did manual work.'

'Save your detecting for what you get paid for,' said Wexford with a grin.

Linda Grover had ordered a raspberry milk shake. Burden watched her suck it up through a straw and look round with faint embarrassment as the straw made gurgling sounds in the dregs. A little drift of pink foam clung to her upper lip. Her hair, soft and satiny as a child's, was yet another golden eye-catcher on this golden day. 'Regular customer of theirs, Kirkpatrick,' he said. 'Buys his evening paper there. I wonder if he bought a knife too?'

'Let's go back and see,' said Wexford. The sun and the warmth made their walk across the street too short. 'Makes all the difference to the place, doesn't it?' he said as they passed up the steps and the cold stone walls of the police station enclosed them.

Drayton sat at one end of the office, Kirkpatrick at the other. They looked like strangers, indifferent, faintly antagonistic, waiting for a train. Kirkpatrick looked up, his mouth twitching.

'I thought you were never coming,' he said desperately to Wexford. 'If I tell you what I was doing in Stowerton you'll think I'm mad.'

Better a madman than a murderer, Wexford thought. He drew up a chair. 'Try me.'

'She wouldn't come out with me,' Kirkpatrick mumbled, 'on account of that damned car. I didn't believe she was going to that party, so,' he said defiantly, 'I went to Stowerton to check up on her. I got there at eight and I waited for hours and hours. She didn't come. God, I just sat there and waited and when she didn't come I knew she'd lie to me. I knew she'd found someone richer, younger, harder—Oh, what the hell!' He gave a painful cough. 'That's all I did,' he said, 'waited.' He lifted his eyes to Burden. 'When you found me yesterday morning at the cottage, I was going to tell her, ask her who she thought she was to cheat on me!'

Black against the sunlight, Drayton stood staring his contempt. What was he thinking? Wexford wondered. That he with his dark glow of virility, a glow that today was almost insolent, could never be brought so low?

'It got dark,' Kirkpatrick said. 'I parked my car by the side of Cawthorne's under a tree. They were making a hell of a racket in there, shouting and playing music. She never came. The only person to come out was a drunk spouting Omar Khayyám. I was there for three hours, oh, more than that . . .'

Wexford moved closer to the desk, folded his hands and rested his wrists on the rosewood. 'Mr. Kirkpatrick,' he said gravely, 'this story of yours may be true, but you must realize that to me it sounds a bit thin. Can you produce anyone who might help to verify it?'

Kirkpatrick said bitterly, 'That's my affair, isn't it? You've done your job. I've never heard of the police hunting up witnesses to disprove their own case.'

'Then you have a lot to learn. We're not here to make "cases" but to see right is done.' Wexford paused. Three hours, he thought. That covered the time of arrival at Ruby's house, the time when the neighbour heard the crash, the time when two people staggered from the house. 'You must have seen the party guests arriving. Didn't they see you?'

'I put the car right down the side turning till it got dark, down by the side of the launderette.' His face grew sullen. 'That girl saw me,' he said.

'What girl?'

'The girl from Grover's shop.'

'You saw her at seven when you bought your evening paper,' Wexford said, trying to keep his patience. 'What you were doing at seven isn't relevant.'

A sulky flush settled on Kirkpatrick's face. 'I saw her again,' he said. 'In Stowerton.'

'You didn't mention it before.' This time impatience had got the upper hand and every word was edged with testiness.

'I'm sick of being made to look a fool,' Kirkpatrick said resentfully. 'I'm sick of it. If I get out of this I'm going to chuck in my job. Maybe someone's got to flog soap and powder and lipstick, but not me. I'd rather be out of work.' He clenched his hands. 'If I get out of this,' he said.

'The girl,' said Wexford. 'Where did you see the girl?'

'I was down the side road by the back of the launderette, just a little way down. She was coming along in a car and she stopped at the traffic lights. I was standing by my car, then. Don't ask me what time it was. I wouldn't know.' He drew his breath in sharply. 'She looked at me and giggled. But she won't remember. I was just a joke to her, a customer who'd kept her late. She saw me standing by that thing and it was good for a laugh. *Lipdew!* I reckon she thinks about me and has a good laugh every time she washes her . . .'

Drayton's face had gone white and he stepped forward, his fingers closing into fists. Wexford interposed swiftly to cut off the last word, the word that might have been innocent or obscene.

'In that case,' he said, 'she will remember, won't she?'

# 11

Sunshine is a great healer, especially when it is the first mild sunshine of spring. Paradoxically it cooled Drayton's anger. Crossing the street, he was once more in command of himself and he could think calmly and even derisively of Kirkpatrick. The man was an oaf, a poor thing with a pansy's job, emasculate, pointed at and pilloried by women. He had a pink and mauve car and he peddled cosmetics. Some day a perfume plutocrat would make him dress up in a harlequin suit with a powder puff on his head, make him knock on doors and give soap away to any housewife who could produce a coupon and sing out a slogan. He was a puppet and a slave.

The shop was empty. This must be a time of lull, lunchtime. The bell rang loudly because he was slow to close the door. Sunlight made the shop look frowstier than ever. Motes of dust hung and danced in its beams. He stood, listening to the pandemonium his ringing had called forth from upstairs, running feet, something that sounded like the dropping of a saucepan lid, a harsh bass voice calling, 'Get down the shop, Lin, for God's sake.'

She came in, running, a tea towel in her hand. When she saw him the anxiety went out of her face and she looked petulant. 'You're early,' she said, 'hours early.' Then she smiled and there was something in her eyes he was not sure that he liked, a look of conquest and of complacency. He supposed that she thought him impatient to be with her. Their date was for the evening and he had come at half past one. That was what they al-

111

ways wanted, to make you weak, malleable in their long frail hands. Then they kicked you aside. Look at Kirkpatrick. 'I can't come out,' she said. 'I've got the shop to see to.'

'You can come where I'm taking you,' Drayton said harshly. He forgot his rage at Kirkpatrick's words, the passion of last night, the tenderness that had begun. What was she, after all? A shop assistant—and what a shop!—a shop girl, afraid of her father, a skivvy with a tea cloth. 'Police station,' he said.

Her eyes went very wide. 'You what? Are you trying to be funny or something.'

He had heard the stories about Grover, the things he sold over the counter—and under it. 'It's nothing to do with your father,' he said.

'What do they want me for? Is it about the advert?'

'In a way,' he said. 'Look, it's nothing, just routine.'

'Mark,' she said, 'Mark, you tried to frighten me.' The sun flowed down her body in a river of gold. It's only a physical thing, he thought, just an itch and a rather worse one than usual. Repeat last night often enough and it would go. She came up to him, smiling, a little nervous. 'I know you don't mean it, but you mustn't frighten me.' The smile teased him. He stood quite still, the sun between them like a sword. He wanted her so badly that it took all his strength and all his self-control to turn and say, 'Let's go. Tell your parents you won't be long.' She was gone two minutes, leaving behind her a breath of something fresh and sweet to nullify the smell of old worn-out things. He moved about the shop, trying to find things to look at that were not cheap or meretricious or squalid. When she came back he saw that she had neither changed her clothes nor put on make-up. This both pleased and riled him. It seemed to imply an arrogance, a careless disregard of other people's opinion, which matched his own. He did not want them to have things in common. Enough that they should desire each other and find mutual satisfaction at a level he understood.

'How's your father?' he said and when he said it he

realized it was a foolish catch-phrase. She laughed at him.

'Did you mean that or were you fooling?'

'I meant it.' Damn her for reading thoughts!

'He's all right,' she said. 'No, he's not. He says he's in agony. You can't tell, can you, with what he's got? It's not as if there was anything to show.'

'Seems to me he's a slave driver,' he said.

'They're all slave drivers. Better your own dad than some man.' At the door she basked in the sun, stretching her body like a long golden animal. 'When they talk to me,' she said, 'you'll be there, won't you?'

'Sure I'll be there.' He closed the door behind them. 'Don't do that,' he said, 'or I'll want to do what I did last night.' You could want it like mad, he thought, and still laugh. You could with this girl. My God, he thought, my God!

There was, Wexford thought, something between those two. No doubt Drayton had been chatting her up on the way. Only that would account for the look she had given him before sitting down, a look that seemed to be asking for permission. Well, he had always supposed Drayton susceptible and the girl was pretty enough. He had seen her about since she was a child but it seemed to him that he had never before noticed the exquisite shape of her head, the peculiar virginal grace with which she moved.

'Now, Miss Grover,' he said, 'I just want you to answer a few routine questions.' She smiled faintly at him. They ought not to be allowed to look like that, he thought wryly, so demure, so perfect and so untouched. 'I believe you know a Mr. Kirkpatrick? He's a customer of yours.'

'Is he?' Drayton was standing behind her chair and she looked up at him, perhaps for reassurance. Wexford felt mildly irritated. Who the hell did Drayton think he was? Her solicitor?

'If you don't recognize the name, perhaps you know his car. You probably saw it outside just now.'

'A funny pink car with flowers on it?' Wexford nodded. 'Oh, I know *him*.'

'Very well. Now I want you to cast your mind back to last Tuesday night. Did you go to Stowerton that evening?'

'Yes,' she said quickly, 'I always go on Tuesdays. I take our washing to the launderette in my dad's car.' She paused, weariness coming into her young fresh face. 'My dad's ill and Mum goes to a whist drive most nights.'

Why play on my sympathies? Wexford thought. The hint of tyranny seemed to be affecting Drayton. His dark face looked displeased and his mouth had tightened. 'All right, Drayton,' he said, not unpleasantly, 'I shan't need you any longer.'

When they were alone, she said before he had time to ask her, 'Did Mr. What's-his-name see me? I saw him.'

'Are you sure?'

'Oh yes. I know him. I'd served him with an evening paper earlier.'

'It wasn't just the car you identified, Miss Grover, not just an empty car?'

She put one hand to smooth the soft shiny knob of hair. 'I didn't know the car. He used to have a different one.' She gave a nervous giggle. 'When I saw him in it and knew it was his it made me laugh. He thinks such a lot of himself, you see, and then that car . . .'

Wexford watched her. She was far from being at ease. On her answer to his next question, the significant question, so much depended. Kirkpatrick's fate hung upon it. If he had lied . . .

'What time was it?' he asked.

'Late,' she said firmly. Her lips were like two almond petals, her teeth perfect. It seemed a pity she showed them so seldom. 'I'd been to the launderette. I was going home. It must have been just after a quarter past nine.' He sighed within himself. Whoever had been at Ruby's had certainly been there at nine fifteen. 'I'd stopped at the traffic lights,' she said virtuously. God, he thought, she's like a child, she doesn't differentiate be-

tween me and a traffic cop. Did she expect him to congratulate her? 'He'd parked that car down by the side of
the garage . . .'

'Cawthorne's?'

She nodded eagerly. 'I saw him in it. I know it was
him.'

'Sure of the time?'

He had noticed she wore no watch on the slender
wrist.

'I'd just come from the launderette. I'd seen the
clock.'

There was nothing more he could do. Perhaps it was
all true. They had no body, no real evidence against
Kirkpatrick after this. A fatherly impulse made him
smile at her and say,

'All right, Miss Grover, you can run along now. Mr.
Kirkpatrick ought to be grateful to you.'

For a moment he thought the shot had gone home,
then he wasn't sure. The look in her big grey eyes was
hard to interpret. He thought it might be a relieved happiness, no doubt because he was terminating the interview. Her departure seemed to deprive the office of
some of its brightness, although the sun still shone. Her
scent remained, a perfume that was too old for her innocence.

'That girl was got at,' Burden said wrathfully.

'You could be right there."

'We should never have let Kirkpatrick out of here
yesterday afternoon.'

Wexford sighed. 'What had we got to hold him on,
Mike? Oh, I agree he probably thought up that alibi between yesterday afternoon and this morning. I daresay
he went straight round to Grover's when he left here.
That girl wasn't at ease.'

'Show me a Grover who wouldn't do anything for
money,' Burden said. 'Like father, like daughter.'

'Poor kid. Not much of a life for her, is it? Cooped
up all day in that dirty little hole and carting the wash-

ing about in the evenings because her mother's playing whist.'

Burden eyed him uneasily. The expression on his chief's face was tolerant, almost tender, and it puzzled him. If he had known Wexford to be almost as uxorious a husband as himself, he might have believed . . . But, no, there were limits.

'If he was outside Cawthorne's, sir,' he said, 'and if he was there at half past nine, he's clear and we're wasting our time with him. But if the girl's lying and he did it, he could have disposed of Anita's body practically anywhere between here and the Scottish border. She could be lying in a ditch anywhere you can name in half a dozen counties.'

'And where the body is the weapon is, too.'

'Or he could have gone home to a place he knew and dumped her in the thickest part of those pine woods in Cheriton Forest.'

'But until we know more, Mike, searching for that body is impracticable, sheer waste of time.'

'I wouldn't mind having a go at Kirkpatrick over it,' Burden said with sudden ferocity. 'Having a go at him in his wife's presence.'

'No. We'll give him a rest for a while. The king-sized question is, did he bribe that girl?' Wexford grinned sagely. 'I'm hoping she may feel inclined to confide in Drayton.'

'Drayton?'

'Attractive to the opposite sex, don't you think? That sulky brooding look gets them every time.' Wexford's little glinting eyes were suddenly unkind. 'Unless you fancy yourself in the role? Sorry, I forgot. Your wife wouldn't like it. Martin and I aren't exactly cut out to strut before a wanton ambling nymph . . .'

'I'd better have a word with him, then.'

'Not necessary. Unless I'm much mistaken, this is something we can safely leave to Nature.'

# 12

The lighter had been lying on the desk in the sun and when Wexford picked it up it felt warm to his hand. The tendrils and leaves of its vine design glowed softly. 'Griswold's been getting at me,' he said. At the mention of the Chief Constable's name Burden looked sour. 'According to him, this is not to be allowed to develop into a murder inquiry. Evidence inconclusive and so on. We can have a couple more days to scout around and that's our lot.'

Burden said bitterly, 'The whole place turned upside-down just to get Monkey Matthews another few months inside?'

'The stain on the carpet was from the fruit of Ruby's imagination, Anita Margolis is on holiday, the couple who staggered down the path were drunk and Kirkpatrick is simply afraid of his wife.' Wexford paused, tossing the lighter up and down reflectively. 'I quote the powers that be,' he said.

'Martin's watching Kirkpatrick's house,' said Burden. 'He hasn't been to work today. Drayton's still presumably hanging around that girl. Do I call them off, sir?'

'What else is there for them to do? Things are slack enough otherwise. As for the other questions I'd like answered, Griswold isn't interested and I can't see our finding the answer to them in two days, anyway.'

Silently Burden put out his hand for the lighter and contemplated it, his narrow lips pursed. Then he said, 'I'm wondering if they're the same questions that are uppermost in my mind. Who gave her the lighter and

117

was it sold around here? Who was the drunk outside
Cawthorne's, the man who spoke of Kirkpatrick?'

Wexford opened his desk drawer and took out his
*Weekend Telegraph*. 'Remember this bit?' he asked.
'About her breaking off her engagement to Richard
Fairfax? I'll bet it was him. Mrs. Cawthorne said he left
the party around eleven and Cawthorne said he dumped
a brandy glass on one of his diesel pumps.'

'Sounds like a poet,' Burden said gloomily.

'Now, then, remember what I said about Goering.'
Wexford grinned at the inspector's discomfiture. 'According to Kirkpatrick he was shouting Omar Kayyám.
I used to be hot on old Kayyám myself. I wonder what
he said?

> ' "I often wonder what the vintners buy.
>     One half so precious as the goods they sell?"

'Or maybe he scattered and slayed with his enchanted
sword.' Burden took this last seriously. 'He can't have
done that.' he said. 'He got to Cawthorne's at eight and
he didn't leave till eleven.'

'I know. I was fooling. Anyway, Griswold says no
hunting up of fresh suspects without a positive lead.
That's my directive and I have to abide by it.'

'Still, I don't suppose there'd be any objection if I
went to inquire at a few jewellers, would there? We'd
have a positive lead if anyone remembered selling it to
Kirkpatrick or even Margolis himself, come to that.'
Burden pocketed the lighter. Wexford's face had a
dreamy look, preoccupied but not discouraging, so he
said briskly, 'Early closing today. I'd better get cracking
before all the shops shut.'

Left alone, the Chief Inspector sat searching his mind
for a peculiarly significant couplet. When he found it,
he chuckled.

> 'What lamp has destiny to guide
>     Her little children stumbling in the dark?'

There ought to be an answer. It came to him at last but it was not inspiring. 'A blind understanding, Heaven replied,' he said aloud to the glass sculpture. Something like that was what they needed, he thought.

Kirkpatrick was leaning against the bonnet of his car which he had parked on the forecourt of the Olive and Dove, watching the entrance to Grover's shop. Ever since breakfast time Detective Sergeant Martin had been keeping his house and his gaudy car under observation. Mrs. Kirkpatrick had gone shopping with the children and just as Martin, from his vantage point under the perimeter trees of Cheriton Forest, was beginning to abandon hope, the salesman had emerged and driven off towards Kingsmarkham. Following him had been easy. The car was a quarry even an intervening bus and hostile traffic lights, changing to red at the wrong moment, could not protect for long.

It was a warm morning, the air soft and faintly scented with the promise of summer. A delicate haze hung over Kingsmarkham which the sun tinted a positive gold. Someone came out from the florist's to put a box of stiff purple tulips on the display bench.

Kirkpatrick had begun to polish the lenses of a pair of sun glasses on the lapel of his sports jacket. Then he strolled to the pavement edge. Martin crossed the road before him, mingling with the shoppers. Instead of making directly for the news-agent's, Kirkpatrick hesitated outside the flower shop, looking at wet velvety violets, hyacinths in pots, at daffodils, cheap now because they were abundant. His eyes went to the alley wall no sun ever reached, but he turned away quickly and hurried into the York Street turning. Martin took perhaps fifteen seconds to make up his mind. He was only a step from Grover's. The bell rang as he opened the door.

'Yes?' Linda Grover came in from the door at the back.

Blinking his eyes to accustom himself to the dimness, Martin said vaguely, 'Just looking.' He knew her by hearsay but he was sure she didn't know him. 'I want a

birthday card,' he said. She shrugged indifferently and
picked up a magazine. Martin wandered into the depths
of the shop. Each time the bell tinkled he glanced up
from the card stand. A man came in to buy cigars, a
woman with a pekingese which sniffed among the
boxes on the floor. Its owner passed the card stand to
browse among the dog-eared books in Grover's lending
library. Martin blessed her arrival. One person dawdling
in the shadows was suspicious, two unremarkable. He
hoped she would take a long time choosing her book.
The dog stuck its face up his trouser leg and touched
bare flesh with a wet nose.

They were the only customers when, five minutes
later, Alan Kirkpatrick entered the shop with a red and
gold wrapped parcel under his arm.

Red and gold were the trade colours of Joy Jewels.
Scarlet carpet covered the floor, gilt *papier mâché* torsos
stood about on red plinths, each figure as many-armed
as some oriental goddess. Pointed, attenuated fingers
were hung with glittering ropes of rhinestone. Schitz and
quartz and other gems that were perhaps no more than
skillfully cut glass made prisms which caught and
refracted the flickering sunlight. On the counter lay a
roll of wrapping paper, bright red patterned with gold
leaves. The assistant was putting away his scissors when
Burden came in and held up the lighter between them.

'We don't sell lighters. Anyway, I doubt if anyone
around here would stock a thing like that.'

Burden nodded. He had received the same answer at
four other jewellers already.

'It's a work of art,' the assistant said, and he smiled
as people will when shown something beautiful and
rare. 'Eight or nine years ago it might have come from
this very place.'

Eight or nine years ago Anita Margolis had been little
more than a child. 'How come?' Burden asked without
much interest.

'Before we took over from Scatcherd's. They were
said to be the best jeweller's between London and

Brighton. Old Mr. Scatcherd still lives overhead. If you wanted to talk to him. . . .'

'Too long ago, I'm afraid,' Burden cut in. 'It'd be a waste of my time and his.' Much too long. It was April and at Christmas Anita Margolis had been lighting her cigarettes with matches.

He walked up York Street under the plane trees. The misty sun shone on their dappled grey and yellow bark and their tiny new leaves made an answering shadow pattern on the pavement. The first thing he noticed when he came into the High Street was Kirkpatrick's car outside the Olive and Dove. If Martin had lost him . . . But, no. There was the sergeant's own Ford nudging the end of the yellow band. Burden paused on the Kingsbrook Bridge, idling his time away watching the swans, a cob and a pen wedded to each other and to their river. The brown water rippled on gently over round and mottled stones. Burden waited.

The girl's face became sullen when she saw Kirkpatrick. She looked him up and down and closed her magazine, keeping her place childishly with one finger poked between the pages.

'Yes?'

'I was passing,' Kirkpatrick said awkwardly. 'I thought I'd come in and thank you.'

Martin selected a birthday card. He assumed a whimsical, faintly sentimental expression so that the woman with the pekingese might suppose he was admiring the verse it contained.

'This is for you, a token of my gratitude.' Kirkpatrick slid his parcel between the newspapers and the chocolate bar tray.

'I don't want your presents,' the girl said stonily. 'I didn't do anything. I really saw you.' Her big grey eyes were frightened. Kirkpatrick leaned towards her, his brown curls almost touching her own fair head.

'Oh, yes,' he said insinuatingly, 'you saw me, but the point is . . .'

She interrupted him sharply, 'It's all over, it's done with. They won't come bothering me any more.'

'Won't you even look inside the box?'

She turned away, her head hanging like a spring flower on a delicate stalk. Kirkpatrick took off the red and gold wrapping, the tissue paper and from a box padded with pink cotton wool, produced a string of glittering beads. They were little sharp metallic stones in rainbow colours. Rhinestones, Martin thought.

'Give it to your wife,' the girl said. She felt at the neck of her sweater until something silvery trickled over her thin fingers. 'I don't want it. I've got real jewellery.

Kirkpatrick's mouth tightened. He stuffed the necklace into one pocket, the mass of crumpled paper into the other. When he had gone, banging the shop door behind him, Martin went up to the girl, the birthday card in his hand.

She read the legend. ' "My darling Granny"?' she said derisively and he supposed she was looking at his greying hair. 'Are you sure it's this one you want?' He nodded and paid his nine pence. Her eyes followed him and when, he looked back she was smiling a little closed-lip smile. On the bridge he encountered Burden.

'What's this, then?' said the inspector, eyeing the card with the same mockery. Drayton, he thought reluctantly, would have been more subtle. He stared down at the river bed and the stone arch reflected in brown and amber, while Martin told him what he had heard.

'Offered her a necklace,' Martin said. 'Showy sort of thing wrapped up in red and gold paper.'

'I wonder,' Burden said thoughtfully. 'I wonder if he always shops at Joy Jewels, if he bought a lighter there years and years ago when it was Scatcherd's ...'

'Had it engraved recently for this girl?'

'Could be.' Burden watched Kirkpatrick seated at the wheel of his car. Presently he got out and entered the saloon bar of the Olive and Dove. 'There goes your man,' he said to Martin, 'drowning his sorrows. You never know, when he's screwed up his courage he may come offering his trinkets to the Chief Inspector. He certainly won't give them to his wife.'

The mist had begun to lift and there was real warmth in the sunshine. Burden took off his raincoat and laid it over his arm. He would have one last go at finding where that lighter came from, make one last inquiry, and if it was fruitless, give up and meet Wexford for lunch at the Carousel. But was there any point, was it too long a shot? He could do with a cup of tea first and the Carousel would be already serving lunches. The thought came to him that there was a little place, not a hundred yards from the bridge, a small café where they served good strong tea and pastries at all hours. He cut up the path between the cottages and came out in the Kingsbrook Road. Just past the bend it was, in the ground floor of one of the Georgian houses.

Strange how heavily the mist seemed to lie in this part of the town, on high ground too and coloured a deep ochreish yellow. He passed the big houses and stopped on the brow of the low hill.

Through the clouds of what he now realized to be not mist but plaster dust, a contractor's board faced him: *Doherty for Demolition. What Goes Up Must Come Down!* Beyond, where the block which had housed his café had stood, was a cliff-face of battered wall, roof, floors, façade torn from it. Among the rubble of what had once been elegant stonework stood a wooden hut on the threshold of which three workmen sat eating sandwiches.

Burden shrugged and turned away. The old town was going, gradually and cruelly. Beauty and grace were inconvenient. They pulled down the old buildings, put up splendid new ones like the police station. New buildings needed new drains and new wiring and digging up the roads killed the old trees. New shops replaced the old, rhinestones and gilt goddesses the best jeweller's between London and Brighton. . . . That reminded him. It was useless to waste time regretting the past. If he was to get no tea he certainly wasn't going to delay his lunch. One more inquiry first, though.

Mr. Scatcherd reminded Burden of a very old and very amiable parrot. The big curving nose came down over a genial mouth and the bird-like impression was sustained by a bright yellow waistcoat and baggy, shaggy trousers suggestive of plummage. The rooms over the shop might have been a perch or an eyrie, they were so airy and lofty, and their windows looked into the tops of whispering greening trees.

He was shown into a living-room apparently unchanged since it had been furnished in the eighties. But instead of the drab browns and reds associated with the nineteenth century, here in the plush and velvet was peacock green, glowing puce and blue. A chandelier that hung from the ceiling winked in the blaze of sun like a handful of diamonds dropped and suspended in space. Fat cushions with gold tassels had cheeks of shiny green shot-silk. There were pieces here, Burden thought as he sat down in a brocade wing chair, that Cawthorne would give his sodden blue eyes to possess.

'I usually have a glass of madeira and a biscuit about this time,' said Mr. Scatcherd. 'Perhaps you'll do me the honor of joining me?'

'It's very kind of you,' Burden said. The former variety of refreshment he had never sampled and he was still regretting the depredations which had deprived him of his tea as well as of the town of its glory. 'I'd like to.'

A sweet smile told him he had been right to accept. 'Just the shade of a garnet,' the old jeweller said when he brought the wine on a japanned tray. 'Not a ruby.' A severity, the didactic crispness of the connoisseur, had entered his rather fluting voice. 'A ruby is quite different. What have you brought me to look at?'

'This.'

The hand that took it was grey and clawed, the nails long but scrupulously clean.

"Could it have come from around here? Or do you only get things like this in London?"

Mr. Scatcherd was not listening to him. He had taken the lighter to the window and he was nodding his head precisely while screwing his old eye up against a pocket glass.

' "*Les grappes de ma vigne*",' he said at last. Burden sat up eagerly. 'That's the name of the design, you know. The grapes of my vine. Baudelaire, of course. Perhaps you are not familiar with the poem. Highly appropriate for a lover's gift.' He smiled with gentle pleasure, turning the lighter over. 'And it was a lover's gift,' he said as he read the inscription. 'A pretty greeting for a lady.'

Burden had no idea what he meant. 'You know it?' he said. 'You've seen it before?'

'Several years ago.' The chandelier flashed pink, violet and green prism spots on the walls. 'Seven, eight years.' Mr. Scatcherd put away his glass and beamed with satisfaction. The rainbow lights flickered on his bald head. 'I know the design,' he said, 'and I well remember the inscription.'

'But that engraving was done recently!'

'Oh, no. Before I retired, before Joy Jewels took over.' A smile of mocking disparagement curved his mouth and made his eyes twinkle as he spoke the name. 'My dear inspector,' he said. 'I ought to know. I sold the thing.'

# 13

'Who did he sell it to? Kirkpatrick?'

Burden hung up his raincoat on the office rack and decided to do without it for the rest of the day. He glanced at the lab reports Wexford was studying and said:

'I don't understand it. Old Scatcherd hasn't sold anything for more than seven years and at that time Anita wasn't here, probably didn't even know such a place as Kingsmarkham existed. Kirkpatrick wasn't here either. Those houses where he lives have only been up a year. Besides, Scatcherd's got a wonderful memory for a man of his age and he's never had a customer called Kirkpatrick.'

'Look, Mike,' Wexford said, giving his reports a glance of disgust, 'are we going to be able to find out who did buy this damned lighter?'

'Scatcherd's looking it up in his books. He says it'll take him a couple of hours. But, you know, sir, I'm beginning to think Anita just found it, picked it up in the street and kept it because the inscription was appropriate.'

'Found it!' Wexford roared. 'You mean someone lost it and Anita found it and then she lost it again at Ruby's? Don't be so daft. It's not a key or an old umbrella. It's a valuable article and I reckon it's the key to this whole thing. If it was lost, why wasn't the loss reported to us? No, you get back to old Scatcherd, assist him with your young eyes.' Burden looked pleased at this as Wexford had known he would. 'You never know what you may discover,' he said. 'Cawthorne may have bought it for her or Margolis himself or at any rate someone who owns a green car. In all this we have to remember that however oddly Kirkpatrick may be behaving he doesn't have and never had a green car.'

When Burden had gone he returned to his perusal of the lab reports. He read them carefully, suppressing a disgusted rage. Never in all his experience had he come across anything so negative. The evidence the carpet afforded would have been satisfactory—only to the manufacturers of Ruby's favourite detergents. Fingerprints on her car corresponded to those in Anita Margolis's bedroom. They were hers and hers alone. The ocelot coat gave even less information. An analyst had suggested that the scent with which it was redolent might be *Guerlain's Chant d' Aromes*. Wexford, who was good on perfumes, could have told them that himself. In one pocket was a crumpled sheet of trading stamps. She had probably bought her petrol at Cawthorne's. Wexford sighed. Who had brought that car back at one in the morning and where had it been all the evening? Why had her killer, Kirkpatrick or another, called himself Geoff Smith when it would have been so much more natural and indeed expected for him to remain anonymous?

A pile of thick books, some of them ancient and all bound in dark green morocco, were stacked at Mr. Scatcherd's feet. Burden stepped over them and sat down in the brocade chair.

'I've been completely through the last three,' Mr. Scatcherd said, showing no sign of a diminution of patience. 'That takes us right back to nineteen fifty-eight.' He had perched a pair of gold-rimmed glasses on his parrot's nose and he glanced over the top of them, smiling pleasantly.

Burden shrugged. It was all getting beyond him. Nine years ago Anita Margolis had been fourteen. Did men give valuable gold cigarette lighters—any cigarette lighters, come to that—to girls of fourteen? Not in his world. Whatever world this was in which he found himself, it was a topsy-turvey one of nightmare inconsistency. The lighter had been sold in Kingsmarkham and in Kingsmarkham its recipient had lived and gone out to meet her death. Simple on the face of it, but for ages and times and a host of confusing facts . . .

'I thought it was new,' he said.

'Oh, no. I knew the artist who made it. He's dead now but in his day he was a fine goldsmith. His name was Benjamin Marks but when I called him Ben it was another master I thought of. Perhaps you can guess whom I mean.' Burden looked at him blankly. "Cellini, inspector,' Mr. Scatcherd said almost reverently. 'The great Benvenuto. My Ben was a naturalist too in his way. It was always to Nature that he went for his inspiration. I remember a standard rose, designed for a lady's powder case. You could see the sepals in the heart of each tiny flower. He made this and inscribed it. It was done to a gentleman's order . . .'

'But whose order, Mr. Scatcherd? Until I know that I'm no further.'

'We shall find it. It helps my memory to talk about it.' Mr. Scatcherd turned the thick watered pages, running a long finger-nail down the margins. 'We're coming up to the end of nineteen fifty-eight now. Do you know, each time I come to the end of a book I feel I'm warm. I have a faint recollection of Christmas and I seem to remember selling a fine ring at the same time.' The last page. Burden could see a date in December printed at the top of it. He had a wild sensation that if the record of the sale could not be found in this book or the next, Mr. Scatcherd would keep on searching, for hours perhaps or days, until he came back to the first entry made by his father in eighteen eighty-six.

The jeweller looked up with a smile but he had worn this continually and Burden could see no particularly encouraging sign of gratification on his wrinkled face. 'Ah, yes, here we are,' he murmured. 'The ring I mentioned. A diamond and sapphire hoop to Mr. Rogers of Pomfret Hall. For his wife, no doubt, or that poor daughter of his. There was insanity there, if I remember.' Nodding sagely, he continued his scanning. 'Not the same day, I'm sure. Perhaps the next day ... Now, inspector, we're getting somewhere.'

Hope surging back, Burden got up to take the book from him but Mr. Scatcherd held fast to it. 'Here we are,' he said again, but this time with a note of quiet triumph. 'Gold cigarette lighter to order: *"Les grappes de ma vigne"*, Benjamin Marks; inscribed: "For Ann who lights my life." Not much help to you, I'm afraid. Such a common name. Still, there's an address.'

Burden was unbearably intrigued. 'What name?' he asked excitedly.

'Smith. It was sold on December 15th, 1958 to a Mr. Geoffrey Smith.'

No doubt about it, Drayton was taking his duties seriously, Wexford thought as he came into the Carousel Café for his lunch. Behind the room divider a hooded coat could be seen lying over the back of a chair, one of its sleeves caught on the fleshy leaves of a rubber plant. Drayton's back was towards the door but there was something concentrated and intense in the set of his shoulders. He seemed to be in animated, not to say amorous, conversation with his companion, for their faces were close. It afforded Wexford considerable amusement to see Drayton raise his hand to cup the girl's white chin and to watch her delicate tentative smile. They had not observed him. Indeed, he thought, it would not be stretching a point to say they had eyes only for each other. A bit hard on the girl, he reflected, and he was wondering how much longer this simulated attention would be necessary when Burden found him.

'What are you eating?'

'Shepherd's pie,' said Wexford. 'Must be ten minutes since I ordered.' He grinned. 'I daresay they've had to go out and shoot a shepherd.'

'I've found him," Burden explained and while he did so the Chief Inspector's expression changed from interest to scowling incredulity.

Burden said apologetically, 'You said yourself, sir, some people really are called Smith.'

'That was a funny,' Wexford growled. 'Where does he live?'

'Sewingbury.' The shepherd's pie came and Burden ordered a portion for himself. 'I don't understand why he isn't on the electoral register. He can't very well be under age.'

'Not unless we're dealing with a little boy buying cigarette lighters for a little girl.' Wexford raised a forkful of his pie to his mouth and made a face. 'I'd like to get our lab to work on this mashed potato,' he said. 'If I'm not mistaken it's been in a packet since it was dug out of the ground.' He pushed the bowl of green pepper salad the Carousel served with everything to the extreme edge of the table. 'Smith could be a foreigner who's changed his name but never got naturalized.'

Burden pondered. He felt he would think better on a full stomach. The mashed potato might be suspect but it was brown and crisp and the savoury smell whetted his appetite. 'We've assumed all the time Smith was a pseudonym,' he said, brightening as the hot steaming plate was set before him. 'Now it suddenly looks as if everything is going to be plain sailing. How about this, sir? Smith's known Anita for years and the friendship was renewed when she and Margolis came to live here. He booked the room on Saturday, going to Ruby's in his black car which he sold the following day or the Monday, exchanging it for a new green one. But when he gave his name to Ruby he had no idea he'd have anything to hide. An attack on Anita was the last thing he planned.' When Wexford nodded, he continued more confidently, 'She broke her date with Kirkpatrick, not on account of his car, but just because she was fed-up with him and because she'd made a new one with Smith. She met Smith somewhere, parked her own car and went to Stowerton with him in his. They quarrelled in Ruby's room, very likely over Kirkpatrick, and he attacked her with a knife or a razor. He managed to get her out of the house and into the car, but she died and he dumped her body or hid it at this place of his in Sewingbury. Later, when there weren't many people about, he collected her car and returned it to Pump Lane.'

'Who knows?' Wexford pushed aside his empty plate. 'It fits. Kirkpatrick comes into it only as a rival and all his worries are genuinely caused by fear of his wife's revenge.'

It was at this point that Burden, reaching for the pepper, saw Drayton. 'Then we can nip that little intrigue in the bud,' he said.

'Before he gets carried away, eh?' Wexford stood up. "Yes, we'll accept Kirkpatrick's story for the time being. I don't fancy Griswold will consider Smith a new suspect, do you?' How preoccupied Drayton looked, almost entranced. 'I don't know that I want my young men amorously involved with a Grover, except in the line of business.' He crossed to the cash desk to pay the bill and dropped on one knee to tie his shoelace. Beneath the table cloth he saw a long bare leg pressed against Drayton's knee. Playing footsie, he said to himself. He took his change and, approaching the two in the corner, gave a slight cough. Drayton lifted his face and instead of cold efficiency Wexford saw a dreamy rapture. 'Feel like a trip to Sewingbury, Drayton?'

The boy was on his feet before the words were out and once more the mask was assumed.

'I'm just coming, sir.'

'Finish your coffee.' By God, that girl was a beauty! The kind that bloomed for half a dozen years and then shrivelled like straw before they were thirty, the golden kind that came to dust.

Geoffrey Smith's flat was one of four in a converted mansion on the far side of Sewingbury, a gracious Georgian house built perhaps at the same time as St. Catherine's convent on to which it backed. A stately staircase took them up to a gallery. The wall facing them had once contained several doors but these had been

boarded up and now only two remained, the entrances
to flats one and two. Number two was on the left.
Wexford rang the bell.

The grandeur of the place scarcely fitted in with
Burden's theory of a knife or a razor. On the other
hand, a customer of Mr. Scatcherd's might well live
here. All the same, Burden was not prepared for the
lofty space which opened before them when the door
swung inwards, and for a moment he looked not at the
woman who stood on the threshold, but at the vast
apartment behind her which led into another as large
and ended finally in a pair of immense windows. It was
more like a picture gallery—but for its bare walls—
than a flat. Light fell from the windows in two huge
twin rectangles and she stood in the darker split between them.

As soon as he met her eyes Burden knew that he had
seen her before. She was the woman who had tried to
sell her jewels to Knobby Clark.

'Mrs. Smith?' Wexford said.

Burden had scarcely expected her to welcome them,
but her reaction astonished him. There was shock and
horror in her eyes. It was as if, he thought, analysing,
she had been tortured for years and then, just as the
respite had come, someone had threatened her with a
renewal of torment.

'*What do you mean?*' she said, and she enunciated
each word separately and slowly.

'I asked you if you are Mrs. Smith, Mrs. Geoffrey
Smith?'

Her tired, once pretty face grew hard. 'Please go,' she
said tightly. Wexford gave her one of his tough implaca-
ble looks and showed her his card. It had seldom
evoked so gratifying a response. The hard look went
with a gasp of relief. She smiled wryly, then laughed.
'You'd better come in.' Suddenly she was cordial, the
ladylike creature Burden had seen in Knobby Clark's
shop. 'I can't think what you want,' she said. He was
sure she had not recognized him. 'But I'm evidently not
in danger from you. I mean—well, before I knew who

you were, I thought you were rather a lot of strange men for a lone woman to let into her home.'

A thin excuse for such a display of disgusted horror. In spite of the sun it was cold inside the flat. In winter it would be unbearable. They could see no sign of a radiator as they tramped through the first huge room and came into the place where the long windows were. Ivory-coloured double doors, the paint chipped on their mouldings, closed behind them. The furniture was much too small and much too new, but not new enough to be smart. No attempt had been made to achieve harmony between furniture and a noble decor. The elegant gleaming windows towered and shone between skimped bits of flowered cotton like society women fallen on evil days.

'I'd like to see Mr. Smith. When do you expect him back?'

'I'd like to see him too.' Now her brown-skinned curly face was alight with a curious half-amused rue. The glasses bobbed on her short nose. Since she had discovered who they were all her fear had gone and she looked like a woman infinitely capable of laughter, a great deal of which might be directed against herself. 'Geoffrey divorced me five years ago,' she said.

'Do you know where he is now, Mrs. Smith?'

'Not Mrs. Smith, Mrs. Anstey. Noreen Anstey. I married again.' She gave Wexford a wise elderly look, a look of wide and perhaps unpleasant experience. 'I think you might tell me why you want him.'

'Routine inquiries, Mrs. Anstey.' She was the last woman in the world to be fobbed off with that one, he thought. Her eyes clouded with reproach.

'It must be something very mild,' she said, the gentle mocking smile sending sharp wrinkles up around her eyes. 'Geoff is one of the most honest people I ever met. Don't you think he looks honest?'

Wexford was greedy for the photograph and when it was handed to him, a large studio portrait, he almost grabbed it. A swarthy, pleasant face, black hair, a pipe in the mouth. The Chief Inspector was too old a hand at the game to give opinions as to honesty on this evidence. He was still studying it when Burden said:

'Have you ever seen this before?' He put the lighter into her hands. They shook a little as she took it and she gave a gasp of delight, bringing it close to her face. 'My lighter!' He stared at her. 'And I thought it had gone for ever!' She tried to make it ignite, shrugged, her face still radiant. 'Where did you find it? This is wonderful! Won't you have a cup of tea? Do let me make you some tea.'

She sat on the edge of her chair and she reminded Wexford of a child on Christmas morning. Smith's photograph was in her lap, the lighter in her hand. He had guessed her age at thirty-eight or thirty-nine but suddenly she looked much younger. There was a wedding ring on each hand. One was chased and patterned rather like the lighter she held, the other more like a Woolworth curtain ring.

'Now, let's get this clear,' Wexford said. 'This lighter is yours? You said your name was Noreen.'

'So it is.' He was sure he could believe her. Every word she spoke had the clear ring of honesty. 'Noreen Ann Anstey. I always used to be known as Ann. First I was Ann Greystock and that was fine; then Ann Smith which is dull but not so bad. But Ann Anstey? It's terrible, it's like a stammer. So I use my first name.'

'Your first husband gave you the lighter?' Burden put in.

'For Christmas. Let me see—nineteen fifty-eight it must have been.' She hesitated and her smile was rueful. 'We were getting on fine in those days. I lit his life.'

'How did you come to lose it?'

'How does one lose anything? It was last November. I had a handbag with a faulty clasp. I always carried it about with me even though I can't afford to smoke these days.' Wexford just glanced at the bare shabby furniture and then was sorry he had done so. Very little escaped her and now she was hurt.

With a brief frown, she went on. 'One day the lighter

was there and the next it wasn't. I'd lost a necklace, a silver thing, the week before. Same old way. Some of us never learn.' She fingered the lighter lovingly and met Burden's censorious eye. 'Oh, I know it's valuable,' she said hastily. 'Everything Geoff gave me was pretty valuable. He isn't rich but he's the soul of generosity. I was his wife and nothing was too good for me. I've sold most of the other stuff . . .' Pausing, she glanced at him again and he knew she was remembering their encounter. 'I've had to,' she said. 'I'm a teacher at St. Catherine's, but I don't manage very well. I don't know why I kept this.' She lifted her shoulders in the manner of one who regrets but regards regret as a waste of time. 'Perhaps because it was so very personal.' Her sudden smile was a flash of philosophy. 'Ah, well, it's nice to have been loved and remember it when it's gone.'

You didn't lose it, Wexford thought. Don't strain my credulity too far. You may have lost it and Anita Margolis may have lost it, but you didn't both lose it and within six months of each other.

'Mrs. Anstey,' he said, 'as his divorced wife, you must know where Mr. Smith is now.'

'He never paid me—what-d'you-call-it?—alimony. It was enough for me that he gave us the flat to live in.' She caught her lower lip in small white teeth. 'Ah, I see why you want him. Some tax thing because he's an accountant. Well, if anyone's been fiddling his returns it's nothing to do with Geoff.'

'Where can we find him?'

'Back where you come from, Kingsmarkham.' Wexford listened incredulously, recalling the visits they had paid to every Geoff Smith in the district. 'Twenty-two, Kingsbrook Road, Old Kingsbrook Road, that is. He lived in Kingsmarkham before we were married and after the divorce he went back there.'

'Have you ever heard him speak of a Miss Anita Margolis?'

The mention of another woman's name did not please her. He could see that by the way the eager smile faded and her hands came tightly together. But she had an answer, an antidote, he thought, for every hint of poison. 'Is she the girl who's been fiddling her tax?'

'Mrs. Anstey, has your ex-husband a key to this flat?'

She wrinkled the already lined brown forehead. Her eyes were teak-coloured but glowing with life. It wouldn't matter what she wore, Wexford reflected, you'd never notice. Her personality, her vitality—for Ann who lights my life—made of her clothes something she put on to keep her warm. For the first time he observed them, a pullover and an old pleated skirt.

'A key?' she said. 'I shouldn't be surprised. If he has, he doesn't use it. Sometimes . . .' She looked up at him under lowered lashes, but not coyly, not artfully, rather as if she doubted his ability to understand. 'Sometimes I wish he would,' she said. 'One doesn't care to mess up someone else's life. It doesn't matter about me. Contrary to the general opinion, there's a whole heap of consolation in knowing one's only getting what one thoroughly deserves. Geoff deserved the best and he got a kick in the teeth. I'd like to know things had got better for him, that's all.' She had been lost and now she seemed to recollect the company she was in. 'You must think I'm crazy talking to you like this. Sorry. When you're alone a lot you get garrulous with visitors. Sure you won't have that tea?'

'Quite sure, thank you.'

'When you see him,' she said, 'you might give him my—er, best wishes. Still, maybe you don't carry messages and maybe he's forgotten the past.' Her face was full of tiny crinkles, a map of experience, and not all those lines, Wexford thought, were capable of being shrugged away.

'For Ann who messed my life,' said Burden when they were in the car. 'What did he do, sir, come back and nick the lighter because he'd found a girl who might appreciate it?'

'Let's not sentimentalize him, shall we? He made a nasty mess himself—out of the girl he did give it to. I suppose he remembered that he'd once given a present to his wife that was highly appropriate as a gift to another Ann. Not all that generous and high-minded, is he, if he sneaked back to his ex-wife's flat and stole it?'

'At any rate, we don't have to worry about him giving it to Anita Margolis nine years ago. He needn't have given it to her till a few months ago. Probably didn't even meet her till then.'

'Fair enough,' said Wexford. 'I go along with that, don't you, Drayton?'

Burden looked offended that Drayton had been considered worthy of consultation. 'I daresay he killed her with one of those flick knives from Grover's shop,' he said sourly. Drayton's back grew if anything slightly more rigid. Faintly amused, Wexford cleared his throat.

'Take the Stowerton Road,' he said to Drayton. 'We'll show this photo to Ruby Branch.'

She contemplated it and Wexford knew that it was hopeless. Too much time had passed, too many faces had been brought to her notice. The identity parade which should have settled things had merely unsettled her. She gave Wexford the photograph, shaking her ginger curls, and said:

'How many more of you are going to come calling?'

'What's that supposed to mean?'

Ruby shifted on the blue and red sofa and stared bitterly at the uncarpeted floor.

'Fellow called Martin,' she said, 'he's only been gone ten minutes. He's one of your lot, isn't he?' Wexford nodded, mystified. 'First there comes this great big car, pink and mauve with letters on it and this fellow gets out . . .'

'What fellow?' Not Martin, he thought. What the hell was going on?

'No, no, that chap with the red tie in your parade. As soon as I saw his car I remembered where I'd seen him before. Twice I saw him on that Tuesday night. Outside Cawthorne's he was when I went by at ten past eight and I saw him again at eleven, sitting in his car, staring at everyone like he was going off his head. But I told your bloke Martin all that just now.'

It was all Wexford could do to quell the laugh that rose in his throat. Ruby's painted face was pink with indignation. Trying to sound severe, Wexford said:

'You wouldn't be saying all this because Mr. Kirkpatrick asked you to, would you? You wouldn't be led into temptation by a nifty rope of rhinestones?'

'Me?' Ruby drew herself up virtuously. 'I never even spoke to him. He was just getting out of that daft car of his when your man drives up. Back he nips like one o'clock and off down the street. That Martin,' she said, very aggrieved, 'he was nasty to me. Some would call it threatening.'

'And others,' said Wexford, 'would call it saving weaker vessels from their baser instincts.'

At Stowerton crossroads Cawthorne was nowhere to be seen, but his wife, bony knees displayed and earrings big as Christmas tree baubles dangling beneath yellow curls, had perched herself on a diesel pump to flirt with an attendant. In the launderette the portholes still whirled.

'You can consider yourself absolved from laundry duty tonight, Drayton,' Wexford said, chuckling.

'I beg your pardon, sir?'

'Miss Grover always comes over here to do her washing on Tuesdays, doesn't she?'

'Oh, yes, sir. I see what you mean.' There was no need for him to flush quite so deeply, Wexford thought. The dark red colour had spread to the back of his neck.

'Kirkpatrick's safe all right.' he said. 'His bribes fell on stony ground.' The metaphor sounded wrong and he added quickly, 'Those two women saw him outside Cawthorne's right enough. He's just a fool who can't let well alone. It's the inside of a divorce court he's afraid of, not a jail.'

'Straight to the Old Kingsbrook Road, sir?' Drayton asked stiffly.

'Number twenty-two's this end.' As they passed the Methodist church, Wexford leaned forward, a dull leaden weight diving to the pit of his stomach. He had feared this when Mrs. Anstey gave him the address, feared it and dismissed his fear as jumping to conclusions.

'Look at that, Mike.'

'As if a bomb had dropped,' Burden said tiredly.

'I know. I feel like that too. Rather nice Georgian houses and the whole block's nearly demolished.' He got out of the car, Burden following him. In the mild afternoon light the last remaining wall stared at them. It was the inside that was displayed, green wallpaper above, the pink, stone-coloured on the ground. A dozen feet from the top an iron fireplace still clung to the plaster, and where the plaster had been stripped, to bare bricks. A great cable wrapped it and the cable was attached to a tractor, lurching through dust. Through the ochreish clouds they could see a painted board, *Doherty for Demolition,* and underneath the slogan, *What Goes Up Must Come Down!*

Burden's eye caught the number on the remaining doorpost, twenty-two. He looked disconsolately from the wall to the cable, the cable to the tractor. Then with a jerk of his head he beckoned to the tractor driver.

'Police,' Burden said sharply into a red pugnacious face.

'O.K., O.K. Only I've got my work to do, same as anyone else. What were you wanting?'

Burden looked past him to the number on the doorpost.

'There was an accountant here, chap called Smith. D'you know where he went to?'

'Where you'll never find him.' The smirk was unpleasant. 'Underground.'

'Come again?'

'He's dead,' said the tractor driver, rubbing his dusty hands.

# 14

'He can't be dead,' Burden said aghast.

'Can't he? I'm only telling you what the old girl in the teaplace told me.' Cocking his head towards where the little café had been, the workman fished in his pocket for a large filthy handkerchief and blew his nose. 'Before her place come down it was. Poor Mr. Smith, she says, he'd have hated to see the old house go. All he'd got left was his wife doing him dirt and him all on his own.'

'What did he die of? A broken heart?'

'Something to do with his heart. The old girl could tell you more than I can.'

'You don't know when he died?' Wexford put in.

'A year, eighteen months. The place stood empty ever since and a proper mess it was in.' Burden knew the truth of this. Where rubble now was he had often sat having his tea and, leaving, had passed boarded-up windows. 'There's the undertakers up on the corner. They'd know. Always go to the nearest, I reckon.

The man went back to his tractor and, puffing heavily as if determined to move the wall by his own unaided effort, edged the vehicle forward over mounds of brick-filled loam. Burden went over to the undertakers. The cable pulled taut. Wexford stood watching it and listening to the groans of crumbling mortar until the inspector came back.

'He's dead all right,' Burden said, picking his way through the debris. 'Died last February twelvemonth. They remember the funeral. No one there but that old

140

woman and a girl who used to do Smith's typing. Our surefire suspect is in a grave in Stowerton cemetery.'

'What did he die of?'

'Coronary,' said Burden. 'He was forty-two.' A low crunching tremor like the first cracking that precedes an earthquake made him look behind him. In the wall of Smith's house a fissure had appeared, running between green wallpaper and pink. From the centre of this rift brown plaster dust began to vomit down the patchy brick. 'As I see it, sir,' he said, 'the Geoff Smith business is coincidence. We have to forget him and begin again.'

'Coincidence! No, Mike. I won't have that. Its arm isn't that long. A man came to Ruby's house and said he was Geoff Smith and after he'd gone a lighter was found in that house that a man called Geoff Smith had bought eight years before. We *know* those things if we don't know anything else and you can't get away from them. It was in Stowerton and a man called Geoff Smith had lived in the next town, knew the place like you and I know it. That man is dead, was dead when the lighter went missing from Mrs. Anstey's flat, dead before Anita came to live here and stone cold dead as a doornail last Tuesday. But to deny he had any connection with the case on the grounds of coincidence is crazy. That way madness lies.'

'Then Mrs. Anstey's lying. She sold Anita the lighter—she admits she's sold a lot of stuff—and happened to tell her all about her first husband at the same time. That wouldn't be coincidence, that'd be normal behaviour for her. Anita told her boy friend the name and it stuck in his subconscious.'

'Why should she lie?' Wexford scoffed. 'What would be the point? I ask you, Mike, did she impress you as a liar?'

Burden shook his head doubtfully and began to follow the Chief Inspector back to Drayton and the waiting car. 'I don't believe her when she says she lost the lighter, at any rate,' he said.

'No, but she thinks she did,' Wexford said quickly.

'The truth is, somebody nicked it. Who? An old mate of
Smith's? You know what we're going to have to do,
don't you? Every friend of Smith's, every friend of Mrs.
Anstey's and all Anita's associates are going to have to
be hunted up just to see if there's the tiniest tie-up between them.'

A shout from behind made them quicken their pace.
'Stand clear!' The tractor gave a final heave, and with a
rumble that grew into a roar, the cable sliced through
the wall like a grocer's wire cutter through a piece of
cheese. Then everything vanished behind a huge yellow
cloud. Where the house had been there was now nothing but a pillar of mud-coloured vapour through which
could be seen a clean blue sky.

'The last of Geoffrey Smith,' said Wexford. 'Come
on. I want my tea.'

There was no future in it, Drayton thought. His am-
bitions had no place in them for such a girl as Linda
Grover. Not even a single rung of his ladder could be
spared to bear her weight. Now, looking back over the
days, he saw that he had been culpable in associating
himself at all with a girl whose father was eyed antago-
nistically by his superior officers, blameworthy for taking her out, appallingly foolhardy to have made himself
her lover. The word with its erotic, insinuating associa-
tions made him shiver and the shiver was not for his future and his career.

It seemed that she was bribable, corruptible. He
knew only that she, like her surroundings, was corrupt-
ing. And Wexford knew it too. Wexford had told him,
although not knowing just what his prohibition en-
tailed, to leave her alone. This was his chance, to obey,
to yield, and in this yielding to put up a resistance to
her spell sanctioned by authority.

He took his hooded coat and went down the police
station steps. The evening was too warm to put it on.
Cawthorne would have to go without his car hire fee
tonight. Drayton made his way to the library where he
got out a book on abnormal psychology.

It was seven when he came out and the library was closing. Grover's would be closed too and he would be safe if he went back to his lodgings by way of the High Street. The Stowerton to Forby bus came in as he approached the stop and he felt a strange urge to get on it and be carried far away into the anonymous depths of the countryside. Instead of the intellectual concentration abnormal psychology would demand, he wanted to lose himself and his identity; he wanted oblivion in the warm quiet air. But even as he thought this, he knew with a sudden conviction almost amounting to horror that he could not escape like this, that the wide green world was not big enough to contain him and her unless they were together. He grew cold and he began to hurry, like a man quickening his steps to stimulate circulation on a cold day.

Then he saw her. She was getting off the Stowerton bus and a young, good-looking man was helping her down with a wheel-basket full of bundled washing. Drayton saw her smile as she thanked him and it seemed to him that her smile was more coquettish and more seductive than any she had ever given him. Jealousy caught at him like a punch at the throat.

Avoidance was impossible. He had lost the will and the desire to avoid. Wexford's words—that apt crack about laundry duties—he recalled as he might remember a sermon so boring, so spurious that it sent you to sleep. But he was awake now, uncaringly reckless.

'Carry your bag, lady? Or should I say, push it?'

She smiled, a shadow of the look she had given the man on the bus. It was enough. The fetters were back. He seemed to feel their cold enclosing touch.

'My boss said I'd be a laundryman tonight,' he said, and he knew he was gabbling foolishly, wooing her anew as he did each time they met. 'He was right. Who's looking after the shop?'

'Your boss thinks a lot of you,' she said and he detected the proprietory note, the tone of satisfaction. "I could tell that in the café today.' Her face clouded.

'Dad's up,' she said. 'His back's awful, but he says he can't trust us to mind the business.'

Drayton felt a curious desire to see the father. He sighed within himself. It was not thus that he had envisaged so crucial and significant a meeting, not in these circumstances nor in this place. Ten years hence, he thought, and a nice educated girl; a tall scholarly father with a degree, pearls round the mother's neck; a half-timbered country house with gardens and perhaps a paddock. She unlocked the shop door and the old grey smell came out to meet him.

Grover was behind the counter, shovelling up sweets someone had spilt. His hands looked dirty and there was rust marks round the rim of the jar he held. Drayton had expected him to be older. The man looked no more than forty, if that. There was no grey in the lustre-less dark hair and signs of age showed only in his face muscles, screwed up in pain. When he saw his daughter he put down the jar and clapped his hand to the small of his back.

'Your mum's just off to her whist drive,' he said and Drayton thought his voice horrible. 'She wants them things ironed tonight.' He spoke to his daughter as if she were alone with him and he gave her a surly glance.

'You ought to be in bed,' Linda said.

'And let the business go to pot? Fine mess you've got these books in.' Though he was dark and she fair, the resemblance between father and daughter was so strong that Drayton had to turn away deliberately to stop himself from staring. If the man smiled he thought he would cry aloud in anguish. But there was little chance of Grover's smiling. 'This is the end of me taking things easy,' he said. 'I can see that. Back to the grindstone tomorrow.' He came out from behind the counter as if he were going to pounce on her and, indeed, his crooked movements to some extent suggested those of a crippled and cornered animal. 'Then I'll get the car out,' he muttered. 'Don't suppose you've cleaned it since I was laid up.'

'The doctor'll have something to say about that,' she

said and Drayton heard weariness in her voice. 'Why don't you go back to bed? I'm here. I'll manage.'

She took his arm as if he were in fact the ancient broken creature Drayton had imagined. Alone in the shop he felt desolate. This was no place for him and as always when here he felt a compulsion to wash his hands. Perhaps she would forget he was there, engulfed as she always was by her domestic duties, and he would be left among the suspect magazines—the hidden knives?—until night came to deepen this darkness. For he knew that he was a prisoner and that he could not leave without her.

It seemed an age before she returned and when she came he felt his face must betray God knew what enslavement, and end-of-his-tether abandonment to longing.

'I had to hang up the washing,' she said. 'Not that it'll dry tonight. I should have taken it in the afternoon like I did last week.' As she came close to him, he put up his hands to her face, touching it as a blind man might. 'No car tonight?' she asked him. He shook his head. 'We'll take Dad's,' she said.

'No,' he said. 'We'll go for a walk.'

He knew that she could drive; she had told Wexford. What puny power remained to him would be utterly lost if he allowed her to drive him about the countryside in her father's car.

'Tomorrow, then,' she said and she looked long into his eyes. 'Promise you will tomorrow, Mark, before Dad gets mobile and—and commandeers it.'

He thought that at that moment he would have promised her his own life if she had asked for it. 'Look after me,' she said, a sudden agony in her voice. Upstairs he could hear the crippled man moving. 'Oh, Mark, Mark . . .'

The river beckoned them with its quiet sheltered path.

Drayton took her in his arms on the spot where he had seen that other man kiss her, but he had forgotten this and everything else which had passed before they met. Even the desire for immediate physical gratification was less strong. He had reached a stage when his paramount wish was to be alone with her in silence, holding her to him, and in silence enclosing her mouth with his.

'I think I was justified in calling you out,' Burden said. He stood up to let Wexford take his seat beside him on the window settle. As usual at this time, the saloon bar of the Olive and Dove was crowded.

'Wouldn't keep till the morning, I suppose,' Wexford grumbled. 'Don't sit down. You can get me a beer before you start expounding.'

Burden came back with two beers in tankards. 'Bit crowded and noisy in here, sir, I'm afraid.'

'Not half so crowded and noisy as my place. My daughter Shelia's having a jam session.'

'No,' said Burden with a smile, 'they don't call it that any more.'

Wexford said belligerently from behind his beer, 'What do they call it, then?'

'Search me.'

They moved into a quieter corner. Wexford lifted the hem of a curtain and looked out at the street. It was dark and there were few people about. Half a dozen youths loitered at the entrance to the cinema car park pushing each other about and laughing.

'Look at all those bloody green cars,' the Chief Inspector said disgustedly. 'For all we know, he's out there, driving around or in the pictures.'

'I think I know who he is,' Burden said quietly.

'Well, I didn't suppose you'd dragged me down here for the sake of the booze. Let's have it.'

Burden looked speculatively at the heavy wrinkled face. Its expression was not encouraging. For a moment he hesitated, fidgeting with his tankard. His idea had come to him, or rather had crystallized, after three hours of arguing it out with himself. When he had formulated it and catalogued the details he had become so excited that he had had to tell someone. The obvious someone now sat opposite him, already derisive and certainly prepared to scoff. The Chief Constable had evidently made up his mind that the whole investigation was so much hot air. Just as the cold light of morning is said to dispel fancies of the night before, so the atmosphere of the Olive and Dove, the sudden burst of raucous laughter and Wexford's doubting look robbed his ingenious solution of everything cogent and left only the ingenuity. Perhaps it would be better if he drank up his drink and went without another word. Wexford was tapping his foot impatiently. Clearing his throat, Burden said lamely:

'I think it's Mrs. Anstey's husband.'

'*Smith?* My God, Mike, we've been through that. He's dead.'

'Smith is, but Anstey isn't. At any rate, we've no reason to suppose so.' Burden lowered his voice as someone passed their table. 'I think it could be Anstey. Shall I tell you why?'

Wexford's spiky eyebrows went up. 'It had better be good,' he said. 'We don't know anything about the fellow. She hardly mentioned him.'

'And didn't you think that was funny?'

'Perhaps it was,' Wexford said thoughtfully. 'Perhaps it was.' He seemed to be about to go on. Burden did not wish to have the wind taken out of his own sails and he said hastily:

'Who does she give the impression of being more fond of, the man who divorced her five years ago or the man she's married to now? She regrets that divorce, sir, and she doesn't mind making it clear to three strangers who didn't even want to know. "It's nice to have been loved and remember it when it's gone," she said. Are those the words of a happily married woman? Then what was all that about being alone a lot? She's a teacher. A married woman with a job isn't alone a lot. She'd hardly be alone at all.'

'You think she and Anstey are separated?'

'I do,' said Burden with decision. Wexford showed no inclination to laugh and he began to gather confidence.

'We don't believe she lost the lighter, but she believes it. If she didn't lose it but just left it lying about or in her handbag, who's the most likely person to have it in his possession? The errant husband. Very probably Smith divorced her on Anstey's account. That means adultery, and a man who'll commit it once will commit it again.'

'Thus speaks the stern moralist,' said Wexford, smiling. 'I don't know that I'd go along with that. Your point is, of course, that Anstey took up with Anita and gave her the lighter. Mike, it's all right as far as it goes, but you haven't got any real reason for thinking Anstey's left her. Don't forget the Easter holidays are on and a married woman teacher would be alone a lot in the holidays.'

'Then why does she say she's only got her salary to live on?' Burden asked triumphantly. 'It's quite true what she says about selling jewellery. I saw her in Knobby Clark's shop.'

'I'll buy you a drink,' said Wexford, and now he looked pleased.

'Scotch,' said Burden when he came back. 'Very nice. Cheers.'

'To detection.' Wexford raised his glass. 'Where's Anstey now?'

Burden shrugged. 'Around here somewhere. Just getting on with whatever job he does.'

'Since you're so clever, you'll no doubt be able to tell me why a man called Anstey gives the name of his wife's former husband when he goes out on the tiles with another girl? Not just Smith, mind, *Geoff Smith*.'

'I can't tell you that,' Burden said, less happily.

'Or why he killed the girl. What was his motive?'

'When we suspected Kirkpatrick, we assumed the motive was jealousy. We lost sight of the five hundred pounds Anita was carrying in her handbag.'

'In that case, Mike, why didn't he wait until they were back in the car, drive to some lonely place and kill her there? You don't murder a woman in someone else's house by a method which leaves incriminating traces behind, when you could do it, for example, in Cheriton Forest. Which brings me to another point. Ruby and Monkey both thought he'd go back. It was because they wanted him caught before he could go back that Monkey wrote to me. Why didn't he?'

'Scared, I suppose. We don't know where he is. For all we know he may have gone home at least for a time.'

Burden shook his head regretfully. 'I don't know,' he said, and he added, repeating himself. 'I can't tell you that.'

'Perhaps Mrs. Anstey can. Drink up. They're closing.'

Out in the street Wexford sniffed the soft April air. The sky which had been clear was now becoming overcast and clouds crossed the moon. They came to the bridge. A swan sailed out from the tunnel, into lamplight and then into their twin shadows. Wexford surveyed the almost empty High Street, the pearly white and yellow lamps and the dark holes made by the unlit alleys.

In the high wall that reared ahead of them an open window twenty feet up disclosed a girl leaning out, her arm dangling as over the rail of a stage balcony. On a bracket below was a lamp in an iron cage, and half in its light, half in velvet shadow, stood a man gazing upwards.

'Ah, moon of my delight,' Wexford quoted softly, 'who know'st no wane . . .'

With a sourness he did not bother to hide, Burden said, 'Drayton was told to leave her alone,' and he scowled at the yellow, cloud-scarred moon.

Indeed the Idols I have loved so long
Have done my Credit in Men's Eye much
    wrong:
Have drowned my Honour in a shallow cup,
And sold my reputation for a Song.

# 15

In the morning the rain came back. From the look of
the sky it seemed to be one of those mornings when it
rains from streaming dawn to dripping, fog-filled dusk.
Wexford, dialling Sewingbury, held the receiver gripped
under his chin and reached out to lower the venetian
blind. He was listening to the ringing tone when Drayton came in.

'That Mrs. Anstey to see you, sir. I passed her as I
came in.'

Wexford put the phone down. 'For once the mountain has come to Mahomet.'

'Shall I bring her up?'

'Just a minute, Drayton.' It was a command, rather
sharp and with a hint of admonition. The young man
stopped and turned obediently. 'Enjoy yourself last
night?'

If possible, Drayton's face became more than ever a
cipher, secret, cautious, but not innocent. "Yes, thank
you, sir.' The rain drummed against the window. It had
grown quite dark in the office as if night was coming at
nine thirty in the morning.

'I don't suppose you've got to know many young
people around here yet?' The question demanded an
avuncular heartiness but Wexford made it sound men-
acing.

'Not many, sir.'

'Pity. God knows, my young daughter seems to know
enough. Always having a'—No, not a jam session. Burden had corrected him on that. '—A get-together at

our place. Quite a decent bunch if you don't mind noise. I daresay you don't.'

Drayton stood, silence incarnate.

'You must join in one of these nights.' He gave the young man a grey cold stare. 'Just you on your own,' he said.

'Yes, sir. I'd like that.'

'Good, I'll get Shelia to give you a tinkle.' Severity had gone and urbanity replaced it. 'Now for Mrs. Anstey,' said the Chief Inspector.

The rain gave him a sensation of almost claustrophobic confinement as if he were enclosed by walls of water. He could hear it streaming from the sills and pouring over the naked stone bodies on the frescoes. Pity it never seemed to wash them properly but just left grey trails on shoulders and haunches. He switched on the lights as Burden came in with Mrs. Anstey in his wake, each as wet as creatures from the depths of the sea. Mrs. Anstey's umbrella hung from her arm and dripped water in a trickle at her heels.

'I had to come,' she said. 'I had an impulse. After you'd gone I got to thinking what on earth you could have meant about some girl you mentioned.' Her laughter sounded itself like water, fresh bubbling, yet a little hesitant. 'I got the first bus.' She shed her grey mackintosh and stripped a hideous plastic hood from her brown hair. There were raindrops on her nose and she wrinkled it as might a little dog. 'Geoff and a girl. I didn't like that. Dog in a manger, aren't I? The fact is, I just have to see him. I've waited long enough. I'm going there now, but I thought I ought to see you first.' Without explanation, she laughed again and this time her laugh held a nervous break. 'Has he got a girl?' she asked and that explained.

The first bringer of unwelcome news, thought Wexford, has but a losing office. How did it go on? Something about his voice sounding ever after as a sullen warning bell. That didn't matter. Only the present pain mattered. For the first time since he and Burden had discussed Smith's death, his particular duty was brought home to him. He was going to have to tell her. That she was only an ex-wife would, he was sure, make no difference.

'Has he?' she said again and now she was pleading.

'I wasn't able to see him, Mrs. Anstey.'

No lying, no prevaricating. None of that would be possible with this woman. Burden had turned his back.

'What is it? There's something bad . . . .' She got up, the plastic thing from her head stretched taut in her fingers. 'He's ill, he's . . .'

'He's dead.' No matter how prepared you were, it was still a shock. You could never be sufficiently prepared. Until the words were said, hope was invincible. 'I'm sorry,' he said quickly. 'I'm very very sorry. It was a coronary, bit over a year ago. I'm sure it was quick.'

'He can't be dead!' The words were an echo of Burden's. He could not have been dead for Burden because that made nonsense of a theory; he could not be dead for her because she had a theory too, a theory of reshaping her life?

'I'm afraid he is.'

'Not dead!' Wexford heard the thin threat of hysteria, the burning electric shock wire.

'Please sit down. I'll get you something to drink.'

With a kind of horror, he watched her feel blindly behind her for the chair she had sat in, find it, kick it away and lurch at the wall. Her fists clenched, she struck her head against the plaster, then the fists themselves came up, pounding and beating on the hard surface.

Wexford took a step towards her. 'Better get one of the W.P.C.s,' he said to Burden. Then she began to scream with a throaty frenzy.

The policewoman took the tea cup from her and replaced the sodden handkerchief with a clean one of her own.

'Bit better now?'

Noreen Anstey nodded. Her face was pink and swollen and her hair, though wet from rain, gave the illusion of being, like her cheeks, soaked with tears. She was all tears, all grief.

Suddenly she said quite coherently, 'I can never ask him to forgive me now.' For a moment she had breath enough only for this. Sobs succeeded it. They were like blood pumping from a vein. 'I won't cry any more.' The sobs were involuntary. Eventually they would subside. 'I'll go to my grave,' she said, 'knowing he never knew I was sorry.' Wexford nodded to the policewoman and she went out with the tea cup and the wet handkerchief.

'He forgave you,' he said. 'Didn't he give you the flat?'

She hardly seemed to hear him. 'He died and I didn't even know.' Wexford thought of the two women at Smith's funeral, the old neighbor and the girl who did his typing. 'You don't even know what I did to him, do you? We'd been married eight years, the perfect couple, the happy couple. That's what everyone said and it was true.' The sobs made a rattle in her throat. 'He used to buy me presents. Unbirthday presents, he called them. You couldn't have that many birthdays. You'd get old too fast.' She covered her eyes, shaking her head from side to side. 'We lived in a house with his office in it. There was a garage next door. I could see it from my window. I'd given up work, teaching was my work. No need when I had Geoff to look after me.' The sentences jerked out, short, ragged, staccato. Wexford moved his chair close and sat looking down into his lap. 'Ray Anstey worked at the garage. I used to watch him. You know the way they lie on their backs with their heads thrown back? My God!' She shivered. 'You don't want to hear all this. I'd better go.' Her things were still wet, the raincoat, the umbrella that had dripped and made a puddle on the floor like a blister. She dabbed feebly at the sides of the chair, feeling for her handbag.

'We'll take you home, Mrs. Anstey,' Wexford said gently. 'But not quite yet. Would you like to have a rest? Two questions only and then you can rest.'

'He's dead. Beyond your reach. Why did you want him?'

'I think,' Wexford said slowly, 'that it's your second husband we want.'

'Ray?'

'Where is he, Mrs. Anstey?'

'I don't know,' she said tiredly. 'I haven't seen him for months. He left me at the end of last year.'

'You said he worked in a garage. Is he a mechanic?'

'I suppose he is. What else could he do?' Her gloves were on the floor at her feet. She picked them up and looked at them as at two wet dead things, dredged up from the bottom of a pond. 'You wanted him all along?' Her face went a sickly white and she struggled up out of the chair. 'It was my *husband* you wanted, not Geoff?' Wexford nodded. 'What's he done?' she asked hoarsely.

'A girl is missing, probably dead . . .'

'The knife,' she said. Her eyes went out of focus. Wexford took a step towards her and caught her in his arms.

'Where did your sister get her car serviced?' Burden said. Margolis looked up from his late breakfast of coffee, orange juice and unappetizing hard-boiled eggs, his expression helplessly apathetic.

'Some garage,' he said, and then, 'It would be Cawthorne's, wouldn't it?'

'Come, Mr. Margolis, you must know. Don't you have your own car seen to?'

'Ann looked after that side of things. When it wanted doing, she'd see to it.' The painter turned the eggshells upside down in their cups like a child playing April Fool tricks. 'There was something, though . . .' His long fingers splayed through his hair so that it stood up in a spiky halo. 'Some trouble. I have a remote recollection of her saying she was going to someone else.' He put the tray on the sofa arm and got up to shake crumbs from his lap. 'I wish I could remember.' he said.

'She took it to that Ray, Mr. M.,' said Mrs. Penistan

sharply. 'You know she did. Why don't you pull yourself together?' She shrugged at Burden, turning her little eyes heavenwards. 'He's gone to pieces since his sister went. Can't do nothing with him.' She settled herself beside Margolis and gave him a long exasperated stare. Burden was reminded of a mother or a nanny taking a recalcitrant child to a tea party, especially when she bent over him and, with a sharp clucking of her tongue, pulled his dressing gown over to hide his pyjama legs.

'Ray who?'

'Don't ask me, dear. You know what she was like with her christian names. All I know is she come in here a couple of months back and says, "I've had about as much as I can stand of Russell's prices. I've a good mind to get Ray to do the cars for me." "Who's Ray?" I says, but she just laughed. "Never you mind, Mrs. P. Let's say he's a nice boy who thinks the world of me. If I tell you who he is he might lose his job." '

'Did he come here to service the cars?'

'Oh, no, dear. Well, he wouldn't have the facilities, would he?' Mrs. Penistan surveyed the studio and the window as if to imply that nothing of practical use to a sane human being could be found in cottage or garden. 'She always took them to him. He lived local, you see. Somewhere local. I'd see her go off but I'd always gone when she got back. *He'd* have been here.' She shoved her elbow into Margolis's thin ribs. 'But he don't listen to what folks tell him.'

Burden left them together, sitting side by side, Mrs. Penistan coaxing Margolis to finish his coffee. The heavy rain had made the path slippery and there were wet petals everywhere underfoot. The garage doors were open and for the first time Burden saw Margolis's own car and saw that it was green.

He was beginning to discern a pattern, a way that it could all have been done. Now he thought he could understand why a black car and a green car had been used and where Anita's white car had been until the small hours. A new excitement made him walk jauntily to the cottage gate. He opened it and the hawthorn bush showered him with water as effectively as if someone had put a tilted bucket in its branches.

This is how it must feel to be a psychiatrist, Wexford thought. Noreen Anstey lay on the couch in the rest room, staring at the ceiling, and he sat beside her, letting her talk.

'He always had a knife,' she said. 'I saw it that first day, the first time he came up from the garage. Geoff was working downstairs. I used to take coffee down to him and then I started taking it to Ray as well. One day he came up instead.' For a while she was silent, moving her head from side to side. 'God, he was beautiful. Not handsome, beautiful, perfect. Like people ought to be, like I never was. Not very tall, black-haired, red mouth like a flower . . .' He didn't want to interrupt, but he had to. He wasn't a real psychiatrist.

'How old is he?'

'Ten years younger than me,' she said and he knew it hurt her to say it. 'He came up that day. We were quite alone and he had this knife, a little flick knife. He took it out of his pocket and put it on the table. I'd never seen one before and I didn't know what it was. We didn't talk much. What was there for us to talk about? We didn't have anything in common. He sat there smiling, making little sort of sly innuendoes.' She almost laughed but it was a gasp Wexford heard. 'I was sick with wanting him.' Her face turned to the wall, she went on, 'I'd had that lighter a few months and I remember lighting a cigarette for Ray. He said, "No, light it in your mouth". He looked at the lighter and he said, "He give you this? Does he give you toys because he can't give you anything else?" That wasn't true, but it must have been the way it looked, the way I looked. I've got a toy too, he said, and he picked up the knife and held it against my throat. The blade came out. I kept still or it would have cut me. My God, I was a teacher of French in a girls' school. I'd never been anywhere or done anything. You'd have thought I'd have screamed. D'you know, I'd have let him kill me, then? Afterwards, after he'd gone, there was blood on my neck from a little scratch and I knew he'd been looking at it all the time he was making love to me.'

'Smith divorced you?' Wexford said to fill up the great silence.

'He found out. That wasn't difficult. I've never been much good at hiding my feelings. Geoff would have forgiven me and started afresh. He couldn't believe I'd want to marry a man ten years younger than myself, a garage hand . . . I was mad to have him. I knew he was a sadist and a moron. He'd cut me, really cut me since then.' She pulled open her dress. On the left breast, where the flesh swelled under the collar-bone, was a small white cicatrice. For all his years of experience, Wexford felt sickness catch at the back of his throat like a fingernail plucking.

'You were always unhappy?'

'I was never *happy* with him.' She said it almost reproachfully. 'I don't think there was a moment when I could say I was *happy*. He loathed Geoff. D'you know what he used to do? He'd give Geoff's name, pretend he was Geoff.' Wexford nodded, guessing this was to come. 'When the phone rang he'd pick it up and say—well, sort of absent-mindedly, "Geoff Smith speaking". Then he'd correct himself and say he'd made a mistake. Once he took some clothes to the cleaners, filthy overalls, and when I went to collect them they couldn't find the ticket. It was made out to Smith, you see. Anything a bit nasty or disreputable he was involved in and he'd always give Geoff's name. A girl came round once—she couldn't have been more than seventeen—and asked if this was where Geoff Smith lived. He'd dropped her and she wanted him back, even though he'd used the knife on her too. She showed me a scar on her neck. I told him he'd go too far one day. He'd kill one of them or she'd go to the police.'

'He's gone too far,' Wexford said.

'He had to see their blood, you see.' She spoke very calmly, without horror. Not for the first time Wexford pondered on the dulling effect of custom, how habit dulled the edge of shock. All pity choked with custom of fell deeds . . . 'I used to think,' she said, 'that one day there'd be a girl who wasn't mesmerized by him but just plain frightened and that maybe she'd turn the knife on him. He wasn't big and strong, you see, not powerful physically. His power was the other sort. I used to take the knives away but he always got new ones. Then he left me.'

'This must have been about the time you lost your lighter.'

Noreen Anstey raised herself on one elbow, then turned and swung her legs on to the floor. 'I've been thinking about that,' she said. 'Ray must have taken it. He took things from Geoff and me when we were still married. I couldn't prove it, but I thought he had, jewellery, things like that.' She sighed, covered her face and then brought her hands down again. 'I suppose Geoff guessed too. There were so many things,' she said, 'we both knew and never put into words. Oh, I'm sorry!' she cried, clenching her fists and pressing them into her lap. 'I'm so bitterly sorry. I want to find where he's buried and lie on his grave and cry into the earth that I'm sorry!'

So many women who were sorry, Wexford thought, Noreen Anstey because she had thrown away love for love's ugly shadow, Ruby Branch because she had betrayed an old crook, and Anita Margolis? The dead have no regrets. She could not be sorry that she had played her dangerous game once too often, played it with a man and a knife.

# 16

'Have you got a friend who could stay with you?' Wexford asked. 'Mother, sister, a neighbour?''

Noreen Anstey seemed to have shrunk. Deprived of her vitality, she was just a little plain woman wilting into middle-age. 'My mother's dead,' she said. 'Ray lost me most of my friends.'

'A policewoman will go back with you. She'll try and find someone to keep you company.'

'And when you find him?' she asked with wistful bitterness.

'We'll keep in touch, Mrs. Anstey. Why do you suppose he ever came to Kingsmarkham?'

She shrugged her shoulders, pulling the creased raincoat tightly around her. Every movement now was a kind of shiver, a hunching and shrinking of her body in a gradual process of contraction. 'If I say to haunt him,' she said, 'you'll think I'm mad. But that would be like Ray. He'd go to—to Geoff and say he'd wrecked two lives, but he'd left me now and all the agony was for nothing. He's a sadist. Then he'd have started it all over again, that business of giving Geoff's name, telling girls he was Geoff and giving them his address.'

'Mrs. Anstey, you thought we were friends of your husband, didn't you? When we called and asked if you were Mrs. Smith. You thought Anstey had put us on to you.'

She nodded limply.

'He must have known Mr. Smith was dead. Would he give his name, knowing he was dead?'

'He might have done. Not to a girl. There wouldn't

159

be any point in that. But if he was going to do something disreputable or underhand, he might then. It would be a joke to him, dishonouring Geoff's memory. And it would be habit too.'

'I wonder why he stayed.'

'I suppose he liked it here or got a good job that suited him. His idea of heaven would be an easy-going employer who'd pay him well and turn a blind eye if Ray took his customers away from him and serviced their cars on the cheap. That was always one of the ways he got to know his girls.'

Wexford did not want to hurt her more than he need, but he did not think she could sustain any further injury from a recital of Anstey's misdemeanours.

'By going round to their homes while their husbands were at work, I imagine?' he said. 'Sitting in their cars with them, the personal touch?'

'He wasn't doing too well in Sewingbury,' she said. 'People got to know too much about him. Some of these garage proprietors give their mechanics a car or let them borrow one. Ray's boss got hard about that when he smashed up a hire car. No, you can be sure he found a job and a good one.' She turned away from him and covered her eyes. 'If Geoff had been alive,' she whispered. 'Oh, if only he'd been alive! Ray wouldn't have been able to hurt him or me any more. When Geoff had seen him, seen him once and heard he'd left me, he'd have come back to me. I often used to think, he'll find out, he'll know sooner or later. We used to be able to read each other's minds. Married people can. He's lonely too, I thought. He's been lonely longer than I have.' She began to cry softly, the calm gentle tears of a grief beyond consolation. 'It's a fallacy that, about reading thoughts. He was dead.' She spoke evenly, as if she were just talking and not crying as well. 'And I sat and waited for him, quite happy really and peaceful. I didn't long for him or feel passionate or anything. I had peace and I thought, one day, this week, next week, sometime— well, it was never, wasn't it?' Her fingers dabbed at the tears. 'May I have my lighter?' she said.

He let her hold it but shook his head at the request. 'In a little while.'

'The name of the design,' she said, 'came from a poem of Baudelaire. Geoff knew I loved that verse. "... *et tes seins*",' she quoted. ' "*Les grappes de ma vigne.*" ' Wexford's French wasn't up to much but he could just understand. She had shown him the scar Anstey, the thief and the sadist, had made with his knife. He turned away his eyes.

It looked as if Russell Cawthorne had a young girl in the office with him. Her back was to the door and she wore a red mac, the glistening hot red of a fire engine with the paint still wet. Burden drove through the rain and up under the trading stamps banner. He and Wexford dived for the office. The girl opened the door for them and illusion snapped, for it was Mrs. Cawthorne's face that appeared between the scarlet collar and the frothy yellow hair.

'Better go into the house,' said Cawthorne. He heaved himself up, grunting. 'Come on, troops, run for it!'

In the living-room the Pre-Raphaelite lady contemplated her lily with pitying scorn. She had seen plenty in that room, she seemed to be saying, most of it unedifying. Mrs. Cawthorne took off the red coat and stood revealed in lemon wool. Her Christmas tree ear-rings hung to her shoulders. Red and shining, they reminded Wexford of toffee apples.

'Ray Anstey was with me for six months,' Cawthorne said. 'He was a good lad, knew his job.' They sat down among the piecrust tables, the wax fruit, the candelabra. My God, thought Wexford, is it all coming back? Is this the way Sheila will do up her house when the time comes? 'When he came he said he wanted something temporary. He'd only come here to hunt up a friend, but then he said the friend had died and he'd like to stay on.' Geoff Smith, Wexford reflected, Smith, the injured, the bait, the perpetually fascinating.

'Much of a one for the women?' he asked.

'I wouldn't say that.' Cawthorne gave Burden a side-long glance. Perhaps he was remembering inquiries into his own proclivities in that direction. He shook himself and added in the tone of a colonel discussing with an officer of equal or even superior rank the naughtiness of a subaltern. 'Good-looking young devil, though.'

Mrs. Cawthorne wriggled. Wexford looked at her. He had seen a similar expression in his seventeen-year-old Shelia's eyes when she was discussing with triumph a boy's unsuccessful advance. Here was the same half-smile, the same mock-anger. But surely he wasn't expected to believe . . .? He was.

'You couldn't say that?' she inquired archly of her husband. 'Then all I can say is, you don't listen to a word I say.' Cawthorne's sick glare made this seem more probable. 'Why, the way he looked at me sometimes!' She turned to Wexford. 'I'm used to it, of course. I could see what young Ray was after. Not that he actually said anything. It was more than his job was worth to go chasing the boss's wife.'

Her husband turned his eyes towards the ceiling where he fixed them on a plaster cherub. 'Oh God,' he said softly.

'When did he leave?' Wexford put in quickly.

His wife's insinuation had temporarily thrown Cawthorne off balance. He went to the sideboard and poured himself a whisky before replying. 'Let's see now,' he said when half the drink had gone down. 'It'd be last Saturday week.' The day he booked Ruby's room, Wexford thought. 'I remember thinking what a bloody nerve he'd got.'

'In what way? Because he left you?'

'Not only that. It was the way he did it. Now I'm in the habit of letting any of my staff borrow a car when they're in need and provided they give me fair warning. It's hard on a young kid, wants to take his girl out.' He smiled philanthropically, the friend of youth, and drained his glass. 'Anstey was one of the kind that take advantage. Night after night he'd have one of the cars and it was all the same to him whether I knew or whether I didn't. Well, on that Saturday morning we were a bit short-handed and I noticed Anstey wasn't about. Next thing he came sweeping in in one of the Minors, all smiles and not a word of excuse. Said he'd been to see a friend on business.'

'A Minor?'

'Black Minor Thousand, one of the three I keep for hiring out. You've seen them out the front.' Cawthorne raised a thick eyebrow like a strip of polar bear fur. 'Drink?' Wexford shook his head for both of them. 'Don't mind if I do, do you?' His glass refilled, he went on, ' "Business?" I said. "Your business is my business, my lad," I said, "and just you remember it." "Oh," he said in a very nasty way, "I wonder how much business you'd have left if I didn't have scruples." Well, that was a bit much. I told him he could have his cards and get out.'

The ear-rings swung as Mrs. Cawthorne gave a small theatrical sigh. 'Poor lamb,' she said. Wexford did not for a moment suppose she referred to her husband. 'I wish I'd been kinder to him.' There was no doubt what she meant by that. It was grotesque. God help him, he thought. Surely he wasn't going to have another regretful woman on his hands? What value they all put on themselves, all sorry, all wanting to reverse hands of the clock.

'Scruples,' he said. 'What did he mean by that?'

Again Cawthorne favoured them with that curious narrowing of the eyes.

'Been taking away your business, had he?' Burden put in quickly, remembering Mrs. Penistan.

'He was a good mechanic,' Cawthorne said. 'Too good.' This last perhaps reminded him of the whisky, for he poured himself some more, first half-filling the glass, then, with a quick reckless tilt to the bottle, topping it to the brim. He sighed, possibly with pleasure, possibly with resignation at another temptation unresisted. 'What I mean to say is, he was too much of a one for the personal touch.' Mrs. Cawthorne's laugh cut off the last word with the shrill screeching whine of a circu-

lar saw. 'Ingratiated himself with the customers,' he
said, ignoring her. 'Madam this and madam that, and
then he'd open the doors for them and compliment
them on their driving. Damn it all, it's not necessary for
a thousand mile service.'

'Harmless, I should have thought.'

'Call it harmless, do you, when a little squirt like that
takes away your business? The next thing I knew—
heard by a round-about route . . .' He scowled, the general in Intelligence. 'I have my spies,' he said absurdly.
'I could see it all. "Why not let me do it privately for
you, madam, I'd only charge ten bob." ' He took a long
pull at his drink. 'And there's not a damn thing I could
do about it, what with my overheads. I'm out of pocket
if I charge less than twelve and six. A good half-dozen
of my customers he got away from me like that, and
good customers too. I taxed him with it but he swore
they'd taken to going to Missal's. But there was Mrs.
Curran, to give you an example, and Mr. and Miss
Margolis . . .'

'Ah!' said Wexford softly.

Cawthorne went pink and avoided his wife's eye.

'You might think she was flighty,' he said, 'but you
didn't know her. It wasn't easy come, easy go with her.
Oh, it came easily enough, but young Anita watched the
spending of every penny. For all we'd been close friends
for a year, she didn't think twice about going to Anstey
on the sly. Still came to me for her petrol, mind.' He
belched and changed it to a cough. 'As if there was anything to be made on juice!'

'Were they friendly?'

'Anita and young Ray? Show me the man under fifty
she wasn't friendly with. He'd have to have a hump or a
hare lip.' But Cawthorne was over fifty, well over, and
his age was his own deformity.

'He left you on the Saturday,' Burden said slowly.
'Where would he go?' It was a rhetorical question. He
did not expect Cawthorne to answer it. 'D'you know
where he was living?'

'Kingsmarkham somewhere. One of my boys might

know.' His sodden face fell and he seemed to have forgotten his former attack on Anita Margolis's character. 'You think he killed her, don't you? Killed little Ann ...'

'Let's find that address, Mr. Cawthorne.'

The ear-rings bounced. 'Is he on the run?' Mrs. Cawthorne asked excitedly. Her eyes glittered. 'Poor hunted creature!'

'Oh, shut up,' said Cawthorne and went out into the rain.

# 17

They stood in the porch while Cawthorne questioned the men. The rain was passing now and the clouds splitting. Over Kingsmarkham they could see that patches of sky were showing between the great banks of cumulus, a fresh bright sky that was almost green.

'One hundred and eighty-six, High Street, Kingsmarkham,' Cawthorne said, trotting up to them and making a final spurt for cover. 'That's his headquarters, or was.'

'One eight six,' said Burden quickly. 'Let's see now. The news block's one five eight to one seven four, then the chemist and the florist . . .' He ticked the numbers off on his fingers. 'But that must be . . .'

'Well, it's Grover's the newsagents.' Cawthorne looked as if it was only what he had expected. 'They let one of their attic rooms, you know. A couple of chaps have lodged there before and when Anstey lost his first billet down the road here, someone suggested Grover's might fill the bill. Mind you, he was only there a month.'

'On our own doorstep!' Wexford said with an angry snort when they were in the car. 'You can see that place from our windows. A fat lot of use our observatory's been to us.'

'It's common knowledge they take lodgers, sir,' Burden said apologetically, but he did not know for whom he was making excuses and he added in his own defence, 'I daresay we've all seen a young dark fellow going in and out. We'd no cause to connect him with this case. How many thousands of little dark chaps are there in Kingsmarkham alone?'

Wexford said grimly, 'He didn't have to go far to see Ruby's ad., did he? He was in the right place to replace his knife, too. What happens now to your theory about the cars? Anstey didn't even own one, let alone swop black for green.'

'Anita got five hundred pounds the day before they went to Ruby's. Mrs. Penistan says she was generous. Maybe she bought him a car.'

They pulled up on the police station forecourt. Burden turned his head to see a man come out of Grover's with an evening paper. As they went up the steps under the broad white canopy, water dripped from it on to their coat collars.

'Maybe she bought him a car,' Burden said again. 'You could buy a very decent second-hand car for five hundred.'

'We're told she was generous,' Wexford said on the stairs. 'We're also told she was hard-headed and careful with her money. She wasn't an old woman with a kept man. Young girls don't buy cars for their boy friends.'

It was warm and silent in Wexford's office. The chairs were back against the walls and the papers on the rosewood desk neatly arranged. Nothing remained to show that earlier it had been the scene of a tragic drama. Burden took off his raincoat and spread it in front of the warm air grille.

'Kirkpatrick saw her at twenty past seven,' he said. 'She was at Ruby's at eight. That gave her forty minutes to change her coat, get down to Grover's, leave her Alpine there for him to mend at some future time and drive to Stowerton. It could easily be done.'

'When Kirkpatrick saw her she was wearing that ocelot thing. You'd naturally expect her to change into a raincoat in the cottage, but the ocelot was *on the passenger seat of her car*. It's a small point, but it may be important. Then we come to this question of time. Your theory only works if Anita and Anstey already had a green car available. Maybe they did. We shall see. But if, at that juncture in the proceedings, they had to borrow or hire a car, it couldn't be done.'

'It could be done if they used Margolis's car,' said Burden.

Drayton and Martin interrupted them and moved in on the conference. The four of them sat round the desk while Wexford put the newcomers in the picture. He watched Drayton's face grow hard and his eyes stony when Grover's shop was mentioned.

'Right,' he said, looking at his watch. 'We'll give them a chance to close up and then we'll all go over. Grover's more or less bedridden at the moment, isn't he?' He gave Drayton a sharp look.

'Up and about again now, sir.'

'Good,' Wexford nodded. 'Now,' he said to Burden. 'What's all this about Margolis's car? Margolis was in London.'

'He'd left his car at Kingsmarkham station and it *is* a green car. Wouldn't Anita be just the kind of girl to go a couple of hundred yards down York Street to the station approach and borrow her brother's car? They could have got it back by the time he wanted it.'

'Don't forget they thought he'd want it at nine, not eleven. No one knew he'd be dining with this gallery manager.'

'So what?' Burden shrugged. 'If ever there was an easy-going slapdash pair it's Margolis and his sister. If his car wasn't there he'd probably think he hadn't left it there or that it had been stolen. And he'd never do anything about that until he saw her. Anstey dumped her body, returned Margolis's car to the station car park and when everyone was in bed and asleep, filled up the Alpine radiator, taking a can of water with him to be on the safe side, and drove it back to Quince Cottage.'

He expected to see on Wexford's face a look of pleasure and approval comparable to that he had shown the previous night at the Olive and Dove. Everything was beginning to fit beautifully, and he, Burden, had dovetailed it. Why then had Wexford's mouth settled into those dubious grudging creases? He waited for comment, for some sort of agreement that all this was at least possible, but the Chief Inspector said softly:

'I have other ideas, I'm afraid.'

The shop was closed. In the alley water lay in puddles that mirrored the greenish lamplight. Two bins had been moved out in front of the garage doors for the dust collection in the morning. A cat sniffed them, leaving wet paw marks on someone's discarded newspaper.

Drayton had not wanted to come with them. He knew who Ray Anstey was now, the man he had seen her kissing by the bridge, the man who lodged with them and who had borrowed his employer's cars to take her out. Perhaps they had used that very car in which Drayton himself had driven her to Cheriton Forest. He had deceived her with Ann Margolis and she him with a young policeman. It was a roundabout, a changing spinning thing that sometimes came to a long pause. He felt that he had reached a halt and that they must alight from it together, perhaps for life.

But he had not wanted to come. Undesired things would be revealed to him and she who would be questioned might speak of a love he wanted to forget. He stood at the rear while Burden banged on the glass and as he waited it came to him suddenly that it would not have mattered whether Wexford had brought him or not. Where else had he to go in the evenings? He would have come here anyway, as he always came.

It was Grover himself who came to let them in. Drayton expected him to be antagonistic, but the man was ingratiating and the oiliness of his greeting was more repulsive than hostility. His black hair was flattened down and combed to cover a small bald spot and it smelt of violet oil. One hand clamped to the small of his back, he ushered them into the shop and put on a light.

'Ray was here a month,' he said in answer to Wexford's question. 'Cawthorne gave him the push on the Saturday and he left here on the Tuesday. Or so Lin and the wife said. I never saw him, being as I was laid up.'

'I believe he had one of your attic rooms.'

Grover nodded. He was not an old man but he dressed like one. Drayton tried to keep his eyes still and his face expressionless as he noted the unbuttoned cardigan, the collarless shirt and the trouser that had never been brushed or pressed. 'His room's been done,' the newsagent said quickly. 'Lin cleaned it up. He never left nothing behind so it's no use you looking.'

'We'll look,' Burden said lightly. 'In a minute.' His cold eyes skimmed the magazines and then he strolled down to the dark corner where the library was. Grover followed him, hobbling.

'I've got nothing to tell you, Mr. Burden,' he said. 'He didn't leave no forwarding address and he'd paid up his next month's rent in advance. There was three weeks to run.'

Burden took a book from the shelf and opened it in the middle, but his face did not change. 'Tell me about Tuesday evening,' he said.

'Tell you what? There's nothing to tell. Lin was in and out all afternoon. We wanted some bread and it's early closing here on Tuesdays—not for us; we don't close. She popped into Stowerton. The wife went to her whist drive around half seven and Lin was off somewhere—the launderette, that was it.' He paused, looking virtuous. Drayton felt angry and bewildered. The anger was for the way Grover used her as a maid of all work. He could not account for the bewilderment unless it was becaue he could not understand her father's lack of appreciation. 'I never saw Ray all day,' Grover said. 'I was in bed, you see. You'd have thought he'd have looked in on me to say good-bye and thank me for all I'd done for him.'

'Like what?' Burden snapped. 'Providing him with a lethal weapon, that sort of thing?'

'I never gave him that knife. He had it when he first come.'

'Go on.'

'Go on with what, Mr. Burden?' Grover felt his back, gingerly probing the muscles. 'I told you I never saw Ray after the Monday. The doctor came before the wife went out and said I was to stop in bed ...'

'Anyone else call? During the evening, I mean?'

'Only that girl,' Grover said.

Burden blew dust off the book he was holding and replaced it on the shelf. He came close to Grover and stood over him. 'What girl? What happened?'

'I was in bed, you see, and there was this banging on the shop door.' The newsagent gave Wexford a sly yet sullen glance. 'I thought it was you lot,' he said. 'It's all very well the doctor saying not to get out of bed on any account, but what are you supposed to do when someone comes banging fit to break the door in?' He winced, perhaps at the memory of an earlier and more acute pain. 'One of his customers it was. I'd seen her about before. Tall, good-looking piece, but older than my girl. You want to know what she looked like?'

'Of course. We haven't come her for social chit-chat, Grover.'

Standing by the paperback stand, Drayton felt almost sick. Burden's reprimand, far from disconcerting Grover, had provoked a sycophantic grin. His lips closed, he stretched them wide, half-closing one eye. This mockery of a smile seemed the ghost of Linda's own. In fact it was the begetter, and Drayton felt nausea rise in his throat.

'Bit of all right she was,' Grover said, again sketching his wink. 'Kind of white skin and black hair with two curly bits coming over her cheeks.' He seemed to reflect and he wetted his lips. 'Got up in black trousers and a spotted fur coat. "What d'you mean banging like that?" I said. "Can't you see we've closed?" "Where's Ray?" she says. "If he's in his room I'll go up and root him out." "You'll do no such thing," I said. "Anyway, he's not there." She looked proper put out at that so I asked her what she wanted him for. I don't know whether she didn't like me asking or whether she was thinking up some excuse. "I'm going to a party," she says, "and I'm bloody late as it is and now my car radiator's sprung a leak." Mind you, I couldn't see no car. Go up to his room, would you? I thought, and him going steady with my Linda.'

Drayton gave a small painful cough. It sounded like a groan in the silence which had fallen. Wexford looked at him and his eyes were cold.

Grover went on after a pause, ' "In that case you'd best take it to a garage," I said, and then I come out on to the pavement in my dressing gown. There was this white sports job stuck in my sideway with a pool of water underneath it. "I daren't drive it," she said. "I'm scared it'll blow up on me." '

'Did she go away?' Burden asked, discreetly jubilant.

'I reckon she did, but I didn't wait to see. I locked up again and went back to bed.'

'And you heard nothing more?'

'Nothing till the wife came in. I do remember thinking I hoped she'd got that white car of hers out on account of Lin not being able to get mine into the garage if it was there. But I dropped off to sleep and the next thing I knew was the wife getting into bed and saying Lin had come in half an hour before. D'you want to see his room now?'

Frowning slightly, Burden came out of his dark corner and stood under the light that hung above the counter. He glanced down the passage towards the side door that led to the alley. For a moment Drayton thought he had seen someone coming, Linda herself perhaps, and he braced himself to face the shock of her entrance, but Burden turned back to the newsagent and said:

'Where did he do this car servicing of his?'

'In my spare garage,' Grover said. 'I've got the two, you see. My own car's in one and the other used to be let, but I lost my tenant and when young Ray said he wanted it I let him have it.' He nodded smugly. Perhaps this was the favour, or one of the favours, for which he had claimed Anstey's gratitude. 'I only charged him five bob a week extra. Mind you, he had plenty of customers. Been doing the same thing at his old digs, if you ask me.'

'I'd like to see both garages,' Burden said. 'Keys?'

'The wife's got them.' Grover went into the passage and took an old overcoat down from a wall hook. 'Or maybe Lin has. I don't know, I haven't had the car out for best part of a fortnight, my back's been so bad.' He got into the coat with difficulty, screwing up his face.

'Keys, Drayton,' Wexford said laconically.

Half-way up the stairs, Drayton met Mrs. Grover coming down. She looked at him incuriously and would have passed him, he thought, without a word.

'Can you let me have your garage keys, Mrs. Grover?' he asked. Linda must have told her who and what he was.

'In the kitchen,' she said. 'Lin left them on the table.' She peered at him short-sightedly. Her eyes were as grey as her daughter's, but passionless, and if they had ever held tears they had long been wept away. 'I'm right in thinking you're her young fellow, aren't I?' Who he was, Drayton thought, but not what he was. 'She said you and her'd want the car tonight.' She shrugged. 'Don't let her dad know, that's all.'

'I'll go up, then.'

Mrs. Grover nodded indifferently. Drayton watched her go down the stairs and leave by the side door. The kitchen door was open and he went in. Out of her parent's presence, his sickness went, but his heart was beating painfully. The keys lay on the table, one for each garage and one ignition key, and they were attached to a ring with a leather fob. Beside them was a pile of unfolded, unironed linen, and at the sight of it he felt a return of the bewilderment he had experienced in the shop. The keys were in his pocket and he had reached the head of the stairs when a door facing him opened and Linda came out.

For the first time he saw her hair hanging lose, curtaining her shoulders in a pale bright veil. She smiled at him softly and shyly but all the coquetry was gone.

'You're early,' she said as she had said that day when he had come to take her to Wexford. 'I'm not ready.' It came to him suddenly that she, like her mother, had no idea why he was there or that others of his calling were down below in the shop. Perhaps she need not know and the knowledge of what probably lay in one of those garages be kept from her a little longer. 'Wait for me,' she said. 'Wait in the shop. I won't be long.'

'I'll come back later,' he said. He thought he could go back to them without touching her, but he could neither move nor take his eyes from the spell of the tiny wavering smile and the golden cloak of hair.

'Mark,' she said and her voice was breathless. She came towards him trembling. 'Mark, you'll help me out of—out of all this, won't you?' The linen on the table, the shop, the chores. He nodded, committing himself to what? To a yet unconsidered rescue? To marriage? 'You do love me, then?'

For once the question was not a signal for evasion and ultimate departure. That she should love him and want his love was to confer upon him an honour and to offer him a privilege. He took her in his arms and held her to him, touching her hair with his lips. 'I love you,' he said. He had used the forbidden verb and his only sensation was a breathless humble longing to give and give to the utmost of his capacity.

'I'll do anything for you,' he said. Then he let her go and he ran down the stairs.

Faded green paint was peeling from the garage doors. From their roof gutters water streamed out of a cracked drainpipe and made a scummy pool around the dustbins. Drayton let himself into the alley by the side door. His hands were shaking because of what had passed upstairs and because here, a few yards from where Grover and the policemen stood, he had first kissed her. He raised his hood against the drizzle and handed the keys to Wexford.

'You took your time about it.'

'We had to look for them,' Drayton muttered.

Whether it was that 'we' or the badly-told lie that gave rise to that chilly glance Drayton did not know. He went over to the dustbins and began shoving them out of the way.

'Before we open the door,' Wexford said, 'there's one little point I'd like cleared up.' Although it was not cold, Grover had begun to rub his hands and stamp his feet. He gave the Chief Inspector a sour disgruntled look. 'Inspector Burden was about to ask you what time Miss Margolis, the girl with the white car, called on you. He was about to ask, but something else came up.'

'Let me refresh your memory,' Burden said quickly. 'Between seven thirty and eight, wasn't it? More like half past seven.'

The hunched shivering figure galvanized into sudden life.

'Half seven?' Grover said incredulously. 'You're joking. I told you the wife and Lin came in just after. Half seven, my foot. It was all of ten.'

'She was dead at ten!' Burden said desperately and he turned to appeal to Wexford who, bland and urbane, stood apparently lost in thought. 'She was dead! You're wrong, you mistook the time.'

'Let us open the doors,' said Wexford.

Drayton unlocked the first garage and it was empty. On the concrete floor was a black patch where oil had once been.

'This the one Anstey used?'

Grover nodded, viewing the deserted place suspiciously. 'There's only my car in the other one.'

'We'll look, just the same.'

The door stuck and Drayton had to put his shoulder to it. When the catch gave, Burden switched on his torch and the beam fell on an olive-green Mini.

It was Wexford who opened the unlocked boot and revealed two suitcases and a canvas bag of tools. Muttering, Grover prodded the bag until Burden removed his hand roughly. Through the rear window something could be seen lying on the passenger seat, a stiff bundle, one arm in a raincoat sleeve outflung, black hair from which the gloss had gone.

Wexford eased his bulky body between the side of the car and the garage wall. He pressed his thumb to the handle and opened the door as widely as he could in that confined space. His mouth set, for he could feel a fresh onset of nausea, Drayton followed him to stare over the Chief Inspector's shoulder.

The body which was sprawled before them had a blackened stain of dried blood across the breast of the raincoat and there was blood on the hilt and the blade of the knife someone had placed in its lap. Once this corpse had been young and beautiful—the waxen features had a comeliness and a symmetry about them even in death—but it had never been a woman.

'Anstey,' said Wexford succinctly.

A dark trickle had flowed from one corner of the dead man's mouth. Drayton put his handkerchief up to his face and stumbled out of the garage.

She had come from the side door and her hair was still loose, moving now in the faint wind. Her arms were bare and on them and on her face gooseflesh had arisen, white and rough, like a disease. Incredible that that mouth had once smiled and kissed.

When he saw her Drayton stopped. In the wind and the rain a death's head was confronting him, a skull staring through stretched skin, and it was much more horrifying than what he had just seen in the car. She parted the lips that had smiled for him and been his fetish and gave a scream of terror.

'You were going to save me! You loved me, you'd do anything for me .... You were going to save me!' He put out his arms, not to enclose her but to ward her off. 'I went with you because you said you'd save me!' she screamed, and flinging herself upon him, tore at his cheeks with the bitten nails that could not wound. Something cold struck his chin. It was the silver chain that Anstey had stolen from his wife.

When Burden pulled her away and held her while she kicked and sobbed, Drayton stood with his eyes closed. He could sort out nothing from her cries and the harsh tumult of words, only that she had never loved him. It was a revelation more unspeakable than the other and it cut into his ears like a knife slitting membrane. He turned from the watching eyes, the man's stern, the girl's unbearable, stumbled from the alley into the backyard and was sick against the wall.

# 18

She was waiting in Wexford's office. Two minutes before, down in the foyer, he had been warned of her presence, so he was able to repress natural astonishment and approach her with the aplomb of a Stanley.

'Miss Margolis, I presume?'

She must have been home. After arriving from wherever she had been, she must have called at the cottage to collect the ocelot coat. It was slung across her shoulders over a puce and peacock trouser suit. He noted her tan and the bronze glaze a hotter sun than that of Sussex had given to her dark hair.

'Rupert said you thought I was dead,' she said. 'But he does tend to be unsure of things. I thought I ought to come and clarify.' She sat on the edge of his desk, pushing papers out of her way. He felt like a guest in his own office and he would not have been surprised if she had asked him in just this imperiously gracious tone to sit down.

'I think I know most of it,' he said firmly. 'Suppose I tell you and you correct the more crashing howlers.' She smiled at him with catlike enjoyment. 'You've been in Spain or Italy. Perhaps Ibiza?'

'Positano. I flew back this morning.' She crossed her legs. The trousers had bell bottoms with pink fringes. 'Dickie Fairfax got though a hundred and fifty quid of my money in a week. You might not think it to look at me but I'm very bourgeois at heart. Love's all very well but it's abstract if you know what I mean. Money's concrete and when it's gone it's gone.' She added thoughtfully, 'So I abandoned him and came home. I'm afraid he may have to throw himself on the mercy of the consul.' Black eyebrows met over the bridge of that pretty hawk's nose. 'Perhaps Dickie's name doesn't mean anything to you?'

'Wild conjecture,' said Wexford, 'leads me to suppose that he is the young man who went to the Cawthorne's party and when he found you weren't there, sallied forth to find you, chanting passages from Omar Khayyám.'

'How clever of you!' If she looked at them like this, Wexford thought, and flattered them like that, it was no wonder they came to her purring and let her devour them. 'You see, she said, 'I had every intention of going to the party but that bloody stupid car of mine broke down. I hadn't a clue there was anything wrong with it until after half past nine when I left for the party. It was boiling like a kettle all the way down the road. Then I thought of Ray. I knew he'd fix it for me ... Oh, but you were going to do the talking!'

Wexford returned her smile, but not enthusiastically. He was growing tired of young women, their ways, their wiles, their diverse characteristics. 'I can only guess,' he said. 'Anstey was out. Then I think you tried to drive to the party but the car died on you ...'

'You've left something out. I saw Ray first, I was trying to get the car out of the alley when the Grover girl came along in hers. Ray was in the passenger seat, looking terrible. She said he was drunk but, my God, he looked as if he was dying! She wouldn't let me go near him, so I just backed the car out and left them.'

'He *was* dying,' Wexford said, 'or dead already.' Her eyebrows went up to meet the bronzy fringe but she said nothing. 'You might have come to us, Miss Margolis. You're supposed to have a reputation for being public-spirited.'

'But I did tell you,' she said softly, 'or I told Rupert. When I left Grover's I got about a hundred yards up the road and the car conked out. Well, I got some water from a cottage and filled up the radiator. I sort of crawled about half way to Stowerton and I was sitting in the damn thing cursing my luck when Dickie came along, singing at the top of his voice about being merry with the fruitful grape. We'd had a sort of affair about six months ago, you see, and we sat in the car talking. I had all that money in my bag. Talk about sugar for the horse! He's always on the breadline and when he knew I was flush he said, what about you and me going off to Italy? Well, it is a bloody climate here, isn't it?'

Wexford sighed. She was her brother's sister all right.

'He was terribly sloshed,' she went on artlessly. Wexford thanked God Burden was otherwise engaged. 'We sat about for hours. In the end when he'd sobbered up he went back to Cawthorne's for his car and I drove mine home. It must have been about one. Rupert was in bed and he hates being disturbed, so I wrote him a note, telling him where I was going and then I remembered about Ray. Go round to Grover's, I wrote, and see if Ray's all right because I don't like it . . .'

'Where did you leave it?'

'Leave what?'

'The note.'

'Oh, the note. I wrote it on a big sheet of cartridge paper and stuck it in front of a pile of newspapers on the kitchen counter. I suppose it got lost.'

'He threw it away,' said Wexford. 'The lights fused and he threw it away in the dark with the newspapers. He had an idea we might have sent someone to clear it all up for him.' He added thoughtfully, 'We thought it infra dig. Perhaps we should be more humble.'

'Well, it might have saved a lot of trouble,' said Anita Margolis. Suddenly she laughed, rocking back and forth so that the glass sculpture shook precariously. 'That's so like Roo. He thinks the world owes him a regiment of slaves.' She seemed to remember that the question under discussion was no laughing matter and she grew quickly serious. 'I met Dickie in the High Street,' she said, 'and we drove straight to London Airport.'

'Why did you change your coat?'

'Change my coat? Did I?'

'The one you're wearing now was found on the passenger seat of your car.'

'I remember now. It was raining like mad, so I put on the one raincoat I've got, a red vinyl thing. You see, Dickie's car makes such a racket I didn't want him disturbing the peace and waking Rupert, so I arranged to meet him in the High Street.'

She looked at him impishly. 'Have you ever sat for three hours in a car in a soaking wet fur coat?'

'I can't say I have.'

'The proverbial drowned rat,' she said.

'I suppose you fetched your passport at the same time.' She nodded as he asked in some exasperation, 'Don't you ever send postcards. Miss Margolis?'

'Oh, do call me Ann. Everyone does. As to postcards, I might if I was enjoying myself, but what with Dickie getting through simply millions of horrid little *lire*, I never got around to it. Poor Roo! I'm thinking of carrying him off to Ibiza tomorrow. He's so very disturbed and, anyway, I can't wear all my lovely new clothes here, can I?'

She slithered languidly from the desk and, too late to stop it, Wexford saw the hem of her spotted coat catch at fragile glass. The blue sculpture did a nose-dive, rising slightly in the air, and it was her lunge to save it that sent it crashing against the leg of his desk.

'God, I'm terribly sorry,' said Anita Margolis.

She retrieved a dozen of the larger fragments in a half-hearted, well-meaning way. 'What a shame!'

'I never liked it,' Wexford said. 'One thing before you go. Did you ever own that lighter?'

'What lighter?'

'A gold thing for Ann who lights someone's life.'

She bent her head thoughtfully and the big crescents of hair swept her cheeks. 'A lighter I once showed to Alan Kirkpatrick?' Wexford nodded. 'It was never mine,' she said. 'It was Ray's.'

'He serviced the car and left the lighter in it by accident?'

'Mm-hm. I returned it to him the next day. Admittedly, I more or less let Alan think it was mine.' She wriggled her toes in gilt-strapped sandals, grinding glass into Wexford's carpet. 'He was always so jealous, a natural bait for a tease. Have you seen his car? He wanted to take me out in it. Just what do you think I am? I said, an exhibit in the Lord Mayor's show? I do tease people, I'm afraid.'

'You have teased us all,' said Wexford severely.

The letter of resignation had been pushed aside with the other papers on his desk. It was still unopened, a thick white envelope with the Chief Inspector's name on it in a clear upright hand. Drayton had used good paper and he had used ink, not a ball-point. He liked, Wexford knew, the good things of life, the best and beautiful things. You could get too fond of beauty, seduced and intoxicated.

Wexford thought he understood, but understanding would not stop him accepting that resignation. He only thanked God that it had all come to light in time. Another day and he'd have asked Drayton if he'd care to make one of a group of young people Sheila was organizing to the theatre in Chichester. Another day . . .

Anita Margolis had left perfume behind her, *Chant d'Arômes* that Wexford's nose detected better than an analyst's tests. It was a breath of frivolity, expensive, untender, like herself. He opened the window to let it out before the coming interview.

Drayton came in five minutes before the appointed time and Wexford was on the floor, gathering up broken glass. The young man had not caught him at a disadvantage. Wexford, in getting down to this menial task, had considered any occupation preferable to pacing up and down because a raw detective constable had made a fool of himself.

'You're resigning I see,' he said. 'I think you're doing the wisest thing.'

Drayton's face was almost unchanged, perhaps a little paler than usual. Four red marks showed on each cheek, but the girl's nails had been too short to break the skin. His expression held neither defiance nor humility. Wexford had expected embarrassment. A violent outburst of emotion, long contained, would not have surprised him. Perhaps that would come. For the moment he sensed a self-control so regulated that it seemed like ease.

'Look, Drayton,' he said heavily, 'no one supposes you actually made that girl any promises. I know you better than that. But the whole thing—well, it smells and that's a fact.'

The narrow contained smile might have been the rejoinder to a wary joke. 'The stink of corruption,' Drayton said and his tone was cooler than the smile. Between them the lingering French scent hung like the perfume of a judge's posy, shielding him from contamination.

'I'm afraid we all have to be beyond reproach.' What else was there to say? Wexford thought of the pompous sermon he had prepared and it sickened him. 'My God, Mark!' he burst out, moving around the desk to stand in front of and tower above Drayton. 'Why couldn't you take the hint and drop her when I told you? You knew her, she talked to you. Couldn't you put two and two together? That alibi she gave to Kirkpatrick and we thought he'd got at her—she was alibi-ing herself! It was eight when she saw him, not nine thirty.'

Drayton nodded slowly, his lips compressed.

Splinters of glass crunched under Wexford's shoes. 'She was on her way to Ruby's house when she saw him and Anstey was with her, only Kirkpatrick didn't notice. Grover told us she went out on Tuesday afternoon, to go shopping, he said. That was when she took the washing, in the afternoon, not in the evening.'

'I began to guess that,' Drayton murmured.

'And you said not a word?'

'It was just a feeling of unease, of something not being right.'

Wexford set his teeth. He had almost gasped with annoyance. Some of it was for his own folly in that, while disapproving, he had entered with a certain romantic and conspiratorial delight into Drayton's love affair.

'You were nosing around that place for God knows how long and all the time that fellow's body was lying in the garage. You knew her, you knew her damn' well . . .' His voice rose and he knew he was trying to spark off in Drayton an answering show of passion. 'Didn't natural curiosity make you want to know who her ex-boy-friend was? They'd had a lodger for four weeks, a small dark lodger who disappeared on the night of the murder. Couldn't you have told us?'

'I didn't know,' Drayton said. 'I didn't want to know.'

'You have to want to know, Mark,' Wexford said tiredly. 'It's the first rule of the game.' He had forgotten what it was like to be in love, but he remembered a lighted window, a girl leaning out and a man standing in the shadows beneath. It distressed him to know that passion could exist and grief beside it, that they could twist in a man's bones and not show on his face. He had no son, but from time to time it is given to every man to be another's father. 'I should go away from here,' he said, 'right away. No need for you to appear in court. You'll forget it all, you know. Believe me, you will.'

'What did she do?' Drayton said very quietly.

'Anstey held the knife to her throat. He relied on a girl's fear and his own attraction to make her acquiescent. She wasn't, you see. She got it away from him and stabbed him in a lung.'

'Was he dead when they got home?'

'I don't know. I don't think she does. Perhaps we never shall know. She left him and ran upstairs to her father, but the next day she couldn't go back. I can understand that. The time would come when her father would want the car and Anstey would be found. Before that happened she hoped for a miracle. I think you were to be that miracle. You were to help her get him away, but we got there first.'

'She had the car keys out ready for me.' He looked down and now his voice was almost a whisper.

'We came half an hour too soon, Drayton.'

The boy's head jerked up. 'I would never have done it.'

'Not when it came to the final crunch, eh? No, you would never have done it.' Wexford cleared his throat. 'What will you do now?'

'I'll get by,' Drayton said. He went to the door and a sliver of glass snapped under his shoes. 'You broke your ornament,' he said politely. 'I'm sorry.'

In the hall he put on his duffel coat and raised the hood. Thus dressed, with a lock of black hair falling across his forehead, he looked like a mediaeval squire who has lost his knight and abandoned his crusade. When he had said good night to Sergeant Camb who knew nothing but that young Drayton was somehow in hot water, he came out into the wet windy street and began to walk towards his lodgings. By a small detour he could have avoided passing Grover's shop, but he did not take it. The place was in total darkness as if they had all moved away and in the alley the cobbles were wet stones on the floor of a cave.

Two months, three months, a year perhaps, and the worst would be over. Men have died from time to time and worms have eaten them, but not of love .... The world was full of jobs and full of girls. He would find one of each and they would do him very well. The daffodils in the florist's window had an untouched exquisite freshness. He would always think of her whenever he saw something beautiful in an ugly setting.

But you got over everything eventually. He wished only that he did not feel so sick and at the same time so very young. The last time he had felt like this was fourteen years ago when his mother had died and that also was the last time he had wept.

# CHEERLEADERS #8

# FORGETTING

## LISA NORBY

SCHOLASTIC INC.
New York Toronto London Auckland Sydney

ISBN 0-590-33689-4

Copyright © 1985 by Lisa Norby
All rights reserved. Published by Scholastic Inc.

12 11 10 9 8 7 6 5 4 3 2 1      8      5 6 7 8 9/8 0/9

Printed in the U. S. A.                01

# CHEERLEADERS

# FORGETTING

# CHEERLEADERS

# CHAPTER

The closing buzzer sounded, and the hometown crowd roared its approval of the final score. Tarenton had beaten the Rivertown team 78 to 68.

Coach Ardith Engborg was looking especially pleased with herself as she called the cheerleading squad together for a brief postgame meeting. "Good work, kids," she said. "I'm glad to see you've finally worked out your little personal difficulties and are pulling together as a squad. Just in time, too, because next week you'll be on your own.

"And I," Ardith added with a grin, "will be leading the cheers for the opposition."

Nancy Goldstein gasped. "Coach Engborg! What are you talking about? Don't tell me you're leaving Tarenton!"

Nancy looked around for support from the

1

other squad members. Silence. What's going on here? she wondered. Does everyone know about this except me?

Finally, after a few seconds that seemed like an eternity to Nancy, Pres broke into a broad grin and patted Nancy on the back. "Relax, Nance. It's nothing like that."

It was easy advice for Preston Tilford III to give out. Dark blond, handsome, and rich — the only son of the richest family in town — Pres Tilford had been born relaxed.

"What Pres is getting around to," Mary Ellen Kirkwood chimed in, "is that next Saturday there is no regularly scheduled basketball game. The students are playing the faculty. For charity."

"I didn't mean to scare you, Nancy," Coach Engborg added. "What I meant was I'll be leading the cheers for the teachers, naturally. So in the meantime, Mary Ellen, your captain, will be in charge. It's a longstanding tradition. Sometimes I forget that you're relatively new in Tarenton."

"Wait till you see Mr. Marburg in his gym shorts," stocky Walt Manners confided with a grin. "One look at those knobby knees and the memory of Founders' Day will be forever burned into your consciousness."

"Don't be too confident," Ardith huffed. "The faculty team has some surprises in store this year. And as for the faculty cheerleaders, I think we look pretty good in our uniforms. We may show you guys a thing or two."

Everyone rolled their eyes mockingly as Ardith

2

finished her announcement and left for her office.

"I think Ardith is trying to psyche us out," Angie Poletti said as she watched the coach make her exit.

"Well, she can't scare me," Walt laughed. "The coach may have a few good cheers in her. But I can't imagine the teachers' squad will be able to come up with any routines to compete with ours."

"Besides," he added, "do you know the best thing about Founders' Week? It means the school year is half over. Think of it! In a few short months we'll be. . . ."

Walt, always the clown, finished his thought by humming a few bars of "Pomp and Circumstance." Inspired, he did an exaggerated rendition of the graduation march shuffle-step, finishing up with a tattoo of tap dancing. "We'll be *liberated*!"

To Walt's surprise, this sentiment fell flat.

"I for one am in no hurry to see the year end," Angie said. "My SAT scores are so low, they broke the computer. I have until June to figure out a way to bring them up at least a hundred points, or I'll be lucky if I can get into obedience school next year."

Besides, Angie Poletti told herself silently, senior year wasn't much fun without a boyfriend. When she was going with Marc, who was away at State, she'd already felt as if she was missing out on a lot of fun. Now that they'd broken up, it was worse. With her luck, she'd end up soloing the rest of the year, and then find herself giving perms in her mother's beauty parlor because she couldn't meet the entrance requirements for State, the only school her mom could afford to send her to.

"I'm with Angie," Nancy said. "I don't care if this year never ends." Nancy, whose grades matched her A-plus figure, had no reason to be anything but optimistic about college. But as everyone knew she had just started going steady with Josh Breitman and she didn't look forward to college splitting them up.

"Me, either," agreed Pres. "Anyway, I am opposed on principle to any form of progress." As Walt had momentarily forgotten, Pres was going with an underclassman — little Kerry Elliot.

"I guess I spoke too soon," Walt said, "but I know one person who'll agree with me. How about it, Mary Ellen? Next year this time, you'll be a New York cover girl."

Privately, Mary Ellen found the prospect scary. A tall, cool blonde, she had the looks as well as the drive that it took to break into big-time modeling. But it was one thing to have dreams, another to realize that sometime she'd have to turn them into a reality. She was determined, though, not to let her friends suspect that she had any doubts. "Sure, you bet," she said, fashioning a convincing imitation of an enthusiastic grin. "And what about you, Livvy? Come September you'll be a senior, and maybe liberated from your mother's watchful eye."

"Huh?"

Long silences were not that unusual for Olivia

4

Evans, but her answer made it clear that she'd been a million miles away mentally.

"Earth to Olivia," Angie joked. "We were talking about next September. You know, about our plans for next year. We were saying you're probably looking forward to it."

Olivia still didn't answer. She'd been sitting with her legs stretched out on the bleacher bench in front of her, and now she seemed to be intently contemplating the tops of her white cheerleading socks. After a painful pause, she shook her small neat head in a gesture like a puppy trying to rid itself of a bothersome collar. "Why don't you guys just cut it out?" she protested. "I'm just not in the mood for all this dumb talk."

And with that, Olivia fled toward the girls' locker room, looking as if she were about to burst into tears.

All eyes turned toward Walt.

"Don't look at me," he shrugged. "I just date her. I can't explain her." Then, swallowing his own surprise and rising to the task of defending his girl, he added, "I'm sure Olivia didn't mean anything. She's just been a little tired lately."

Mary Ellen, however, had watched with a feeling of rising panic as Olivia ran out of the gym. For the coming week, squad morale would be her responsibility, and it would be just her luck if some major problem was brewing. Worse yet, the trouble *would* have to involve Olivia, the one member of the squad she found it hardest to figure out.

A born sophisticate, Mary Ellen was the opposite of petite, boyish Olivia when it came to looks. Underneath, they probably had more in common than either girl cared to admit. But Mary Ellen, who hid her insecurities behind an unchippable facade of pep and optimism, found it difficult to sympathize with anyone who let herself be so moody and vulnerable in public. Mary Ellen would have died a thousand times before she'd let Pres and Walt, or even the other girls for that matter, see her pouting like that.

In the meantime, Mary Ellen already felt sure that the coach's little speech had been meant as a hint to her. She was the team captain, after all, and she'd had a few very weak games recently.

"I think we really ought to have a special practice tomorrow afternoon," Mary Ellen said slowly. "We missed one practice last week because they were giving the freshmen physical fitness tests in the gym, and Thursday was wasted because the heating system wasn't working and it was so cold."

There were a few feeble protests to the idea of a Saturday practice. Nancy already had something scheduled for the morning and had been planning to spend Saturday afternoon shopping for a new outfit for the Eismar twins' party that evening. Pres objected to any extra work all together. But no one seemed seriously ready to protest against Mary Ellen's decision.

"Don't worry about Olivia," Walt volunteered. "I'll make sure she shows up."

"Okay, it's all set," Mary Ellen said, feeling more confident. "See you here tomorrow."

Knowing how quickly Olivia could shower and change when she was in a hurry, Walt went straight around to the outside door of the locker room. Sure enough, Olivia was already escaping down the hall toward the exit, having managed to avoid explaining herself to Mary Ellen, Nancy, and Angie.

"Livvy, wait up," Walt called.

As he ran in Olivia's direction, Walt couldn't help thinking that in her bulky down parka, quilted boots, and brightly colored knit mittens, Olivia looked like a little kid bundled up to go out and play in the snow. He thought the effect was cute. In fact, Olivia's looks and personality combined little-girl vulnerability and grown-up seriousness in a way he found fascinating. He could never explain this to Olivia herself, though. Olivia had been very ill as a child, and she was still sensitive about her small size and her mother's overprotectiveness.

Despite whatever had been bothering Olivia back in the gym, she seemed composed enough now. She even agreed that the Saturday practice was probably a good idea. Walt helped her up into the passenger seat of his jeep, and they made small talk about the game on the drive to her house.

But when they'd pulled up in front of the Evans

place and Walt pulled Olivia close for a good-night kiss, he felt as if he were hugging a statue.

"Olivia, is something wrong?" he asked.

"Of course not. It's nothing," Olivia insisted, though not very convincingly.

"Olivia, I'm your boyfriend. It isn't fair to shut me out of your problems. We've got to be able to talk about what's on our minds."

"I told you it's nothing." Olivia pulled her coat around her and grabbed her tote bag. "I just don't feel that great. It's probably a touch of the flu. No sense in your catching it, too."

"I wouldn't mind. Not if I caught it from you."

Olivia laughed in spite of herself. "That's quite a compliment. But not very practical." She gave Walt a quick kiss on the forehead, affectionate but about as unsexy as a kiss could possibly be. "See you tomorrow, okay?"

Walt waited until Olivia was safely inside her front door, and then gunned the engine as he pulled up the steep, snow-covered street leading back to the main road. Why had he ever been dumb enough to think that life would be simpler once he had a steady girl friend?

Just a few weeks ago he and Olivia had almost broken up because he'd caught her making out at his party with one of the sound men who worked on his parents' TV talk show. Even when he was at his angriest, part of him had known that Olivia wasn't at fault. Olivia wasn't a drinker at all, and Boomer — that was the guy's name — had given her a couple of strong drinks. If anyone was to blame, Walt thought gloomily, it was Mrs. Evans. Olivia's upbringing was short on more than just experience. She was naive in the ways you'd least expect. Not only hadn't Olivia realized that she wouldn't be able to handle drinking, she seemed to have no notion of just how fast an older guy like Boomer could move in on a girl.

Now that that little misunderstanding was out of the way, Walt had expected that everything would go smoothly. But it wasn't like Olivia to be so cold and distant — not with him at least. And worrying about him being exposed to her flu germs! That sounded like Olivia's mother, not her.

Something was definitely bothering Olivia, Walt decided. And the worst part of it was, she didn't trust him enough to confide in him. It was bad enough to be a loner more or less by choice, but to be shut out by someone you really cared for was even worse.

It must be your fault, Walt lectured himself. You spend so much time playing the clown that you don't communicate with the one person who means the most to you. From now on you've got to do better. Either that, or resign yourself to being "good old Walt" for the rest of your life. Everybody's buddy, but nobody's love.

# CHAPTER

The voice of Bruce Springsteen broke rudely into the pastel tranquility of Nancy Goldstein's bedroom. Nancy groaned as she slid out of bed and pulled her peach-colored robe around her shoulders. The dial of her clock radio said five A.M.

I must be crazy, Nancy thought, getting up in the middle of the night like this, just to prove to Josh that I'm not spoiled.

It had all started when Josh announced he was taking over a rural paper delivery route for a few weeks, while Mark McCorkle, an older neighbor of his who normally had the business, was doing a stint with the Army reserves. "Rural routes like that pay pretty well. I figure I can clear more than a hundred dollars a week," Josh had told her. "Mark thought of me because my van has four-wheel drive."

"But doesn't the morning *Call* get delivered in

10

the middle of the night?" had been Nancy's immediate reaction. "Why would you want to work such crazy hours just for a silly hundred dollars a week?"

That was the remark that had started her and Josh's first big fight. "A hundred may not sound like a lot to you, but if you had ever tried getting a part-time job around this town you'd know better. And for your information, I need the money. I borrowed from my college fund to get new tires for the van, and I want to pay it back."

"Why?" Nancy had asked in all innocence. "Won't your parents replace the money? They know you needed those tires."

"You really are spoiled, did anyone ever tell you that?"

"I am not, Josh Breitman!"

"Yes you are."

"Am not. I'll prove it, too. I'll help you deliver those papers," Nancy had vowed bravely. "I probably ought to anyway, since I'm the one who kept after you to replace those tires in the first place."

The offer had sounded so noble when she made it. Now that she was about to have to keep her word and venture out into a north country's winter dawn, Nancy was beginning to have her doubts.

It's like that song from *A Chorus Line*, Nancy told herself as she jumped out of the steaming shower and dried herself on a thick pile bath towel with her initials NLG embroidered on it in

11

gold. "What I Did for Love." The thought made her giggle. Delivering newspapers probably wasn't what the songwriter had in mind.

Of course it was probably true that she was spoiled. And if Josh thought so, that meant a lot of other kids at Tarenton High must have the same idea.

Just about the only two people in the world who didn't agree were Nancy's parents. "I don't know what we're doing wrong," her father had complained when Nancy had announced her Saturday schedule last night at dinner. "We give you all the advantages, and you insist on getting up at dawn to do hard labor. And then cheerleading practice in the afternoon. Why don't you cancel both things and come skiing with us up at Uncle Bernie's winter lodge? He and the kids were looking forward to seeing you."

Of course, since she would be working with Josh her dad hadn't put up a real fuss. The fact that her mom and dad considered Josh the ideal match for their only daughter had almost kept Nancy from ever giving him a chance. Fortunately, Josh had been persistent.

Now it was hard for Nancy to imagine how she had ever been able to resist Josh's dazzling smile and curly mop of dark hair — even if he did come equipped with a parental stamp of approval. Josh was the only boy she had ever ached to impress . . . and she was going to do it, even if she had to get up before dawn for three weeks running to show him how loyal she could be.

* * *

What Nancy Goldstein considered a taxing Saturday schedule was more or less a normal day for Angie Poletti. Angie had let herself sleep in until six, but she was dressed and out jogging with the first light of sunrise. Angie's morning runs were a well-kept secret from her friends. She'd made so many cracks about physical fitness nuts that she would never hear the end of it if the kids on the squad ever knew *she* was running. Unfortunately, it was either run or give up chocolate — a fate worse than death.

Coming back from her run, her face stinging from the cold air, Angie had just enough time to take a quick shower. She washed the breakfast dishes, thoughtfully left for her by her younger brother Andrew, and did a quick cleaning job on the kitchen. Her mom was already downstairs, setting up the beauty parlor that she operated from the house.

"I've got an hour or so to spare," Angie said as she came down the back stairs into the beauty salon. "I could help you set up, if you want."

"Good." Rose Poletti was an older, broader version of her daughter. Angie had inherited the same tendency to chunkiness, which she was already trying to compensate for by counting calories. Unfortunately, her sweet tooth worked against her, Even now, the box of glazed donuts that her mother had on hand, so that her morning customers could have breakfast while getting their hair done, looked mouthwateringly tempting.

13

"Go ahead, have one," Rose urged. "You're already skinny, and all you think about is getting skinnier still. You should have a boyfriend, a girl your age. Then you wouldn't have so much time to worry about dieting."

"You don't have to tell me. It's not my fault." Angie knew her mother meant well, but tact was not her strong suit.

Rose shook her head. "I know you're still mooning over that Marc. Forget him. Get yourself someone who appreciates you."

Angie laughed defensively. "You make it sound like I could just hop over to the store and pick up a new fellow. A specialty store, maybe — Boys 'R' Us."

Rose laughed appreciatively. "That's good. But seriously, at your age there's always another fellow waiting around the corner. How about that nice young man who's been tutoring you?"

"Arne? Arne Peterson?!"

"Sure. Him."

"Arne's the class brain. He and I have nothing in common."

"Don't put yourself down." Rose Poletti shook her head disapprovingly. "You're bright."

"That's not what I meant. We're not in the same crowd. We have nothing in common."

Rose rolled her eyes upward and stared in mute appeal at the fluorescent light fixture on the ceiling. "Okay, forget it. It was just a suggestion. What do I know?"

"Sorry, Mom," Angie apologized. "You know

a lot. It's just that these things either click or they don't. Maybe I'm still not ready to be interested in someone else. I need time."

Was she being honest with her mother? With herself?

A few hours later, when Arne Peterson had arrived and settled in at the dining room table to help Angie with her math, she still wasn't sure. To begin with, Angie wasn't happy about having to make time during busy Saturdays for math tutoring. Her grades at school were decent and getting better. It seemed so unfair that she had messed up dismally on her SATs.

And now, after only three tutoring sessions, she was already beginning to feel more interested in her tutor than in her lessons.

What she'd said to her mother was true enough. Arne Peterson was not the kind of guy she normally gave a second thought. He mostly hung around with the kids from the science club, and as far as Angie could tell, his closest relationship was with his pocket calculator. He wasn't even handsome. Not really. His arms and legs seemed a little too long for his body. And his blond hair had a tendency to stand up in spiky clumps — an effect that looked fashionably punk, except that Angie was sure it wasn't achieved intentionally.

So why was she starting to feel so weird whenever Arne bent over her shoulder to check her math exercise book? Maybe it was his voice, which was deep and mellow, almost hypnotizing. Or maybe it was his hands, so big and powerful-looking, yet sensitive at the same time.

This is crazy, Angie scolded herself silently. Arne just doesn't compare to Marc. It would be one thing to forget Marc so soon if Prince Charming came along. But to give up mourning for him just for Arne!

"Angie. . . ." Arne's voice cut into her thoughts, almost as if he had been reading her mind.

"Oh yeah." She was startled back to reality. "I guess I was daydreaming."

"It's a simple quadratic equation. You know how to do those, don't you?"

Angie stared down at the jumble of x's and y's and symbols on the page in front of her. "Uh huh. At least I did last year. But I guess I've forgotten. Math is so abstract, I just can't seem to make it stick in my mind, you know?"

Arne listened to her explanation politely, as if the idea of math being abstract were something he was hearing for the first time.

He put his hand on her shoulder while he launched into a lengthy discussion of quadratic equations. His touch made Angie feel alive through and through.

I don't even know if he's attracted to me, she thought. He must be, or he wouldn't waste his time on such a dummy. He wouldn't touch my shoulder like that.

Or maybe not. On second thought, Angie reflected, maybe all the little signals she hoped she was getting were all in her imagination.

The sound of rock music drifted up from the

16

salon downstairs. Mrs. Poletti liked to have the radio on when she worked; she said it made her cut hair better. Angie snapped her fingers and gave her hair a little shake. "Do you like to dance?" she asked Arne, feeling very brave. "I mean, you don't just do math all the time, right?"

"Of course not." Arne's grave blue eyes looked down into her blue ones. "But I've never been much for dancing. My hobby is astronomy. I'm grinding my own telescope lens."

Angie wanted to scream. Give me a break, she thought. I'm getting a crush on a guy whose idea of a good time is grinding lenses.

Angie checked her watch, looking for an excuse to bring this torture to an end. "Twelve-thirty!" she gasped. "I've got cheerleading practice in half an hour! I'm going to be late."

"Cheerleading? Oh, that's right. You mentioned you were on the squad."

You could say one thing for Arne: Even if he wasn't part of the in crowd, he wasn't one of those guys who nursed hopeless dreams of dating a cheerleader, either. He hadn't even known Angie was on the squad. And now that he did know, he wasn't exactly bowled over by the news.

My luck again, Angie thought.

"If you want, I could give you a ride to the school . . . if you need one, that is," Arne offered.

"Great. You'll be saving my life."

Arne's Japanese subcompact was so small that the shoulders of his and Angie's parkas touched. There had to be some reason why Arne was letting these tutoring sessions stretch out longer and longer each time, Angie thought to herself. And it couldn't be that he was attracted to her for her mind.

As if answering her question, Arne switched on the radio, rolling the dial to a station that played nothing but mellow songs. "I like slow music better," he said. "How about you?"

Angie felt herself turning red, for no reason at all that she could think of. "Sometimes. It depends on my mood."

"That's what I thought," Arne said, though it was obvious he hadn't heard her answer. "I figure you for the romantic type of girl."

They reached the school parking lot just in time to see Josh drop Nancy off near the side entrance of the building and drive off. "Thanks a lot for the ride, Arne," Angie said. "I'll see you next Saturday."

"If not sooner," Arne answered. Then he turned away from her gaze and drove off quickly, as if he had just said something dangerously compromising.

"You girls are really doing well for yourselves. My, my." It was the voice of Vanessa Barlow, followed by Vanessa herself, who emerged from the shadows of the doorway looking pleased with herself as usual. "First, Princess Nancy starts dating a guy who makes her keep him company on his little paper route. And now we have the spectacle of Angie Poletti, no less, hanging out with Arne Peterson. Awful Arne himself."

18

"There's nothing wrong with Arne," Angie said a bit too quickly. "Besides, I'm not dating him. He's tutoring me in math. And awful," she added, "is a word you should definitely reserve for your self-portrait."

Vanessa cocked her head to one side and graced Angie with one of those names-can-never-hurt-me smiles. It was obvious, though, that she was surprised. Nancy was the type to make a quick comeback, but not Angie. She usually took longer to work up a show of temper.

"I guess you set her straight," Nancy remarked when Vanessa had gone. "But it's true, isn't it? You're really falling for Arne?"

"Of course not," Angie denied, but not very effectively. She just wasn't the poker-faced type. Arne had probably noticed her feelings, too, and was embarrassed to be around her. No wonder he acted a little funny.

"If you say so," Nancy agreed. "Personally, though, I don't think Arne would be such a bad bet. He may be on another planet mentally, but he's got that sexy voice. And he's changed in the last year. Vanessa's always the last to get the news when anyone improves his act."

"Speaking of Vanessa," Angie said, changing the subject, "what's she doing here at school on a Saturday?"

"Who knows?" Nancy said. "And who cares? Come on, let's get changed so we can get this practice started and over with."

19

# CHAPTER

$P$res had arrived in the gym early, but Mary Ellen was already there ahead of him. She was seated in the first row of bleachers, busily studying the black loose-leaf notebook that Ardith used to keep track of practice sessions and squad routines.

"Hi, Melon," Pres greeted her, plopping down companionably on the bench beside her.

"Please don't call me that. You know I hate it," Mary Ellen answered without looking up. "And especially not today. I'm running practice, remember?"

Pres shrugged. "Okay, teach. Your wish is my command."

"If only that were true," Mary Ellen shot back. In fact, Pres and she met all her qualifications for Tarenton High's ideal couple. The only problem was that *he* didn't see it that way. Now that she had more or less given up on ever convincing him to change his mind about the two of them, Mary Ellen had reached the point where she could make jokes about the subject without feeling more than a tiny twinge of regret.

"Don't worry," Pres joked back. "You already have one willing slave." He pointed in the direction of the gym door, where Patrick had just appeared, pounds of camera gear hanging around his neck.

"Don't bother to welcome me with open arms," Patrick said, cutting off Mary Ellen in midquestion. "I'm here to take some candid shots for the yearbook."

"You are *not*," she contradicted him. "You must already have enough candid shots of the squad to fill six volumes."

"Have it your way," Patrick agreed pleasantly. "We'll just use the ones we have that make you look fat."

"I do *not* look fat!" Mary Ellen protested. "But okay. Stay if you want. Just don't interrupt our work."

"Wouldn't dream of it." Patrick draped himself across several rows of seats, making himself at home.

Pres tried not to let either of them see his smile of amusement. No matter how hard Mary Ellen tried to hate Patrick, she could never quite manage it. If Patrick ever wised up and stopped chasing her for just five minutes, Mary Ellen would have to admit to herself her feelings for

21

him, and the roles in the chase would reverse.

While Mary Ellen was working hard trying to ignore Patrick, the other members of the squad had drifted in.

The group warmed up with a few calisthenics just to stretch their cold muscles, and then ran through some standard cheers, trying out ways to change the words to suit their next opponent.

"How about this one?" Mary Ellen suggested:

"We've got the team that's on the beam —
That's on the B . . . E . . . A . . . M,
We've got the team, that's on the beam —
We're the Tarenton Five!
Come on, Wolves. Eat those teachers alive!"

Everyone repeated the cheer enthusiastically, except for Olivia. Mary Ellen gritted her teeth, waiting for Olivia to come out with another dumb complaint about her cheers being "too violent."

Olivia, however, was silent. I guess she's finally given up on that one, Mary Ellen thought. It was a good thing, too, because Mary Ellen was counting on the new stunt Olivia had been practicing to liven up next week's routine.

"Olivia, do you think you're ready to try the vault?" she asked, a bit nervously.

Olivia looked slightly bored but agreeable. "Why not? I guess it's time."

As Pres, Angie, and Nancy got into position to practice the move, Mary Ellen held her breath. The stunt looked dangerous to her, although

Olivia said it was easy for anyone who had as much gymnastics training as she had. And Ardith had already approved the move, provided that Walt and Mary Ellen stood by to spot Olivia in case she fell.

The trick started with Pres, in a half split, supporting Angie and Nancy on either side of him, while they held their outside legs up high, forming the outsides of the human "W." Olivia, getting a running start from a springboard behind the formation, vaulted right over Pres's head, did a full twist in the air, and landed on her feet.

Mary Ellen, who was by no means a natural athlete, could never quite get over her amazement that anyone as frail looking as Olivia could launch herself into the air like a guided missile. But Olivia, when they'd practiced the routine in the past, kept insisting that it wasn't really hard at all. "Pres has the tough part," she had insisted. "If he can stand being a human pommel horse, I can do a simple midair twist."

Standing to one side waiting to spot Olivia, Mary Ellen caught Walt's eye and realized that today he also looked a little worried.

In fact, he couldn't keep quiet. "Are you sure you're up to trying this today, Olivia?" he asked her. "Maybe we should wait until you're feeling a hundred percent."

"Walt, I'm perfectly all right," Olivia said through clenched teeth. "And I do *not* need a nursemaid."

Mary Ellen could see Pres, poised to take

Olivia's weight as she vaulted over him, frowning in worry. For her part, she tried to look totally confident. There was no sense making Olivia more uptight than she already was.

"W . . . O . . . L . . . V . . . E . . . S . . . ," Mary Ellen and the others chanted, "Let's go . . . Wolves!!!"

On cue, Olivia launched herself from the springboard and came flying over Pres's head. For a second, Mary Ellen thought it was going to work perfectly. Then she realized Olivia had overrotated a bit. Instead of landing on her feet, she toppled onto the mat knees first, arms flailing wildly in a futile effort to catch herself at the last minute.

"Damn!" The word, so unexpected from Olivia, rang through the gym.

"Are you okay?" everyone asked at once.

Olivia, however, was already picking herself up. "Of course I'm all right. I just got a little brush burn on my knee, that's all." Olivia looked around, as if challenging anyone around to contradict her. "What's more, I wouldn't have missed, if you all hadn't made me so nervous."

"Sure," Mary Ellen agreed. Anything to keep the practice moving. "Do you want to try it again right away, or should we take a five-minute break?"

Mary Ellen was certain that Olivia would insist on doing the trick again immediately. "Never quit on a failure" — that was Olivia's motto when it came to gymnastics, as they had all heard time and again. But for all her insistence on being fine, Olivia did seem shaken. In fact, Mary Ellen thought, she looks positively green.

"A break, if you don't mind," Olivia said weakly. "I'll be right back."

Olivia managed to keep her composure as she walked across the gym. But as soon as she was safely inside the girl's restroom she leaned against the cool tiled wall and let herself slump down into a squatting position. The truth was, she was not all right. She felt slightly queasy. Almost as if she was going to be sick . . . again.

I must have the flu after all, Olivia told herself. She'd been sick to her stomach three times now in the last week, which wasn't like her at all. Unless, she thought, unless. . . .

The thought Olivia had was so scary that she could hardly bring herself to consider it. It just *couldn't* be. She hadn't even done anything that should even make her *think* she was pregnant. Or had she? On the other hand, her period was already a week late — something that had never happened to her before, flu or no flu.

No matter how hard she tried to blot the scene from her consciousness, Olivia's mind kept going back to that party at Walt's house last month. She remembered being angry with Walt because he'd been ignoring her. And she remembered letting Boomer give her two drinks of that awful stuff that tasted like slightly off lemonade. The problem was that she had no idea what had happened next. The next thing she knew, she and

Boomer were stretched across a pile of coats in one of the Manners' upstairs bedrooms, and Walt was standing in the doorway looking furious.

Walt had found it hard to believe that anyone, even Olivia, could black out after just two drinks. But that must have been what happened. Of course, when he came into the room, she and Boomer hadn't been doing anything worse than kissing. . . .

But what about *before* that?

Aside from Boomer, of course, the only other person who really knew the answer to that was Vanessa Barlow, who had come into the room sometime earlier and surprised them. Olivia didn't even remember *seeing* Vanessa. But Vanessa had obviously gotten an eyeful.

A few days after the party, Vanessa had approached Olivia when she was at her locker and said, in a secretive whisper, "I've got to hand it to you, Olivia. I always thought you were the backward type. I would never have guessed you were *so* experienced. And with someone you hardly knew. . . ."

Olivia had walked away in a fury. But what if she really had done exactly what Vanessa was implying? After all, Vanessa couldn't know that she had no memory of that evening.

For the last week, Olivia had been trying with all her might to fight her rising panic. What would she do if it turned out to be true? She could never, *never* confide in her mother. Mom thought of her as completely innocent, a little girl who still needed to be told not to go outside without her mittens on. Something like this would destroy her.

Then there was Walt. Poor Walt, who treated her as if she were some sort of fragile china doll: okay to touch, but always with respect. He had forgiven her for kissing Boomer, because he had convinced himself that what happened was all Boomer's fault. She couldn't hurt him again by telling him that the whole scene might be even worse than he thought!

Olivia struggled to her feet and went over to the sink where she splashed cold water on her face and arms. She was starting to feel a little bit better at last. The only thing to do was to go back to practice and pretend that nothing was wrong. She could use the excuse of having the flu, for a few more days at least. But if nothing had changed by then, she had no idea where she would turn.

# CHAPTER

$P$res wasn't entirely sorry that Olivia hadn't been feeling up to working any more on the new routine. Mary Ellen had called practice off earlier than he'd expected, and he was home before his parents returned from their Saturday afternoon bridge game at the club.

That's why, when he came into the foyer, he found the day's mail still sitting on the silver tray on the antique rosewood credenza, right where their maid Louise always left it. The letter from the Princeton University Office of Admissions was sitting right on top of the pile, where the first person to look over the mail couldn't possibly miss it.

Pres quickly scooped up the letter. He didn't even feel curious enough to look inside and read the bad news. It was the rejection he'd been waiting for. He was just relieved that he'd been able to intercept it before his folks got home. The news that he definitely would not be going to Princeton was something he wanted to bring up with his parents when *he* was ready. And tonight, when he was looking forward to taking Kerry to the Eismar twins' party, was definitely not the time for a major family blowup.

As Pres was by now sick of hearing, all Tilfords — or at least all Tilford males — attend Princeton. It was a family tradition, so unbreakable that it might as well have been carved in stone over the Tilford front door. Princeton, as his father liked to brag, was "part of the Tilford heritage."

That being so, it didn't matter a bit to the senior Tilford that his son was not Princeton material, had no hope of ever getting in, and did not want to go even if he could. Pres's dad had even insisted that Pres apply for the early decision program. So one night, more than a month ago, Pres had spent a miserable hour or so filling out the application form. He'd done a fairly sloppy job — not that it mattered, considering his unimpressive grades and test scores. And he'd purposely left blank the space for listing relatives who were alumni — which he would have done even if he had wanted to get in.

Ever since he could remember, the name Tilford had been like a free admission pass to life. It got him whatever he wanted, impressed girls, and even — he suspected — enabled him to slide by in school when another student who worked as little as he did might have been pressured to shape up. He had no idea what he wanted to do with his future. But he knew what he *didn't* want — and that was to go off to a competitive eastern college where he would, inevitably, have to keep on relying on the Tilford name to get by.

Pres was about to take a peek at the contents of the letter, just to confirm what he already knew, when he heard his father and mother outside the front door. Hastily he stuffed the envelope into his jacket pocket.

"Have a good day, dear?" his mother asked distractedly, as she came into the hall.

"Fine. I just got back from practice," Pres said.

"Cheerleading practice!" Preston Tilford II snorted. "In *my* day, cheerleaders were girls."

"In your day," Pres shot back, "they didn't even have cheerleaders. They had knights in armor, riding in jousting tournaments. And ladies sat on the sidelines waving handkerchifs to urge them on."

"Doesn't sound so bad to me," his father grumbled, not at all insulted. "I always thought the middle ages would have been a good time to live. People in those days knew where they belonged." He paused to give Pres a look of pointed rebuke. "Among other things, sons obeyed their fathers."

"What are your plans for this evening, dear?" Felicia Tilford asked, deftly changing the subject.

"I'm taking Kerry to a party at the Eismars'."

"Oh yes, Kerry Elliot," his father said, as if he had considered a dozen possible Kerrys before coming up with the last name. "A sweet girl, I suppose."

"Why, Dad, when you say it, does it sound like a backhanded compliment?"

"Don't be so sensitive, Preston," his mother intervened again. "You know your father and I both like Kerry very much. As long as your relationship with her doesn't become serious."

Pres could feel himself steaming up fast. "And if it does? What would be wrong with that?"

The elder Tilfords exchanged pained looks. "Nothing dear," Felicia Tilford ventured. "It's just that . . . well . . . the Elliots aren't really our sort, are they?"

"You mean they don't belong to the country club? And they aren't rich?"

"Of course not," Mrs. Tilford said, insulted. "I would never put it so crudely."

"But that's what you mean, isn't it? You're a snob. But you're too refined to say so in so many words."

"Preston Tilford III," his father said, "you apologize to your mother this instant."

It was too late, though. Pres had already bolted from the house. As he was fastening the seat belt in his sporty red Porsche, he noticed the letter from Princeton sticking halfway out of his right-hand jacket pocket. Disgustedly, he flung it into the space behind the seat. Based on past experience, it would be at least a few days before his

31

parents forgave him for that outburst. The subject of his plans for college — or, rather, his nonplans — would have to wait.

Maybe it had something to do with the fact that the Eismar twins' parents were used to doing everything in duplicate, but Eismar parties always seemed to outdo everyone else's. There was twice as much food. Twice as many guests. And the music was twice as loud.

"Dad's on the premises somewhere," Cathleen Eismar told Pres and Kerry as she welcomed them at the front door. "But I think he must be hiding upstairs in the guest room. I saw him take a radio and a set of earphones in there about an hour ago."

"I hope he's all right," Kerry said, her voice full of concern, as she took a can of soda from an ice chest that was filled to overflowing with soft drinks of every kind.

"Oh, he'll survive," Cathleen predicted. "He always does."

Pres could hardly wait for Kerry to take a few sips of soda before leading her into the room where the dancing was going on. Kerry might not be the best dressed girl at the party — or even, by some people's standards, the prettiest. Her family might not have money or social clout, either. But Pres wanted her. Something about Kerry — maybe it was her gentle nature or the perpetually windblown look of her curly hair — made Pres want to hug her close and never let go.

Pres danced with Kerry for nearly an hour before he felt ready to share her with the rest of the party. Then they wandered into the large eat-in kitchen at the back of the Eismar house: a comfortable room with windows facing the backyard, where several spotlights illuminated a picture-pretty winter scene.

Nancy and Josh were seated on the couch in front of the fireplace, talking with Angie and Shelley Eismar, the other twin. Pres, indulging his pre-Kerry habit of evaluating girls by their looks and clothes, couldn't help noticing that Nancy was as sexy as ever. She was dressed in a buttery soft skirt of plum-colored leather, with snakeskin-trimmed boots to match, and a hand-knit sweater of plum-colored yarn shot through with silver threads. But Nancy, who loved a party, did not seem to be in her usual high spirits.

"I just don't feel up to dancing tonight," she was telling Josh, who was obviously impatient to get out into the living room where the main action of the party was going on. "Why don't you ask Angie?"

But when Josh did just that and the two of them disappeared in the direction of the music, Nancy looked even more down. "I've been up since five this morning helping Josh deliver papers," she confided to Kerry, "and now he's off having fun with someone else. And look! I even broke two fingernails. All just to prove I'm not spoiled."

Kerry didn't know quite what to say. Nancy's

tone suggested that there was more to this issue between her and Josh than she let on, and Kerry didn't want to get drawn into an argument she didn't understand. Diplomatically, she offered sympathy for the broken nails.

Shelley, meanwhile, was filling Pres in on the guest list. "Walt called at the last minute to say that he and Olivia couldn't come because she wasn't feeling well. I told him to come by himself if he wanted to, but he said he'd rather not. Is something wrong there? I can't imagine Walt missing a party."

Pres mumbled something noncommittal. He had the feeling there was something wrong, but he hated gossip like this on basic principle.

Shelley went on, paying no attention to Pres's lack of response. "Vanessa Barlow isn't here, either. Not that I'm exactly in mourning over that, but it always makes me wonder, when Vanessa is out of sight for very long, what she's up to."

"Well I just wish some others would take their cue from Vanessa," Cathleen Eismar added, joining the group around the couch.

"Why? What do you mean?" Pres asked.

"I mean that!" Cathleen pointed in the direction of the door to the hallway. There on the love seat, strategically located where every single guest at the party was sure to notice them sooner or later, Patrick Henley was amorously nibbling at the ear of Mindy Norris.

Mindy was new in school, a tall, leggy girl with

long, straight red hair. "The story on Mindy," Shelley explained, "is that she transferred from some really strict school in Canada. She seemed so shy that I was almost afraid to invite her here. But I guess she isn't quite as shy as I thought."

Cathleen sighed. "I guess not. The question is, Is Patrick really interested in Mindy? Or is this another ploy to make Mary Ellen jealous?"

"Whatever it is," Nancy put in, "Mary Ellen is sure to see them there. *That* will be something."

The words were scarcely out of Nancy's mouth when Mary Ellen appeared alone. Mary Ellen's face went chalk white when she saw the couple on the love seat. She was about to hurry past, but Patrick looked up in time to catch her glaring at him.

"Mary Ellen Kirkwood," his voice boomed out. "This is Mindy Norris. I don't know if you two have met.

"Mindy's dad is the new administrator of Haven Lake Medical Center," Patrick went on. "And *she* thinks my garbage truck is cute."

"Oh, I do!" Mindy said in all innocence. "We weren't even allowed to go out on dates in cars at the stuffy school I used to go to. And Patrick's truck is so . . . funky. Don't you think so, Mary Ellen?"

Mary Ellen gulped out something inaudible and hurried back in the direction of the living room. It made no sense at all that Patrick's being with Mindy should ruin the party for her. I ought to be happy, Mary Ellen scolded herself.

Maybe now he'll stop chasing after me all the time. My problem will be solved.

Patrick was loud, brash, and totally wrong for her, Mary Ellen reminded herself. It wasn't just that he worked for his father's garbage collection company. He actually made a point of letting everyone *know* it, driving his dates around town in his own truck and even wearing a HENLEY TRASH T-shirt to school.

More important, Patrick made no bones about the fact that he intended to spend the rest of his life right here in Tarenton, as a partner in his father's business, and eventually taking it over. Any girl who married him would be marrying Henley Trash, too. It was a package that Mary Ellen, with her dreams of a modeling career and all the rewards that went with it, could never imagine herself accepting.

None of this kept Mary Ellen from feeling miserable at the thought of Patrick with another girl. Joining a group of kids who were discussing the Tarenton basketball season, Mary Ellen did her best to pretend interest in the status of Hank Vreewright's problem knee and Donny Parrish's free-throw percentage. It was impossible, though, to ignore the nagging little voice inside her that kept asking: When Patrick kisses Mindy, does he feel the same electricity that he felt with me?

After an hour of sheer torture, Mary Ellen decided that she had put in enough time at the party to be able to leave without seeming too obvious. Gratefully accepting a ride from Hank, the owner of the problem knee, she grabbed her coat from the hall closet and said a quick good-bye to the twins.

When she left, Patrick and Mindy were still on the love seat, staring into each other's eyes with a devotion that spelled love at first sight in no uncertain terms.

"I think Patrick is disgusting," Kerry said when she and Pres had left the party and were headed home in the Porsche.

"Why?" asked Pres, genuinely surprised. "He's been chasing Mary Ellen for months and she can't make up her mind. If he's found another girl, good for him!"

"But he doesn't need to flaunt it," Kerry pointed out. "Patrick knew that Mary Ellen would feel lousy when she saw him with Mindy. If he really cared for Mary Ellen, why would he want to hurt her like that?"

"I suppose," Pres said. In fact, he had always admired Patrick, one of the few guys at Tarenton High whose style was even bolder than his own. That he was starting to agree with Kerry was a sign of just how fast Pres Tilford, Tarenton's gift to the female population, was changing.

"One thing I do like about Patrick," Kerry said, "is that he knows what he wants to do with his life. I think that's important, don't you?"

The thought flashed through Pres's head that if he wasn't careful, he was going to end up in the same fix Mary Ellen had been in with Patrick.

He was crazy about Kerry, but sometimes he wondered if the Pres Tilford that Kerry liked bore any resemblance to the real boy.

"You know what I think is important?" Pres said, changing the subject. "This."

Pulling the car to a stop on the broad shoulder of the lake road, he took Kerry into his arms and kissed her passionately. She responded, but just up to a point. She was always wary, always careful not to go too far with Pres, who wanted to go farther.

# CHAPTER

"Look at old Hubie! He's pink! I can't believe it!"

The cry went up on busload after busload of students arriving at Tarenton High on Monday morning. And it was true. Over the weekend someone had spray-painted the statue of Hubert Tarenton, the town's founder, a brilliant day-glo pink.

During homeroom period, the seldom-heard voice of Tarenton's superintendent of schools, Dr. Fredrick Barlow, boomed out over the P.A. system:

"It is true that years ago there was a so-called custom of painting the statue at the school entrance during the week of the student-faculty game. I recall participating in such a . . . um . . . ritual myself when I was a student. However, when I became superintendent of schools I dis-

39

covered that cleaning and restoring the statue was costing the district several hundreds of dollars each year. Therefore, it was time for this so-called tradition to come to an end.

"The rule against defacing the statue, or, for that matter, any school property," Dr. Barlow went on, his voice rising to a pitch of near hysteria, "is *clearly* printed in your student handbook. The culprits will be apprehended. And when you are, your parents will have to reimburse the school board for the cost of undoing this wanton damage. In fact, you'll be lucky if you aren't suspended. . . ."

"So much for so-called tradition," Patrick Henley said when he ran into Pres later in the halls.

"Yeah," Pres drawled. "Now that I've heard Dr. Barlow's side of the story, I'm kind of sorry I wasn't the one who did the deed. It doesn't seem fair that he's going to suspend some poor bozo for doing the same thing he got away with when he was a student."

"You didn't do it, then, huh?"

"Not me. It never occurred to me. I never even heard of such a tradition, or whatever you want to call it."

Walt Manners, who happened to be passing on his way to bio class, was called aside and questioned.

"Uh uh," he said, "I've got more important things on my mind right now than some dumb prank."

The three boys exchanged puzzled looks. It was

not necessarily true that one of the three was involved in *every* practical joke pulled at Tarenton High. But usually it was a safe bet that at least one of them knew who did it.

"I can't figure it out," Patrick mused. "No one has bothered that statue for as long as we've been in school. If something like this was in the wind, you'd think we would at least have had some hint."

"Well, we may never know," Walt said. "Unless Dr. Barlow is a better detective than I think."

"He isn't," said Pres. "But don't think we won't find out eventually. The word'll get around. There's no such thing as a secret at Tarenton High."

Unfortunately, that was all too true, as Angie was just beginning to find out. While they dressed for their first period volleyball class, Evie Caird had been filling her in on what happened yesterday at the church both Evie and Olivia Evans attended.

"It happened right in the middle of the closing hymn," Evie confided. "I was sitting in the back of the church, just across the aisle from Olivia and her mom, and I noticed that Olivia didn't look too hot. Then all at once, she turned green and ran out the vestibule door."

"That's too bad," Angie said sympathetically. "But I knew Olivia had the flu. She said so at Saturday practice."

"I don't think so." Evie looked mysterious.

"What do you mean?"

41

"Right after services I went into the ladies' room, and I heard Olivia and her mother talking. Mrs. Evans was asking Olivia what was wrong with her. 'This is the third morning this week you've been sick to your stomach,' she said."

Evie paused significantly. "Morning sickness. Get it?"

Angie glared at her in disapproval. "That's *crazy*. I *told* you she has the flu."

"Well," Evie replied, "I wouldn't say this to just anyone, but I don't believe that. For one thing, have you heard of any cases of flu around school lately? I haven't. If it's the flu, then Olivia is a one-woman epidemic. And besides, if it *is* the flu, then why is Olivia in school today?"

Angie was furious. Nothing would ever make her believe there could be any truth to what Evie said. But if the story started to get around, it would hurt Olivia — and Walt, too. "Look Evie," she said, "that's just speculation, and anyway it's none of our business. And just think of what Vanessa Barlow could do with a story like that. She would have Olivia tried and convicted on the basis of one little remark. And it would be all over school in no time."

Evie, who had been carried away by her access to inside information, looked embarrassed. "I didn't mean any harm," she said. "I just told you because you're on the squad with Olivia. Of course I would never pass anything like this on to Vanessa."

Angie breathed a sigh of relief.

"But," warned Evie, "I'm sure I wasn't the only person who noticed Olivia's sudden exit from church. People are sure to wonder, so don't blame me if you hear talk."

Olivia was in school, but she certainly was not in a talkative mood. When Angie caught her just before lunch period and tried to strike up a conversation, Olivia pleaded that she had a French quiz that afternoon and was too busy to chat. "I'm planning to skip lunch and hole up in the library," she explained, producing an apple from her purse, as if to prove that she wasn't simply feeling too sick to eat.

Maybe there really *is* something wrong, Angie thought as she headed toward the cafeteria alone. She still didn't believe Evie's theory, of course. On the other hand, it wasn't like Olivia to devote her lunch period to cramming.

The thought of Olivia virtuously having nothing but an apple for lunch had given the green light to Angie's appetite. On her way through the cafeteria line she automatically loaded up her lunch tray with cheese ravioli, a salad, a hunk of garlic bread, and a chocolate brownie, then headed on automatic pilot for a table where Nancy and Mary Ellen, who had just come from the same class, were sitting together.

"Thanks for bringing food for all of us," Nancy joked, eyeing Angie's overflowing tray. "But you didn't have to, really. We have our own."

Angie guiltily compared her lunch with Nancy's tuna fish sandwich and Mary Ellen's salad on pita bread, which she'd brought from home. "I guess I overdid it," she admitted.

The truth was, though, she felt ready to eat every bite, and probably would if Nancy and Mary Ellen didn't shame her out of it. Ever since the party Saturday, she'd been trying to eat her way out of a bottomless depression. Watching so many of her friends paired off and having a good time had made Angie ache all over again for Marc.

Angie prided herself on being a good sport. She would never stay away from a party just because she didn't have a date — or sulk, like Mary Ellen, because the guy she liked was ignoring her. But it often seemed to her that being a good sport didn't pay off the way it should. She'd been loyal to Marc all the time he was away at State, and what good had it done her? She still got dumped.

"So what's new?" Mary Ellen prompted, pulling Angie back from her private thoughts.

"Not much." She certainly didn't feel like talking about herself, so she ended up filling Mary Ellen and Nancy in on what Evie had told her that morning. "It's just typical of Evie that she would jump to conclusions," Angie added. "Just because poor Olivia felt under the weather in church. Naturally, it couldn't possibly be true. And think of the damage a rumor like that could do!"

"It sure could," Mary Ellen agreed. "The whole squad would suffer."

44

Angie was taken aback. It hadn't ever occurred to her to think about the squad.

"Of course it would be awful for Olivia, too," Mary Ellen added quickly.

"That's right," Angie agreed. "Anyway, I'm sure Olivia and Walt aren't even sleeping together. They haven't even been going together for very long."

"I'm sure you're right," Nancy said, a bit too quickly.

In her own mind, Nancy wondered whether how long you went with someone had anything to do with it. She wasn't sleeping with Josh, but that didn't mean that there hadn't been moments when she'd been seriously tempted.

Nancy waited until Angie had finished her food and left, before confiding her thoughts on the subject to Mary Ellen. "You know, Olivia and Walt would be just the types to let things get out of control and end up in trouble. Olivia is kind of naive about sex, and she's always trying to prove that she isn't. And Walt has never had a serious steady before . . . so it could be true."

Mary Ellen had to agree that sometimes Angie took too much for granted. What difference did it make if Walt and Olivia hadn't been going steady since junior high? She herself had gone out with guys for months and never felt seriously tempted. When she was with Patrick, though, she knew that if they ever stopped fighting for five minutes, they would get serious fast.

In fact, the whole subject made Mary Ellen

feel panicky. All weekend long she'd been brooding about Patrick and Mindy Norris. What if *they* ended up getting serious fast? Unless she made her move for Patrick right away, she might lose him forever. She had almost made up her mind to do something really decisive, like telling Patrick that she wanted to be his girl after all. Thinking about Olivia's situation — or at least, what Olivia's situation might be — was fast scaring her out of that impulse.

Mary Ellen was so caught up in her worries that when she ran into the real live Patrick Henley in the parking lot after school that day, she felt as if he must know what she'd been thinking about.

But of course, he had no idea. Following Mary Ellen out of the school building, Patrick had been concentrating on how sexy Mary Ellen's walk was, and how cute she looked in her waist-length aviator jacket with a long white silk scarf around her neck. He was trying hard to convince himself that he was interested in Mindy, but was not doing a real good job of it. Mary Ellen was the real thing; the tall peaches-and-cream blonde who was his idea of perfection. For the life of him, he would never understand why Mary Ellen worried so much about clothes, since she would always look a hundred times better than any other girl, no matter what she had on.

"Hey, Melon, wait up," he called.

Mary Ellen wheeled around as if she'd heard a shot. "Patrick!"

"In the flesh. Can I offer you a ride home in my chariot?"

Maybe it had something to do with the winter light, but silhouetted against the snow-covered parking lot and the dull gray afternoon sky, Patrick looked like a technicolor vision. His ruddy complexion and dark eyes made her heart melt with longing.

So Mary Ellen accepted the offer and found herself, minutes later, seated in the truck outside her own modest frame house, madly making out with the guy she'd been vowing to forget.

They kissed for minutes that seemed like hours, and when it was over Patrick made a little sound that was a sigh of mingled happiness and frustration. "Mary Ellen, you're the one for me," he whispered. "Mindy means nothing to me. Trust me."

"Trust you to do *what*?" she blurted out.

Patrick drew back, the mood shattered. "What do you mean, 'to do what?' To do anything . . . or nothing. Whatever."

"That's just typical, Patrick Henley. You want me to trust you, but you yourself don't know what you're talking about."

"Mary Ellen, come on. Cut this out."

"Why should I? And why do you get so defensive? Don't I have a right to know what you mean when you say things like that?"

"Sure. I guess. But I don't even know what we're arguing about —"

"Well I do," Mary Ellen said. And with that,

47

she jumped out of the truck cab and sprinted for the safety of her front door.

"There goes one crazy girl," Patrick muttered to himself as he sped away. "When will I ever learn?"

# CHAPTER

6

Olivia's mother would have been shocked if she had known what Evie Caird read into her conversation with her daughter after church. Mrs. Evans was worried, but she was convinced that Olivia's problems had a much simpler cause: Olivia was so busy worrying about cheerleading and that new boyfriend of hers that she was neglecting to take care of herself.

"Mother, I'm *fine*," Olivia kept insisting not very convincingly. "I just had an upset stomach. It could happen to anyone."

"That's true, it could," Mrs. Evans replied in her always-logical way. "But it doesn't. I, for example, haven't had an upset stomach in years."

"But you don't have someone hovering over you, constantly watching for symptoms," Olivia said.

"Don't talk back to your mother, dear," said

49

Mr. Evans automatically, between mouthfuls of something Mrs. Evans called "healthy meatloaf," a leaden concoction of ground meat and wheat germ glued together with a yogurt sauce.

If Mom served this stuff for breakfast, I'd know why I didn't feel good, Olivia thought sullenly. But no such luck. She'd been having her usual fruit juice and corn flakes every day.

"You've been so busy running around that you probably haven't even been taking your medicine."

"Mom, I have."

"It's bad enough that you insist on cavorting around like a jumping bean in that dusty gym. But you should at least take your medication regularly."

Sometimes Olivia felt that in her short lifetime she'd taken enough medicine to keep a whole hospital stocked for a century. As a child, Olivia had been constantly in and out of hospitals, going through heart operations, as well as what seemed an endless series of tests and procedures. Now she was fine . . . except for her mother.

"I *am* taking my medicine," Olivia repeated.

"So why are you sick?"

Exasperated, Olivia planted her fork in her meat loaf and noticed that the food was dense enough to hold the heavy utensil upright. "I am *not* sick, Mother. I was sick yesterday. Today, I'm fine."

"Leave the girl alone, Marcia."

Olivia's father so seldom interfered with her

and her mom's constant bickering, that Olivia was more stunned than grateful.

"I was just trying to be a concerned mother," Mrs. Evans sniffed. But she dropped the subject.

Later, in her room, Olivia took her little pillbox out of her nightstand drawer and examined the contents. For once, her mother may have been right. She had missed a few pills, and for that matter, she wasn't even entirely sure that she was taking enough of them. She thought Dr. Curry had told her to take one every evening, but the medicine was new and she wasn't really sure if he had said to take one pill in the morning *and* one at night. Unfortunately, she'd lost the prescription label that belonged with the original container. The pills were small, and there were an awful lot of them left, considering that she was supposed to see Dr. Curry again next week.

Vowing to be more conscientious in the future, Olivia stuffed the pillbox into her oversized hobo-style purse, so she'd be sure to have it with her in case she forgot her morning pill again.

At the Goldstein house across town, Nancy was also getting flack from her parents.

"I think it's admirable that you want to help Josh," Mr. Goldstein was saying, "but we never see you anymore. You're always in a rush."

"It's just for a few weeks, Dad."

"Well, at least relax and have dessert with us this evening," her father said. "Don't be in such a hurry."

In some homes, Nancy knew, everyone ate on the run and family members hardly talked from one day to the next. She'd always been glad that it wasn't that way in her home. Nancy was an only child, and her parents looked forward to spending time with her. And usually, though she felt a little ashamed to admit it, she enjoyed being with them.

The last few days, however, had been hectic. Between getting up at dawn to help Josh with his paper route, and cheerleading practice, and schoolwork, she'd had little time left over. Then on Saturday night, she'd gone to the Eismars' party with Josh, and she'd spent all day Sunday helping him fix his van — or, rather, handing Josh tools while he tinkered with the balky carburetor. Even tonight, it made her nervous to sit there eating her piece of sponge cake and making small talk, when she ought to be upstairs doing math homework so that she could get to bed at a decent hour.

Getting up at five A.M. didn't seem to be bothering Josh at all. As long as he got five hours of sleep at night he felt fine. But Nancy, after just three days of the routine, was dead on her feet. She'd nearly dozed off today in history class.

When she finally finished her dessert and helped her mother load the dishwasher, Nancy went upstairs to attack her homework. The math took twice as long as it should have, because she was so tired she could hardly concentrate. By the time she washed her hair and looked over her clothes for school the next day, it was midnight. Only five hours till wakeup time!

Nancy lay in bed, eyes wide open, worrying that she was going to sleep through her alarm the next morning. It was crazy. All day she'd been wishing she could curl up and take a nap, and now that bedtime was actually here she couldn't sleep!

When she finally did drop off, she dreamed that someone was in her bedroom, grabbing clothes out of her closet and throwing them on the bed, saying in a very disapproving voice, "That Nancy Goldstein is *so* spoiled." As the dream came into focus, she recognized her tormentor: Vanessa Barlow!

At five, when her clock radio switched on, Nancy woke up feeling furious with Vanessa. How dare she, of all people, call her spoiled! Nancy slowly opened her eyes and sat up. Her clothes were hanging in her closet as neatly as ever, but the bedcovers were a twisted mass. She'd been fighting an imaginary Vanessa all night.

Josh arrived in his van at five-thirty, looking disgustingly cheerful. He'd already picked up his cargo of papers from the distributor and stacked them into the back of the van. Grumbling hello, Nancy climbed into the passenger seat and sat in silence until they reached the beginning of the country road where the first customers lived.

The last several mornings they'd worked out a neat routine. Josh drove down the road close to the customers' roadside mailboxes, stopping just long enough for Nancy to reach out and stuff each paper into the box. They'd finished about half of this morning's papers when Nancy looked down and noticed that she'd forgotten to change into her old gloves. Her new camel-colored suede gloves were stained black with newsprint ink.

"Damn!" She felt so frustrated, she wanted to cry.

"Nancy, what's wrong?" Josh pulled over to the side of the road, his face filled with concern.

"Look." She held up both gloved hands for inspection. "They're ruined. Nothing will get all this gunk off, and it's all my fault."

Josh sighed with relief. "I'm sorry, but you sounded so upset I was afraid it was something really serious."

Josh had spoken too soon, however. The serious problem of the morning was still ahead of them. When he tried to get the van back into gear to continue the route, the engine let out a few feeble coughs and died.

"That stupid carburetor again!" Josh said, in the tone of voice a person might use for a favorite pet who'd done something naughty.

While Josh tinkered with the engine, Nancy sat in the front seat shivering and fuming with anger at the same time. "What'll we do if you can't get this thing started?" she shouted out the open window.

"Don't worry, it'll start," Josh assured her. "It may just take some time."

"That's fine for you," Nancy snapped back. "You have gym first period and you can always make up a class. But I stayed up last evening doing my math, and now I won't even get to turn it in. I might as well have left it to do today."

Josh put down his tools and crawled back into the van beside Nancy. "I'm sorry," he said again. "Maybe we should rethink what we're doing. I really appreciate you helping me like this. But the job is *my* responsibility. *My* problem. There's no reason for you to make yourself miserable trying to help me. I'll be fine, really."

Nancy burst into tears. Not because of anything Josh said, but because she was so tired her crying valve seemed to be broken.

"Nancy!" Josh pulled her close, and she buried her head inside his sheepskin jacket, feeling the warmth of his body.

"But there *is* a reason," Nancy mumbled. "To show you I'm not as spoiled as you think."

"What?"

Nancy sat up and repeated what she'd said.

Josh looked incredulous. "Spoiled? Who said you were?"

"You for one."

"I did?"

Nancy reminded him of the conversation they'd had when he first told her about the job.

"Okay," Josh conceded. "Maybe I did say

that. But I didn't mean it seriously. I was just teasing. I like you just the way you are, Nancy. Or were, before you started on this sleep deprivation kick."

"But you were right," she protested. "It's true. I've never worked in my life. Never had a job."

"So what? You will soon enough. You don't have to prove anything to me."

One thing about Josh, Nancy thought, he knew how to be supportive. Some guys got really defensive when a girl started to show emotion, but not him. Seeing her cry had made the tears well up in his eyes in sympathy, and he wasn't even embarrassed. He must care about her.

Suddenly she started to feel very silly. "I'm sorry, Josh," she said, relief flooding over her.

"It's okay, it's okay." Josh kissed her tentatively on the cheek, then on the lips.

"But who else said you were spoiled?" he asked when they'd finished making up. "You said me, 'for one.'"

"Vanessa . . . but it was only a dream." Embarrassed, Nancy told him about her nightmare.

Josh laughed. "I guess you can't hold Vanessa responsible for what she does in your dreams. Seriously, though, you're the exact opposite of Vanessa. You care about your responsibilities. And you care about other people. Vanessa only cares about herself."

They were kissing again when a red Porsche came around the bend and pulled up beside them. "Whoa, there," Pres drawled in pretended concern. "All this mad passion at seven-thirty in the morning. Sex and lust on the delivery route. I'm not sure the citizens of Tarenton are ready for this."

"Are you here to criticize? Or would you like to lend us a hand with the van?" Josh asked unperturbed.

"I'd rather help with Nancy, but. . . . What's the problem?" Pres said, reverting to his normal voice.

After a brief consultation, Pres adjusted the carburetor while Josh started the engine. The van's engine made a few hungry, gulping noises, then shuddered into gear.

"I think it'll be all right now," Josh said. "If you don't mind, Pres, maybe you could take Nancy to school with you. There's no reason for both of us to be late."

Giving Josh a good-bye kiss for good measure, Nancy hopped into the passenger seat of the Porsche, and she and Pres drove off. Pres couldn't help thinking that Nancy looked more at home in his Porsche than in Josh's old van. Under her down coat she was wearing a fawn-colored cashmere turtleneck, and she had little ruby posts in her pierced ears. Tiny rubies, but no doubt real ones. Her dark hair was cut perfectly in a layered style that was chic and soft-looking at the same time. And for a girl who'd spent the last two hours delivering papers, she smelled terrific.

"White Shoulders," he said appreciatively.

"Huh?" Nancy seemed taken aback.

"Your cologne," he explained.

"That's right!" Nancy was amazed. "Can you really tell one cologne from another?"

"Every time," Pres said. "Some guys are geniuses at math. Some at football. I am a connoisseur of women."

And recently, Pres told himself, his greatest and only talent had been going unused. The old Pres would have been busy right this minute trying to figure out a way to put the moves on Nancy. That she was already going with Josh would only have made the challenge sweeter. Josh was okay, but Pres still hadn't forgotten that he was the guy who had almost replaced him on the cheerleading squad, when he was on probation over that tiff with his parents.

And surely, he thought, Kerry can't expect me to be a totally faithful. I'm only human. . . .

Pres began to wonder what Nancy would do if he moved his hand off the gear shift knob and onto her cute, shapely knee. . . .

"Pres!"

Nancy's exclamation made him start guiltily. Had he been thinking out loud?

But Nancy's attention was focused on a white envelope that she'd found on the floor of the car, when she'd bent down to fish a comb out of the purse she'd stashed under her seat. "Look! It's from Princeton. And it's never even been opened."

"Oh yeah," Pres said unenthusiastically. "That."

"But aren't you curious? I didn't know you were thinking about going to Princeton."

"I'm not thinking about it. My parents are."

"I don't get it," Nancy said.

"Princeton is a family tradition that has become obsolete, kind of like painting the founder's statue," Pres explained. "And that," he added, pointing to the offending envelope, "is no doubt a rejection letter. Not that I care. Believe me, I'm relieved. But the right moment to break the news to my folks has not yet arrived."

"Well, if you know what the letter says, then you won't mind if I open it," Nancy said.

Pres couldn't think of a reason to protest, so he drove on, scowling as Nancy did just that.

"I hate to disappoint you," Nancy said after she finished scanning the letter, "but it isn't a rejection at all."

"Don't tell me they accepted me!"

"Nope." Nancy shook her head. "They just want you to know that you didn't finish filling out the application. You forgot the essay on 'Why I want to attend Princeton.' "

"But I *don't* want to attend."

Nancy made a face. "You know that. I know that. But Princeton seems to have this crazy idea that you wouldn't bother to send in an application if you weren't interested in going there."

"Why don't they stop bugging me?" Pres said illogically as they pulled into the school parking lot. "Obviously, anyone who's too dumb to send in the essay in the first place doesn't belong at

Princeton." Pres grinned with pleasure at his own reasoning and strode off, whistling happily.

Nancy smiled to herself as she climbed out of the car and headed for her locker. That was classic Pres, all right. Anyone else would be worried about messing up on such an important application, but he thought the whole thing was a big joke. She couldn't help admiring Pres, in a way, but she could never be like that herself. And she was glad Josh wasn't like that, either.

# CHAPTER

"Who's playing for the faculty Saturday night?" Mary Ellen asked when the squad had gathered for Tuesday afternoon's practice session. "Karlsson and Marburg always do. But who else?"

"Maybe we should send a spy to their practice over at the 'Y,'" Walt suggested. "I'll volunteer. I could dress up as a janitor and pretend to be cleaning the floor."

Walt was half serious. Being a spy was one of his fantasies. Or a detective like Mike Hammer. His role as the class entertainer got boring sometimes. It might be more fun to be a tough guy.

"Sorry, Walt, but I don't think that's necessary," Angie said. "I already know that my cousin Tom is playing forward. It's supposed to be hush-hush, but his wife mentioned it to me by accident."

"Mr. Gaetano," Mary Ellen groaned.

"And what's wrong with my cousin?" Angie shot back.

"Nothing," Mary Ellen explained. "It's his name that creates problems. I thought it would be cute to make up some cheers using the faculty players' names. But it's impossible! *Nothing* rhymes with Gaetano. Or Karlsson, for that matter. Or Marburg."

"Just as well," Nancy mumbled. Mary Ellen's attempts to make up new cheers were always a total failure, in her opinion. Especially rhyming cheers.

"I heard that," Mary Ellen said, glaring at Nancy.

"Well, there's always Mr. Lutz," Angie interjected before the two could get their tempers up. "The phys. ed. student teacher. He's playing center."

"Good," Walt said brightly. "Lutz the Klutz, he's their man, if he can't mess up, no one can!"

Pres sank to his knees, pretending to gag.

"I hate to say it," Angie said, "but I think Pres is right. We're probably lucky the other names don't rhyme."

"Unfortunately," added Walt, "Lutz isn't such a klutz. He was all-state last year. And Mr. Gaetano isn't a bad player, either, for such an old guy."

"He's thirty," Angie put in.

"That's what I said," Walt added, shrugging off the remark. "What I mean is, the faculty team is usually pretty much of a joke. But this year I think Varsity is going to have to work to avoid being embarrassed. Maybe we should think less about clowning around, and more about practicing our regular routines."

"Good idea," said Olivia, who had been quiet so far. "I'm ready to work on the flip. How about it?"

Mary Ellen felt a stab of uncertainty. "I don't know," she said. "I was thinking about leaving that one till next week when the coach is back with us." She grinned awkwardly. "I'm such a lousy spotter."

"Ardith said it was okay for us to go ahead," Olivia insisted.

Mary Ellen looked to Nancy for support.

Nancy, confused, looked at Angie.

"What's gotten into you girls?" Pres complained. "I'm the one that risks getting knocked on the head in this one. Why are you all so chicken?"

"That's right," Walt insisted. "Come on. We're wasting time."

Mary Ellen wasn't sure whether to feel worried or ashamed. Obviously, what she'd been thinking about Olivia wasn't true. It was just ugly gossip. She should have realized that anyway. But if Walt, who ought to know, wanted Olivia to do the routine, there was obviously no problem. And now, by hesitating like that, she'd let it show that she wasn't sure there wasn't some truth to the story.

At the same time, she wished that this hadn't

come up during the one week that Coach Eng-borg wasn't around. She loved being captain of the squad, but sometimes she hated the responsibility that went with it.

Worried and at the same time annoyed at Olivia for putting her on the spot, Mary Ellen called out the letters of the "Go, Wolves!" cheer. At exactly the right moment, Olivia hit the springboard and sailed over Pres's head, landing with perfect balance.

"That a girl," Walt beamed.

The rest of the practice went pretty well. The squad practiced cartwheels and a fairly new move that involved Nancy and Angie standing on the guys' shoulders and then jumping down into their partners' arms in perfect synch.

Later, when Mary Ellen called a five-minute break, Walt disappeared into the supply closet and emerged carrying an old wolf suit that was used years ago by the football team's mascot. "It won't be as much fun as playing spy," he said to Mary Ellen. "But how's this for a funny routine? I can dress up in this suit and pretend to be a wolf, flirting with the women on the faculty cheering squad."

"Sounds pretty funny to me," Pres said. "Try on the suit."

Walt struggled into the outfit. "I think whoever wore this suit was a little bit shorter than I am."

"And *thinner*," everyone said in unison. The suit fit, but very snugly.

"It looks like the body of a teddy bear joined to the head of a wolf," Angie observed.

"I think he's cute," Olivia giggled.

"At last!" Walt joked, his voice booming out of the papier-mâché wolf's head. "I've been trying to get her to say that for weeks. Now at last I've figured out what turns her on."

"I think we've worked enough for today," Mary Ellen said when the laughter died down a little too soon. "Why don't we give ourselves a break and knock off early?"

While the others headed for the locker rooms, Walt pulled Angie Poletti aside. "Hey Ange, will you help me get out of this suit and put it away?" Walt asked.

Angie agreed, although feeling uneasily that Walt didn't really need the help. She was not too surprised, when they got into the supply room, to find out that she was about to be interrogated.

"You're my friend, Angie," Walt began. "So will you please tell me why everyone is acting so weird?"

"I don't know what you mean," Angie lied.

"You do to. It has something to do with me and Olivia, but I can't figure out what. Has my deodorant stopped working or something?" Walt, still dressed in the wolf suit, lifted a furry arm and sniffed tentatively.

Angie laughed. "Walt, it's nothing. There was this dumb story going around. But I know it isn't true. And so does everyone else."

"So tell me."

65

While Angie filled Walt in, he frowned and shook his head in amazement. "Poor Olivia! It's bad enough having the flu, without Evie Caird circulating nasty stories."

"She didn't exactly circulate it. It never got beyond the girls on the squad," Angie assured Walt.

Actually, Evie hadn't said anything to anyone but her. But Angie decided to leave out the little detail about her being the one to pass the story on to Nancy and Mary Ellen.

"Well, take my word for it, it isn't true," Walt insisted. "In fact, it couldn't be, much as I hate to admit it."

"I knew it all along," Angie added quickly. "That's what I told Nancy and Mary Ellen."

Walt laughed. "That's my girl," he said, tweaking an imaginary handlebar mustache. "I knew I could count on you to keep secret what a fast mover I really am."

Angie blushed. "You know what I mean. I didn't meant it *couldn't* be true. I just meant that it *wasn't* true."

"I know, Angie," Walt said. "And thanks. Anyway, its all history now. Just make sure Nancy and Mary Ellen get the message."

Walt decided not to mention the misunderstanding to Olivia when he drove her home after practice. After not being up to par for several days, Olivia seemed to be feeling all right again. Since she didn't seem to have noticed the awkward way the other girls acted during practice, he didn't see any reason to upset her by bringing the subject up.

"I can't wait until Saturday," Walt said, settling on the first topic that came to mind.

"The game should be pretty funny," Olivia said. "And I like the wolf suit idea."

"Oh, sure. But I was thinking about the party."

Walt had invited some friends over after the game. It was the first time he'd done that since the big party at his parents' house last month — the one that had almost split up him and Olivia. This time, however, he was going to make sure that nothing went wrong. He'd already promised Olivia that there would be just kids from school — none of his parents' friends — and absolutely no alcohol.

"I'm going to stop at the supermarket and stock up on soda pop and chips," Walt said. "Do you want to come with me?"

"I'd better go straight home," Olivia excused herself. "If you don't mind. I've got a lot to do."

"No problem."

It was only after he'd dropped Olivia off at her house and loaded up the jeep with party food that Walt began to wonder whether Olivia was feeling all right after all. She'd been unusually quiet during the ride, even for her. And since when had Olivia ever been eager to get home early? Not since he'd known her.

It was probably his fault for mentioning Saturday's party. Still, he couldn't stop having friends over for the rest of his life just because of one silly incident that had happened at his last party. He wasn't upset with Olivia anymore about that. And Boomer was a creep.

"Boomer," Walt said aloud. The name just seemed to hang there. *Boomer*.

It couldn't be. . . .

Was it possible that he'd been too fast to re-assure Angie? He knew that Olivia had seen Boomer at least once after the party. He'd run into the two of them that night at the pizza joint. What if they'd actually slept together? Boomer was in his midtwenties, and by reputation, a total snake where women were concerned. And Olivia. . . . He'd already seen that two drinks knocked Olivia out. Obviously Boomer knew it, too.

Walt wanted to kick himself. He'd acted so jealous after finding Olivia and Boomer kissing at that party . . . and so disgusted with Olivia for being dumb enough to let Boomer give her a drink. . . . If something had happened between Olivia and Boomer, it was a safe bet that she would never tell him about it.

The thing was, he wasn't angry with Olivia. He didn't even care that much what the other kids on the squad thought about him. All he cared about was Olivia, and whether she was all right.

As soon as he got home and unloaded the groceries, Walt bounded upstairs to his room and dialed the Evans' house. He got a busy signal. Fifteen minutes later he tried again, and the phone was still busy. After an hour and a half of calling at fifteen-minute intervals, Walt decided that someone must have taken the phone off the hook. Either that or someone was having a marathon phone conversation — something he was pretty sure Mrs. Evans would never allow.

Finally he decided to drive by Olivia's house, just to see if everything was all right. When he arrived, the family car was not in the driveway, but there was a light burning in Olivia's bedroom.

Walt rang the doorbell at least five times before giving up. He felt sure that Olivia was home alone and was just not answering the door. It's your own fault, Walt lectured himself on the lonely drive back home. If you hadn't been so busy worrying about your own bruised ego, maybe Olivia would be ready to confide in you.

So much for my tough guy pose, Walt thought. Angie was right. I'm really more the teddy bear type. A teddy bear in wolf's clothing.

He couldn't help wondering, though, how he was ever going to get the message through to Olivia that he was on her side. But what *was* her side? What was really wrong with Olivia? And how would he cope with what it might be?

# CHAPTER

8

The route Angie took out of gym after practice didn't normally take her past the school science labs. She was trying to tell herself that she had no particular reason to go this way tonight, but it was hard to ignore the way her heart beat just a little bit faster when she saw the light in the workroom that the astronomy club used for its meetings. Sure enough, when she just happened to glance through the open door on her way past, there was Arne Peterson, bent over one of the work benches, his long legs wrapped around the high stool he was sitting on.

"Hi," Angie ventured.

"Oh hi, Angie."

"Having fun?" Angie no sooner said the words, than she wanted to call them back. Would Arne think she was being sarcastic?

"Not really. You couldn't exactly call grinding a lens fun."

"Then why do you do it?" Angie asked.

"Because I want to have a better telescope than I can afford to buy," Arne explained.

"Actually," he amended, "that's only half the reason. I guess I just like making things. I want to prove to myself that I can do it. Come on in, I'll show you what I'm working on."

Angie didn't understand three quarters of what Arne had to say about building a telescope, but she loved listening to his velvety voice. She would gladly have stood there and listened to him count the bricks in the wall.

"It's hard to describe what the finished scope will look like," Arne said finally. "If you could see the one I have at home, you'd get a better idea. It's much smaller than this one will be, but you can still see a lot of things that you can't see with the naked eye."

When he'd finished discussing telescopes, Arne seemed to run out of conversation pretty quickly. "I like your uniform," he said, indicating the red and white cheerleading outfit that Angie was still wearing. "My family isn't big on spectator sports, so I never got into the habit of going to games."

"That's okay," said Angie.

Actually, she was almost shocked. Sports and school spirit meant a lot to Angie. And she had several older cousins who'd played for Tarenton teams, so she'd been going to games since she was in grade school. She knew there were kids in school who didn't pay any attention to that kind of thing. But it was hard for her to picture herself being all that interested in someone who had never so much as attended a single game.

"I'll have to come out to see a basketball game sometime," Arne mused, as if it were a totally novel thought. "I'd like to see you cheer."

It suddenly occurred to Angie that this was the perfect opportunity for her to suggest that Arne come to the game on Saturday. She could even ask him to come with her to Walt's party afterwards.

Angie wouldn't normally have considered asking a boy out on a date. Especially a first date. Not that she disapproved, but she just wasn't the type to feel confident about making the first move. This time, she almost felt as if Arne was hinting that he wanted to be asked. But what if she was wrong?

The next thought that crossed Angie's mind was even more bothersome. What if Arne didn't fit in with Walt and her other friends? What if the kids on the squad thought she was only going out with Arne because she was lonely — and desperate to be dating someone again? What if Arne thought that?

The barrage of doubts made her chicken out. "You really ought to go to the games and support the team," she said. But what had almost been an invitation came out sounding like a lecture, instead.

"Yeah," Arne agreed, his voice gone flat. "I probably should. But I guess the team will manage without me."

When she got home, Angie had a quick dinner, put a load of laundry in the washing machine, and plopped down in the living room to watch TV.

"Anything good on?" her brother Andrew asked as he passed through on the way to his room.

"There's *The A-Team*," Angie began, and automatically ran down the evening schedule of the three major networks, throwing the local independent station in for good measure.

Andrew whistled in amazement. "With you in the house, we don't need *TV Guide*," he said. "But I think I'll skip it all and go over to Donny's to read his cycle magazines."

When he'd gone, Angie felt disgusted with herself. This was her senior year in high school, supposedly one of the most exciting times in a girl's life. Not that she hadn't had good times, but she'd spent an awful lot of evenings at home in front of the TV, too. At first, it had been because Marc was away at school. Then, she'd been trying to get over him.

Mom's right, she thought. It's time I closed the book on Marc once and for all.

Switching off the TV, she wondered what Arne was doing tonight. As she mentally played back their conversation from this afternoon, she realized that Arne's mention of going to a game hadn't been the first time he'd hinted at a date. He'd been about to ask her over to his house to see his telescope, but she'd acted bored with the whole subject. Actually, she *didn't* care much about telescopes. But what did she have to lose? Anything would be more interesting than sitting home in front of the tube.

Once Angie got up the nerve to call Arne's house, the rest was easy. All she had to do was mention that she just might be interested in coming over, and suddenly it was all arranged. Arne picked her up in his little Japanese car less than half an hour later.

The Peterson house was a big old frame structure set on a hill, with a view overlooking Narrow Brook Lake. Angie was about to say how peaceful the setting looked, when she noticed that there were five cars already in the driveway. "I didn't realize you had company," she said worriedly. "Maybe this isn't a good time for me to visit."

"We don't have company," Arne said a bit mysteriously. "If you think five cars is a crowd, just wait till you see the inside of the house."

Arne led the way in through the closed-in porch to the living room. "Well, this is it," he announced.

The house looked like a combination library and sporting goods store. There were books and papers piled everywhere, a glass-front case with fishing rods on the living room wall, cross-country skis stacked in the kitchen, assorted plaid hunting jackets, and boots and briefcases strewn about. Arne let out a deep throaty laugh. It was the first time Angie had ever heard him laugh wholeheartedly about anything.

"I'm sorry," he said when he finally managed to compose himself. "I was just thinking about how all this must look to you. Your place is so neat all the time."

"That's all right," Angie said. "It's kind of cozy here." And at second glance, it was. Under the surface clutter, the house was basically clean and comfortable. A large cast iron stove stood in the living room, the fire inside visible through an open grate. The furniture consisted of well worn but inviting oversized easy chairs, and a sofa with walnut legs and burgundy velvet upholstery, which was probably an antique.

"My parents have been divorced for years, and just my father and my four brothers live here. None of us is that crazy about housework."

"I'm sorry," said Angie. "I mean, about your parents being divorced. Not that you don't love housework."

"Oh, that was a long time ago," Arne said. "My dad and my oldest brother are in the upstairs study, working on a report. They're both geologists. You probably know my youngest brother, Charley. He's a freshman at school. And this is Alex. Arne pointed to a picture of an

75

older, bearded copy of himself, dressed in climbing gear and standing on what appeared to be the summit of a mountain.

"That was taken on Mount Rainier," Arne explained. "Everyone in my family seems to be involved with rocks in one way or another. I guess that's why I decided to go in for astronomy. *Someone* needs to concentrate on what's overhead." Arne looked a bit embarassed at what was obviously an often repeated family joke.

"The telescope's out here on the porch," he added. "Better keep your coat on."

At first, Angie couldn't see anything but her own eyelashes when she tried peering into the telescope, but gradually her eyes adjusted and Arne pointed out Jupiter and some of the constellations.

"I thought all stars looked alike," Angie said. "But they don't. I can see they're different colors."

"That's right," Arne said, explaining a little about white giants and red dwarfs.

It wasn't as boring as Angie had expected it to be. The sky around Narrow Brook Lake was usually pretty clear. It wasn't like living in the city where you can hardly ever see stars. But somehow, she'd always taken that for granted. Looking through the telescope, with Arne's arm around her shoulders — comfortably, as if it very much belonged there — Angie felt overcome by the strangeness and wonder of the night sky. "It's all so far away," she said.

"I guess so," answered Arne, misinterpreting

her comment. "You can't really see too much from here. But someday I'd like to go into space and take pictures of Earth from out there. That would be neat."

They stayed on the porch with the telescope for a little while longer, but it was so cold outside that even with her coat on Angie began to shiver.

"Would you like to stop for a slice of pizza on the way home?" Arne asked. "I had dinner a while ago, but I'm usually ready for a second go round about now."

They stopped at a pizza place near the north end of the lake, not the usual high school hang-out in town, and each had two slices of pizza with anchovies.

"Well, that's one thing we have in common," said Arne, polishing off his second slice.

"That's right," Angie laughed. "A lot of kids don't like anchovies. And if you don't like them, you can't stand them."

"Oh, right," he agreed. "But I meant food. It seems to me a lot of girls don't eat at all."

"I shouldn't eat at all," Angie said guiltily. "I just can't help myself."

"But you look great. You can handle it because you work out."

"Ugh! Exercise! I'm the lazy type."

Arne looked at her in surprise. "But you work out. You run. I've seen you in the mornings, running up by the park."

Angie flushed. She'd been caught. "I run once in a while," she admitted reluctantly.

Arne shook his head in amusement. "For a cheerleader, you certainly don't do much cheering for yourself. To hear you talk, you're lazy, dumb, no good at math — all kinds of things you really aren't."

"Then what am I?" Angie asked defensively.

"I told you the other day." Arne reached across the table and put his large hand over hers. "I think you're the romantic type."

Angie would always wonder what she and Arne would have said next if their attention hadn't been distracted at just that moment by the waitress, seating another couple at the table next to theirs.

Arne apparently knew the guy, and the two of them got into a brief conversation.

The female half of the couple took her seat facing Angie and immediately gave her and her companion a good once-over. "Why, Angie and Arne!" she gushed. "Isn't that sweet!"

"Hello, Vanessa," Angie replied. "What brings you out tonight? The full moon?"

"Now, now." Vanessa shook her mane of dark hair and studied the menu while she waited for her date to return his attention to her.

Their privacy gone, Angie and Arne paid the check and left almost immediately.

"Who was that guy with Vanessa?" Angie asked as they walked to Arne's car. "He looked familiar, but I couldn't quite place him."

"That was Ron Lutz," Arne said.

"You mean *the* Mr. Lutz who's a student teacher at school?"

"The same."

"I bet Vanessa's father doesn't know she's dating a student teacher," Angie mused. "That's strictly against the school rules. Even if he is just a first year graduate student, I'm sure he still counts as faculty, technically."

"I'm sure there are a lot of things about Vanessa that her father doesn't know," Arne said in a voice that indicated he might know at least a few of them.

"But don't spread the word about this, Angie. Okay?" he added. "Ron Lutz is a nice guy, and I wouldn't want to get him in any trouble. Vanessa has been chasing him for weeks and I guess he finally broke down and invited her out. But I have a feeling his interest in her won't last very long."

Angie promised, and they drove back to her house in silence, enjoying each other's company without feeling any pressure to keep up the small talk. But when they pulled into Angie's driveway, Arne seemed overcome by his old, shy self. He said good-bye quickly, giving Angie a peck on the cheek that hardly counted as a kiss at all.

The next morning, she was almost suspicious that some of the things she remembered Arne saying must have been in her imagination. Arne Peterson, the math grind, talking about romance? Never!

She had practically convinced herself that her

memories of the evening were at least partly self-delusion, when she got to school and opened her locker to hang up her coat.

There, neatly taped inside her locker door, was a single pink rosebud.

# CHAPTER

Vanessa knew. Vanessa had seen her with Boomer before Walt had, before Olivia ever remembered anything.

The thought had been preoccupying Olivia for days. Aside from Boomer, whom she didn't dare face and never wanted to see again, Vanessa Barlow was the only person in the whole world who knew what had happened in the Manners' spare bedroom the night of the party. True, Vanessa might not be a very nice person, but she was a girl. Surely, for the sake of female solidarity, Vanessa would tell her the truth once she understood how important it was.

During practice on Tuesday Olivia had felt sure that the other girls were already acting as if they suspected something was wrong. Even Walt had seemed strange in the jeep driving her home. Being with Walt and not telling him the truth about what was on her mind was, in some ways, the hardest part of this whole messy situation, Olivia thought. She cared so much for him it drove her crazy to see the hurt look on his face when he knew he was being shut out.

In fact, it was so hard lying to Walt — or rather, not telling him the whole truth — that Olivia had promised herself that she would avoid him, at least until she could confront Vanessa and clear up her confusion. On Tuesday evening, she had called the Barlow house at least six times, always without giving her name. But Vanessa's mother had said that her daughter was out at her girl friend Tricia's house. And naturally, when she'd called Tricia's number, whoever answered the phone claimed Vanessa wasn't around. Sure this was a lie, Olivia had even sneaked out to check, only to find out that it was true. Tricia had been home alone watching a concert on cable TV, and insisted that she hadn't seen Vanessa in days.

Tonight, Wednesday, Olivia felt sure she was going to have better luck. Unable to face Walt, she'd stayed home from school all day, telling her mother she had an upset stomach — which had actually been true, at least at eight o'clock that morning. And when she'd called the Barlows' house after school, Mrs. Barlow, who seemed used to fielding anonymous queries about Vanessa's whereabouts, had told her that Vanessa had taken her car into town to go shopping and catch an early movie at the Tarenton Theater.

Fortunately, Olivia's mother did volunteer work at the hospital on Wednesday nights. Her father was downstairs, in the little room off the living room that he grandly called the den. But Olivia had seen him take a mystery novel in there after dinner, and when her father read mysteries the house could burn down around him without him missing a page.

Taking no chances, Olivia carefully unhitched the storm window in her bedroom and dropped her parka, scarf, and gloves out onto the hedges below. That way, she could go downstairs in her regular clothes and claim to be getting a snack in the kitchen if her father heard her.

As it turned out, the ruse was unnecessary. There was no sound coming from the den except the music of her father's favorite jazz program on the public radio station. Olivia let herself out the kitchen door, and ran to the hedges to retrieve her outdoor gear. Then she sprinted to the bus stop at the end of the block, just in time to catch the half-hourly bus that ran to the town center.

Fifteen minutes later she was outside the theater, stomping her feet and clapping her mittened hands to keep warm while she waited for the six o'clock show to end. The film, she noted with dismay, was called *Valentine's Day Victim*. JUST A HEARTBEAT AWAY FROM HORROR!!! screamed the posters displayed outside by the ticket booth. And judging by the full color stills featured in the preview case, the movie was as gory as it sounded.

Olivia made a face. She didn't care much for blood and gore movies to begin with. She'd been too close to blood and cutting when she had her own operations to consider the subject thrilling. But it was even harder for her to imagine wanting to go to this kind of movie by yourself! Trust Vanessa to do something that strange.

Olivia had even begun to wonder whether Vanessa was really at the movie . . . or really alone. But when the film let out, Vanessa emerged on schedule, and very much by herself. She was wearing jeans and a parka and, for Vanessa, hardly any makeup — just the mascara and ounces of eyeshadow that she was never, ever seen without.

"Vanessa, can I talk to you for a second?" Olivia hailed her.

"Well, hello, Olivia," Vanessa purred, her eyes automatically darting around to see if Olivia was with a guy who might be observing her without her full makeup on.

"It's really important, or I wouldn't bother you. . . ." Olivia began.

Unfortunately, she had concentrated so hard on finding Vanessa, that she hadn't given much thought to what she would actually say once she was face-to-face with her. She felt completely tongue-tied.

"Well, what do you want?" Vanessa asked, none too sympathetically.

"Uh, the th-th-thing is . . ." Olivia stuttered, ". . . well, you know how it is when you're with an older guy. Sometimes things get out of hand. And I guess it's possible to do things you don't really know you're doing. And I was wondering if you could just tell me . . . I mean, really. . . ."

Vanessa's eyes looked as if they were about to strike sparks. "What are you talking about, Olivia Evans?" Vanessa challenged. "I suppose that Angie Poletti has been giving you an earful?"

"Angie?" Olivia said, confused. "Angie has nothing to do with it. I just want to know what happened. You know . . . the night of the party."

A calculating expression crossed Vanessa's face.

"You figure it out," Vanessa said and sailed toward the parking lot and Mrs. Barlow's Cadillac.

Feeling ridiculous and dejected, Olivia caught the next bus back to her neighborhood and sneaked back into her house through the kitchen door. She was no sooner inside than she heard her dad calling her name. Quickly hanging her coat on the peg by the steps to the basement, she opened the refrigerator door and pretended to be studying the contents of the vegetable compartment. "I was just looking for something to nibble on, Dad," she said as her father came into the kitchen.

"That's good, dear," Mr. Evans answered distractedly. "Glad to see you're feeling better."

Olivia selected an orange from the bin and turned around, hoping her dad wouldn't notice that her cheeks were still flushed from the cold.

Lucky for me, Olivia thought, Dad doesn't notice much. Ever since Olivia was a child he had seemed almost to avoid getting involved with her daily problems, abdicating the whole responsibility for his fragile daughter to his wife.

"You'd better call that boyfriend of yours soon," Mr. Evans said, as he turned to head back to his study. He's been calling here all evening for you. I *told* him you were asleep."

Olivia spun around and watched her father's back disappearing into the study. Was she crazy, or had there been a hint in his voice that he knew very well that she'd been out of the house? Was it possible that he was covering for her?

The questions at least helped Olivia to keep her mind off her own problems for the rest of the evening. She hadn't any idea what she'd do, now that talking to Vanessa hadn't worked. All she did know for sure was that she was going to have to go back to school tomorrow. She couldn't fake being sick two days in a row, without having her mother get worried enough to drag her off to the doctor. Somehow, she'd just have to manage to get through the day without spending any time alone with Walt.

Although they missed seeing Olivia, Patrick and Mindy had been to the same early show of *Valentine's Day Victim* that Vanessa had seen. Both horror movie fans, they had agreed that the movie was all right. Otherwise, though, their date was not going well.

86

"You've been acting like an old stick in the mud all evening," Mindy pouted as Patrick drove her home. "I don't know what's wrong with you."

"Nothing's wrong," Patrick said, telling a white lie. "Can't a guy be in a quiet mood for once?"

Mindy made a sour face, which indicated she did not expect guys to have quiet moods when they were supposed to be entertaining her.

Patrick concentrated on his driving, meanwhile debating the question of whether Mindy owed her auburn hair to genes or to a good henna job. Her hair looked good, but Mindy's complexion was a bit too sallow for a natural redhead. The combination made her look attractive but slightly decadent, like one of those shady ladies in a forties mystery movie who pretends to be a helpless victim when she is really the killer all along.

Actually, the comparison was turning out to be fairly accurate, Patrick decided. When he met her at the party on Saturday, Mindy had acted shy and sweet, if perhaps not awfully bright. Now, as their second date was coming to a close, he was finally figuring out that Mindy was anything but helpless. As long as she was the focus of attention, Mindy was fun. But when there was a hint that she might not be the center of the universe, she could turn nasty in a second.

Why do I have such terrible luck with women? Patrick asked himself silently.

If he'd thought about it a little longer, at least part of the answer might have come to him. He had only paid attention to Mindy in the first place because he thought that with her dramatic looks, Mindy would be sure to arouse Mary Ellen's jealousy. Now that the strategy had failed and Mary Ellen was down on his case again, he'd ended up going out with someone he'd chosen for all the wrong reasons.

"You're brooding," Mindy accused again. "I know you've got some other girl on your mind. And I know who it is, too. It's that cheap looking brunette we saw in the movie theater."

"Vanessa," Patrick said automatically.

"That's right. Vanessa."

"It isn't *her*," he insisted, not realizing he'd just denied that he was thinking about any other girl at all.

"You can't fool me," Mindy insisted.

Patrick decided to take the easy way out. "Okay, I can't. You win. I'm crazy about Vanessa. I thought you would make me forget her, but it hasn't worked. Sorry."

A few minutes later, Patrick deposited Mindy at her front door and drove off, feeling sorry for himself.

Mindy, meanwhile, was wasting no energy on self-pity. She was already trying to figure out what she could do to win Patrick back from her brunette rival.

# CHAPTER

 10

It was Thursday evening and Pres had been sitting in front of the typewriter for at least an hour, staring at the sheet of paper that contained his attempt to write the essay on "Why I want to go to Princeton."

Pres had written:

> Attendance at Princeton is a Tilford family tradition. My father went to your school, and he would be very happy to see me follow in his footsteps — for once. My girl friend Kerry would be happy because she likes guys who set goals and work to carry through on them. My mother would be happy, too. I, Pres Tilford III, would not necessarily be happy.

On the other hand, I have no idea what would make me happy. Sometimes I think I would like to travel around the country for a year or so after graduation. Maybe be a ski bum at Aspen. Or try to learn how to surf. If I did that, though, I would probably find myself missing Tarenton. I know I would miss Kerry. Part of me would be happy to stay right here in my hometown forever. But then I will get sucked into working for my father's company, Tarenton Fabricators, which I know I would hate.

So, all things considered, I am not that fired up about the idea of going to Princeton. But I don't think I would dislike being a Princeton student any more than I would dislike the other alternatives open to me.

Pres reread the statement for about the twentieth time, wondering what the reaction to it would be at the Princeton admissions office, if he actually had the nerve to put it in the mail to them. Admissions officers probably weren't used to that much honesty. The poor jerk who read the statement might end up having a heart attack or a stroke, and then he'd be responsible.

The wastebasket beside Pres's desk was stuffed full of essay drafts he'd tossed away. Any one of them, Pres knew, would be more likely to please the Princeton admission office than this one. Honesty was definitely not the best policy when it came to dealing with the adult world. Although he'd never been the world's greatest student, Pres wasn't a Tilford for nothing. He knew how to write and say the kinds of things that colleges wanted to hear — lines about how he'd like to broaden his intellectual horizons, and prepare himself for a career as a socially responsible businessman.

In disgust, Pres turned off the power on the electric typewriter, leaving the paper where it was. Reaching for the push-button extension phone on his desk, he dialed the number of the Elliot house. "Hey, Kerry," he said. "Can you get out for a little while? I need some fresh air. I've got a case of claustrophobia from sitting around this house."

After driving around the lake for a while as Pres let off steam, he and Kerry ended up stopping in Burger Benny's at the mall. There they ran into Josh and Nancy.

Although Pres would have rather been alone with Kerry, she immediately accepted Nancy's invitation to share their booth. "What's up?" she asked.

Nancy explained that Josh — who looked as fresh and energetic as ever — had just come from his gymnastics class. "In the meantime," Nancy said, "I'm only just beginning to feel human

91

again." She explained to Kerry that she'd given up helping with the paper route after her discussion with Josh on Tuesday morning. "Working at the crack of dawn is just not for me," she laughed. "I'm a night person, basically, and so are my parents. It has something to do with our biological clocks."

"Looks to me as if your biological clock is running fine." It was the kind of crack Pres couldn't resist making, even in the presence of Kerry and Josh. He wasn't sure whether it was a good sign or not that Kerry, instead of looking jealous, merely groaned in mock agony at the bad joke.

"Do you know what else he said this evening?" Kerry told Josh. "He said that he felt *claustrophobic* sitting around his house! Can you believe it? You could put all three of our houses inside the Tilford place and still have room left over."

Pres, who might have been upset if anyone but Kerry made a remark like that, merely looked guilty. "There's more than one cause of claustrophobia," he said.

"That reminds me," Nancy wondered, "what did you decide to do about that letter from Princeton?"

"Oh, nothing much," Pres mumbled, hoping to quickly move the conversation on to another subject.

But Kerry was too sharp to fool that way. She knew him too well. "What letter?" she asked.

"You didn't tell me that you had heard anything from Princeton."

"Well, it's no big deal," Pres said uneasily. "They just wanted some more information."

"Which Pres may or may not give them," Nancy joked. "You should have heard him, Kerry. Anyone else would be nervous about getting accepted. Pres's attitude is 'take me or leave me.' "

Kerry listened, pretending to be amused, as Nancy outlined in detail her conversation with Pres that morning in the car. In spite of the polite smile on Kerry's face, however, Pres knew there'd be a moment of reckoning as soon as they were alone together.

And he was right. No sooner had Nancy and Josh left than Kerry confronted him. "Why didn't you tell me about all of this?" she asked, obviously hurt.

"I don't know," Pres answered inadequately. "I figured I'd deal with it myself."

"Of course, you'll deal with it yourself. That isn't the point. It's just that I thought you cared enough about me to share your problems with me. I don't want to be just another girl you hang around with when you want a good time. I thought our relationship went deeper than that."

"Kerry, give me a *break*," Pres pleaded. "I do feel that way about you. I'm just not ready to discuss this yet."

"Apparently," Kerry said, uncharacteristically

huffy. "But explain to me one thing: If you don't want to go to this school, then why apply at all? Don't tell me it's because you don't have the nerve to face your own parents!"

"First you want to hear about it. Then you say, 'Don't tell me it's because, . . .'" Pres shot back. "So what am I supposed to do?"

"I'm sorry," Kerry apologized. "But you've had plenty of fights with your folks in the past. Why are you suddenly avoiding this confrontation?"

"Because," Pres explained, "I don't know what I want. It'd be easier to tell Mom and Dad I don't want to go to Princeton because I have some other plan in mind. It's a lot harder to argue when you've got *no* plan. Sometimes even *I* think I'm just being negative. That's one reason I didn't want to talk about it with you. Especially after hearing you say how much you admired people who know what they want."

"Oh oh. I did say that, didn't I." Kerry looked caught. "But I didn't mean it as a put down of you. I don't know what I want to do with the rest of my life, either. And I probably wouldn't be comfortable with someone who was never in doubt. It's easy to admire people like that from a distance. But I'm not one of them. And I'm sort of glad you're not, either."

"You are?" Pres was astounded. Not so much at Kerry's words as at the way her big eyes had filled with tears as she spoke. The girl really cared about him.

Kerry was not the most beautiful girl he'd ever dated. Not by a long shot. And certainly not the best dresser. She had come out for their drive tonight in a pair of well-worn corduroys, clean and pressed but still a bit baggy in the knees and seat; a Tarenton High sweatshirt under her coat; and a pair of blue and silver running shoes that she wore all the time. Kerry would never be a fashion plate, and he could see why his folks did not quite approve of her. She was definitely not the country club type.

Yet Kerry was the first girl he had known who cared about *him*. Not about his name. Not about his family's position in the town. Kerry, Pres thought ruefully, was not even that interested in the fact that he was a hunk. She liked him for his inner self — a self she seemed to see more clearly than even Pres did at times.

What did I do to deserve a girl like this? Pres wondered. *Nothing*, came the answer. He had just hit it lucky. Now all he had to do was to avoid doing something stupid that would drive her away.

"I'm sorry I didn't tell you," Pres apologized, drawing Kerry close and kissing her.

"Pres!" Kerry protested. "Not here! Not where everyone can see!"

Pres looked up, realizing that his demonstration had attracted the attention of the other Burger Benny customers. A group of grade school girls in the next booth had actually stopped squabbling with their mothers long enough to study the scene with giggly interest.

"Okay then," Pres said, unembarrassed but understanding Kerry's feelings. "In that case, let's go somewhere else."

On their way out of the restaurant, they ran into Mary Ellen Kirkwood and her little sister Gemma, arms loaded with packages. They stopped just long enough to say hi before heading out to the car.

"Sometimes," said Pres, as they drove toward their favorite spot along the scenic shore of the lake, "I wish that we were the only two people living on this lake. It must have been nice during pioneer times. People got married young in those days. And then they built themselves a house in the woods where their nearest neighbor was miles away."

"And their parents were miles away, too." Kerry added, picking up on Pres's thought.

"Right," said Pres. And this time, his attempt to kiss Kerry was not interrupted.

When he got back home later that evening, however, reality came washing back over him like a tidal wave.

His father greeted him at the foot of the stairs, waving the paper containing Pres's last attempt at an essay. "Is this yours?" he asked accusingly.

"Of course it's mine." Pres bristled. "It was in my room. On *my* desk. In *my* typewriter. Naturally it's mine. The question is, What is it doing in *your* hand?"

"Don't get smart with me young man," his father said angrily. "Your mother went in your room to pick up your laundry, which she wouldn't have to do if you'd left it in the hamper for Lucy to take care of the way you're supposed to. And naturally, she was curious when she saw mail from Princeton on your desk."

"Naturally," Pres said, too tired to fight over what still seemed to him to be an outrageous invasion of his privacy.

"I certainly hope you weren't planning to submit this," his father pushed on.

"Planning? I don't have any particular plans," Pres said too honestly.

"Well, young man, I'll give you until Saturday to write a suitable essay, and I want to look it over before it's mailed. Is that too much to ask? Just a few paragraphs?

"And don't worry about the rest. I've already contacted the head of the alumni committee to discuss your case personally. He was in my class. An old football buddy. I think that Princeton will overlook any shortcomings in your record, if they realize that I am considering making an appropriate gift to the scholarship fund."

"A little bribe, huh, Dad?" Pres said sarcastically. "Think you can get away with that?"

"I don't know," Mr. Tilford glowered. "I wouldn't have to try, though, if you bothered to look out for your own interests. What exactly do you expect to be doing next year at this time,

97

if I don't pull some strings to get you into a decent college?"

Pres shrugged. "Who knows?" He reached for the possibility that would needle his Dad most effectively. "Sometimes," he said with forced brightness, "I think I'd be happy hauling garbage for Henley Trash. I could be another Patrick Henley."

"You've got a lot to learn," his father glowered. "Did it ever occur to you that Patrick Henley wouldn't be hauling trash if his father didn't own the company?"

As a matter of fact, Pres had never thought about it quite that way. He wasn't the only kid in town whose future was being determined by who his parents were, after all. Maybe he should just give up fighting fate.

Tired and confused, he took the piece of paper from his father's outstretched hand and headed for his room.

"Saturday afternoon," his dad reminded him. "We'll discuss this further then."

Pres went up to his room and stretched out on the bed. He thought of calling Kerry for consolation, but didn't. Instead, he thought about calling Vanessa or Mary Ellen or any girl to hold and kiss and not worry about going too far. Finally, he fell asleep.

# CHAPTER

11

$M$ary Ellen had taken Gemma out to the mall to help her buy some art supplies for a school project. Gemma's class was building a model robot and Gemma had ended up chairman of the committee that was putting together the robot's body out of plastic, assorted hardware, and painted papier mâché.

Normally, canvassing hardware stores and art supply outlets was not Mary Ellen's idea of a fun shopping trip. This was the third trip she'd made with Gemma over the last several weeks, too. But at least they'd taken care of most of the basic materials and now they were down to the more creative part of the project. Gemma, after long deliberation, purchased two tea strainers to use for the robot's eyes, and Mary Ellen bought some hardware that would fasten them securely to the robot's head.

After picking up a few more last minute items on Gemma's list, they decided they could make a quick stop for a snack at Burger Benny's and still have time left over to window-shop the boutiques.

Some people have hobbies that give them a lift when they're depressed. Some exercise. Some eat. Mary Ellen window-shopped. No matter how bad things might be going with her life, surveying the latest arrivals at the stores and imagining how they would look on her — even if she couldn't always afford to buy — was guaranteed to raise her spirits.

Mary Ellen and Gemma were examining some new fake snakeskin purses at Luxe Leathers when they ran into Nancy and Josh on the upper mezzanine.

"It seems like we all had the same idea this evening," Nancy said, greeting them. "Did you see Pres and Kerry? They're around somewhere, too."

"We saw them in Benny's," Mary Ellen began.

". . . but they were too busy to talk," Gemma finished. "They're in love," she said, rolling her eyes and hugging herself, in case Nancy and Josh failed to get the idea.

"I hope they still are," Josh joked.

"That's right," Nancy said. "I'm afraid I may have put my foot in my mouth." She explained how she'd brought up the subject of Princeton, not realizing that Kerry knew nothing about it.

"All we need is for Pres to have problems, too,"

Mary Ellen said, the good mood generated by her shopping excursion quickly slipping away.

Mary Ellen considered mentioning that Nancy had seemed half asleep during the last two practices. But the problem seemed to be solved now so, tactfully, she passed on to the real problems on the squad. "And who knows *what*'s going on with Olivia and Walt. Olivia was back in school today, but she managed to do an invisible woman act every time I tried to talk to her. She's even been avoiding coming to lunch. And Walt isn't himself, either. It's weird."

"Olivia hasn't been feeling well, that's all," Nancy said. "There's nothing to those suspicions that Evie had. Angie talked to Walt, and he said so."

Nancy considered this. Angie was Walt's best friend on the squad. She couldn't picture him lying to her. On the other hand. . . .

"So why don't you talk to Olivia, Mary Ellen?" Nancy suggested. "You're the squad captain."

"I'm a captain, not a den mother," Mary Ellen snapped. "Besides," she added more reasonably, "I just can't see Olivia confiding in me. We've never been that close."

"Well, Olivia and *I* certainly aren't close," Nancy said, recalling how they'd practically had it out with each other when they both had crushes on the same guy: dumb Jimmy Hilbert, who'd hardly been worth all the fuss.

Mary Ellen and Nancy exchanged looks. No one on the squad was close to Olivia, except of course for Walt. In fact, neither of them could think of any girls who were close enough to Olivia to share really personal confidences.

"Face it," Mary Ellen said. "Olivia is a loner. I guess she likes it that way. We can't force her to talk to us if she doesn't want to."

As if Mary Ellen didn't have enough problems, on Friday morning there was a notice in homeroom, asking her to report to Mrs. Oetjen's office before her first period class.

When she presented herself at the door of the principal's inner sanctum, she found Mrs. Oetjen with Superintendent Barlow, who was waiting to talk to her.

"I can't help feeling," Dr. Barlow said, launching into the heart of his accusation, "that you must have some notion of who is responsible for defacing the statue of our founder, Hubert Tarenton."

"Me! Why me?"

"Because you are the captain of the cheerleading squad," Dr. Barlow suggested, as if this were some suspicious secret he'd unearthed and was confronting Mary Ellen with for the first time.

"Of course, but what—" Mary Ellen sputtered.

"I understand that school spirit can get out of hand," Dr. Barlow went on, oblivious to Mary Ellen's protests of innocence. "If you make a full confession, I'm sure Mrs. Oetjen will be prepared to be lenient with you. We won't consider suspension, though of course you'll be off the squad for the rest of the year."

"Don't you think we should have some evidence that Mary Ellen is actually guilty, Dr. Barlow," Mrs. Oetjen interrupted, "before we start deciding on the punishment?"

Mary Ellen shot the principal a look of gratitude. At least someone was on her side.

"But there is evidence," Dr. Barlow insisted. "My own daughter saw Miss Kirkwood here purchasing spray paint at the art supply store at the mall only last week."

*Vanessa!* Suddenly it became clear to Mary Ellen who was behind Dr. Barlow's decision to single her out. But if Vanessa had seen her at the store last week, she must have seen her with Gemma — and who would be dumb enough to bring a little sister along on an errand that needed to be kept a secret! Even Vanessa had to know that Mary Ellen wasn't guilty, but of course that wouldn't stop her from doing her best to make trouble.

"That paint," Mary Ellen protested aloud, "was for my kid sister's robot. And I can prove it. Call her and ask her. Call my mother. For that matter, call Gemma's teacher."

"I don't think that will be necessary, dear," Mrs. Oetjen reassured her. "Buying a can of paint is no crime."

Mary Ellen felt relief flooding over her. Mrs. Oetjen was not looking particularly pleased with Dr. Barlow at the moment.

As principal of Tarenton High, Mrs. Oetjen knew Vanessa Barlow well enough to be suspicious of any evidence that came from her. Unfortunately, Vanessa's father was superintendent of schools, so it was necessary for her to be more tactful than she might like to be. "I think there's no point in discussing this any further, until we have the facts," she said dryly, not bothering to hide the implication that Dr. Barlow had come poorly prepared in the fact department this time around.

"But I do hope that we find the culprit soon," she added, "so that Dr. Barlow will not find it necessary to take up any more of his valuable time coming down here to the school to deal with it."

Mary Ellen had to bite her tongue to keep from smiling at that one. By the time she got to her first period class, however, she was beginning to worry all over again. Even though Mrs. Oetjen clearly didn't believe the accusation against her, Dr. Barlow was on the warpath and he wasn't going to rest until someone took the blame for painting that statue. And with Vanessa whispering in his ear, it was obvious that he would continue to be suspicious.

Opening her English textbook, Mary Ellen tried her best to concentrate. All she wanted was to get through this week without any major complications. Coach Engborg had trusted her to handle the squad business, and she wanted so much to prove that she could handle the responsibility.

Nancy, meanwhile, had been giving a lot of thought to her conversation with Mary Ellen at the mall. It was true that Olivia's problems were not her responsibility. She and Olivia had never been great buddies, and that wasn't her fault, either. She had even invited Olivia to some of her parties in an attempt to get to know her better. But somehow the chemistry for true friendship had never been there.

On the other hand, it bothered her that everyone seemed to be too busy worrying about their own petty little problems to even talk to a member of the squad who might be in serious trouble.

"Did you really mean what you said the other day about me being a caring person?" Nancy asked Josh, when they met on their way to the cafeteria for Friday lunch.

Josh looked surprised. Girls were always bringing up something you said days ago and then asking if you really meant it. "Of course I did," he insisted, recovering his composure. "I wouldn't have said it otherwise."

"In that case," Nancy said abruptly, "I'm afraid I can't have lunch with you today. There's something important I have to do."

"Huh? . . . Sure, okay," Josh said to Nancy's back as she abruptly turned around and headed down the hall in the direction they'd just come from. What had he started now? Shaking his head in confusion, he headed off to the lunchroom alone.

Nancy found Olivia hiding out in the stacks of the school library. She had taken over one of the little study desks that were placed back there for hermits who couldn't stand to work around others. But Nancy noticed right away that the pages of Olivia's notebook were blank and her history textbook was open to a chapter they'd covered back in September.

"Do you think we could have a talk?" Nancy asked, grabbing a chair from the next desk and moving it so that Olivia had no hope of making a quick exit.

Olivia looked as if she'd rather walk barefoot over a bed of hot coals, but she was trapped.

Stuck for a way to begin, Nancy found herself talking about herself and Josh. She mentioned how she had almost not given Josh a chance because she'd held it against him that her parents were always trying to pair them up. She talked about how, even now, they sometimes had trouble communicating. About how she'd thought she needed to prove herself to Josh by helping him out with his job and his van, when actually he was just as happy to be taking care of those things on his own.

"What I'm trying to say," she summed up finally, "is that as much as I care for Josh, sometimes I need another girl to talk to. And I was wondering if you feel the same way once in a while, too."

Having tried her best, Nancy stopped talking and waited for Olivia to tell her to get lost. The truth was, she'd always been a little afraid of Olivia, who seemed so tough physically and so self-assured. It was almost as if Olivia didn't need or care about the social acceptance that Nancy craved.

And Olivia, for her part, had always been wary of Nancy. So cute and sexy and always dressed in the latest styles, Nancy seemed to have self-confidence to burn. The idea of choosing Nancy — Miss Perfect with her real ruby earrings and her perfect hairdo — as a confidante would never have occurred to her.

But Olivia, at this point, was feeling desperate. Almost before she knew it, she was pouring out the whole story. About the party at Walt's, and how she couldn't really remember what had happened. About her recent symptoms. And her failure to get any information out of Vanessa, who'd walked in on her and Boomer that evening. "I know I'm probably worried about nothing," she added. "But I can't help worrying. It's awful to think that you might have actually had sex with a guy, and you don't even remember it."

"I'm sure everything is all right, too." Nancy hugged Olivia in sympathy. "And I can understand why you don't want to talk to Walt about this. But why did you waste your time going to see Vanessa? The person who really knows what happened is Boomer."

Olivia drew back. "I couldn't ask *him*!" she gasped. "I mean, I've thought about it a hundred times. But I can't get up the nerve to call him. It would be so embarrassing."

Nancy snorted in indignation. "He's the one who ought to be embarrassed, not you. I bet he purposely tried to get you drunk, knowing that you weren't used to drinking. How else could anyone get smashed on two drinks?"

That was a question Olivia had been asking herself ever since the party. And she wasn't that sure it was one hundred percent Boomer's fault, either. But Nancy was basically right. What difference did it make what Boomer thought about her? He had acted like a total louse.

"Maybe I'll call him. . . ." she thought aloud.

"Forget it," Nancy advised. "It will be too easy for him to evade the issue over the phone. See him in person."

Olivia thought it over and decided that Nancy was right. The best place to find Boomer would be at his job, at the local TV station. She didn't know where he lived, and wouldn't want to go there even if she did. She had only one important class this afternoon, then two study halls. She could tell the nurse she was weak from the flu and leave school early.

"Not only are you right," Olivia said finally, "but I'm going to talk to him this afternoon. Why let this hang over the weekend?"

"What about practice?" Nancy wondered automatically. "We're supposed to practice today after school, remember?"

"I know practice is important," Olivia said. "But some things are more important. Anyway, I can probably get to the station and back in time." She squeezed Nancy's hand. "If I'm late, just make some excuse for me. Okay?"

Nancy swallowed hard as she watched Olivia gather up her books and papers. She looked so determined.

I just hope I gave the right advice, Nancy told herself as the class changing bell brought their conversation to an abrupt end. That's the trouble with getting involved. What if Olivia would be better off not knowing what happened?

# CHAPTER

"I'm looking for Boomer Henderson," Olivia
told the woman at the receptionist desk downstairs.

"Fine." The woman gave Olivia an appraising
look that suggested she was not the first girl to
come around looking for Boomer during working
hours. "Go right up. He's in Studio Nine."

Too nervous to ask just where Studio Nine
might be, Olivia hurried past the receptionist's
station and into the elevator. She pushed the
button for the ninth floor at random. Where
else would Studio Nine be?

She had never felt so dumb in her life. What
would Boomer think when she admitted that she
couldn't remember what happened that evening
at Walt's party? Of course Nancy had been right,
in a way. She didn't care what Boomer thought

about anything. Or shouldn't. But it was easier to say it, than to put it into practice. The thought of having to confront him face-to-face made her feel slightly ill.

Olivia got off the elevator at the ninth floor and found herself in an empty hallway. The doors to the various offices on the floor were all closed. Some were unmarked, and one announced itself in gold lettering as being the office of the station director. Obviously, she was in the wrong place.

Back in the elevator, Olivia tried the eighth floor.

Then the seventh.

At the sixth, a heavyset, pleasantly frazzled looking young woman in jeans an a WNBL T-shirt got on the elevator. "Can I help you?" she asked, spotting the lost look on Olivia's face.

"It's on the fourth floor," she explained when Olivia told her what she was looking for. "And don't ask me why it's called Studio Nine. There are no studios one through eight. Just nine and ten. Nothing is logical around here."

The woman shrugged. "I hope you're not planning to steal Boomer away from us for the weekend. He's supposed to go out on location to film a story tonight."

For no reason she could think of, Olivia felt her face turning pink. "Of course not," she said.

"Sorry. Didn't mean to embarrass you," the woman apologized. "Boomer's friends usually aren't that easy to shock."

The woman studied with her interest, as if trying to figure out her age. Olivia felt relieved when the slow, creaky elevator finally stopped at the fourth floor and she could escape. If only she were tall and a sophisticated dresser like Mary Ellen — or better still, like Vanessa — she could go anywhere and no one would question her. But with her looks she would probably still be taken for a kid when she was twenty-five.

After wandering around the halls for a few minutes, she found the studio. The door was locked, but it didn't matter. A sort of indoor window set into the wall beside the door allowed her to look inside and see that the studio was empty. She paced in front of the door for a few minutes, feeling edgy and too warm in her heavy winter clothes. Finally, she took off her coat, but this didn't help much. She was still wearing her thick rose-colored cowl-neck sweater, wool slacks, and boots — even leg warmers. And the studio was overheated.

Ten minutes passed. Olivia was about to give up when she heard a noise at the end of the hall. Two models, a tall brunette and a short blonde, both in tennis whites, appeared, and behind them four young men in shirtsleeves, loaded down with various kinds of cameras and sound gear.

Even before she recognized one of the crew as Boomer, Olivia heard the blonde say, "Hey, Booms, are you taking me out to celebrate when we finally get this wrapped up?"

"Not tonight, beautiful," Boomer said cheerfully. "Got to work. How about tomorrow?"

The blonde made a face. "I suppose so," she said sulkily. "But why do you always have to work on Friday nights?"

"Give us a break, will ya?" another of the men complained. "Let's film the commercial, and you kids can arrange your social lives later."

The group had reached the door to the studio by this time and were standing practically on top of Olivia, yet no one seemed to have noticed her. Boomer has his arm around the blonde, his attention focused on the attractive shoulders and hint of cleavage revealed by the scanty tank top blouse she was wearing.

Olivia cleared her throat, which felt as if she had swallowed about a dozen cotton balls. "Excuse me, Boomer, can I talk to you for a second?" she said. The words, which she'd tried to make come out cool and confident, sounded timid instead. She felt like a little kid trying to get the attention of a group of adults.

Boomer was annoyed, then softened a bit as he recognized her. This was obviously not, however, a good time.

"Hi, there," he said. "Uh, it's Libby, isn't it?"

Olivia felt her anger rising. "Livvy," she corrected him. "Olivia. Remember?"

"Oh, yeah. Sure. Of course I do." Boomer smiled, as if the memory was just coming back to him that very second and turning out to be not unpleasant. "Did you come to look around the studio?" he asked. "Maybe I can give you a tour?"

113

The blonde looked unhappy about this. The others merely impatient.

"Come on, Boomer," said the man who had complained before. "We've got work to do. You can play studio guide later."

Boomer made a face. "Slave drivers," he said cheerfully, pointing to the others.

Olivia was losing patience. "I didn't come for a tour. But I need to talk to you. Just for a few minutes."

"We're late already," the other man answered for him. "And if we have to pay these girls overtime, the sponsor will be spitting tennis balls, not selling them."

"Sorry," Boomer said to her. "But this should only take a few minutes. Can you wait till we're through?"

Olivia wanted to say no. But the others were already half pushing, half dragging Boomer and his gear through the door of the studio. As soon as he was inside, the door slammed shut, and the red light over the door began to flash on and off. PLEASE DO NOT DISTURB WHEN LIGHT IS FLASHING warned a sign tacked to the outside of the door. FILMING IN PROGRESS.

Olivia stood and watched through the window as the crew busily set up their equipment. A tennis net was strung in front of the painted sky-blue background. And one of the men who had spoken out in the hall, apparently a director, was showing the models how to stand. A speaker by the door had been left turned to the on position, making it possible for her to hear what was being said inside.

"Be a sport. Come to Olsen's, the one-stop sports shopping center for your year-round sports needs," the brunette said experimentally, then shook her head. "What a mouthful! I'll never get it right, Louie."

Louie, the director, was encouraging. "Of course you will honey. You said it perfectly."

Olivia, outside, wished there were a chair in the hall so she could sit down. She had already messed up. First by avoiding this conversation so long out of cowardice. And then by barging in at what was obviously a bad time. But she had come this far, and she wasn't going to quit now. They were just filming a commercial, and how long could that last anyhow? Maybe a minute. Certainly, no more.

If only it weren't so hot and stuffy! The smell of a thousand cigarettes and cigars hung in the corridor, and there were butts and assorted dust balls coating the edges of the tiled floor. She hadn't seen an outside window since she entered the building, or for that matter, breathed a breath of air that didn't smell as if it had been closed up inside the building for decades.

I'm going to have an attack, Olivia worried.

Noticing a water fountain at the end of the hall, Olivia fished into her purse and found her pill box. She took one pill, followed by a quick gulp of water. Despite her uncertainty about the dosage, she had been sticking to her one-pill-a-day regime. Obviously, though, that wasn't working. Olivia hesitated, then reached for a second pill and swallowed it. That should do the trick, she told herself hopefully.

Back at the studio window, she could see that nothing remotely resembling progress had been made.

On the first take, the brunette said her line perfectly. Then the blonde chimed in with, "Whether your game is skiing or tennis, ice hockey or sports, Olsen's has it all!"

"Not sports, honey," Louie said with a show of exaggerated patience. "Fishing. They're all sports."

They tried again. This time the blonde got it right, but Louie didn't like the way she was holding the tennis racquet.

On the third take, it was the brunette who flubbed her line, calling Olsen's the "one-stop sports stopping center for your year-round shorts needs."

When everyone had finished giggling, they tried again. There were several more takes, each one producing a new tongue-twisting variation on the line.

Olivia was feeling warmer by the minute. Her stomach felt queasy, the way it had been feeling most mornings recently, but a bit worse. Her pulse was too fast, too. She could feel it thumping inside her head.

The next thing Olivia knew, Louie's voice over the speaker was saying, with infinite disgust,

"Take fifteen. And this time let's do it right."

Had there been fifteen takes already? It didn't seem possible. She checked the clock on the studio wall, then her own watch, confirming that she'd been standing in the hall for over forty minutes. Yet the last take she remembered clearly was take number five. She felt disoriented, as if while she wasn't paying attention a little chunk of time had been stolen right out from under her.

And then she felt just plain sick. Sprinting for the ladies' room she'd noticed at the end of the hall, she made it inside the door and then sank gratefully onto a folding chair that sat in the far corner of the room, back by the sinks. She no longer thought she was going to be sick to her stomach. But she felt faint, as if some inner plug had been pulled and the blood was rushing out of her head to settle in her feet.

In a flash of clarity, she recalled someone telling her that the thing to do if you felt you were going to faint was to sit on the floor and put your head between your knees. As quickly as she could, she crouched in the corner and put her head down.

But it was too late. Suddenly, she just didn't feel like fighting to stay conscious anymore. She closed her eyes and let the blackness wrap itself around her.

# CHAPTER

13

"This is our last practice before the faculty game tomorrow night," Mary Ellen was saying, "and we've really got to pull our act together. I know the game doesn't count toward the team's record, but there will be a lot of people here. People who don't normally attend school games and who've paid good money for their tickets to support the United Fund. We owe it to them to look sharp.

"There's another reason why we want to do ourselves proud," she added. "We've got to show Dr. Barlow that we represent the positive side of school spirit." Briefly, she recapped her experience in Mrs. Oetjen's office that morning.

"But none of us had anything to do with painting that statue," Angie said.

"I know that and you know that," Mary Ellen agreed. "But Dr. Barlow believes Vanessa. Let's just not give him any more reasons for being down on us."

Walt was having trouble paying attention to Mary Ellen's pep talk. Olivia had still not shown up for practice, and he was getting worried about her. She'd been avoiding him for days, and acting strangely silent and withdrawn when they were together. He'd tried every way he could think of to let her know that he was on her side, that he wanted her to confide in him, but nothing had worked. Finally, he'd just decided it would be better not to push things. When Olivia needed him, he'd be there, and in the meantime he was going to give her breathing space.

In the meantime, he'd been doing his best to pretend nothing was wrong, to avoid drawing attention to Olivia's odd behavior. It hadn't been easy, especially knowing what some of the others must be suspecting about his part in Olivia's problems. This afternoon, he was too worried to care, however. Olivia had been in school this afternoon, looking fine physically. And practice was important to her. She wouldn't just not show up unless she had a very important reason.

"Walt!"

Mary Ellen's shriek of impatience brought his attention back to the group. "Olivia's not here," he said, stating the fact that everyone else had been tactfully ignoring. "Do any of you have any idea where she could be?"

"It's all right," Nancy said. "She told me she might be late."

Walt wasn't satisfied. For some reason, he had a very bad feeling about this whole thing. "But why?" he insisted. "Didn't she say why?"

Nancy was annoyed. "She did. But I'm not supposed to tell."

Mary Ellen's expression changed to an obvious mixture of curiosity and suspicion.

"Now you've drawn attention to it, made it seem like a big deal," Nancy rebuked Walt.

"That's all right," Walt said. "You don't have to tell me another thing. Excuse me. You guys practice without me for a few minutes. I've got some phone calls to make."

Mary Ellen didn't know whether to scream or cry. Here it was the final practice of the week, her last chance to show that she was in control, and everything was falling apart. It was bad enough that one member of the squad hadn't shown up at all. Now a second had simply walked out on her. How could they practice their routines with just four people?

At the pay phone out in the hall, Walt dialed the number of the Evans home. He was fairly sure Olivia wasn't there, but it was worth checking just in case.

"She said she had practice," Mrs. Evans answered when Walt asked if Olivia was home.

Walt could hear a note of suspicion creeping into Olivia's mother's voice. "Wow, that's right," he said quickly. "I forgot all about it. That's where she is all right. Thanks, Mrs. Evans."

Walt felt a slight twinge of guilt about lying, but he'd already learned that the honest approach was not rewarded by Olivia's mom. She got hysterical over the littlest things. It was no wonder Olivia couldn't talk to her about major worries.

Now that he was sure Olivia wasn't at home, Walt's thoughts turned back to Boomer Henderson. Needless to say, he had been thinking about Boomer a lot over the last few days. Was it really possible that Boomer and Olivia had slept together? Maybe they were still seeing each other. It had even crossed his mind more than once that Olivia and Boomer might be planning to run off together. Of course, Olivia had *said* that she never wanted to see Boomer again. But what if it was all a lie to keep him from getting suspicious?

Without thinking further, almost in a rage, he dialed Boomer's home number. Boomer's roommate, Larry Wilson, answered. "Hi, Walt," he said, "I just got home a few minutes ago and Boomer is nowhere around. I assume he's working."

Like Boomer, Larry worked for the local TV station as a technician and had crewed occasionally for the breakfast hour talk show that Walt's parents broadcast from home five mornings a week. Walt felt pretty sure that Larry wouldn't lie to him. Not one hundred percent sure, though. Paranoia was beginning to make him doubt everyone and everything.

"You really don't know where they are?" he asked Larry, for good measure.

"Who's *they*?" Larry said in all innocence. "I told you I didn't know where Boomer was. What's the matter?"

"Never mind. Forget it."

Walt hung up on Larry and dialed the TV station. Fortunately, the receptionist there knew him, too.

"I'm looking for my girl friend," he explained, "and I thought she might have stopped in to see Boomer. She's a petite girl. Light brown hair. Wearing a rose-colored sweater and leg warmers and a light blue parka."

"I remember her," the receptionist said. "But she must be long gone by now. Boomer and his crew left a while ago. In fact, there's no one left upstairs. There are just a few engineers here with me on the first floor, running a typed feed from the network. The news show crew will be back later, but they're out on a meal break right now."

Walt thanked the woman and hung up the phone dejectedly. Now what?

He wandered back into the gym where the rest of the squad was running through a fight cheer. "Do you think we can get started now?" Mary Ellen asked him.

"I don't think so," Walt answered, ignoring Mary Ellen's tone of exasperation. "I'm really worried about Olivia."

"Olivia is a big girl," Pres said. "Maybe she stopped in at a coffee shop. Maybe she's visiting someone. What's the big deal?"

Nancy, however, didn't like the feel of the situation at all. What if Olivia had learned something from Boomer that really upset her? She could be wandering around town somewhere, depressed and scared. It was a cold day to be out without a car, too. "I agree with Walt," she said. "Olivia was quite sure she'd be back here at school by this time. Something must be wrong. I think we should go look for her."

Walt shot Nancy a look of gratitude.

"I'm with you two," Angie agreed. "Knowing that Olivia is all right is more important than practice."

"I'll go along with that," Pres said after a short hesitation. He had less of an idea than anyone what the big fuss was about, but it sounded more interesting and important than doing a few more cartwheels to add to the thousands he'd done already this year.

"Wait a second," Mary Ellen protested. "I'm running this practice. You can't just all decide to quit on me and go running off."

"In that case," Walt said slowly, "it is up to you to declare practice over."

"Oh." Mary Ellen thought about her options for a second. "All right. I think we should call it quits for today and go looking for Olivia."

"Good work, teach." Pres thumped Mary Ellen on the back, earning an icy look in return.

Briefly, Nancy filled the others in on the fact that Olivia had been planning to go down to the TV station after sixth period to have a talk with Boomer Henderson. She didn't say why. "After she left the studio, she probably would have taken the Crossely Road bus back here," Nancy concluded. "Why don't I call Josh and he and I can retrace the route in the van. Maybe she stopped in a store somewhere. Or maybe the bus isn't running for some reason."

"Good idea," said Walt. "The other possibility is that she got a ride with Boomer in the TV station van that he drives. I don't know where they'd be going, but you can't miss that van. It's bright orange and has the station's call letters printed on the side."

If it were true, if Olivia was with Boomer, Walt wasn't sure he wanted to be the one to find them. He suggested that Mary Ellen and Pres scout around town in the Porsche, to see if they could spot the station's van.

"I suppose one of us should stay here at school in case she shows up here," Angie said sensibly. "I'll do that. The rest of you make sure you have the number of the pay phone in the hall and call me if you find out anything."

"Good idea," said Walt. "In the meantime, I'm going down to the station to see if I can get any more information.

When he arrived at the station, the news was not encouraging. Mrs. Bultner, the receptionist, admitted that she had not actually seen Olivia leave the station. But then, she'd been away from her desk on a coffee break for at least fifteen minutes. "Come to think of it," she added after a moment's thought, "your friend might have left with Boomer after all. There was a young woman with him. I didn't really get a look at her because I was on the phone. I just heard their voices laughing together about something as they went out."

This was exactly what Walt was hoping not to hear.

"You didn't happen to hear them say where they were going?" he asked.

Mrs. Bultner shook her head. "No. But Boomer was supposed to be working tonight. He didn't sign out on his time sheet." Unfortunately, she added, she didn't know anything about specific assignments. "That's the station manager's job," Mrs. Bultner said a bit stuffily, as if she felt she could keep track of people better than any mere station manager. "That would be Lynn Lacey."

"I know Lynn," Walt said. "Where is she?"

Mrs. Bultner didn't know the answer to that one. Lynn had gone out to have an early dinner — or a late lunch, depending on how you looked at it — and she wasn't expected back for nearly an hour.

It was lucky for Walt that he knew Lynn by sight. He checked four other places around the neighborhood before he finally spotted Lynn, reading a newspaper and eating a hamburger in the back room of Banratty's, a rundown-looking combination bar and restaurant.

Lynn had started out as an assistant producer on Walt's parents' show and had known Walt

125

since he was in junior high. She was pleased to see him, and too preoccupied to be especially curious about why he happened to be tracking her down.

"You should try the hamburgers here," she suggested as Walt sat down in the booth facing her. "The food outshines the ambience by a mile."

"I've got no time for that," Walt said. "I'm looking for a friend of mine. It's important. And I think she might be with Boomer."

"Oh, right." Lynn brightened. "I think I saw her. A petite girl. She seemed a little bit nervous."

"That sounds like her. Did you see her leave the studio?"

Lynn shook her head. "She was on her way to find Boomer. I gave her directions."

"Too bad. I think maybe she left with him. Do you know where Boomer was supposed to go when he finished at the studio?"

"Do I ever?" Lynn laughed. "He was supposed to tape a couple of interviews about farm mortgage rates. The piece is already mostly done and we just needed some more quotes for the sound track. Very dull stuff. I don't know why anyone would want to tag along." Lynn was beginning to look very unhappy. "I hope he didn't decide to give himself the night off and go out with your friend instead," she said. "He's done that kind of thing before, and I need that tape."

"I'll find out," Walt promised. "Do you know

specifically where the interviews were supposed to be?"

"I have the addresses back at the studio. Just give me a second to finish my coffee, okay? This has to last me until I get off work at midnight."

On the way back to the station, Walt started to have second thoughts. Why was he so ready to believe that Olivia would have gone off with Boomer? Did he really trust her so little? He thought about how angry Olivia had been about the way Boomer had treated her. About her sudden sick spells over the last week or so. About how she panicked when she was closed up in stuffy indoor spaces. And suddenly, he knew where she was.

"Do you think we could take a look around the upper floors of the station?" he asked Lynn Lacey as they walked briskly away from the restaurant. "I have an idea that Olivia is still up there somewhere, and she may need our help."

"But the elevators are still running," Lynn protested. "Why would she be hanging around up there?"

"I don't know," Walt admitted. "Call it a crazy hunch. But let's see what we can find."

Olivia had regained consciousness only a few seconds after she fainted.

When she came to, she felt a lot better, but she was still a bit dizzy and extremely tired. She was too shaky and exhausted to worry about waiting around to talk to Boomer. She was too tired to think about heading for the bus, too, for that matter. If I can just rest for a few minutes, I'll feel better, she promised herself, dazedly. Looking around her she noticed a small alcove off the main rest room, furnished with an old high-backed couch. She climbed onto the couch gratefully and stretched out, promising herself that in five or ten minutes she'd get up and head back to the school.

The next thing Olivia knew she was waking from a deep but not at all restful sleep. She felt headachy and dull. The only light in the room was seeping in through the space underneath the door to the outside hall. Someone had turned off the ceiling lights.

How long had she been asleep? Not all that long. According to her watch it was just after five o'clock.

She grabbed her coat and tugged at the door. It was locked! The corridor outside was deadly silent. There was not even a window to let in a glimpse of the outside world.

No doubt the two models had been told to lock up the rest room when they were finished with their filming, Olivia realized. They wouldn't have noticed her curled up on the couch. Now surely the whole crew was gone from the building. What next? Would she be locked up here all night? Or all weekend? It was Friday evening and she had no idea whether this floor of the station was in use on Saturdays or not.

Would there be a cleaning person or a security guard coming around tonight? But even if that happened, how would they know she was trapped in the rest room? She tried pounding on the door and shouting. No one answered.

Olivia tried not to panic. She tried to figure out a way to make her presence known to anyone passing in the hall. She couldn't scream all night long.

In a flash of inspiration, she peeled off one of her leg warmers and started stuffing it under the crack between the floor and the bottom of the door. Fortunately, the space was wide enough for the thick wool garment to fit through. With luck, anyone who came into the hall would see the pink leg warmer protruding from under the door and come close enough to investigate. Close enough so that she could call out and get the person's attention.

Olivia sat down near the door and waited. Fifteen minutes went by. Then half an hour. She was starting to think she had a long vigil ahead when suddenly she heard Walt's voice at the end of the hall.

"Hey, that looks like Livvy's," he was shouting to someone. "Let's check it out!"

Olivia almost cried with relief. "Walt!" she shouted. "I'm in here! I'm locked in!"

# CHAPTER

A little more than an hour after being rescued by Walt, Olivia found herself seated in Dr. Curry's office, and the target of a stern lecture.

"You've been very foolish, young lady," Dr. Curry began. "I would have expected you, of all people, to be more careful."

Olivia's heart sank. Was it possible that it was really true? Could she be pregnant after all? She had just about convinced herself that it was impossible, and now the doctor was pulling her hopes out from under her.

Olivia was so miserable she scarcely noticed when Dr. Curry held up a familiar looking white pill and started waving it in her face. "This is the cause of all your problems, young lady," he said with a scowl.

Slowly, the words began to sink in. Olivia studied the pill with interest, then dawning comprehension. "It is?" she said, unable to keep from breaking into a grin of relief.

"I don't know what you're smiling about," Dr. Curry huffed. "You're luckly the reaction wasn't more serious. I would have thought that with your medical history you would know enough to get in touch with me right away when you started having a bad reaction to a new medication."

"But I didn't know it was the medicine!" Olivia protested, explaining about the first time she had blacked out at Walt's party.

"Alcohol could complicate the reaction," Dr. Curry agreed, "but regardless of what you thought the cause was, you still should have contacted me sooner. At any rate, I'm changing you back to your old prescription. You shouldn't have any trouble from now on."

When she left the doctor's office, Walt was outside in the waiting room. Olivia hugged him gratefully. "You'll never believe it!" she told him. "It was my new prescription that was causing all my crazy symptoms! But I'm really lucky that you found me when you did. I was afraid of having an attack locked in that stuffy room, and if I had been there much longer I might have taken another pill. The doctor says that it could have been really serious. Especially with no one around to help me when I blacked out.

"Just wait till I tell my mother," Olivia rattled on. "The worse I felt, the more she kept nagging me to take more pills. I think Dr. Curry was almost as angry with her as he was with me."

Walt had already called Angie at the school and told her to let the others know they could give up their search and go on home. "I'm glad this crisis is all over," he said, almost as relieved as Olivia.

Suddenly it occurred to Olivia that there was one question that still wasn't resolved. "I never did get to have my talk with Boomer," she reminded him. "So I still don't know what happened at the party. You know what I mean, Walt. I'm scared that I —"

"At the party?" Walt was mystified. "*Nothing* happened at the party!"

"Are you sure?"

"Of course. Nothing except that you and Boomer were making out in the spare bedroom. Believe me, if it had been anything more than that, Vanessa would have made sure the whole world knew about it. Anyway, I came upstairs a few minutes later and saw you two for myself. It wasn't that big a deal.

"I thought," Walt added, "that you had gone on seeing Boomer *after* the night of the party. I was even half convinced that the two of you were ready to run off together."

Olivia was having trouble taking it all in. "Didn't you trust me any more than that?" she asked.

"I should have trusted you more. But it's hard to trust someone who's purposely shutting you out."

"You're right." Olivia gave Walt another hug,

then she kissed him sweetly. "I'll never shut you out like that again. Oh, Walt, I feel so relieved. I thought . . . maybe . . . I couldn't remember . . . and when I started feeling sick. . . ."

Walt held Olivia close. "I know what you thought. I worried, too . . . and wished if it had happened it could have been me."

Pres was delighted when Mary Ellen called him that evening to say that Olivia was all right and would be able to cheer with the squad at the student-faculty game. That afternoon, driving around with Mary Ellen in their futile search for Boomer's van, he had given her a pretty hard time.

"Olivia could be kidnapped. She could have fainted and be freezing in a snow bank," he'd teased. "And all you would care about, really, is whether she'd be rescued in time not to ruin the squad's appearance."

"That's not true," Mary Ellen had protested. "But I *am* responsible for our performance tomorrow night. You wouldn't be so casual if Ardith had left *you* in charge."

Later, when they had called Angie at school and were told that Olivia was found, he had started to think over what Mary Ellen had said. It was true that Mary Ellen sometimes took herself too seriously. The girl was a bundle of ambition. Whether the subject was her long-term goal of becoming a model, or a little thing like the squad's performance on a given night, Mary

133

Ellen drove herself hard — and expected everyone else to care just as much about success.

On the other hand, Pres had to admit to himself, Mary Ellen had taken on the responsibility. Which was more than he would ever do.

"Look," he had said when Mary Ellen called with the message about Olivia, "I apologize for riding you so hard. You were right to care about the squad."

Mary Ellen, stunned to hear Mr. Cool himself admitting that he was in the wrong about anything, had been speechless.

"Now if I can only get one small matter ironed out with my folks," Pres went on, "I'll be ready to cheer tomorrow night, too."

"What?" Mary Ellen had yelped, suddenly finding her voice again. "Don't tell me you're going to have a fight with your parents and end up grounded on the night of the game!"

"I promise I won't. But for once, I'm not going to avoid the issue by procrastinating, either."

After hanging up with Mary Ellen, Pres took his last attempt at an essay for his Princeton application out of his typewriter, rolled the paper into a neat ball, and lobbed it into his wastebasket. Downstairs he found his father, smoking his after-dinner cigar in the library.

"There's no sense waiting until tomorrow to discuss this," Pres said, confronting his dad.

"Good." Mr. Tilford looked up from his magazine. "I gather that means you've finished your essay. Can I read it?"

"There's nothing to read. I've decided to withdraw my application."

"But I told you that I would help you to get in. The Tilford name still means a lot in certain circles. All you had to do was write one little essay —"

"You don't understand, Dad. I'm not worried about being rejected. I'm worrying about being accepted. I don't belong at Princeton and I don't want to go there in any case. I may not have any firm plans for the future, but at least I know where I don't belong."

Pres squared his shoulders and waited for his father to do his firecracker act: a few preliminary sputters followed by a loud explosion.

To his surprise, no outburst occurred. Instead, Mr. Tilford puffed away on his cigar in meditation and then shrugged. "I was afraid you'd decide something like that."

"You were?"

"I can't say I'm happy. Naturally, it's a disappointment to know that there won't be a Tilford at the old school. But it's your life."

"It is?" Pres stuttered, then recovered. "Uh, yeah, I do . . . I mean . . . yes, it's my life."

After his momentary demonstration of humanity, Mr. Tilford returned to his old crusty self. "I suppose you intend to make a fool of yourself at this charity game tomorrow night. Cavorting around with those girls like a demented jumping jack."

Pres had heard this line of complaint before. "Of course," he said.

135

Mr. Tilford laid his cigar aside and set his face in an expression that was half smile, half grimace. "Well, I'm afraid to say that I will be on hand to witness your performance. Your mother bought some tickets to help the United Fund. Of course, we don't necessarily have to use them. But I like to get full value for my money."

"Naturally."

Pres could hardly believe it — after all his father's complaints that cheerleading was unmanly, and certainly unseemly for a Tilford male.

"No matter what he says, I really think my dad's beginning to mellow," Pres told Kerry later when he picked her up at her house that evening on the way to the movies.

Kerry smiled at the unlikely image of a mellow Mr. Tilford. "Maybe he's secretly happy you decided not to apply to Princeton," she suggested. "Not that he didn't want you to go there. But because he's happy to see you starting to make your own plans for the future."

"Who knows?" Pres wasn't big on analysis. As long as the crisis was over and the waters were unruffled again, he was content. "I'm actually looking forward to tomorrow night's game," he said, changing the subject. "It's going to be funny to see Ardith and a bunch of teachers trying to lead cheers. And for once, there's no pressure since the game doesn't count."

"I'm not so sure that it's going to be quite that

relaxed." There was a worried look in Kerry's big dark eyes.

"Why not?"

"I had swimming class today," Kerry explained. "The class that Vanessa's in. And down in the locker room I heard her telling some of the other girls that Olivia Evans is definitely pregnant. It seems that she almost fainted in church last week and Evie Caird overheard Mrs. Evans complaining about how Olivia has morning sickness practically every day."

"But that isn't true. She was sick because she had a reaction to some new medicine." Pres filled Kerry in how Olivia hadn't shown up for practice that afternoon because she had fainted in the TV studio downtown. "We all spent a couple of hours after school looking for her," he finished. "Walt found her and took her to the doctor, and the doctor says she'll be fine for tomorrow's game."

"I'm glad Olivia's all right," Kerry said. "But that won't necessarily stop the rumor. What is she going to do? Wear a sign that says, 'I'm not pregnant?' "

"Well, sooner or later, everyone will know that it isn't true. Whether she wears a sign or not," Pres said.

"But they won't know that tomorrow night," Kerry pointed out. "Vanessa has been spreading the story all day, and unless I miss my guess, she'll find some way to embarrass Olivia at the game."

Kerry shivered. "I wouldn't want to be in Olivia's shoes tomorrow night. Not for anything."

137

# CHAPTER

A ngie had her own worries about Saturday night.

The news that Olivia was all right and that Walt's after-game party was still on had forced her to make up her mind about Arne. She had been debating with herself all week about whether to ask him to the game and the party. Part of her really wanted him to be there. But another part of her had been uncertain. Arne had never hung around with her friends, especially her friends on the squad. What would they think of him? Despite Nancy's hint a few days ago that she thought Arne was basically all right, Angie wasn't sure. For all she knew, Nancy had only said that to make her feel better about Vanessa's nasty remark.

The other side of the problem was just as worrisome: What would Arne think of her friends?

The two of them had been getting along so well the last few days. She hated to risk everything by taking Arne to a party where he might suddenly figure out that they had nothing in common — where it might dawn on him that she was not the sweet, romantic girl he took her for but just plain Angie Poletti, accepted by her friends as an all-around good sport and pal.

But then she realized, she wanted to be with him no matter what!

Waiting for Arne to pick her up before the game, Angie paced nervously. Normally, she felt good in her cheerleader's uniform. The red and white pleated skirt and white letter crew neck made extra energy start to flow almost as soon as she put them on. But they certainly weren't romantic!

Wanting to please Arne she had experimented with her hair. First she tried braiding the sides and pulling them back off her face the way Mary Ellen sometimes did. But the effect, instead of being both girlish and sophisticated at the same time, the way it looked on Mary Ellen, had merely made her look like a recently arrived refugee from some remote farm village. Next she had stood for half an hour in front of her mirror with a curling iron, trying to reproduce the flipped back waves that Nancy Goldstein often wore. This time, the results were even more hopeless.

For the daughter of a professional beautician, Angie thought disgustedly, I certainly don't have an expert touch when it comes to fixing my own hair. It was no use asking her mother for help, though. Her mom would only tell her that her usual style was best for her, and that an hour before going out on Saturday night was no time to start thinking about a change.

Now that she had showered and dressed and blow-dried her hair back into her usual casual style, Angie continued to feel nervous. When Arne rang the front door bell, instead of merely honking in the driveway to let her know he had arrived, she nearly jumped out of her skin.

During the drive to school, she managed to settle down at least partly. Arne, his usual studious self, plied her with questions about basketball rules and the fine points of making shots. "What I don't understand," he kept saying, "is how the referee decides who fouled whom. I mean, when two people run into each other, how can you tell who is responsible?"

"Don't worry about it," Angie laughed. "The ref will have no trouble deciding. Anyway, you don't have to understand everything that goes on right away. The game is supposed to be fun."

"But don't you think things are more fun when you understand the fine points?" Arne persisted. "I do."

I ought to be annoyed, Angie thought. But for some reason, she found herself liking Arne more and more. He sees everything so differently, that it makes me see things differently, too, she reflected. I even see myself differently when I'm with him.

Unfortunately, when they arrived at the school parking lot, Angie was confronted by her first hint that the evening might not go smoothly after all. They were hardly out of the car before Angie was confronted with a tearful Evie Caird.

"Please don't blame me," Evie blurted out. "I didn't mean to tell her. I didn't."

Angie had no idea what Evie was talking about. "Blame you for what?"

"For telling Vanessa about Olivia being pregnant," Evie explained. "I tried to keep it a secret. But Vanessa heard the story from someone who goes to my church. And she kept pumping me for the details, until finally I guess I said too much."

"I guess you did," Angie agreed when she finally figured out what Evie was referring to. "Especially since none of it is true. For your information, Olivia's problem was a reaction to medicine. She is definitely not pregnant."

"Oh." Evie sounded almost disappointed. "But what will we do about Vanessa? She's planning to tell Coach Engborg the whole story, so that Olivia will get kicked off the squad and she can take her place," Evie added breathlessly.

Angie winced. Vanessa's dreams of replacing Olivia were just so much wishful thinking. But that didn't mean that Olivia wouldn't be humiliated to have Ardith hear the rumor about her.

"Tell you what, Evie," Angie said. "Try keeping what I just told you a deep, dark secret. If you do as good a job this time as you did the last, the whole school will know the truth about Olivia by the fourth quarter of the game."

Trying hard to keep her cool, Angie turned to Arne and walked with him into the school. Overhearing that little conversation couldn't have given Arne a very good impression of the squad, she reflected.

"Don't worry," Arne said, patting her on the shoulder as if he had read her mind. "Just enjoy your cheering and relax. I have an idea that Vanessa will have other things to worry about tonight besides spreading dumb stories about your friend."

Angie was about to ask Arne what he meant by that prediction when he gave her a quick kiss on her cheek and headed for his place in the stands. "See you later," he said cheerfully.

Still mystified, Angie headed down to the corridor leading to the basketball court where the rest of the squad was warming up. Olivia obviously had no hint of what Vanessa was saying about her. After only a day without her troublesome prescription, she looked better than she had in weeks. Walt, too, was in a good mood, prancing around in the old wolf suit, which he had fit over his uniform.

"This is going to be a big hit," he predicted. "The only problem is, I can't see much of anything."

Angie decided that this was definitely not the moment to sound the alarm about Vanessa. They were going out on the court any minute now. Why ruin everyone's good mood when there was nothing to be done?

When the time came, Mary Ellen led the squad onto the floor, warming up the crowd with the "Go, Wolves" fight cheer. The section of the bleachers usually reserved for fans of the visiting team was filled with grown-ups from town, each of whom had paid seven dollars toward the United Fund drive. The student cheering section was large and enthusiastic as it responded to the squad's lead, but it roared even louder when the faculty team's cheerleaders took to the floor.

Mary Ellen and the others, at first wondering why the faculty cheerleaders were getting such a big response, studied their competition. Ardith Engborg was the squad captain, of course, and was followed by Mrs. Curry, a tall, slender woman in her twenties who taught Latin and Spanish. Behind her was Mr. Underhill, the physics teacher, also young and athletic, a predictable volunteer for Ardith's group. The next, and last, member of the faculty squad was a spry looking woman who wowed the crowd by doing a smart series of cartwheels.

"Who is that?" Mary Ellen and Nancy asked in unison.

Angie giggled. "Don't you recognize Mrs. Oetjen?"

143

"*That*'s who it is," Pres agreed, whistling softly in amazement. "I can't believe it."

Tarenton High's principal, usually so dignified in her tailored suits and high heels, was almost unrecognizable. Her gray-streaked hair, which she invariably wore pinned up in an elaborate hairdo, hung in a single thick braid down her back. Her legs, encased in opaque blue tights and blue and silver running shoes, were surprisingly youthful. And in the absence of the oversized horn-rimmed glasses and gold earrings she always wore around school her face looked softer and less stern.

In spite of the cheers and laughter from the crowd that had greeted Mrs. Oetjen's cartwheels, there was still one person on the court who had yet to recognize the mystery cheerleader. Walt, half blind inside his wolf suit, saw only an anonymous teacher in a blue and white uniform. Deep into his wolf act, he sauntered over toward the newcomer and, miming an exaggerated leer, made a show of pinching the energetic cheerleader.

The crowd loved it. Mary Ellen and the others on the student squad gasped. Had Walt gone too far this time?

Fortunately not. Mrs. Oetjen immediately pinched Walt back and then chased him across the floor, waving her finger in his face in the familiar gesture she used to warn students who earned her displeasure. This time, the action drew laughter, not just from the student section, but

144

from the adult fans who were young enough to recall being lectured by Mrs. Oetjen in the same fashion.

When the two teams took the floor, the clowning settled down a bit. As Walt had predicted, the team of Ron Lutz and Tom Gaetano, on the faculty side, managed to make it a real contest — at least for the first half. At one point the faculty even managed to pull three points ahead of the varsity.

By the second half, however, the faculty's two-man offense had begun to tire. The varsity pulled ahead steadily and surely, and the game began to turn into a show — an amateur version of a Harlem Globetrotters' performance. Mr. Marburg, looking bizarre as usual, his storklike legs supporting a substantial middle-aged paunch, came off the bench to do some fancy dribbling. At one point, Walt even took to the floor, escorting a tiring Mr. Marburg to the basket and waving the varsity guards aside to give him a clear shot at the hoop. When he missed the shot anyway, Walt shook his head in mock exasperation and had him try again until he finally made a score the third time around.

Through it all, Mary Ellen and the others on the squad cheered their hearts out. The relaxed atmosphere of the game gave them a chance to try some fancy routines they hadn't yet had the nerve to do outside of practice. Olivia even did her vault over Pres, Angie, and Nancy, landing perfectly with a smile on her face that said, "See how easy it is?" Across the floor, Ardith Engborg slipped out of her role as leader of the opposition cheers long enough to give Olivia, Mary Ellen, and the others a cheer of approval.

The game ended in a warm glow of good spirits all around. Even Angie had forgotten the dire prediction of trouble made by Evie Caird earlier in the evening. Having held back her impulse throughout the game to cheer for Tom Gaetano, who was still her favorite cousin in spite of being a teacher and the mainstay of the faculty team, she ran across the court to congratulate him.

The one person in the auditorium who was not sharing the general mood of celebration was Vanessa Barlow. To begin with, Vanessa was furious at the young student teacher Ron Lutz. She had been harboring a crush on Mr. Lutz ever since he arrived at Tarenton High, and she was spitting mad that he had finally taken her out one evening last week only to explain, gently but firmly, that she was too young and immature for him to consider as a girl friend.

*Immature!* That word, in particular, made Vanessa cringe. She considered herself by far the most sophisticated senior girl in school, and with her sultry dark hair and well developed figure she certainly looked the part. Ron Lutz, she had belatedly decided, was a jerk.

And then there was Olivia Evans. Vanessa had felt all year long that Olivia, the quiet one among the cheerleaders and the one who had been the dark horse candidate to make the squad originally, was filling the place that had been meant for her. Personally, she had some doubts about whether the story of Olivia's pregnancy was true. But even if it wasn't, in her mind Olivia was an upstart, a little snit who deserved all the trouble that came her way.

As the majority of the spectators headed for the exits, Vanessa joined the knot of friends and onlookers who had gathered at courtside to watch as Patrick Henley took some final photos for the yearbook.

Patrick snapped Dr. Barlow handing over a check representing the evening's proceeds to the local chairman of the United Fund; then the faculty team; the two teams together; and finally the two cheerleading squads, posed in a two-tier pyramid with Mrs. Oetjen bravely standing on Walt and Pres's shoulders.

"Well, that's about it," Patrick said finally, after he had used up the last of his roll of film. "I think we have some good mementos of the evening."

Vanessa waited for the group to break up, her eagle eyes focused on Mrs. Engborg. She could hardly wait to get the coach alone and give her an earful about Olivia!

She was just about to step forward and claim the coach's ear when a voice called out to her from up in the bleachers.

"Oh, Vanessa! There you are! I'm glad I caught you!"

Mindy Norris, with her husky yet penetrating voice and her dramatic looks, knew how to upstage anyone, even Vanessa Barlow. When she was sure that her words had attracted the attention not just of Vanessa but of the entire group gathered on the court, she paused significantly and pulled a boldly labeled can of pink spray paint from its hiding place inside her coat.

"I think this belongs to you, Vanessa," Mindy announced triumphantly. "We wouldn't want the evening to end without our anonymous spray paint artist getting some credit, would we? Maybe Patrick should take your picture, too."

"Where did you get that? You had no right to go into my locker!" Vanessa snapped, forgetting in her anger that she was all but confessing her own guilt.

"My own daughter!" wailed Dr. Barlow, who was slowly but surely turning the color of a boiled lobster.

Mindy, still waving the spray can tauntingly, looked tremendously pleased with herself. Vanessa, her temper out of control, raised her arm and moved toward Mindy who cried out, as Pres and Walt grabbed hold of Vanessa.

Patrick watched the whole scene with a growing feeling of dismay. "I think there are some moments that we're better off not recording," he whispered to Mary Ellen and he closed his camera case with a snap. "What do you say to the two of us getting out of here?"

Mary Ellen looked at Patrick speechlessly. In theory, there was no reason why she should feel sympathy for Patrick Henley. If he was embarrassed by Mindy and Vanessa's tactics, so what?

Nevertheless, she was feeling that pull that always seemed to disrupt her emotional balance when Patrick was around. She just couldn't help herself.

"Okay," she said after a long moment's thought. "Let's go."

Patrick took her hand — that's all he had to do, just take her hand — and she felt all the familiar feelings cloud her head. He looked at her yearningly. "It's always you, Mary Ellen. Always."

Luckily for Olivia, the gossip about her that Vanessa had been doing her best to get started had been all but forgotten. The sensational confrontation between Vanessa and Mindy was going to be the one and only topic of gossip among Tarenton students for a while. It was certainly the main topic at Walt's house, where he and Olivia, the rest of squad and their dates, and a dozen other friends were having their after-game party.

"What I don't understand," Nancy said as she and some of the others took a break from dancing to discuss the situation, "is how Mindy Norris got into Vanessa's locker."

Arne, seated on the couch with his arm around Angie, could not help smiling broadly. "I cannot tell a lie," he said. "I showed her how to do it. For a while back in junior high, I had this thing about being an escape artist. Another Houdini. I learned a good deal about lock picking. Of course, normally I wouldn't use it to break into

149

anything. But I figured this was for a good cause. So I gave Mindy a few lessons."

Angie smiled to herself, remembering the rose that had been left in her locker on Wednesday morning. She'd just assumed that she must have left her lock open by mistake. She should have known better than to underestimate Arne.

"But why did Vanessa paint the statue in the first place?" Nancy persisted. "And how did you figure out she did it?"

Vanessa, Arne explained, had been nursing a major crush on Ron Lutz for weeks. "She was hanging around him all the time," he added. "It was really getting embarrassing for him. She showed up at school on Saturdays when he was coaching the junior varsity basketball team. She even followed him when he went to the movies once after school."

Both Olivia and Nancy nodded. Each of them had run into Vanessa in those places and wondered what she was doing.

"I remembered Ron's brother telling me that when Ron was a senior he was part of the last group at Tarenton High ever to paint the statue," Arne told the others. "I figured that Vanessa had heard the same thing and was hoping to impress Ron. As you can imagine, the gesture backfired. Ron was scared he'd get in trouble for putting Vanessa up to the prank. When Angie and I saw Ron and Vanessa at the pizza joint that evening, it looked like a date. But really, Ron was warning Vanessa to get off his case and behave herself."

Mindy, Arne went on to explain, had figured out on her own that Vanessa was the culprit. An ambulance driver from the hospital had been making a call near the school the the previous Saturday night and noticed a car in the student parking lot. He had been about to report it when he realized that the car belonged to Mrs. Barlow, the wife of the superintendent of schools. Later, when the statue was found painted, he mentioned the coincidence around the hospital. Mindy had heard the story from her father.

Mary Ellen, who had arrived at the party with Patrick in time to hear Arne's explanation, gave a sigh of relief. "So Vanessa probably would have been caught in time anyway," she said. "No wonder she was trying so hard to shift suspicion in my direction."

Patrick was shaking his head in amazement. "Mindy is clever," he agreed. "But not too smart. She only wanted to get Vanessa in trouble because she was jealous. She thought I had a secret yen for Ms. Barlow."

Patrick grinned at the thought. "Luckily, she never figured out who her real rival was. It's Mary Ellen who lights my fire."

Mary Ellen squirmed. "Forget it, Patrick," she said automatically. "You know there's nothing between us."

A look of general disbelief went around the

room, and Mary Ellen suddenly realized that she had been holding Patrick's hand even as she spoke.

"Well, nothing *major*," she insisted.

A wave of music almost drowned out Mary Ellen's words, as someone across the room pointedly turned up the volume on the stereo. "Come on, you guys," Shelley Eismar called out, "let's forget the talk. It's time to party."

"I couldn't agree more," said Walt, as he put his arm around Olivia's shoulders and led her out toward the end of the room that had been cleared for dancing.

Nancy and Josh followed after a few seconds, joined by Pres and Kerry.

By the time the pounding beat of the song had died out, the record moving on to a slow, romantic ballad, Angie and Arne were still seated.

"I warned you that I'm not much of a dancer," Arne confessed, still holding Angie close. "In fact, I could use some tutoring in a few other areas. Like kissing."

Angie smiled. "Well, I think any subject is more interesting if you really get involved and learn all the fine points. Don't you agree?"

"Exactly," said Arne. And he gave Angie a gentle slow kiss that showed just how fast he could learn.

"Come on, Mary Ellen," Patrick pleaded good naturedly. "Forget that you're not supposed to like me just long enough for us to have one little dance together."

Mary Ellen started to protest as Patrick pulled her to her feet. But why fight it? In theory, she was the golden girl of the squad, the one who could have any almost any guy in school. Yet somehow her heart kept choosing Patrick, the part-time trash collector and full-time show-off.

Tomorrow, Mary Ellen told herself, I'm going to figure out why I lose my cool every time this guy looks at me. But tomorrow will be soon enough.

*How do the girls react to being called nasty names? Read Cheerleaders #9,* PLAYING GAMES.

153

## Join the Team!

They're talented. They're fabulous-looking. They're winners! And they've got what you want! Don't miss any of these exciting CHEERLEADERS books!

## Watch for these titles! $2.25 each

- ☐ QI 33402-6 **Trying Out** *Caroline B. Cooney*
- ☐ QI 33403-4 **Getting Even** *Christopher Pike*
- ☐ QI 33404-2 **Rumors** *Caroline B. Cooney*
- ☐ QI 33405-0 **Feuding** *Lisa Norby*
- ☐ QI 33406-9 **All the Way** *Caroline B. Cooney*
- ☐ QI 33407-7 **Splitting** *Jennifer Sarasin*

---

**Scholastic Inc.**
P.O. Box 7502, 2932 East McCarty Street,
Jefferson City, MO 65102

Please send me the books I have checked above. I am enclosing
$_____(please add $1.00 to cover shipping and handling).
Send check or money order–no cash or C.O.D.'s please.

Name _____

Address _____

City_____ State/Zip _____
CHE851      Please allow four to six weeks for delivery.

# Introducing

**CHRYSTAL FALLS**

*A NEW BOOK EACH MONTH!*

**The continuing struggles of the "Mill" kids and the "Hill" crowd...a fabulous new series!**

Chrystal Falls looks like an ordinary town...but it's the setting for forbidden loves, secret jealousies, frightening accidents and stormy courtroom battles. You see, in Chrystal Falls, you're either a rich kid from the Hill, or a working-class Mill-towner—and you don't go falling in love on the wrong side of the tracks, unless you're looking for trouble.

Meet Chelsea Chrystal, the "princess" of the Chrystal family dynasty...Karen Pickett, a Mill girl who seethes with hatred for the Hill...Pete Carter, the brooding Mill boy whose anger gets in the way of his love for Dawn Newhouse, the new girl in town who lives on the Hill. **Chrystal Falls: where there's a right side of town, and a wrong side of love.**

### Read BOOK 1: THE WRONG SIDE OF LOVE
Paperback $2.50 each .At your bookstore in September!

📖 Scholastic Books

CHR851.